SHORT ODDS

RAY WOOD

ZP

ZP

PROLOGUE

It was a perfect summer's day and the racecourse was at its best. The grass of the infield was neatly trimmed and as green as a shamrock. The track had been groomed like a Persian carpet and it stretched unblemished between the flawless white ribbons of the rails. The fresh paint on the stands glowed in the hot sun, and although the architecture of Ellerslie, Auckland's most prestigious racecourse, would never be called charming, the high-spirited racegoers were glad of the shade under its sweeping roof.

It was a good crowd. Both the members' stand and the public stand were at least three-quarters full and the atmosphere was buoyant. It wasn't the Melbourne Cup but many of the racegoers were dressed for fashion and there was a good sprinkling of fancy hats.

A middle-aged man with Oriental features sat in the middle of the crowd about halfway up in the public stand. Small wrinkles at the corners of his eyes stood out as white lines against his deeply tanned face. His hair was closely cropped and lighter in colour than his thick eyebrows. He was neatly dressed in a striped shirt, pressed khaki trousers and polished brown loafers. He was holding a racecard and a pair of binoculars, and his dark eyes were always moving, watching the constant flow of people around him with interest.

Loudspeakers announced the start of the first race and the attention of the crowd focused on the horses as they walked around the parade ring. It was a colourful sight, with the bright silks of the jockeys contrasting with the gleaming coats of the horses. Two of the trainers were giving last-minute instructions to their jockeys while the other jockeys mounted their horses and began the walk to the track.

The man raised his binoculars and studied the activity in the parade ring. Tui Dancer, the race favourite, was easy to pick out. With his glossy black coat, a white blaze on his face and two white socks, he moved easily, his muscles sharply defined and his head erect. In the background, the man was aware of the announcer's commentary on the form of the horses and heard him say that Tui Dancer had won his last four races, the most recent by two lengths. He looked at the tote board and saw Tui Dancer's odds were 6 to 4. He returned his gaze to the binoculars and looked at the other horses. Hot Vanilla, the second favourite at 4 to 1, was grey with white stockings on his hind legs. He sidestepped when his trainer gave a leg up to his jockey but quickly settled when the jockey got his feet in the stirrups.

There was considerable activity in the stands as punters moved to the betting booths and refreshment areas. Lowering his binoculars to his lap, the man watched the horses trot and canter past the starting gate and then walk back. This race was over 2,200 metres and the starting gates were to the right of the stands, about halfway along the finishing straight. All the horses entered the gates smoothly. Tui Dancer was in the third gate, Hot Vanilla beside him in gate four. The man checked the tote board again and saw that Tui Dancer's odds had lengthened to 9 to 4 and Hot Vanilla's had shortened to 3 to 1. Last-minute bets favoured Hot Vanilla.

There was a brief pause before the bell rang, the gates opened and the horses sprang forward. The man watched closely as the horses swept past the stands, their hooves tossing divots high as they accelerated and headed for the first turn. Tui Dancer was well placed and moving easily in third behind a bay mare and the hard-pulling chestnut outsider. Hot Vanilla was boxed in two places back, his jockey looking for a path to the front. The man raised his binoculars and watched as Tui Dancer moved to the outside and eased into second place at the 1,500 metre mark. Hot Vanilla found a gap and moved along the rail and was handily placed in fourth.

Along the back straight, Tui Dancer increased his pace and moved into the lead, a full length ahead of the bay mare. Hot Vanilla also made a move and by the 1,200 metre mark was in third place, a length and a half behind Tui Dancer. Around the final bend Tui Dancer slowly pulled away, his lead increasing to two lengths over Hot Vanilla, who had moved into a clear second place. The man kept his binoculars trained on Tui Dancer as he came around the bend. He saw the jockey glance over his shoulder to judge the position of the field and saw him touch Tui Dancer with his whip.

Just before the end of the bend, with 400 metres to go, the gap began to narrow. The man watched closely and could see no abrupt change in Tui Dancer's motion, but with every stride it was apparent he couldn't maintain his pace. The crowd was screaming as the race tightened and the horses entered the final straight.

The man lowered his binoculars and watched the horses race towards him. With 250 metres to go Hot Vanilla stuck his nose in front. With 150 metres to go Tui Dancer was in third place. When he crossed the line he was in fourth. The noise of the crowd was deafening with shouts of joy and groans of dismay.

The man watched the horses walk back past the stands. Hot Vanilla's jockey guided him to the winner's enclosure and Tui Dancer headed for the unsaddling boxes along with the other unplaced horses. As he did so, the man retained his focus on Tui Dancer. The horse still moved easily, with no sign that he'd had a hard race. The man's eyes were thoughtful and his mouth twitched in what might have been a smile. He stood as the announcer called the runners for the next race and apologised as he moved along the row of seats to the aisle. He worked his way through the crowd to the exit and in a few minutes was in his rental car heading back to his hotel. There were five more races on the racecard but he'd seen what he'd come to see.

CHAPTER 1

The backs of the cattle gleamed in the moonlight and the stillness was broken by an occasional soft moo or snort and the clop of hooves as the animals jostled each other in the pen.

'God damn it, Dennis,' said Fraser, softly but harshly, 'get that fucking door open.'

'Get that fucking door open,' mimicked Dennis under his breath as he struggled with the latch. The metal catch was bent slightly and hard to move. Perched on top of the fence in the dim light he was having trouble getting a proper grip. He pushed harder and at last the latch opened with an audible click. 'Shit!' he swore as the latch took some of the skin off one of his knuckles.

With the latch undone, Dennis opened the truck's doors and scrambled over the fence to join Fraser behind the cattle. The animals were moving nervously but had so far been remarkably quiet. A small black heifer on the far right of the herd stopped and peed vigorously onto the dry earth. The smell of fresh urine and old shit was pungent on the still night air.

'Okay, let's get them in the truck and get out of here,' said Fraser. He slowly shifted to his right, Dennis sidled to the left, and with soft voices and quick gestures they began to urge the cattle forward and up the short ramp into the truck.

The first cow, a large black and white heifer, was reluctant, snorting and blowing and backing from the ramp. But the pressure continued from behind as the other cows tried to push forward and finally she scrambled up the ramp, her hooves finding purchase on the slats nailed across the slanting boards, the clatter loud in the darkness. Once she was in the back of the waiting truck the others followed one at a time, tossing their heads and mooing plaintively at this unaccustomed activity. Only the last again proved reluctant, jumping nervously left and right, her wide eyes brilliant white in the moonlight as she looked desperately at the two men until she, too, went up the ramp.

'That's it!' said Fraser. 'Get the door closed. This has taken way too long already.'

Dennis jumped forward and swung the big doors closed with a thump, shoving the latch back into place with no sign of the trouble he'd had opening it. He rubbed his hands on his jeans and wiped the sweat off his forehead with the back of his sleeve. He climbed over the wooden fence and dropped to the ground next to the ramp.

In fact, the entire operation had gone easier than either of them had hoped. They had waited until after 11 p.m. before arriving at the paddock and parking their truck at the small wooden loading yards just off the road. They had quickly entered the paddock through the gate and gone looking for the cattle they had seen the day before. The moon was waxing three-quarters full and it wasn't hard to spot the small herd at the water trough about a hundred metres away towards the back of the paddock. Fraser and Dennis had split up and walked to the rear boundary fence before moving together and gently herding the animals towards the truck. One of the cows, the large black and white one, kept trying to duck around Dennis and he'd had to run and wave his arms to control her without letting the rest of the herd slip back between him and Fraser. The two men were careful to make no noise. They used no whistling or shouting to urge the cattle on and kept them moving steadily at a walk. As they moved across the paddock the night air was rich with the fecund smell of cows and grass and dew and the paddock gleamed like pewter in the moonlight. Everything seemed to happen very slowly, but in fact the cattle were used to being moved and it had only taken about fifteen minutes to get them into the yards, and another fifteen minutes to load them in the truck.

Fraser moved forward and was standing by the driver's door of the truck. The back of the truck had tall, slatted wooden sides and no roof and now held an even dozen cattle. Fraser cocked his head to one side and listened intently. The song of crickets rose and swelled in the cool night air. And there was something else …

'Shit,' he exclaimed and grabbed for the door handle. 'Goddammit, Dennis, get in the truck!' Dennis sprinted for the passenger door and swung it open just as Fraser fired up the diesel and ground the gears into first. The engine rattled for a moment as it took the load and then the truck lurched forward, swinging Dennis' door shut and throwing him back into his seat as Fraser wrenched it onto the road. Dennis looked across the cab at Fraser's tense face, almost invisible in the soft backlighting of the headlights.

'What's the matter? Are you crazy? Be careful or you'll spook the cattle and we'll roll this thing.' Fraser was concentrating on his driving, swinging the steering wheel savagely as he pushed the truck up through the gears along the winding road. 'Screw the cattle,' he said, 'if we don't get our asses out of here we'll be the ones who get spooked.' As he said it he switched the headlights to high beam, and the sides of the road, a steep muddy cutting on the left and a fence-lined paddock on the right, suddenly sprang into stark relief.

No sooner had he done so than the glare of oncoming headlights came around a sharp corner ahead and suddenly hit them both in the eyes. The car dimmed its headlights and was past them in seconds, before Dennis could see what model it was. Fraser glanced in the side mirror several times and urged more speed from the labouring truck.

Dennis craned his head to look in the wing mirror on his side but already the taillights of the car had disappeared around a curve. He was thrown against the passenger door as Fraser took another corner at speed. 'For Christ's sake, slow down! You'll kill us if you don't watch out.'

'Shut up,' growled Fraser, as he slammed the gearshift into fourth and gunned the engine. 'I figure we've got about an hour to get out of here and off the road.'

'An hour? What are you talking about?' asked Dennis incredulously. 'Who do you think was in that car? A cop? No way, man. I couldn't make it out, but no way was it a cop car. I'd have seen the lights on top. Anyway, whoever it was, they couldn't have seen anything.'

Fraser groped in his pocket for a packet of cigarettes and pulled one out with his teeth. 'Give me a light,' he told Dennis and drew deeply when Dennis held a Bic lighter to his cigarette. 'It's like this, you dimwit. It doesn't matter who saw us. This isn't the fucking city where everyone is anonymous and no one wants to get involved. This is the country. It's full of cows, and trees, and bloody farmers who won't mind their own business. In the country everyone notices everything. And tells everyone else. It's all they have to talk about,' he laughed sourly.

He drew on his cigarette again and continued: 'Remember the *Rainbow Warrior*? Remember those French frogmen? They came here and blew up that greenie boat, right? And everyone was so surprised when they were caught. "Oh my," they said, "how could those great French spies have been caught by little old New Zealand?"' Fraser glanced over at Dennis and grinned fiercely. 'Why do you think those professional spies didn't get away with it? All their specialised training and equipment and preparations weren't worth shit. What was their big mistake?' he asked, but didn't give Dennis time to answer: 'They thought they were operating in a city. They thought they could waltz around New Zealand in fucking rubber suits and no one would notice. Hell, half of Paris probably walks around in rubber suits, but not here. This whole country is just one small town and everyone has one eye out the window. Those dickheads didn't have a chance.'

He stuck his cigarette in his mouth, downshifted and used both hands to swing the truck onto the main road. 'So this is the way it is. Uncle Mike or Aunt Mary or whoever was in that bloody car is going to get home and start to wonder what a truck carrying a load of cattle was doing parked up by their good friend Trev's farm in the middle of the night. And since everyone knows Trev never goes to sleep before 1 o'clock it won't take long for them to decide to call Trev and get him to check out his animals. Then Trev has a look in the paddock and calls the cops. And then the cops get on the radio and if we're not off the road then we have some fucking difficult questions to answer.'

Dennis looked pensively into the night flashing past the windows of the speeding truck. 'How do you know the farmer's name is Trev?'

———

Their lips moved close, paused, and then met, fleetingly, brushing at first, then again, nibbling, caressing, as light as a moth. Bridget felt his hands on her back, strong and firm but gentle, caressing her through her blouse. With an act of will she opened her eyes, raised her hands and gently pushed against Hugh's chest. 'Hold it, cowboy. You've had your dance tonight,' she said, shaking her head.

Hugh leaned back slightly and said, 'Hold it? Hold what?' He cupped her buttocks and asked 'This?' Then moved his left hand around and stroked her and asked, 'Or this?'

Bridget tossed her head, swinging her hair away from her face, and looked away. Her hair was thick and brown and hung past her shoulders, untied this evening, though she often wore it up. She wore blue jeans and a plain white blouse, with no makeup or perfume. The lamp on the small side table threw shadows across her face, highlighting her straight nose, rounded cheeks and dark brown eyes. She smiled briefly and gripped Hugh, gently at first, and then squeezed hard enough to get his attention. 'This needs to stay right here. You're on your way home, remember?' She pushed again against his chest and moved away from him, out of the bedroom and into the large lounge. Her bare feet made no sound on the wide, dark wooden floorboards. Hugh watched her trim, athletic body retreat and felt the emptiness she left behind. The furniture in the lounge was fine and heavy and old, inherited from her parents. Hugh thought it was perfect for a patrician homestead but that it didn't gel with the more carefree spirit of its current owner.

He followed her and stood close behind her as she looked out of one of the two tall windows in the lounge. The small panes divided the moonscape into fragments of black and silver, patches of porch and railings and posts and a trimmed lawn running to the drive and the stable block, its red exterior grey in the moonlight. In the near distance the silhouette of a large macrocarpa tree was haloed by the Milky Way.

Hugh resisted touching Bridget and forced his gaze from the window. To his right, through the opening between the rooms, he could see the large dining table that dominated the formal setting of the dining room. The soft light from the overhead fixture highlighted the hard gloss of the native timber and the remains of Bridget's dinner – a single plate and wine glass – at the end of the long table where she had left them when Hugh arrived. Three heavy iron candlesticks were arranged along the length of the table.

Bridget looked at his reflection in the window pane and said, 'You know we can't go on like this.'

Hugh lifted his right hand to her shoulder and touched her cheek with his fingers. 'Well, this is new. We haven't had a fight yet.'

'We're not having a fight now. We're having a discussion.'

'A discussion. Well, that's different. A discussion. Like adults. With a topic and everything?'

'Yes, a topic. Our relationship. The topic's our relationship.'

'Oh, our relationship. Yes. That's important to discuss. From the beginning? The part where it was your idea to start having sex with a married man?'

'No, not so much that part. More the part where we decide it's been fun but it's time to move on.' Bridget turned towards him and leaned against the window frame, arms crossed over her breasts. Her left foot tapped the floor softly and a small crease appeared on her forehead as she frowned. *Was it really my idea?* she thought.

Hugh was at least fifteen centimetres taller than her, with close-cropped hair, almost a grey fuzz, and a full, solid face with deep-set brown eyes beneath thick eyebrows. The lines at either end of his lips seemed to lift them, giving him the appearance of always being faintly amused. He was dressed in a check shirt and corduroy jacket that hid his broad shoulders, khaki slacks buckled around his stocky waist, and elastic-sided boots. She had to admit that it *had* been her idea, and in spite of tonight's reservations she wasn't sure she wanted to stop. He was sexy as hell even though, at 52, he was almost twenty years her senior.

Her mind drifted back to the night three months earlier when she'd checked her heifers before she went to bed and saw that one was having difficulty giving birth. A foot had emerged but there was no sign that the calf was following. Hugh had always been her vet and it was no surprise that he responded to her late-night call. He'd pulled the calf free at nearly midnight and when it took its first steps Bridget had cried and hugged Hugh and kissed him – in relief at first and then, to her subsequent astonishment, with increasing ardour. He had responded and it had been difficult for them to focus on making sure there were no complications from the birth. Both knew that what they had shared could only lead to one thing.

Over the course of three months she and Hugh had been together at least a dozen times. He'd drive up in his Range Rover in the middle of the afternoon and it wasn't only the animals that received his attention. Or worse, she found herself calling and asking him to come and look at animal ailments that, in other times, she would have ignored or dealt with herself. They'd made love in the stables and in just about every room in the house.

Hugh spread his hands and looked at her enquiringly. 'Fun? It's been fun? That's what this has been?'

'Yes. Fun. I want to be with you. But …'

Hugh frowned, his tanned face revealing a network of lines radiating from his eyes and across his forehead. 'But? If you're worried about Barbara, don't be. I haven't told anyone but you know that things haven't been going very well with us. Our daughter Alice graduated and went to Sydney. Barbara got the accounting job at the dairy factory and I have more clients than ever. I'm hardly ever home. It turns out there isn't much keeping us together.' He continued, 'You were married once. How long were you married?' He didn't pause to give her a chance to answer. 'It doesn't matter. At the end did you ever get the feeling, not of being lonely, exactly, but like something's missing? Something that was there before, that maybe you weren't even aware of until it was gone?'

Bridget held up a hand. 'Huh! Missing? The only thing missing in my marriage was my husband. I woke up one day and the jerk had run off with another woman.' As she was speaking she was thinking, *Where is this coming from? Hugh's never shown any signs of real emotion. Why is he suddenly talking about his marriage? Is something going on? Is he going to leave his wife?* A final thought only added to her confusion *Get a grip, girl. I've been through marriage once. Is there any way Hugh is someone I might want to try again with?*

Thrusting those thoughts aside, she continued: 'So, back to our relationship. From the start we agreed there would be no ties. We both wanted a good fuck and as long as Barbara didn't find out then no one would get hurt. That's great in theory, but the fact is you're married. Really married. You know Barbara still loves you, and I think you still love her. And the problem is I think I'm beginning to want more than sex. Or less.'

She waited for him to respond and when he kept quiet she smiled softly and said, 'It's late and we both have a lot to do tomorrow. It was good of you to come around and check on Ginger.' She looked directly into his eyes and continued, 'Let's not worry about anything deep and meaningful at the moment.'

Hugh straightened and said, 'Meaningful. Damn, that reminds me. I've been meaning to tell you that the stallion at the McKerrow place looks like the best bet for covering Ginger. He's got the right temperament and bloodline. Ginger should be ovulating in a few days and we need to be ready to move her. I'm going to be pretty tied up looking after Tui Dancer when he comes tomorrow, but we'll manage somehow.'

Bridget nodded and glanced at the heavy stainless steel watch on her wrist. 'That's a plan. You'd better go. You've been gone hours.' Hugh took her in his arms and held her close. Bridget returned the embrace and nestled her head against the soft fabric of his shirt, feeling the swelling of his chest as he breathed, and the regular beat of his heart. But her eyes were open and she stepped back when he released her.

Hugh walked to the front door where his bag lay on an old wooden chair. Bridget switched on the porch light and they both stepped out into the summer night. Hugh went down the steps and over to his Range Rover parked on the drive nearby. He opened the door and said, 'Thanks, Bridget. It was a great evening.' He slid behind the wheel and closed the door, rolling down the window to say, 'You'll have to come and see Tui Dancer while he's at my stables.'

Bridget leaned against one of the columns supporting the porch roof and watched Hugh back away from the house. He tooted his horn and waved as he swung into the drive that led to the main road. Bridget waved back and then stood in the light on the porch with her hands in her back pockets, watching the red tail lights flicker and disappear among the trees that lined the drive. She heard the noise change as the vehicle left the gravel and turned onto the tarmac, heading towards town. A gentle breeze brought the fragrant smells of summer to her – grass, trees, animals, dew, moonlight and dust.

A soft nicker came from the stable block tucked against the hill about fifty metres from the house. Bridget stepped off the porch onto the grass and walked towards the building. She walked lightly with the free and easy motion of someone used to hard physical activity. The dew had already begun to settle on the grass and her boots darkened with the moisture.

The stables were a conventional structure with two large sliding doors and a pitched roof. She reached them and slid the door on the right open just enough to step inside. Inside it was pitch black except for the sliver of moonlight that came through the door. She reached back and opened the door fully, revealing the interior in silver-grey highlights. To her left, through an open interior door, was the bonnet of her flat-decked ute. Against the far wall was a tool bench, and against the back wall, on the right side, was another workbench and an assortment of saddles, bridles and other riding equipment. To the right were four loose boxes and a small pile of hay bales. The horse's head sticking out of the second box was swivelled to look at her, the large eyes and nostrils black in the subdued lighting. She breathed in the familiar smell of hay and horse, and smiled.

'How's it going, Ginger?' Bridget asked as she walked towards the mare, who she owned along with an ex-racehorse called Blackbird. Of the two horses, it was Ginger who was her true passion. As a filly, Ginger Snap had been owned by one of Bridget's best friends and her husband. She had an impeccable pedigree and had won a few races as a 2-year-old. Unfortunately, her decline in form the following year mirrored the decline in the state of the couple's marriage. After a brief but bitter divorce Bridget's friend had demanded the mare because she knew she meant so much to her ex-husband. But a few months later she realised that revenge on her husband was actually a significant financial drain. She'd shared her troubles with Bridget over a bottle of wine and by the end of the evening Bridget had bought Ginger Snap for a song.

Blackbird had been a moderately successful racehorse who'd developed a tendency to break blood vessels. He'd been retired and given to Bridget by other friends who weren't interested in horses that couldn't earn their keep. Free from the rigours of racing, Blackbird had become a very nice riding horse.

Bridget loved horses and horseracing and had decided to keep Ginger on the farm and breed from her rather than race her any more. She and Hugh had been looking for a suitable stallion to send her to for months but it had been hard, at times seemingly impossible, to find the right horse at a price she could afford. Bridget could keep the farm going for another year, but if she was going to secure her long-term future then she needed more money. She knew that breeding horses was a lottery but she was running out of options and a foal from a top stallion might be her salvation.

That was what Hugh had stopped in to see her about that night. He had been negotiating with Phil McKerrow for a week and they had finally come to an arrangement that was agreeable to everyone. Phil's stallion, Great Escape, wasn't ideal but, as Hugh had explained, the chances of a classy foal were still good.

When she reached the box Bridget pulled a mint from her pocket and offered it to the mare. The soft lips sucked it off her palm and nuzzled her for more. Bridget patted the firm muscles in Ginger's neck and thought about Tui Dancer, the horse Hugh had mentioned. *Now* there *was a horse,* she thought. Tui Dancer had showed promise as a 2-year-old but, after being sold to new owners, rumoured to be Chinese, and going to a new trainer, he had won or been placed in every race he had entered. Until recently, that is. He'd faded badly in his last two races and there was speculation in the media that he'd been pushed too hard. Tui Dancer had all the characteristics that Bridget was looking for but if he were to be available for stud then his fees would be stratospheric, ten times more than Bridget could ever afford.

The first thing Hugh had told her when he arrived was that Tui Dancer was being brought to his own stables for a couple of days. Max Treadlow, Tui Dancer's trainer, wanted Hugh to give the horse a thorough examination and see if he could identify why he was no longer winning.

Bridget fantasised briefly about what it would mean to have one of Tui Dancer's offspring, but she quickly brought herself back to reality. She wasn't the type of woman who wasted time on thinking about what could be or might have been: there were far too many practical things demanding her attention. The fact that she had dreamed at all about foals from Tui Dancer showed how desperate she was becoming.

'That's enough for you, girl,' Bridget said and stroked the white blaze on Ginger's forehead. 'It's time for both of us to hit the hay.' She gave the ears a last scratch and turned away. She closed the stable door behind her and walked back to the house. At the porch steps she paused and looked at the sky, the moon, the rolling hills surrounding her home bathed in the soft light, and knew again why she had stayed here after the divorce.

———

Gordon rolled down his window and felt the night air rush in and clear his head. The country road wound away in front of his headlights, the fences along either side holding back the black emptiness of the paddocks. Occasionally the dark branches of a windbreak lining the paddocks would protrude into the headlight beams, but mostly he drove down the narrow two-lane tunnel of the night, a hole in the darkness opening before him and closing noiselessly as he passed.

It had been a long day and he was tired. He'd taken the call about the milk tanker accident at 6 a.m. and had left his flat without breakfast, or even coffee. He'd been at the scene until the driver was cut free an hour later and had then followed up with interviews at the hospital and the police station. The afternoon had been spent talking to a citizens' action group concerned about rising rural crime. He'd had a dinner of fish and chips in his flat and then a few beers at the cricket club. Gordon's name was painted on one of the large wooden plaques that lined the walls, as a past captain of one of the club sides more years ago than he liked to think about. On a cold day he could still feel the deep, arthritic ache in his left knee and right elbow, his only lasting souvenirs of a career as a fast bowler. He still knew some of the faces around the bar but he hadn't played on a side in years, other than the odd social match at a barbeque. If he were honest with himself, unless he was actually playing, cricket held no real attraction for him anymore. Gordon was thinking that it might be about time to find another place to drink. The beer was cheap but he could drink among strangers at any bar and the unattached female clientele of the club was approximately zero. He saw Dani Painter at the bar sharing a beer and a yarn with one of the younger players. She was female and unattached. He'd heard she was making a name for herself on the women's side, but he wasn't sure that dating a policewoman would be a good idea.

Gordon knew he spent too much time working and not enough time getting exercise. Repeatedly he told himself that next week he'd get back into a groove, play golf twice a week, give up fast food and join the cricket team again as a fielder. But 'next week' had been receding into the future for the last two years and his trousers were beginning to feel tight around the waist again, even after going up a size.

He'd watched the league match in the UK on the big screen in the club bar, coverage switching to the West Indies-Sri Lanka match during half-time and after the rugby was over. Since they'd got Sky and the big-screen TV, attendance at the club had increased dramatically. Norm Atkinson, another ex-player once renowned for his bowling pace but now better known for his staying power at the bar, had kept the patrons amused during the games with his monologue on the future of rugby and the Kiwi cricket team's prospects on the upcoming tour. Norm had retired before Gordon's glory years and the two, although sharing a bowling background and having less than ten years difference in age, had never been close. Gordon enjoyed a party and a bit of fun as much as the next guy, but he'd found that Norm's humour too often cut a little close to the bone.

Norm's commentary finally ran out of steam when highlights of the previous night's netball test match came on. He got another beer, looked around the bar, and sat down next to Gordon. 'Gordon. Hell of a mess. I don't know what those selectors think they're doing.'

Gordon wasn't entirely sure whether Norm was talking about rugby, cricket or netball but he knew it didn't really matter. Norm wasn't asking for his opinion, only for permission to continue. 'Um-hmm, Norm, you know how it is,' he replied.

'They chucked out all the old girls. Too slow. Can't jump. Some other bullshit. And they got these young ones,' Norm said disgustedly. 'They've got the legs but they don't have the guts.'

'Yeah, well, everything goes through cycles, Norm.' Gordon knew that one of Norm's hobby horses was 'cycles'. According to Norm everything, from sports to politics to the weather was controlled by cycles. And identifying the causes of those cycles – international cartels, the Labour Party, the oil price, global warming – was the never-ending source of much of Norm's conversation.

Norm took a long pull of his beer and looked around the room. A few people were still at the bar and a pair were playing darts, but the crowd had mostly gone home. He turned back to Gordon and looked at him closely. To Gordon's surprise he didn't rise to his conversational bait but said, 'Is something the matter with you, Gordon? Time was you would have been up there with me, leading the lads in a bit of fun.' Norm liked to play the fool but he was one of the best stock agents in the region and more than one person had regretted underestimating him. Gordon didn't say anything and Norm continued, 'You haven't been the same since you got back from Oz. If you're in a bind you know you can count on me. What are mates for, right?' Norm leaned closer and Gordon could smell the beer on his breath. 'That little girl take you through a cycle or two, did she?'

Gordon hid his face in his beer and hoped that Norm would let it drop, but Norm wasn't going to be deterred. His earnest face with its lines and jowls wrinkled in concern and he carried on, 'Gordon, mate, you think you're the only one to do something like that? Huh? How many guys do you know wouldn't have done the same bloody thing? I mean, a beautiful young woman, a movie star for Christ's sake. What are you going to do?'

'TV,' said Gordon.

'Huh?' Norm had been building up momentum and was momentarily thrown off of his stride.

'She was in TV, not movies.'

Norm was not to be deterred by a few stray facts. 'Whatever. What I'm trying to tell you, none of us are getting any younger. And let's face it, who wouldn't have been bloody well tempted? Hell,' he snorted, 'half my customers wish they could do the same thing. Only problem is, the sexiest thing they ever see probably wears overalls and boots.' Norm poured himself another beer from the jug and continued, 'Sometimes you can't help going a little crazy.'

'Bridget didn't go crazy,' Gordon replied, and took another drink of his beer.

Norm's face assumed a knowing look and he winked at Gordon. 'Ah, guilt. It's always the guilt. You think you ran away and left Bridget and ruined her life. And maybe, what's even worse, you have a sneaking suspicion that you *didn't* ruin her life. That now she doesn't need you anymore. It's not that she hates you that's eating your guts; it's that she doesn't give a damn.' Norm took another look around the room and leaned even closer to Gordon. Gordon tried to recoil but he was trapped in the corner and couldn't retreat. Norm raised a finger, looked slyly at him, and said, 'Well, buddy, there are a few things you should know.'

He looked around again and continued softly, 'Rumour has it that Bridget may not be doing as well as she'd like everyone to think. I hear that she hasn't done too well at the cattle sales. He paused for a moment and said, 'I also hear that she's not entirely without companionship. If you know what I mean. But it's not exactly what you could call a prospective relationship.' Norm tried to leer and wink at the same time but couldn't pull it off and ended up looking as though he'd squeezed lemon juice into his eye. He recovered doggedly and carried on, 'Times are tough, Gordon. She may need you more than you think she does. More than she bloody well thinks she does.'

'Yeah, well, thanks for those encouraging words, Norm.' Gordon managed to push Norm out of his face and got room to breathe. 'You've made me feel a whole lot better. You've told me that I'm as dumb as your customers. That Bridget's going broke, and that she's in a dead-end relationship with some jerk. That's all great news. Just great. I don't know how I can thank you.' Gordon drained his beer and stood up. 'I'd better be going before you tell me how lucky I am to have terminal cancer.'

Norm looked hurt as Gordon sidled from behind the table and walked out the door. 'Funny bugger,' he said to himself. 'Bloody hell, I didn't know he had cancer.'

It was close to 11 p.m. when Gordon finally left the club. Once in the car he suddenly didn't feel like going home to the flat with rented furniture and nothing on the walls. He checked his cell phone for messages and started the car. Turning right at the end of the drive he headed away from town, into the country, wandering the roads without conscious purpose, listening half-heartedly to talkback radio and wondering what the hell he was doing. He was 38 years old, twice-divorced, a poorly-paid reporter for a small-time local paper with no prospects for advancement. He had a 6-year-old Honda with a bad whine in the rear end and no other significant assets. Assets? The whine threatened to break into a shriek as he accelerated downhill and he tried not to think about his liabilities.

Gordon drove automatically, the white line almost hypnotic as it disappeared beneath his right headlight. He saw no traffic, no sign of life other than the occasional light in a distant farmhouse. After driving for some twenty minutes he came to a T-junction where a stop sign gleamed in the bright headlights. He stopped and tried to work out where he was. A yellow AA sign was just out of view to the right. He eased the car that way until he could read the sign. Suddenly he knew that he hadn't been driving entirely without purpose. His subconscious, at least, had been busy. Gordon accelerated away from the intersection, his uncertainty gone, concentrating on the winding road that weaved between the steep hills on either side.

He slowed for a particularly tight corner and was almost blinded by the high beams of an oncoming vehicle as he straightened out again. 'Asshole!' he exclaimed and swung as far as he dared towards the verge. The vehicle thundered past and he got a glimpse of a light-coloured cab and a white face in the driver's window before it was past, disappearing around the corner before he could get a proper look in his rear-view mirror. Gordon muttered 'Asshole' again and wiped the perspiration from his forehead. *What were a couple of lunatics in a stock truck doing out at this time of night?* he wondered. *If I'd seen the licence number I'd report them to the police for dangerous driving.*

Then he forgot about the incident as he rounded a familiar curve and slowed to look for the mailbox and drive. Suddenly there it was, a large red metal mailbox and a metalled drive leading off hard to the left. He coasted to a stop and craned his neck to look back along the drive towards the house that he knew so well. He caught a glimpse of light between the trees, but as he looked it went out and there was nothing but darkness. He looked up the drive for a long time, but the night stayed dark. The hollow feeling returned as he put the car into gear and eased back onto the road. It had been a long day and it was time for bed.

———

Elliot stood in the long dark grass outside his shed and listened to the breeze in the willows that lined the stream just below his house. He was of average height, lean but solid, with grey hair going a little long in the back and looks that could be anything from a weathered 50 to a well-preserved 80. In fact, he had just celebrated his seventieth birthday, and although he was slowing down he still felt pretty good. He could just make out the sound of the water tumbling over the small dam he'd put across the stream to make a pond when he'd moved onto the property. The dew on the grass had soaked his socks and they were cool against his ankles. The stars were bright and the sky clear, not as clear as on a winter's night with a hard frost, but they were visible right down to the horizon.

Across the valley he saw the lights of a car leave Bridget's house and highlight the trees along her drive. Soundlessly they disappeared over the hill. Her porch light gleamed like a glow-worm in the distant darkness. Elliot had been Bridget's neighbour for almost ten years and knew her well. She had moved in with her husband, full of optimism and dreams about what they would do with the land. But one knock had led to another and sometimes he was amazed that she had stuck it out. Elliot had helped the couple at first, and then Bridget when she was on her own. But he recognised her independence and never offered help unless he thought she really needed it, and took her frequent refusals without comment. When Gordon had left he was sure that she wouldn't be far behind, but that was almost three years ago and she was still there. He shook his head as he continued to look at the blackness, relieved by a single point of light where her house lay against the fold of a hill.

Elliot walked softly across the packed earth of his yard and paused at a small fenced enclosure. The fence was about a metre high, made of wrought iron, and it enclosed a patch of grass about six metres square. In the daylight, the grass was a patch of verdant lushness amidst the barren dirt and parched grass of his homestead. At one end stood a simple headstone. The inscription was unreadable in the darkness but Elliot didn't need to read it to know what it said.

Beth had died five years ago, but he still missed her and often came out to visit her grave in the evening. He had first met her when he moved to New Zealand in 1954 after serving in the Malayan Emergency. That conflict had taught him much about himself and more than he wanted to know about cruelty, war and politics. It had not been a hard decision to come to New Zealand rather than return to Cornwall when he was demobbed.

On the passage to New Zealand Elliot had met Roger Fox, the owner of a meat works in the Waikato, and Roger had offered him a job. The work was hard and unpleasant but the pay was fair and he knew he would move on when he had the chance. At nights he dreamed of a farm, with deep green fields covered with white sheep. Shortly after he arrived he'd met Beth at a dance and it didn't take long for things to proceed from there. He had saved his soldier's pay and his wages at the works, and Beth's parents helped them buy the farm he still lived on. It had been back-breaking work in the beginning, fighting back the scrub and bush and turning the land into neat paddocks. But they had persevered, had two kids, a son and a daughter, and for almost forty years he and Beth had worked as a team, turning their farm into one of the best in the district.

His kids had come back for the funeral, of course, but neither was interested in the farm or intended to stay in New Zealand. His son had a family and a career as an engineer in Sydney and his daughter had just been transferred to London by her employer, an international accounting firm. Elliot was proud of his children and only a little sorry that the farm wouldn't be passed on to one of them. It was ironic, he thought, that he and Beth had struggled to give them an education and opportunities and now they were turning their backs on the farm, uninterested in the life that had made them who they were. He was realistic enough to know that the farm wasn't really big enough to be economic anymore. But Elliot didn't think about that; he only wished he could see his kids and grandkids more often. The iron fence beneath his hands was rusty and he idly picked flakes off as he thought about the past. The night smelled of hydrangeas and jasmine and resonated to a pulse that only he could hear. For a moment he swayed and had to grip the fence more tightly, but the feeling of loss and sorrow and a sense of imminent danger passed quickly and he turned back towards his house.

The sound of a truck came to him faintly from the road and he looked up in time to see its headlights swing across the pines in the paddock by the bridge where the road crossed the stream. He caught a glimpse of a light-coloured cab and a slatted back before the truck swung out of sight around the spur of the hill and the sound receded again. The truck seemed to be in a hurry. He had no sooner turned to go back towards his house than he heard another sound from the road and saw the lights of a car travelling in the opposite direction. Elliot watched the lights swing across the landscape as the road contoured around the hill and then stop at the entrance to Bridget's place. Her porch light clicked off and left the hillside in darkness. The car waited at the end of the drive for almost a minute and Elliot watched it closely, deciding whether he needed to call and tell Bridget someone was looking at her house. Before he got seriously concerned it pulled back onto the road and picked up speed, following in the path of the vehicle that had left her house earlier.

CHAPTER 2

Barry slapped the rump of a cow and its hooves quickened their clatter on the concrete floor of the large building. The harsh light from the bare overhead bulbs in the high ceiling made the other cows' eyes look wide and frightened and glinted dully off the galvanised steel stalls in the centre of the shed. 'You boys cut it pretty fine this time,' he said as he looked at the small herd, milling nervously in the far corner of the shed. The animals were mooing softly as they moved, unsure of where to turn for safety. 'I don't want your truck to be seen here and it's going to be daylight soon.'

Fraser was leaning on the open shed door. He tossed his cigarette butt out into the gravel of the parking area and grinned. 'Don't be an old woman, Barry. It's barely midnight. We'll be out of here soon enough. We don't want to be seen any more than you do.' He winked at Dennis. 'We've already had one close call tonight. You just worry about giving us the money and getting those ear tags removed. And the sooner you turn those animals into hamburgers the better.'

Fraser and Dennis stepped outside and waited for Barry to turn out the lights and join them. Dennis leaned close enough that Fraser could smell the sweat on his clothes. 'I don't like it, Fraser. Barry's never acted this nervous before. What's going on? Can we still trust him?'

Dennis could see Fraser's teeth gleam in the moonlight as he smiled. 'Trust him?' he snorted. 'I wouldn't trust him with a bent paperclip. But he'll do what we need. You leave the worrying to me, Einstein, and everything will be all right.'

They stepped apart as Barry closed and latched the shed door. He turned to them, keeping his back to the door, glancing from one to the other, then looking quickly away towards the distant hills shining silver and black in the moonlight before returning his gaze to the dark figures in front of him. 'Good looking stock,' Barry said, 'I won't ask where they came from.' He licked his lips and gave a weak smile. 'But, I'm not sure how much longer I can keep this going. I'm getting a bad feeling about it, you know?'

Fraser glanced at Dennis, moved to put his arm around Barry's shoulders, and began to walk with him towards their truck. 'Feelings? Bad feelings? Are you having trouble with the product? Is someone asking questions?'

Barry shook his head. He was very conscious of the hand on his shoulder and the strength of the man beside him. Barry was big, bigger than Fraser by at least twenty kilograms and almost certainly much stronger. He could easily pick up a whole carcass and carry it from the freezer to the cutting room where, in his hands, a saw and cleaver would quickly turn it into chops and steaks. But he knew that there was something different about Fraser, a commitment to violence, an ability to put absolutely everything he had into a fight, that made him dangerous. More dangerous than Barry could ever be. Even if he had one of his cleavers in his hand, Barry would be reluctant to provoke the man who walked so easily beside him.

'No, no, nothing like that,' Barry replied. 'Things are still sweet. I have enough stock going through my shop that no one's going to be interested in a little extra. Or able to trace them if they were. And there's the cash sales as well. Lots of people are finding themselves short of money when it's time to buy groceries and are bloody interested in a no-tax discount. My regular cash customers will just about take care of this lot by themselves.'

They reached the side of the truck and halted. Fraser dropped his arm and faced Barry, whose troubled eyes searched Fraser's face for some hint, some sign of reassurance. Barry paused and rubbed his hands down his stained trousers before continuing, 'There's nothing exactly. Just a feeling. That something's going to happen. I'm worrying all the time about these damn deals. I can't keep it up. My wife says I'm driving her crazy and if I don't get it together she's going to take the kids and leave.'

Fraser pulled a pack of cigarettes from his pocket and shook one loose. He offered it to Barry, who refused, and then to Dennis who took it and applied his lighter. Fraser also took a cigarette and played with it in his fingers while he thought for a moment. 'Partner, how long have we been doing business together? Two and half, three years?' He didn't wait for Barry to reply, but carried on. 'Now, when we started this little business arrangement we didn't worry about lawyers or contracts or bills of sale, did we? It was all built on mutual trust – and an interest in making money.' He winked at Dennis out of the corner of his eye. 'That's the kind of business we wanted – no books, no taxes, no worries. And, best of all, strictly low risk and high reward. Right? What could be easier? We grab a few surplus animals now and then, carefully chosen so they won't be missed until it's too late, and then, like you were just telling us, you do a public service and feed a few solo mums and pensioners.

'Now you tell us you're feeling a little nervous. That you're getting a bad vibe. But Dennis and I aren't quite ready to stop trading just yet. Things have been going like clockwork so far and there's no sign that's going to change. So you just relax and hang with us for a little while longer. If you get nervous, think of that nest egg you're putting away. And if you get real nervous, think of what your partners might do to your other assets if they were disappointed in your performance.'

Dennis had offered to light Fraser's cigarette but Fraser had refused. He now pulled out a book of matches, struck one, and lit the cigarette. He held the match in his calloused fingers for a moment and then, grinning at Barry, tossed the still-burning match into the long grass beside the drive. The match seemed to go out and then, like magic, a small flame blossomed and began to spread slowly through the grass.

'You crazy mother-fucker!' Barry cried and leaped forward to stamp out the flames. 'What do you think you're doing?' In a few seconds the fire was out, leaving a thin trickle of smoke rising in the calm night air. Barry stood in the centre of the small charred patch, panting heavily and staring with a volatile combination of fear and hatred at Fraser. His fists were clenched at his sides, his face was flushed and his blond hair had fallen across his eyes.

Fraser opened the door of the truck and turned to swing up into the cab. 'Hop in the truck,' he said cheerfully, 'we'll give you a ride to the house. We'd better get our money and be on the road before it gets light.'

After breakfast Bridget picked up her bag, grabbed her sunglasses, got in her ute, an 8-year-old Toyota flatbed, and headed for town. She had to buy groceries, arrange delivery of some posts, strainers and wire to replace a dodgy stretch of fencing, and she needed to talk to her banker about extending her line of credit. The morning was still and clear, with no sign of the summer haze that often built up in the afternoon.

She pulled out onto the main road and switched on the radio. She drove leisurely along the winding road, humming softly with the music. The ute had almost three hundred thousand kilometres on it but the radio was still good and she turned up the volume.

Her last paddock was less than a kilometre down the road. As she reached the large windbreak that marked the paddock boundary she slowed slightly so that she could check on the cattle she'd moved there a week ago.

Bridget's eyes swept across the expanse of grass and then, when she didn't see anything, they darted more hurriedly from front to back and left to right, searching for any sign of the cattle. The paddock was gently undulating but there was no place where the cattle could be out of sight.

'Oh shit!' Bridget exclaimed, as she swerved to the shoulder of the road and skidded to a halt. *Those bloody cattle went through the damned fence before I could replace it*, she thought. *They'll be making a mess of Elliot's alfalfa.*

She was out of the ute in a flash, jumped the ditch and leaned on the wire fence. Her eyes carefully searched every inch of the paddock, every inch of the boundary fence, but there was no sign of any animals or any break in the wire. She went to a post and quickly climbed over the fence, then walked to the water trough adjacent to the far boundary. The area around it was muddy and covered with hoofprints and cow pats. She kicked one softly with her boot and saw it was still soft.

Straightening up, she looked again around the paddock. Nearly two hectares of grass stretched between the windbreaks and from the road to the back fence. Nothing was out of order, there just weren't any cattle. 'Bloody hell,' she muttered, 'where have you silly buggers gone?' She walked over to the gate by the small loading pen adjacent to the highway. There were more fresh prints and cow shit inside the loading pen. She looked closer at the gate into the pen and saw that the latch was undone.

Her eyes narrowed and she opened the gate and walked up the loading chute. The latch on the chute gate wasn't shut, either, and two strips leading up to the chute were beaten flat in the long grass between the road and the yards. She latched the gate slowly and her face darkened. She hit the wood with the flat of her hand and shouted 'Goddamn it! God damn you to hell!'

———

Hugh woke at dawn and couldn't get back to sleep. All he could think about was the arrival of Tui Dancer. Everything was ready, but still he worried. The owners' instructions had been clear and everything had to go right. Tui Dancer was owned by a powerful Chinese syndicate with a string of successful horses in their stable. Hugh had been looking after Tui Dancer since they'd bought him and, although his services had been somewhat unconventional and closely monitored, they had paid very well. He also knew that excuses weren't an option and the owners would replace him in a heartbeat if they weren't happy with him.

Hugh's father had been a carpenter for the railways; a nine-to-five job that had suited his talents. He'd also been a passionate rower, winning national championships before his children were born. Ben, Hugh's older brother by five years, had no interest in physical activity but had excelled at university and was now the chief financial officer for one of Australia's largest companies.

Hugh looked up to his father and brother and had always lived life flat out. It didn't matter what it was – his job, his family, his rugby – he gave it everything. But in his eyes he was never quite as good, never got the gold medal or the academic kudos or the financial rewards. The flat-out pursuit of a goal could involve considerable risk-taking – but always calculated risks, he assured himself and his wife, Barbara. Hugh skated on the edge but had never fallen over – so far.

Now, when Hugh woke up and faced the new day he felt a cold tendril of real fear. Treating Tui Dancer had started as just another business challenge, but working with the Chinese syndicate had taken him to new levels of risk and responsibility and, for the first time, Hugh wasn't sure he was in control. Deep down, he suspected that if he failed to deliver on his promises he might suffer more than just being fired.

At 6 a.m. he got out of bed, put on his clothes and went out to have one last look at the barn which housed his stables before Tui Dancer arrived. The morning was clear and the dew sparkled on the long grass beside the drive. He paused to look at the green of the pines on the hills that marked the back of his property, and smelled the rhododendrons that still flowered by the back porch.

In the barn he turned on the light and walked straight to the stable he'd prepared the day before. The barn was old, his father and two uncles had built it in the 1930s, but the interior had been refinished a few years ago as his practice grew and he needed the space to look after animals. There were five stables along the back wall and two more to his left along the side wall. To the right were his office, with the door closed; next to it another room with a large, padded operating table, an overhead hoist for lifting animals onto it, and cabinets with medical supplies, the door closed and locked; and beyond that a large open storage area piled high with tools and equipment used around the farm.

Hugh pushed open the stable door and went inside. The air had a faint smell of disinfectant and a spicy freshness from the thick bed of wood shavings on the floor. The walls were some two metres high, made of stout timber reinforced with heavy bracing. To the left was a feed trough and water bucket, and several large rings were set into the walls in case it was necessary to secure an animal. Hugh stepped back into the barn and stared into the dawn, thinking of Tui Dancer and the challenge he faced. He continued to stare and a plan formed slowly in his mind.

Barbara and Hugh had separate beds and she hadn't woken when he got up. She got up at 7 a.m., her usual time, put on her robe and went to the kitchen. It was not unusual to find her husband gone; the hours of darkness seemed to be the preferred time for cows and horses to have difficult births. She made coffee and toast and sat at the breakfast table, reading the latest issue of a news magazine. The sun beamed in on her through the big kitchen windows and she could feel sweat start to form under her arms and across her forehead.

When she refilled her coffee cup she noticed that Hugh's truck was still parked by the back door. She wrinkled her forehead, cocked her head slightly and listened, but couldn't hear any noise coming from the barn. She tugged at the belt on her robe, slipped on her shoes by the back door and walked across the yard to the barn. 'Hugh?' she called out as she pushed the door open. 'Hugh, are you there?'

She opened the door wide and walked uncertainly towards the back of the barn, her eyes adjusting to the dim light. 'Are you all right?' she asked. Her voice was anxious, strained. 'Hugh, what's the matter?'

Hugh turned from the stable and walked towards her. 'Nothing, Barb. I couldn't sleep and came out to see that everything's set for Tui Dancer.'

Barbara was silhouetted in the morning light but even in shadow he could see her slender frame that still looked stylish in anything she wore. Her skin was remarkably smooth, with just enough lines to show she'd enjoyed life. Her tousled medium-length grey hair was the only sign that she wouldn't see 50 again.

He put his arm around her shoulder and they walked back towards the entrance to the barn. 'You remember that I told you Tui Dancer's arriving today?' he asked. 'I've been thinking about what to do with him. The owners want his stay here to be a secret. People are in and out of here all the time and I'm worried that someone might see him. I was wondering if it might be a better idea to hold him somewhere nearby, somewhere more low profile, so there's less chance of news of his examination getting out. Those racing reporters would like a scoop and it would only take one person with sharp eyes and a big mouth to give it to them.'

'Do you really think that's likely, Hugh?' she asked. 'And anyway, who cares if anyone knows that Tui Dancer's here?'

'Barb, as far as the public knows, Tui Dancer's at his trainer's for rest and observation. That he's recovering from overwork. And his owners have been very explicit that's the only message they want out there. Any indication that there's something wrong with him could affect his future stud fees. They don't want any hint of a physical problem that might be passed on to his foals.'

'Okay, Hugh. But if he has a problem then don't people need to know about it?'

'Sure, Barb, but we don't know that yet. We need to do the tests first and see. The owners will decide what to do if we find a problem.'

'But if he can't stay here, then where do you have in mind?'

Hugh paused in the open door and looked around the yard before turning back to Barbara. 'It's got to be nearby and have facilities suitable for a horse like Tui Dancer. I was thinking of taking him to Bridget's place.'

Barbara nodded slowly and took Hugh's arm as they walked together towards the house. 'Yeah,' she said, 'that could work. Have you asked her yet? I'm sure she'd be keen to have him. She wouldn't get many chances to have a horse like that at her stables.' As they went through the kitchen door she asked, 'Have you had breakfast yet?'

———

Gordon was lingering over a cup of coffee in Vern's Café, the only place in town that knew the difference between an espresso and Esperanto. He wasn't a country boy; he'd grown up in Auckland and appreciated a good coffee. The interior was bright and the tables were almost full with morning customers. He had already paid and was about to go when he saw Bridget's ute hurtle up the street and jerk to a halt in one of the angled parking spots in front of the police station across the road. Drawing surprised looks from the other patrons, he stood up and almost ran to the door. Hauling it open he nearly collided with a slow-moving pensioner on the footpath who shouted out, 'Hey, watch where you're going!' But Gordon was moving fast, dodging the parking meter and ducking between the parked cars on his side of the street and he hardly heard the old fellow. He glanced in both directions and darted across the street, catching up with Bridget just as she stepped onto the footpath.

'Bridget! Hey, Bridget! What's the hurry?'

Bridget whirled and her angry face didn't relax when she saw him. 'Gordon. Shit. I don't have time for you right now,' she said and turned back towards the police station.

Gordon skipped in front of her and blocked her progress. He was about her height but more solid and had no trouble holding out his arms and stopping her on the footpath. 'Come on, Bridget. What's happened? What's the hurry?' he repeated. Bridget put her hands on her hips and her anger seemed to rise even further. The conversation hadn't started as well as Gordon had hoped, but he hadn't had a chance to speak to Bridget since he'd returned to town three months ago. He desperately wanted to talk to her, but he began to wonder if perhaps this wasn't the right time. His arms dropped to his side and his shoulders drooped slightly. 'Bridget, come on. Just give me a minute. We have to talk.'

'Gordon, I can't think of a single thing that I have to say to you.' Bridget pushed her sunglasses up onto her head and looked at him. Her voice was like ice and her deep brown eyes were locked on his.

Gordon could sense that she was about to push past and he raised his hands again entreatingly.

'Bridget, what do you want me to say? That I'm sorry? That I was wrong? That I'm a complete idiot? Do you think that I enjoyed making a fool of myself? I know we can't forget it, but can't we at least talk about it?'

'Talk? There's nothing to talk about. Don't forget it was you who ran off with the Australian television bimbo, not me. And you seemed to be enjoying yourself quite a lot with her before you left. You think you made a fool of yourself? Well how much of a fool do you think I felt when the whole town knew what was going on except me?' She pulled her sunglasses back down. 'Now, if you don't mind I have to report some stolen cattle.' Bridget stepped sideways, past his still outstretched hands, and moved towards the police station.

It took almost a second for Gordon's professional reflexes to overcome his personal distress, long enough for Bridget to step past and reach the door. Far too late he spun on his heel and called after her, 'Cattle? Stolen cattle? Hey, Bridget, that's a story! When did you …?' His question was cut off by the closing of the station door.

———

Dani Painter enjoyed being a cop. Most of all, she enjoyed being a small town cop. When she'd joined the force eight years ago she'd served her first three years in Auckland, and had hated it. She'd expected the long hours, the discipline, and even the violence. But the personal abuse and the seemingly endless stream of mindless viciousness began to make her wonder about her job and even ask herself *What's the point?*

She began to drink, broke up with her boyfriend, and was on the verge of resigning when this job came up. She knew little about police work in a small town but figured she had nothing to lose. It couldn't be worse than policing in Auckland and she wasn't quite ready to toss in her career. Dani applied and was surprised when she was accepted. Looking back, she wondered whether the panel had seen something in her that she hadn't seen herself, because she had to admit that she enjoyed the job and had been good at it.

Although she had grown up in Auckland, Dani found that she immediately fitted into the life of the small town. She was of average height, trim and fit with dirty blonde hair, cut medium length and gathered in a short ponytail. She had a good memory for names and she enjoyed talking to people about the weather and the crops and the animals and all the other mundane things that were important to the community. She'd joined the cricket club and had started making friends at the gym. Of course there was just as high a percentage of bad apples here as in Auckland, but they didn't seem to have the same propensity for violent anarchy. Fights in the pub, drunk drivers, dope growing, graffiti, child or wife abuse – the offences were the same but Dani didn't feel as though the fabric of society, or more particularly the fabric of *her* society, was threatened by them.

The police station had originally been a modest state house brick bungalow. It had been modified so that the lounge became the public waiting room, with several chairs and a large, scarred desk, and two of the bedrooms became offices. The station was a small one with a sergeant and four constables. Dani was on watch, seated at the desk in the front room, and had just finished reading the bulletins from Wellington when the door opened and Bridget Crawford burst in. Dani raised her head and watched as Bridget strode across the room to stand in front of her desk.

When Gordon had done a runner with the Aussie sheila and left Bridget to look after the farm, Dani had wondered what Bridget would do next. She'd seen Bridget struggling with her herd once when she'd been on her rounds, had offered to help and hadn't been offended when Bridget had told her 'Thanks, but I can manage.' She eyed Bridget's wind-blown hair, flushed features and flashing eyes when she walked through the door. Bridget had her complete attention when she said, 'I want to report a crime.'

'A crime?' Dani repeated, reaching for a pen and report pad. 'What's the problem? What's happened?'

'Cattle rustlers,' Bridget replied. 'I've lost a dozen cattle from my north paddock. And I want you to catch them and roast their balls.'

Dani leaned back in her chair and scratched her chin with the cap on her ballpoint pen. Cattle rustling wasn't exactly one of the common crimes she dealt with. However, everyone knew it happened, and lately it had been becoming more common. Usually, though, rustling was just a couple of sheep or a cow bowled for a barbeque. It was also bloody hard to do anything about because by the time the crime was discovered the evidence was on the grill. So, on Dani's personal crime scale, based on a feeling for the severity of the crime and the chance of solution, Bridget's announcement of cattle rustling ranked somewhere behind murder-suicide and ahead of auto-theft. 'Okay,' she said, 'take a seat and tell me what happened.'

Bridget glanced behind her and moved one of the chairs closer to the edge of the desk. Sitting, she swept her hair back behind her ears, braced herself with her hands on her knees and looked Dani in the eye. Dani had her pen and pad ready and was looking at her expectantly.

'Well,' Bridget began, 'I was driving into town and couldn't see the cattle in my north paddock. I was afraid that they had broken out and were in Elliot's alfalfa so I stopped the ute and had a look. There was no sign of them and no breaks in the fence. You know that loading ramp I have on the yards in that paddock? The gate on it was open, there was fresh shit inside, and tracks in the grass verge leading up to it. I know the cattle were there yesterday so the bastards must have come by last night and taken them.'

Dani asked, 'There's no chance the gate was left open by mistake? Or some kids opened it as a prank and your cattle wandered off down the road?' The prospect of the paperwork that was likely to come out of this interview was definitely not appealing.

Bridget gave her a withering look. 'I do not leave gates open. It's nearly a metre drop from the end of the ramp. The nearest kids live five kilometres down the road and think that exercise is a dangerous disease. And if cattle were wandering down the road then someone would have seen them and reported them. Have you had any calls about stray cattle?'

'Um, not yet,' Dani conceded, 'I guess you may be right about them being stolen.' She sighed, looked up from her notes and said, 'There were twelve cattle?'

'Yeah, and those sons-of-bitches stole every one. Now I want to know what you're going to do about it.'

'Okay. When was the last time you saw them?'

'I saw them when I went to town yesterday afternoon. When I drove by this morning they were gone.'

Dani finished writing her notes. 'Right, I'll come out this morning and have a look and see if there's any other evidence. But I've got to tell you, Bridget, that rustling's not an easy crime to solve.'

'Fuck easy,' said Bridget, 'I want my cows back or I want those guys in jail. Preferably both.' She got up to leave. 'Thanks for your time, Dani. I can meet you at the paddock if you want me to. Let me know when you'll be there.' Bridget put her sunglasses on as the door closed behind her.

Gordon was still waiting outside, leaning on a parking meter. He stepped over to her before she could reach her car. 'Bridget? Hey, what's this about cattle rustling? Did you lose some stock? Is there anything I can do to help?'

Bridget eyed him warily as she stepped around him. 'Yeah, some bastards took some cows from the north paddock. And no, there's nothing you can do.' She stepped off the curb and opened the door to her ute.

'Bridget, hey, wait, Bridget,' said Gordon. 'Give me a second here. Maybe if we put something in the paper it will prompt someone to come forward and you'll get some information about who did it.'

Bridget didn't pause as she slipped into the driver's seat and started the engine. She put the ute in reverse but, before backing out, looked out of the window at Gordon. 'Okay. Put a story in the paper if you want to. But I don't have time to talk. Dani has the details. Tell her I said it was okay to give them to you.'

Gordon stepped back onto the footpath as she reversed and drove off down the street.

———

The phone was ringing as Bridget unlocked her front door. She ran to grab it on the extension in the kitchen and gasped, 'Hello?'

'Hey, Bridget, it's Hugh.'

'Hugh!' she exclaimed. 'I just got in and had to dash for the phone. How's Tui Dancer? Has he settled in okay?'

'Well,' Hugh said, and Bridget could sense the tiredness and tension in his voice, 'that's what I'm calling about. He hasn't arrived yet. He's not due until late this morning. But I'd like to ask you a favour.'

'Sure,' Bridget replied without hesitation, 'what can I do?'

'I was wondering,' Hugh paused, and then went on, 'I was wondering if I could keep Tui Dancer at your place. Just for a couple of days. I know it would be an inconvenience but I'll pay you, of course.' He paused again and continued tiredly, 'I'm sorry. I'm in a bit of a bind and don't know what else to do. Will you help?'

'Of course. You know I'd be thrilled to have Tui Dancer here, even for a night. I can get one of the spare stables fixed up in no time.' Bridget thought quickly and then continued, 'But I don't understand. Why isn't Tui Dancer staying with you? You have all the facilities there to look after him, better than I do.'

Hugh sighed. 'Well, the owners are very sensitive about bad publicity and they don't want anyone to know he's not with his trainer. I know it's unlikely but I really don't want to risk anyone finding out he's here. I figure no one will be looking at your place. We'll be able to bring him in, give him an exam and get him back to the trainer without anyone knowing he's gone.' He paused for a second, 'Besides, your stables are well set up, they're close to mine and as I'm already your vet no one will think it odd that I come to your place.'

'Okay, no worries,' Bridget said brightly. 'That'll be amazing. Is there anything special that you'll need?'

'You're a treasure,' Hugh responded, 'I hoped I could count on you.' His voice picked up slightly and he continued more briskly, 'No, there's nothing special you need to do. I'll bring over anything I can think of but he should be fine with your usual expert care.'

'Okay. I'll get started on the stable right now. When do you think you'll arrive?'

'The van's due here soon, so I'd guess just after lunch. That will give us plenty of time to get him settled and I can have a look at him before dark.'

'That's fine, I'll see you soon then.'

'Right. And thanks, Bridget. I owe you a big one for this.'

'Oh,' she replied airily. 'A big one. A big favour. To be repaid with interest. I can't wait.'

CHAPTER 3

The big van was painted a royal red and had Meridian Transporters in large gold letters on the sides. It pulled into Hugh's drive at 11.30 a.m. and stopped near the barn door, the small cloud of dust raised on the gravel drive washing over it and dissipating as it passed the cab. The driver, Sam Norris, and his assistant, Ben Greeling, got out of the cab and stretched in the sunshine, looking appreciatively at the tidy array of grounds and outbuildings.

'Whaddya reckon?' asked Ben as he walked around the front of the van to stand beside his partner. 'Looks pretty sweet.'

'Sweet as,' Sam replied, pushing his sunglasses up onto his long wavy hair. 'But we're not here to buy the place. Just get this horse unloaded and we're back on the road.'

As he finished speaking Hugh appeared in the barn entrance, wiping his hands on a rag. Hugh walked to where the two men stood and shook their hands as he greeted them. 'Hugh Jacobs,' he said and nodded as the other two introduced themselves.

Sam gestured to Ben and said, 'Go ahead and get the back open mate.' He looked at Hugh and continued, 'We'll have him out in a jiffy. Do you want him to go straight in the stables there?'

Hugh cleared his throat. 'I'm sorry, but there's been a change of plans. We're going to take him to one of my neighbour's. It's not far from here.'

Sam frowned and crossed his arms. 'I'm not sure I can do that. My papers say to deliver the horse to you. I don't think I can take him somewhere else just on your say-so.'

Hugh had forgotten about the instructions the transport company would have been given. They accepted liability for horses during transport but only to the designated destination. He turned towards the house and said over his shoulder, 'Come on inside and get something to drink. I'll call Max and clear it with him. Max is the horse's trainer. If he says it's okay, will that be good enough for you?'

Sam shrugged and said, 'I guess. We'll have to call it in to our office, but if it's in writing it will probably be okay.'

———

Bridget was just collecting the last of the old wood shavings from the floor into a large bucket when a familiar voice called out, 'Bridget? Bridget, are you there?'

'Back here, Elliot,' she replied. She recognised the voice of her neighbour Elliot Hayes and moved towards the front of the stables to meet him. The lean, weather-beaten body was framed in the doorway, looking intently towards her as she approached. 'How are you doing?' she asked as she reached him and gave the old man a brief hug.

'I'm fine. I just dropped in to ask if you knew that the cattle in the paddock up by my place are missing? There's no sign of a break in the fence and I haven't seen them in my paddocks.'

Bridget nodded angrily and stepped out into the warm sunshine. 'Yes, I noticed it when I drove to town earlier. I've just got back from talking to the cops. Looks to me like they've been stolen.'

'Stolen?' Elliot asked incredulously. 'That's crazy. Who'd steal a few cattle? Hell, the price of beef is so low I'd just about pay somebody to take mine off my hands so I didn't have to feed them.'

'Well, all I know is that it looks as if someone backed a truck up to the loading chute and took them some time last night. I reported it to the police in town. Dani said it's not all that uncommon, but she wasn't terribly optimistic about catching the bastards, either. The worst thing is I feel so betrayed,' she went on. 'You know what I mean? It's like we were living in a place where everyone could be trusted and things like this couldn't happen. Now that's spoiled and I'm not sure I can trust anybody. Besides being really pissed off I feel like I have to start locking my doors and worrying about security.'

Elliot raised his cap and scratched his head. 'Yeah, it's a bad business, all right.' He rubbed his hand along the side of his jaw. 'I'm not sure what we can do about it, though.'

'Do about it?' exclaimed Bridget. 'I'll tell you what we can do about it. We can get the cops to track them down and put them in jail. And if they can't do the job then we can bloody well look after ourselves.'

'Vigilante justice?' Elliot asked wryly. 'I doubt that that will be necessary.'

'Hmph,' said Bridget angrily. 'Vigilante my ass. Wait until it's your cattle that are missing. All I know is that I'm bloody mad and someone's going to pay.' She relaxed suddenly and laughed. 'Hell, you're right. I need to get a grip. I may make as much off the insurance as I would have at the sale yards.' She gestured towards the stables and said, 'Hey, while you're here, can you spare a minute to help me clean out one of these boxes?'

'Sure. What's the occasion? You haven't bought another racehorse have you?' Elliot asked, with a twinkle in his eye. Elliot was firmly convinced that racehorses were like lotteries, a tax on stupidity.

Bridget laughed again. 'No. Not me. Hugh's supposed to be looking after one, though. Tui Dancer, a real top horse. His stables are full, though, so he asked me to look after him for a day or so until he can return him to his trainer.' She put a hand over her mouth and said, 'Oops. But it's supposed to be a secret. Hugh doesn't want anyone to know that he's coming here instead of staying at his place. So don't say anything, please.'

Elliot grinned: 'No worries. Your secret's safe with me.'

The dim light in the stables seemed to enhance the rich smell of animals and feed and wood shavings. Bridget grabbed the bucket of soiled shavings she'd just filled and carried it out of the stables. She and Elliot then grabbed a bag of fresh shavings and took it into the box, spreading it in a thick layer on the floor. Bridget checked that there was fresh water and said, 'Thanks Elliot. I told Hugh it was no problem, but there's going to be a hell of a lot of work to do for the next few days.'

Elliot put his hand on her shoulder and gripped it tightly. 'Look, I know how hard you're working to make a go of this place on your own. I don't have a lot on at the moment so I'll come around and give you hand for a while.'

'But,' Bridget began, but was interrupted as Elliot carried on.

'No, there are no "buts". Haven't you learned by now that you can never win an argument with a pensioner?' Elliot asked with a smile. He stepped outside and Bridget followed. 'At least you won't have to worry about me making the moves on you like some of the young blokes around here,' he said and was delighted to see Bridget blush slightly and turn away.

Bridget slapped him on the arm and said, 'You're terrible!' She glanced at her watch and said, 'Oh no! Look at the time! It's almost one o'clock and Hugh said he'd bring Tui Dancer around after lunch.' She turned to Elliot and said, 'Come inside. I'll give you lunch. It's the least I can do and we might need a hand when Tui Dancer arrives.'

———

'Hey, Fraser,' Dennis said, trying to get Fraser's attention. His voice was raised because he had his earphones in his ears. He was sitting on an old sofa in the front room of their rental house. The sofa was covered in a sheet, yellowed and stained by neglect, to conceal the holes in the torn upholstery. A badly worn scrap of carpet lay on the dusty floor and the walls were covered in a gaudy floral wallpaper, the height of fashion in the 1970s but now faded and hanging loosely from the walls. The afternoon sun streamed through the open window that looked out onto the porch, the sunburnt weeds in the yard and the suburban street. The view was dry and dusty and worn out, like the day after a travelling fair left town and the grass had been trampled by thousands of too hot feet and the tired soil showed no trace of the water from melted snow cones. The curtains were long gone, but another sheet, the mate of the one on the sofa, had been hung on the curtain rod and pulled to one side.

Fraser was sitting on the one nice piece of furniture in the whole house, an orthopaedic reclining rocker that he'd bought at a furniture auction. He was reading the evening paper and didn't look up when Dennis spoke to him. His wavy blond hair, long on top and shorter on the sides, was combed back from his forehead and behind his ears. The blond hair, pale eyebrows and light blue eyes gave him a Nordic appearance, though as far as he knew his ancestors and relatives were exclusively English and Scottish. Perhaps his looks were a souvenir of the Viking raids more than a thousand years ago. He was average in height and his compact frame looked almost small in the big chair.

Dennis had originally found Fraser's indifference to him and what he said tremendously annoying, but had eventually given up expecting anything else. He had finally accepted Fraser's behaviour, mistaking self-centeredness for deep thought. And besides, nothing he could do, except leave, would alter their relationship.

'Hey, Fraser,' Dennis repeated, and carried on without waiting for a response, 'Do you want chicken or burgers for dinner?' He didn't really expect an answer and focused again on the music.

Fraser lowered the paper to his lap and looked across the room at Dennis. He saw a medium-sized guy slouched on the sofa, the hair long and unkempt, bleached golden by the sun. It was hanging over his ears and almost into his eyes. The ears were pronounced but not comical and he had what looked like a five-day beard. How he kept it that length was a puzzle to Fraser as he'd never seen Dennis either shave or trim his beard. Dennis was wearing faded denim jeans and a purple T-shirt with Lakers written in flowing gold script across the front. One leg was crossed over the other and he was wearing dark socks with holes in the toes. His dirty white sneakers lay on the floor beside the sofa. His earphones were connected to the phone on the arm of the sofa and he was engrossed in an eight-month-old issue of *Woman's Weekly*. Fraser reflected, once again, that Dennis was the perfect partner, someone who didn't mind letting him be the boss. Dennis did everything he was told without asking questions.

Fraser's thoughts were interrupted by the sound of knocking on the front door. Whatever Dennis was listening to was obviously so loud he couldn't hear the knocking. Fraser had once sneaked a look at Dennis' playlist and had been horrified by the vile mixture of everything from gangster rap to Korean pop. Dennis could just as easily be listening to Ice Cube, the Natural Dread Killaz or Johnny Cash. Fraser put the paper aside, got up and went to the door.

'Hello?' The girl had long brown hair hanging loosely past her shoulders and was dressed in jeans and a T-shirt that said Free Tibet (with purchase of another Tibet of equal or greater value). The push of her breasts against the shirt made Fraser think of Tibet, or at least the Himalayas. She had broad cheekbones, dark eyes, incredibly smooth skin and a dimple in her chin. She was above average height and looked Fraser in the eye as she stood easily on the doorstep. She looked about 18 but Fraser figured she must be older.

Fraser stood in the doorway with one hand on the edge of the door, ready to close it firmly if this turned out to be another visit from the Mormons, although it seemed unlikely they would send someone dressed so impertinently to proselytise. He looked over her shoulder to see if anyone was with her and said, 'Yeah? We have enough Tibets, thanks.'

She laughed, shook her head and pulled some strands of hair behind her ear with her left hand. 'No, that's okay, I'm looking for Dennis. Is he here?'

Fraser looked at her again and thought, *Dennis? Why would an attractive girl be looking for Dennis? And how did she find us anyway? Nobody knows where we're staying. Nobody.* He hesitated for a second, weighing the potential trouble she represented against his curiosity about how she had found them, and then stepped aside and said, 'Sure, come on in. He's in the lounge.'

The girl stepped past him and Fraser caught a hint of her scent, though it was so faint he wasn't sure he hadn't imagined it. Earthy rather than floral. Sandalwood? Cinnamon? Fraser shook his head and followed her to the lounge.

The girl moved through the short hall and when she entered the lounge and saw Dennis she quickly stepped towards him. Dennis was facing away from the door but caught a glimpse of her movement out of the corner of his eye and swung to see her. When he saw who it was, a smile lit up his face and he stood up quickly, the cell phone dragging the earphones from his ears as it fell to the floor.

'Hey, Venus!' he said as he gave her a big hug. The girl responded with equal enthusiasm, keeping her hand on his arm as they pulled apart. 'Venus! Hey! Wow, it's been a long time. How are you? How's your mom? What are you doing here?'

'I'm good, I'm good. How are you?' she replied.

'Fuck, this is amazing!' Dennis said. 'I thought you were still in uni in Wellington. What happened?'

The girl shrugged and looked away from Dennis. 'Well, you know, one thing led to another and I decided it was time for a change.' Her face brightened and she looked back at him and said, 'And here I am.'

Fraser moved into the room behind her with a half-smile on his face. 'Venus? That's your name? For real? Were you named after the tennis player?'

The girl laughed again and shook her head. 'Shit no. My mom's a physicist, not an athlete. She named me after the planet. She says I'm her morning star.'

Fraser's grin widened. 'You're lucky your mom stuck with the inner planets. Being named Uranus or Pluto wouldn't be so much fun.'

'Yeah, and it's easier to spell than Ganymede,' Venus responded. She'd had a lifetime of dealing with dickheads who thought her name was funny.

Fraser knew when he was outgunned and let that one slide. He responded, 'So how do you know Dennis?'

Venus looked at Dennis and said, 'We grew up together. We were best mates. We went to the same high school until we graduated. I went to uni in Wellington and Dennis sort of disappeared.'

'Didn't I hear that your parents split up?' asked Dennis. 'That must have been tough.'

Venus nodded, 'Yeah, it sucked for a while but it was really for the best.'

'You said your mom's a physicist? She's at the university? You've been living with her?' Fraser asked.

Venus shook her head and grimaced. 'No way. I haven't lived with either mom or dad since high school. Anyway, she's in Switzerland and my dad's in California.'

'Switzerland? California? Shit, they must really hate each other,' said Fraser.

'No, they actually like each other,' Venus said. 'They just can't live together. Mom's at CERN, the nuclear research lab in Switzerland. She went to Berkeley for her Ph.D. and met dad there. He's a software developer. They moved to Auckland and had me but in the end New Zealand was just too small for both of them. When I went to uni they divorced and got their dream jobs.'

Fraser's smile dropped and he asked, 'So, Venus, this is all interesting and it's great to meet you and all, but, um, how did you find us? It's not like we're in the phone book.'

Venus walked across the room and sat on the old sofa. She looked Fraser up and down and asked, 'Who are you again?'

Dennis jumped in, 'Fraser. His name's Fraser, Venus.'

Venus gave Dennis a quick smile and said, 'Fraser. Okay. Well, Fraser, nobody has a listing in the phone book. Probably not since you were born. You've got to move with the times. I was finishing my Ph.D. in computer science and decided to look up Dennis. I knew Dennis used to have a cell phone. Like most people he hasn't changed his number in at least five years. Using a few database backdoors it wasn't hard to find the area where that phone's calls were being made. So I drove here and switched from digital to analogue.' She saw Fraser look at her blankly and laughed. 'I started doing things the old-fashioned way. It took a few hours of talking to people to narrow the search down to this street. I mean, it's a small town and not many people look like Dennis.'

Fraser looked doubtful. 'You were doing a graduate degree and decided to look up Dennis? This Dennis? Why would you do that?'

Venus shrugged and said, 'Someone famous once said life's like a bowl of shit. Sometimes you have to stop eating the lumps.' She tossed her hair back and continued, 'I was having a very lumpy period at the university. I'd reached a major roadblock in my project. The flat I was in broke up and my thesis advisor was, well, a little more interested in my bits than bytes, if you know what I mean. The thought of a formal complaint and bringing all the mess out into the open was more than I could bear, so I thought a little break from academia was required. Like I said, Dennis was my best mate once and I decided I'd like to see him again.'

Dennis nodded and said, 'Bummer. Definitely time for a change.'

Fraser knew there was a lot more to Venus' story than she was sharing. He looked at her doubtfully and said, 'Yeah, right.' He continued to look at her, getting nothing but an innocent face in return. 'Huh,' he grunted. 'That's it? You're sticking with "*lumpy*"?' He gave the word air quotes. 'Things got lumpy and you decided to come and see Dennis?'

Venus thought about what else to say. Her thesis advisor was the hotshot prodigy of the department and her research was at the cutting edge of artificial intelligence. Venus thrived while she worked closely with him on the challenging project, but every meeting was in his office with a closed door, every conversation was punctuated by his touches and laden with innuendo. The thrill of a revolutionary breakthrough outweighed the predatory behaviour until she discovered that her advisor was sleeping with her roommate, a first-year student in his Introduction to Computers class. Venus didn't want a confrontation. She didn't want to complain to the Vice Chancellor (*Now there's an appropriate title*, she thought). She just wanted to complete her research and get her degree.

But there were limits to what she could tolerate, and screwing first-year students was way over that line. Feeling totally compromised, she'd sent her advisor an email saying she was taking a break, and walked out of the university and her apartment.

Standing in this run-down house Venus didn't know where she was going, what she was doing. She knew she couldn't go back to the university. Not yet. She loved her parents but they were far away. She had no other relatives in New Zealand, no close friends, no one to turn to. It was sad, it was scary, but she realised now why she'd come here. Dennis was all she had. She looked at Fraser and decided none of that was any of his business. She said, 'Yep. That's about it.'

Dennis was oblivious to the undercurrents of the conversation and said, 'Yeah, we're mates. It's great to see her.' In fact she and Dennis had always been best mates. They had the same irreverent sense of humour and enjoyed taking the piss out of anyone they considered a pompous jerk. In high school their matey relationship had evolved to include romantic and then sexual dimensions. Venus had been immensely happy and it had been a wrench when Dennis told her that he wasn't going to university with her.

'You know I'm no good in the classroom,' he'd said, 'you stick with the books and I'll find a trade. I'll always have work and I'll support you when you're an unemployed egghead.'

'But I love you!' Venus had protested. 'How can I go away without you?'

'Well,' said Dennis, 'to start with I'll still be here. You'll be studying in the city and I'll be training in the suburbs, in Porirua.'

'Porirua?' asked Venus. 'What the hell will you do in Porirua?'

'I've got an apprenticeship as a mechanic,' he'd said with a grin. 'I promise to wash the grease from my hands when you introduce me to all your new friends.'

In fact, Dennis had trained as a motor mechanic, a landscape gardener and an agricultural contractor but hadn't managed to stick with any of them. Their relationship had survived for nearly a year, but Dennis' move to the South Island for an agricultural job had been the death knell. Venus had been angry and sad and swore she never wanted to see him again. But when something good happened in her life or problems arose, like her pompous dickhead supervisor, Venus couldn't help occasionally thinking about what Dennis would say.

Fraser thought Venus' story was pretty thin and knew there were many things she wasn't saying, but decided it didn't matter. He said, 'Okay. That's very sad and all. And I'm sure Dennis is really glad to see you. I'm impressed that you used Dennis' cell phone to get here. But you really need to understand that we're doing some sensitive shit and are trying to fly under the radar, if you know what I mean.'

Venus just laughed and shook her head. 'Get into the twenty-first century, boys. Do you have any idea how hard it is to keep the whole fucking world from knowing what you had for breakfast? I'm good, but I'm not MI5 or the CIA. If you want to fly below the radar then you have to seriously raise your game.'

Before Fraser could respond, his cell phone buzzed in his pocket. He pulled it out, looked at the screen and frowned. The screen showed 'number blocked'. Like this house address, nobody was supposed to have his cell phone number unless he gave it to them. He looked at Dennis and Venus sitting on the sofa and, without speaking, got up and moved into the hall. He stepped into the kitchen before hitting the answer button. He didn't speak but just listened to the phone.

'Mr Lyman? Fraser Lyman, is that you?' a male voice asked.

Fraser thought about saying no or hanging up, but decided he needed to find out who had his number and how they'd got it. 'Who are you?' he asked. 'What do you want? How did you get this number?'

'That is of no importance,' the voice said, 'but what I have to tell you could be *very* important. If you give me a few minutes of your time I think you will learn something that will prove very interesting. And very lucrative.'

'Look,' Fraser said, 'I don't care who you are or what you have to say. I want to know how you got my name and number.'

The voice paused for a moment, then said, 'Let's just say we have a mutual friend who suggested your name, and I have friends who are very good at finding people.' There was another brief hesitation in the voice and then it continued, 'Our friend explained to me about your unfortunate experience in the business world. He thought you might have potential and has kept an eye on you. We both think that your foray into animal husbandry is a waste of your talents. But really, that's of no consequence. I have your phone number. I know what car you

drive. I know where you live. Is it 81 or 83 Tawa Street, Mr Lyman?
Just joking,' the voice added, though Fraser could detect no humour in
its tone, 'We both know it's 85.'

Neither party spoke for a while. 'Are you there, Mr Lyman?' the
voice on the phone asked. 'Is there anything you'd like to say?'

'No.' Fraser replied. 'Not really. I just want to know what the fuck
you want.'

'Really, Mr Lyman, such language,' the voice said. 'I want you to
know that we're serious. We have significant resources at our disposal.
We know who you are. We know how to find you.'

Fraser fought a moment of panic. First a girl finds him and now
some anonymous voice on the phone had done so, too. In a few
minutes he'd gone from complacency to alarm; from thinking he was
invisible to feeling that there was a spotlight on him. Fraser flashed
back to Venus' arrival and thought about what the voice had said. If
some girl had found him, then maybe that meant the voice didn't have
as many resources as it said. Unless that girl was very, very good – or
if she was working with the voice. Shit. Fraser ran his hand through his
hair and tried to think.

His thoughts were interrupted when the voice continued: 'I know
that you have certain skills that would be useful to me, and I can offer
you rewards that will be useful to you. If you will agree to listen to
what I have to say then I think we can very quickly come to a mutually
agreeable arrangement.'

Fraser was still shaken but he was recovering fast. This wasn't his
first encounter with 'serious' people. He didn't know who the voice was
or who was behind it, but he was sure it would be risky to cross him.
He quickly decided he had no option. 'Okay,' he said, 'let's hear what
you have to say.'

There was no hint of satisfaction in the voice when it continued, as
though it, too, knew Fraser had no option and was only waiting
patiently for him to reach the same conclusion. 'I know you have some
expertise in, shall we say, acquiring things through unofficial channels.
In particular, I know you have expertise in stealing livestock. I want

you to use that expertise to steal a horse. I will pay you a great deal of money to do this. Are you interested?'

Fraser thought for a long moment. Finally he said, 'Yeah, maybe. I need to know more about the horse. Stealing a horse from a top stable is very different from stealing a cow from a paddock. Those places have security systems for Africa.'

The voice responded smoothly, 'Don't worry. Security will not be a problem. The horse will be in a stable but the security will be minimal.'

'Okay, if you say so, but even if the security isn't tight it's still a big risk. You mentioned payment of a large sum of money. How large would that be?'

Again there was no change in the voice. 'You will be paid ten thousand dollars for your efforts. You will be paid one thousand dollars when you agree to take the job and the rest when it's completed.'

Fraser was quiet while he thought it over. 'Maybe I can do it. But I need more information, a lot more information, before I can decide.'

'Certainly,' said the voice. 'I can't give you specific details until the operation starts, but I can give you the broad outlines. 'First, the horse. The horse is one of New Zealand's top racehorses, named Tui Dancer. He has had an excellent season but has recently lost form. He is being sent to a veterinarian in your district for assessment.' The voice paused momentarily and then said, 'Am I going too fast for you, Mr Lyman? Do you need to take notes?'

Fraser grunted, 'Uh, yeah, hang on a minute.' While he pawed through the debris on the kitchen counter he thought about the bizarre conversation he was having. His initial fear had faded and he was getting angry at the arrogance and condescending tone of the voice. He didn't know who this guy was, but he decided that it was important to say something to disrupt the flow of conversation. He finally found a pen. There was no paper but he found an envelope that the electricity bill had come in. He said, 'Okay. I got it. Tui Dancer. Racehorse. Local vet. Go on.'

'The horse is a big black stallion,' said the voice, 'with two white socks ...'

'Hang on,' laughed Fraser, 'you're shitting me. I know horses wear shoes, but white socks? Is this a horse or a schoolgirl?'

The voice took a deep breath, struggling to conceal a sense of irritation. 'Socks. They are white markings on two of his feet. And he has a white blaze ...'

'A white blazer?' Fraser misheard deliberately. 'Sounds like *Strictly Ballroom*.'

There was a moment of icy silence on the phone and then the voice replied in its normal, controlled tone. 'A blaze, Mr Lyman. It's a white mark on the face.' There was another moment of silence and then the voice said, 'You were highly recommended, Mr Lyman. I was told you were reliable and trustworthy, and also creative. That you are able to read a situation and adjust your actions accordingly. But now I'm not so sure. Perhaps you are not the person I'm looking for after all. I am offering you a job. A serious job. And a serious amount of money. I suggest you should reflect on our conversation and decide whether your feeble attempts at humour are ... appropriate. I suggest that you may conclude that it is in your interest to concentrate on what I'm telling you. It could be the difference between considerable financial benefits and something ... far less welcome.'

It was Fraser's turn to be silent. He felt the icicle of fear again and was no longer sure that disrupting the flow of conversation had been such a good idea. Eventually he said, 'Okay, let's keep it simple. Big black horse, two white feet, white mark on its face. Anything else?'

Fraser listened without interruption while, over the next few minutes, the voice expanded on where the horse would be found and what should be done with him. The voice concluded by saying, 'We will talk again to discuss the details of your actions once I have confirmed the horse's location and the routine there. Do you have any questions?'

'Yeah,' said Fraser. 'The money. It's not enough. I could drive a truck through parts of your story. There are half a dozen ways things could go wrong. Seriously wrong. And if things turn to shit then it's me holding the can. And besides, I can't do this on my own. I'll have to have help and they'll want a share.'

There was no anger in the response, which Fraser found almost more frightening. 'Do not attempt to negotiate with me. If I wanted to I could have you behind bars, or dead, before you hang up the phone.' The voice was silent for a moment. 'However, I am a fair man and I am prepared to pay a fair amount for your services. You will be paid twenty thousand dollars, with the same terms as before. I trust you find that acceptable.'

Fraser did a fist pump and spun half around before he replied. He kept his voice neutral as he said, 'Yes, but half up front and half on completion. That will be acceptable.' He paused and when there was no response he said, 'When and how will I get the first payment?'

———

Fraser returned to the lounge. He picked up the newspaper where he'd dropped it in his chair and sat down. He quickly found the sports section and scanned the pages until he found the article he was looking for. He skimmed the article. The basics agreed with what the voice had told him.

Dennis and Venus were deep in conversation and neither made any indication that they'd noticed his return. Fraser put the paper down and said, 'Dennis? Hey, Dennis? That call I just got – it was from an interesting bloke. What would you say to branching out into something different?'

Dennis said, 'Branching out. Hmmm. Sounds interesting. You mean we won't steal cows anymore?'

Venus grinned crookedly and said, 'Ah, ha! I wondered what you guys were up to. Now let me guess. The reason you're – she made quote marks with her fingers – "flying under the radar" may have something to do with the, shall we say, off the books nature of your income?'

Fraser pinched his nose between his thumb and forefinger, closed his eyes for a second, and sighed. He was still pissed off that she'd managed to find them so easily. 'Venus? Honey? Could you just shut the fuck up, please? You don't need to worry about the nature of our income. Now I have something I need to talk to Dennis about and it's not for your ears. So could you go to the kitchen and make a cup of tea or something?'

Venus looked at him for a second and then stood up. She left the room without a word and they heard her footsteps retreat down the hall to the kitchen. Fraser turned to Dennis and said, 'Dennis, you heard Barry last night. He's cracking up. I think it's time to make a change. And this may be our big opportunity.'

Dennis squeezed his hands together between his knees, the big knuckles white against the brown skin. 'Okay, opportunities are good. So what are we changing to?'

Fraser unfolded the paper and began to read. 'Tui Dancer, whose successful campaign last year earned total winnings of over one million dollars, has been withdrawn from forthcoming engagements after a string of disappointing finishes. Trainer Max Treadlow said, "We are sure this is a temporary setback and we have every confidence that Tui Dancer will be back on the track as soon as possible."'

Fraser put the paper in his lap and looked at Dennis. 'A million dollars in winnings. A million fucking dollars for running around a stupid track. Not even going anywhere. The article also says that foals from a top stallion went for over two hundred and fifty grand at last year's sale.' Fraser leaned forward and put his forearms on his thighs. 'Does that give you any ideas, Dennis?'

Dennis shrugged. 'Horses? I don't get it. We don't know anything about horses. Or about racing.'

Fraser snorted. 'We don't need to know anything about racing. We're going to steal a horse.'

'Steal one?' Dennis asked. 'What for? What could we do with a stolen horse? Even Barry couldn't help us with a horse.'

Fraser shook his head. 'This is one deal that we definitely don't need Barry's skills for – though his big shed may be handy.' He leaned back in his chair and crossed his legs. 'That phone call just now. The guy said he wants us to steal Tui Dancer. He'll pay us twenty thousand dollars to steal him.'

'You're shitting me. You want to steal a horse and keep it until we get the ransom? You don't know anything about animals. You can't even open a can of dog food. How are we going to look after a bloody horse?'

'We'll only have it until the owners pay the ransom. Even you can throw some hay or whatever feed it has into the stable.'

'Oh, yeah, right. And where are we going to keep it? The neighbours might notice a little thing like a fucking horse in the back yard. Or do you think Barry's going to go along with this? No way. He's shitting himself when we bring him a few cows. What's he going to do if we show up with a bloody million dollar racehorse?'

Fraser waved a hand and said, 'Where we keep the horse is a detail. If we pull this off then we're set for a long time and Barry won't have to worry about us. If we need him then I reckon that the promise of seeing the backside of us might be enough to get his cooperation one last time.' Fraser grinned but Dennis didn't see any humour in the look. 'But if it's not, then I think we may be able to persuade him anyway.'

Dennis didn't look convinced. 'Well, okay, say we get Barry to agree to look after the thing. What are we going to do? Just waltz up to whoever's keeping the horse and say "Please, sir, may we take your horse and hold him for a million dollar ransom?"'

Fraser rubbed his chin and smiled slowly. 'I don't know for sure yet, Dennis, but that doesn't sound too bad. I've always been a fan of keeping it simple.'

Dennis' forehead was creased with worry and he settled back on the sofa and crossed his arms on his chest. 'Man, you may think you know what you're up to here but it sounds like bullshit to me. A million dollar horse is a different ballgame from a few fucking cows. No one bothers looking for a few cows. But you know someone's going to come looking for a racehorse.'

Fraser sighed and said, 'Dennis, listen to me here. I'm sick of fucking cows. I'm sick of this fucking house. I'm sick of thinking small. Trust me. If we pull this off then we're sweet for a very long time.'

Dennis was silent for almost a minute, studying the floor between his feet. He finally looked up at Fraser and said, 'Okay, maybe. But I'm serious. This is way different from stealing a few cows. I don't care what you say, I'm not happy about looking after a horse. Do you know anything about horses? Have you ever even ridden a horse?'

Fraser shook his head and said, 'Dennis, it's like I said. All we have to do is keep the horse alive. We don't need to be some kind of cowboys to do that for a couple of days.'

'Yeah, right. And what about getting it into the truck or trailer or whatever the fuck we're going to use to move it? And getting it out of the truck into a stable? It's not like cows that just walk where you point them. Horses need reins and shit. Can you put one of those bridle things on a horse?'

'Does this mean you're out?' Fraser asked coldly.

'No,' replied Dennis. 'What it means is we need help. We need someone who knows about horses. Someone who can manage the fucking thing so we have something to ransom.'

Fraser thought for a moment. 'Hmmm. Maybe. But it would have to be somebody we trust. Do you know anybody who's had experience with horses?'

Dennis snapped his fingers and said, 'Venus! Shit, Venus! She's bloody awesome with horses.'

Fraser looked sceptical. 'Venus? This Venus? She's a bloody student. What could she possibly know about horses?'

'I tell you, she's awesome. She's been riding since she was about five years old. Her aunt and uncle had a stud farm. Near Cambridge. She used to go there all the time. She spent most of her summers there as a kid. I went there once with her and couldn't believe it. She was doing all kinds of crazy shit – dancing around a horse ring, jumping wicked obstacles. She flew over fences in the paddock that were taller than me. She competed a lot and did bloody well, I think. She couldn't ride full time, though, so she never made a national team or anything.'

'Damn. Who'd have guessed?' Fraser thought some more and then said, 'Okay, let's talk to her.'

Venus returned to the room and sat on the sofa. Fraser stood in front of her and Dennis was standing by the door to the hallway. 'Venus,' asked Fraser, 'do you know anything about horses?'

Venus looked at the two men warily and then said, 'Wow, there's a conversational leap. Horses? My dad used to like a bet on the horses. He said never to bet on a rocking horse or one named for royalty.'

Fraser interrupted, 'Cut the shit, Venus. Dennis says you used to ride horses. A lot. Is that true?'

'Yeah, I guess,' she replied suspiciously. 'So what?'

'So you know how to put a bridle on a horse and lead it around and shit like that?'

Venus nodded, 'Yeah. I can do that. But like I said, so what?'

Fraser considered her for a long moment and then explained, 'Okay, here's the deal. Dennis and I may have the opportunity to acquire a horse and we're looking for someone who can help us look after it, just for a few days. Nothing difficult. Just help move it to our mate Barry's place and then help keep it fed and watered. Do you think you could do that?'

'Who's Barry?' asked Venus.

'Who he is doesn't matter. Can you look after the fucking horse?'

Dennis glanced at Fraser and said, 'Barry's a mate. A butcher. He helps us out now and then.'

'A butcher?' Venus queried. 'They have horse butchers in France. They're called *boucher chevalin*.'

Fraser looked at her oddly and shook his head. 'The fuck. What kind of people eat horses? This is one deal that we definitely don't need Barry's butcher's skills for. He's got a big shed and he knows how to keep his mouth shut. That's all we need.'

He asked Venus again, 'So, are you interested in helping us?'

She looked at the two men for a long moment. 'From our earlier discussion I assume that this horse is also off the books and needs to fly under the radar, right?'

Fraser hesitated and then nodded. 'Right.'

Venus thought some more and asked, 'And what do you want me to do? Anything besides babysit the horse?'

Fraser appraised Venus, smiled and answered, 'No, that's it. Unless you want to cook for us?'

Venus had picked up the *Woman's Weekly* and was flipping through it. She replied without looking up, 'Cooking my ass. I saw your kitchen when I went in there a few minutes ago. The only things you guys eat are meat pies and hamburgers. You think frozen dinners count as gourmet meals.'

She turned more pages but wasn't seeing them as she thought, *Fraser's a total piece of work and I wouldn't trust him to clean my sneakers. But in spite of that he's not bad looking. Hot in a bad boy sort of way. And he's got something different going on in his head. Dennis is my best mate but he's not the sharpest pencil in the box. If things turn to custard then there's a good chance Fraser will pin it all on Dennis and just walk away. How much do I care about Dennis? Do I care anything at all about Fraser? What's the risk of getting caught? Can I bail out if I want to? Am I doing something stupid just to forget those creepy hands?* She closed the magazine and tossed it on the sofa beside her. She looked at Dennis and said, 'Dennis, your friend Fraser is an arrogant shit. Does he have a fucking clue? Is there any way I should take him seriously about this?'

Fraser started angrily: 'What do you mean …?' but he was cut off when Venus raised her hand to him and said, 'Shut up, Fraser. I asked Dennis a question and want an answer.'

Dennis looked back and forth between Fraser and Venus. He was clearly uncomfortable. 'Um, Venus, I know what you're saying.' He glanced again at Fraser and continued, 'Fraser can be a bloody annoying sometimes. But he's really smart. He does all our planning and we've never been caught. He's always reading the papers and magazines and asking me about shit I don't have a clue about.' He swallowed and said, 'If Fraser thinks we can steal a horse then I reckon we can do it, if we have your help.'

Venus stared coolly at Fraser and thought for a long moment before she said with a hint of sarcasm, 'Okay, I'll help you. I've always wanted to have a horse. We could feed him apples and sugar cubes and brush his hair like My Little Pony. But there's one condition – I need to know the plan. And if I don't like it then I walk away.' She tilted her head and said, 'You do have a plan, don't you?'

Fraser replied, 'Venus, this is not some kid's pet pony. Forget the apples and shit. We're talking about a highly strung racehorse. And don't worry, you won't have time to get attached to the bloody thing.' He pulled a pack of cigarettes from his pocket and shook one loose. Before he lit it he looked at Venus and said, 'And thanks for asking. We don't have a plan. Yet. That's another thing you're going to help us with.'

———

Dani Painter pulled her police car to a stop in front of Bridget's porch and got out. She took off her hat and wiped her forehead while she looked around at the grounds, the stables and the implement shed. A row of agapanthas were making a terrific show along the drive, and roses had been trained to climb the posts supporting the roof of the porch. The sun was a blinding disc in a sky innocent of clouds. As Dani watched, Bridget and an older man whom Dani recognised as Elliot Hayes emerged from the stables and walked briskly towards the house. Bridget was wearing her usual work attire, khaki trousers and a check shirt. Elliot always amazed Dani with his vigour and apparent immunity to age. The pair reached the car and Dani shook hands with them both.

'Hi, Dani,' said Bridget. 'Elliot's been helping me while I've been bending his ear about the theft.'

Elliot smiled and said, 'Bridget got pretty excited during her description of what happened. I'd hate to be in those rustlers' shoes if she catches them.'

Dani returned the grin and glanced at Bridget. 'She's got a way with words, all right. I think I got the same description earlier today.'

'Give me a break, you guys.' said Bridget, 'You'd be bloody mad too if you'd just been rustled. Particularly if there's damn-all chance that they'll get caught.'

'Actually, that's why I've dropped in,' said Dani. 'I thought I'd have a look at the paddock and see if there were any clues that might help us find them. You never know, they may have made a mistake that will tell us who they are.'

'Well,' said Bridget, 'thanks, Dani, but I'm not going to hold my breath. If these guys dropped an envelope the only address would probably be "occupant", but it looks like they were smart enough not to leave any meaningful evidence. I told you about the tyre tracks, but I don't think they'll be much help.'

'You're probably right but I'd like to have a look anyway. Would you mind showing me which paddock they were stolen from?'

Bridget turned to Elliot and said, 'You don't need to come with us, Elliot. Why don't you stay here and have a cup of tea and keep an eye out for the horse transport?'

'Sounds good to me,' he replied.

Dani watched the old man go into Bridget's kitchen and said, 'He's quite a guy, isn't he?'

'He's one in a million, that's for sure,' replied Bridget. She turned back to Dani and said, 'I'm ready now. Shall we go?'

They drove the short distance to the paddock and Dani parked the police car near the loading chute, careful not to disturb any signs that might be there. They got out of the car and Bridget stood to one side with her hands in her back pockets and watched Dani carefully examine the area in front of the chute, stooping down now and then to take a closer look at the ground, and once turning over some clods of earth with her ballpoint pen. After a couple of minutes she stood up and walked over to Bridget.

'There's definitely been a truck in here recently, but there's nothing distinctive I can see. The ground's too hard to have taken an imprint of the tyres and even if it had that's really only useful if we have a truck that we suspect is involved.' She sighed and looked across the paddock. The leaves on the poplars along the riverbank shimmered green and grey in the light breeze and a pair of skylarks soared and sang over the grass. 'I'll have a look out there as well, but I'm not very hopeful. Either these guys know what they're doing or they've been very lucky, or both.'

Bridget pointed to the gate latch. 'They had to go through the gate. Is there any chance of getting prints off the latch?'

Dani shook her head. 'I doubt it. Did you touch it?'

'I don't think so, but I was so mad I can't remember for sure.'

'Well, I could get a technician out here to have a go but I've never seen them get anything useful off something as rough as that.' Dani swung over the fence and looked again across the paddock.

'Is there anything I can do?' asked Bridget.

'Sure. Stay on my right side and look at everything. Don't move forward until you're sure there's nothing more to see. It's not likely we'll find anything, but you never know.'

For the next forty-five minutes the two of them walked back and forth through the paddock, examining the ground for any sign of the thieves. The soil was as hard as by the road and the only signs of the cattle were those Bridget had first seen, a few fresh hoofprints and cow pats by the water trough and in the loading chute. When they'd finished they climbed back over the fence and walked to the police car.

Dani paused before getting in and looked at Bridget. 'I'm sorry, Bridget,' she said, 'we'll do what we can but there's not much to go on. I'll ask around; someone may have seen something. You never know. I'll let you know if I learn anything.'

'Thanks, Dani,' said Bridget. 'I know it's only a bunch of cattle but it's really pissed me off. I appreciate your help and, believe me, I hope you get a break and catch the bastards.'

'I hope so as well, but you've got to realise that it's going to be a long shot. You seemed pretty upset earlier. Are you okay? We'll do whatever we can to find the thieves.'

Bridget gave a small smile and shook her head. 'Thanks again, Dani. Really. I'll be right.' She looked away from Dani and folded her arms across her chest, her strong fingers clasping her biceps. 'You know how it is, every farmer is always moaning about something. But when I took over the farm from Gordon I swore I wouldn't do that. No moaning, no excuses. This is no different. We'll get past it.' She tossed her hair back over her shoulders and said, 'We'd better get going if we're finished here.'

———

Robert Hughes stuck his head out of his office and called out, 'Gordon, could you come in here a minute?' Gordon didn't look up from his screen but waved in acknowledgement. Robert was his boss, the editor of the local paper. After six months of working together they were not friends but had come to an understanding. Gordon had spent his lunch hour talking about the last council meeting with one of the local politicians who enjoyed seeing his name in print. He finished typing the lead paragraph on his story about the council's plan to cut library and swimming pool hours, stood up and walked into Robert's office. Robert said, 'Close the door, would you?' and gestured to a chair. 'Have a seat.'

Gordon shut the door and sat in the old rimu and leather chair across from Robert's battered desk. The native timber frame creaked as his weight settled onto the seat. He was wary about these meetings with Robert. The editor was a canny man with no illusions that he was running the *New York Times* or even the *New Zealand Herald*. He had been in his position for over thirty years and knew what people expected in a local paper – news about themselves and the events that affected them. The only investigative journalism he believed in was tracking down who was speaking at the Rotary dinner the next week or what was likely to be on the council's agenda at the next meeting.

Gordon knew that the only times he was called into Robert's office were to be told bad news, like being assigned to cover the fashion show on Sunday or that the newspaper was being sued because of his article about prize-fixing at the social club's Friday night housie session. So Gordon watched Robert's face closely and did not get comfortable in his chair as he waited to hear whatever bad news was about to come his way.

Robert leaned far back in his chair and reached for the pipe lying on his desk. He tamped the tobacco remnants with his brown-stained forefinger and picked up his lighter. He fiddled with the lighter before speaking. 'Gordon. Well. That was a good piece yesterday. What are you working on at the moment? Still that item on the council's decision to put in parking meters?'

Gordon shifted in his chair. He could feel a request for overtime coming on. 'No,' he replied, 'I finished that one and gave it to Judy yesterday.' Judy was Robert's wife, a large woman who filled in most of the journalistic positions between reporter and editor. 'She should have it to you today or tomorrow.'

Robert nodded. 'That's fine. What else is on?'

'Not a lot. I'm following up on some more council activity and there's the usual stuff about meetings and sports, but nothing very interesting. I heard some cattle were stolen from Bridget's place last night but haven't had a chance to follow it up.'

Robert leaned forward and put his pipe in the ashtray on his desk. 'Stolen cattle? Now that could be interesting. What do you know so far?'

Gordon shrugged. 'Not much yet. I ran into Bridget on her way to see the police. That's when I heard about it. I had a quick chat with Dani but she wasn't talking. She was going out to look at the scene after lunch and I thought I'd check with her later this afternoon.'

'That's good. That could be very good. Follow it up and keep me informed on what you find.' Robert leaned back in his chair again and gave Gordon a long look. He fidgeted with the stem of his pipe and said, 'You've only been here a few months but I think you know what the score is with the paper.'

Gordon didn't think he knew what the score was at all, but thought he'd better say something. It didn't look as if he was going to be asked to work overtime after all. He cleared his throat, 'Um, I don't quite know what you mean, Robert. Things seem to be going pretty smoothly to me.'

'Come on,' Robert shook his head, 'you're a reporter, for Christ's sake. You can't be that unobservant.' He rocked slightly in his chair and ran a hand over the top of his head. His black hair was fashionably long and combed back from his forehead.

He must be pushing 70 but there's no sign of it. Once again Gordon wondered if Robert dyed his hair. 'Sorry, I don't know what you're getting at. All I see is the day-to-day stuff. If there's something else going on I don't know what it is.'

'You mean you haven't noticed that the ads that pay for the day-today stuff, as you call it, have dropped dramatically? That the size of the paper has shrunk by a third? That the whole bloody town is going down the gurgler and there's no one left to pay the piper?' Robert pulled a stack of back issues of the paper from a pile by the side of his desk and held up the one on top. 'Lead story – freezing works closes down, 150 jobs to go. Byline – Gordon Crawford.' He tossed the paper aside and picked up the next one, scanned the front page and opened it to the first inside page. 'Three columns – drought continues, orchardists predict loss of 60% of their crop. Byline – Gordon Crawford.' He tossed that paper aside as well and picked up the next one. 'Lead story – small branch banks unprofitable say head office, future of local bank to be reviewed in next six months. Byline – Gordon Crawford.' He dumped the whole stack back on the floor and exclaimed, 'Jesus, Gordon! You can't be that thick! You can't tell me that you haven't seen the writing on the wall.'

Gordon folded his arms and sank back in his chair. 'Sure, I've noticed that there's been lots of bad news. But things are bad everywhere right now.' He gestured at the pile of papers strewn across the floor. 'Those stories could be written about any small town in the country. Hell, about the major centres as well. I had no idea the downturn was impacting on the paper.'

Robert grunted, 'It sure as hell is. We're just about flat-ass broke. And the only light at the end of the tunnel is an oncoming train.' He paused, picked up his pipe, and put it down again. 'The fact is that I'm going to sell the paper. I've had an offer from one of the big dailies that wants to try running a local edition of its paper. I think it's a crazy idea, but that's not my problem. Now, the thing is they want to sack everybody immediately and use their own staff to run the paper. But I told them I owed more than that to you and the others and that I wouldn't sell on those conditions. I tried to get them to guarantee all of you positions on their paper but they refused. In the end the best I could do was to get them to guarantee jobs for six months. After that they'll review how things are going – keep those of you who they want and let the rest go. I'm sorry, Gordon. You're the best reporter I've got. I'm sure you'll impress them with your ability and make a place for yourself.' He poked at one of the pieces of paper on his desk and said gruffly, 'Hell, we both know you're wasted on a paper like this anyway. Given half a chance you'll take off and become a high-flying city reporter. I'll make sure you get a good recommendation whatever happens.'

Gordon was stunned and couldn't speak for a moment. Finally he gathered himself and sat up in his chair. 'Yeah, uh, yeah, thanks. I'm sure you did what you thought was best.'

Robert nodded sagely and said, 'Yes, it's what's best for all of us in the end. You'll see.'

Gordon stood up and turned towards the door. 'See you around.' He opened the door and said as he closed it behind him, 'I think I'll take the rest of the day off. Maybe have a beer, before the pub joins the rest of the failures and closes for good.'

CHAPTER 4

The dust from the arrival of Hugh's Range Rover had hardly settled before the red van containing Tui Dancer pulled up in front of Bridget's stables. Bridget had greeted Hugh warmly when he arrived. She dropped her hand from Hugh's arm and turned to look at the van and its famous cargo as it came to a stop. She couldn't see inside, but could faintly hear the sound of horse's hooves on the wooden floor. She glanced anxiously at Hugh's face and saw the mixture of worry and excitement there. 'It'll be okay, Hugh,' she said and squeezed his arm again. 'It'll be okay,' she repeated, 'nothing's going to go wrong.'

Hugh smiled down at her and put his big hand over hers. 'I know. Thanks to you.' He gently disengaged her hand and gave it a squeeze as he stepped forward to supervise the unloading.

Elliot stood on the porch. He had watched Hugh park his Range Rover beside the stables and the big van drive past and stop near it. He'd seen Bridget give Hugh a kiss and hug before they walked over to the van. A small smile appeared briefly on his lips as he stepped down and followed the pair across towards the stables.

Sam and Ben climbed down from the cab and walked over to meet Hugh and Bridget. Sam nodded to Hugh and asked, 'Is it all right to unload now?'

'I reckon,' said Hugh, 'do you need any help?'

'Naw,' Sam shook his head. 'He's lively but no real problem.' He cocked his head towards the stables. 'Do you want him in there?'

'Yeah. We'll show you where when you come in.'

'Right,' said Sam as he turned towards the back of the van. 'Let's go, Ben. Drop the tailgate and let's get him out of there.'

The two men worked quickly and in a short time they had backed Tui Dancer out of the van and onto the gravel yard. Bridget had moved to watch them and she involuntarily caught her breath as the magnificent horse emerged. He was a big animal, with a glossy black coat contrasting with a white blaze on his face. He tossed his head as he came out into the sunlight, almost jerking the lead rope from Sam's hands, and his large eyes seemed to take in the entire yard with one glance.

This is the stallion I want, thought Bridget longingly. She trailed behind as the horse walked majestically towards her stables. *Damn, damn, damn. So near and yet so far. Oh, Ginger, you don't know what you're going to miss.*

With Hugh showing the way, Sam and Ben soon had Tui Dancer in the back stable. While Sam coiled the lead rope Bridget, Hugh and Elliot looked through the open top of the stable door as Tui Dancer explored his new surroundings. He inspected the fresh hay and took a few mouthfuls, had a quick drink of water and moved to the door to accept his due adulation. 'I'll give him a small feed when he's settled down,' said Bridget.

Sam finished his work, slapped his palms against his thighs, and headed towards the main stable door. 'Right,' he said, 'let's get a move on. We've got another long haul tomorrow.'

Hugh, Bridget and Elliot followed Sam and Ben outside. Hugh walked to the cab of the van and shook hands with the two men before they climbed in. Bridget moved up alongside him and put her arm around his waist and they watched the van disappear down the drive.

Elliott walked up behind them and said, 'Well, guess I'd better be going. I'll be back tomorrow morning to make sure the horse is settled. We can work out a proper schedule then.'

Bridget dropped her arm from Hugh's waist and turned to Elliott.

'Thanks for everything, Elliott. We couldn't have been ready without you.'

'No worries,' said Elliot, and walked to his car.

Bridget watched Elliott reverse his car and she waved as he drove out the drive. Hugh came up behind her and put his arms around her once more. She turned in his arms, they stared at each other for a moment and then kissed. Their arms tightened and the kiss deepened and they only broke for a moment before renewing their passionate embrace. Several minutes later they stepped apart, still looking at each other and holding hands. 'Well,' said Bridget.

'Well indeed,' said Hugh with a smile. He tugged her gently towards the stables and they walked together back to Tui Dancer.

Bridget leaned her forearms on the lower half of the stable door and looked at the stallion. She sighed, leaned her head against Hugh's arm and said wistfully, 'One day I'll have a horse like that.'

Hugh ran his hand over her smooth hair and pulled her closer to his side. 'No doubt about it.' She pressed her body against his and they kissed. After a long time she tilted her head back and looked up into his brown eyes and said, 'Come into the house. I think we need to celebrate.'

———

Gordon sat at his desk with his head propped on one hand and doodled on a yellow pad with the other. He drew a series of interlocking circles which he then connected and made into a cow. He added several more cows and then drew a horse. After twenty minutes of thought he put his pen and notebook in his pocket and headed out the door. He got into his car and drove the few blocks to the police station. Parking in front of it, he walked quickly through the front door. Inside, Dani Painter looked up from her desk, gave him a smile and waved towards the chair in front of her. 'Well, well, well,' she said, 'what can I do for you today? It wouldn't have anything to do with some stolen cattle, would it?'

Gordon sat in the chair and returned the smile. 'Ah, Dani, with those investigative skills you'll make detective yet. You read me like a book. And with your omniscience you'll already know that I'm here to ask you about the criminal mind.'

Dani sat back in her chair and folded her arms. 'A book? More like a magazine. Or a leaflet. Probably a leaflet.'

Gordon widened his eyes in mock disbelief, 'Another illusion shattered. But the reason for my visit is – I'm here representing the press. As always, in the ongoing search for truth.'

Dani chuckled and said, 'Truth, lies. So hard to tell sometimes.'

Gordon leaned back in the chair and put his left ankle on his knee. 'You are such a cynic. Today I need some info. I prefer the truth but a good lie is not to be ignored. Off the record, if you want. There's a real story here. More than just Bridget and a few cows. This is today's version of the Wild West. The same theme – the struggle between the landowners and the outlaws, the haves and the have-nots, the privileged and those marginalised by society.'

'Jesus, give me a break. We're talking about a couple of scumbags and a dozen cows, not the Apocalypse.'

'Yeah, yeah, just listen, will you?' Gordon uncrossed his legs, leaned forward and put his hands on his knees. 'What I'm getting at is this: where is the real interest in this story?' He began to tick off his fingers, 'One – a beautiful woman. Two – rural crime. Three – the linkages. Other people have to be involved. Someone must have butchered the animals. Someone must have bought the meat. How does anyone know if they're buying stolen meat or not? Hell, people are so concerned about organic this and genetically-modified that – what are they going to think if their meat's been butchered in somebody's toilet? How do I make this a story? What do I need to know to strike fear in consumers' hearts?' He paused for effect and continued, 'First, the facts of the case. And second, whatever you can tell me about modern-day cattle-rustling.'

Dani looked away from Gordon, out of the window at the patch of blue sky above the half-curtains. She was silent for a long moment and then said, 'Fear in their hearts? Is that really what you want?' She shook her head slowly and sighed. 'Right. The facts of the case. Last night persons unknown stole twelve cattle from one of Bridget Crawford's paddocks. There were no clues to their identity but there are several indications that they backed a truck up to the loading chute, herded the animals inside and drove away unseen. At the moment there are no suspects.'

She picked up her ballpoint pen and began tapping it on the desk. 'Stock stealing doesn't make the headlines because it's usually not a big crime. A couple of sheep or a cow disappears out of a herd and no one gets hurt. At least physically. It's getting especially bad near the cities. With rising unemployment lots of characters are seeing the countryside as a supermarket offering a five-finger discount. And it's not just animals, it's tools, tractors … hell, a joker in Taranaki not only lost a tractor, he lost the implement shed as well.

'So anyway, most of the stock is stolen for personal consumption. And we have about zip chance of stopping that. But there's an increasing trend towards larger thefts, like Bridget's. It's still relatively small-time, a few dozen animals max, but it's definitely more than for personal consumption. Now, I can't imagine a cocky building a herd that way so you were right a minute ago: those animals must be getting killed and butchered somewhere. And someone's buying the meat.

'MAF have cracked down recently on farm-kills so it's not easy for Joe Blogs to go into the unlicensed meat business. What's left? I'd guess that it's going to butchers looking to make some quick money on the side. And who's to know? How can you prove whether a steak came from a stolen cow?' Dani shook her head. 'You ask me, I don't think we'll ever catch these guys. Not unless somebody gets greedy, or unlucky.'

Gordon rubbed his chin and felt his interest quicken. This was a lot more challenging, and interesting, than reporting on next week's Rotary speaker. But Dani was right. He couldn't see where to start, yet. And the theft of a dozen cows wasn't headline news. But the broader issue of rustling, why people did it and the impact on the farmers who lost the animals, was much more interesting. And he could see that it could be his ticket to a permanent job on the new paper. He got up and put his pad in his pocket. 'What about Bridget? How's she taking all this?'

Dani knew about Gordon and Bridget's history and was careful with what she said. 'She was angry at first, of course, but when I spoke with her this afternoon she seemed to have calmed down. I think she'll be okay, especially if we catch the crooks. Is she going to be part of your story?'

This time it was Gordon's turn to be cautious. He scratched the back of his neck and looked away for a second. 'Probably, but we'll have to see how it goes.' He shook Dani's hand and headed for the door. 'Thanks. You've been a big help. You're probably right about not catching them but for Bridget's sake I hope you do. I'll do some poking around on my own and if I turn anything up I'll let you know.'

Dani looked and sounded sceptical: 'Poking around. Yeah, you do that.' She still remembered the time Gordon had learned about the marijuana growers who were making a fortune on a plot behind the council greenhouse and the only notice the police had received was on the front page of the paper. The door closed and Dani returned to her weekly report.

———

The faded green Falcon station wagon pulled up beside Barry's shed and Fraser switched off the engine. He and Dennis sat in the front seat, Venus in the back. No one moved or spoke for a minute or more. The light was just starting to fade and the air was still. They could faintly hear the sound of cattle in the paddock beside the shed. Fraser left the keys in the ignition and opened his door. 'Let's get to it,' he said.

The three of them got out of the vehicle and walked to the door of the shed. Fraser opened it and stood on the sill, taking in the big interior. On the far side Barry, dressed in waterproof gear, was hosing down several stalls, flushing a potent mixture of manure, urine and straw towards the drain in the back wall. Catching the opening of the door out of the corner of his eye, he turned his head and saw Fraser standing in the doorway. Fraser raised his hand and waved and Barry scowled in response. He swung the hose in short, angry strokes and finished the job in a few minutes. He closed the valve on the nozzle and dropped it to the wet floor.

Fraser, Dennis and Venus entered the building as the last of the sludge went through the drain, closing the door behind them. The lights were high up in the roof, at least six metres overhead, but their halogen bulbs cast a harsh light on the interior. Barry strode towards them and they met near the centre of the building.

'What the fuck are you doing here now?' Barry asked, with his hands on his hips. He pointed at Venus and said, 'And who the fuck is she?'

Fraser smiled and folded his arms before answering. 'What's the matter, Barry? We just stopped in to say Hi, see how you were doing.'

'The fuck you did. You bloody gangsters don't give a shit about anything except yourselves. And you haven't answered my question. Who the fuck is she?'

'Mate, get a grip. She's cool. She's a mate of Dennis'.' Fraser swept his arm from Barry towards Venus, 'Barry meet Venus. Venus, Barry.'

Barry glowered at Venus for a second and then turned his attention back to Fraser. 'I don't care if she's Princess Diana's love child, I don't want to see her, or you, or Dennis ever again. Get it?' He raised his arm and pointed his finger towards the door. 'And there'd better not be any bloody cattle outside, either. You can threaten all you like but I'm out. I'm through. I'm not taking any more stock from you.'

Fraser shook his head slowly and clicked his tongue against the back of his teeth. 'Tch, tch, tch. Barry, Barry, calm down. Get a grip on yourself. Of course you're out. Isn't he, Dennis?' Fraser looked at Dennis who nodded solemnly. 'Isn't that what I said on the way over? Didn't I say that Barry was out?' Fraser walked slowly towards the back wall of the shed, turning to face Barry after a few strides. He smiled gently and spread his hands to either side. 'Hey, you don't want any more cattle? No problem. I admit Dennis and I were a little disappointed yesterday when you told us, but now we see your point of view. And besides,' Fraser's smile broadened, 'how could we do business with someone we couldn't trust? That's all we came to say, partner. That we understand and that it's been a pleasure doing business with you.'

Barry licked his lips and shuffled his gumboots on the wet concrete. He cleared his throat and said, 'You mean it? You don't have a truckload of cattle outside? It's all over?'

'Well, partner, I didn't exactly say *that*.' And, as Barry's face drained of colour, Fraser proceeded to tell him exactly what he had in mind.

CHAPTER 5

Elliot arrived at precisely eight o'clock, dressed in clean khaki trousers and a pressed blue cotton work shirt. He knocked on Bridget's kitchen door and entered when she called out, 'Come on in.'

Bridget was sitting at the kitchen table, drinking a cup of coffee and reading the previous day's paper. She smiled when Elliot walked in and asked him, 'Would you like a cup of coffee? I'm still not organised yet.'

'Sure,' he said. He looked around the room as Bridget got up to get a cup and pour some coffee from the coffee maker sitting beside the stove. The benches were clear and, except for the breakfast dishes in the sink, there was no mess anywhere.

Bridget turned and said, 'Have a seat. What's the weather doing?'

Elliot pulled out a chair and sat. He took the cup of coffee and set it on the table. 'Well, it's cool at the moment but you can tell it's going to be another hot one.'

Bridget sat back down, blew on her cup absentmindedly and took a sip. 'I'm glad you came over. I know it's a nuisance for you but I seem to be swamped at the moment.'

'What's on the agenda, then?'

'Where do I start? Most importantly, check on Tui Dancer. I also have to talk to the insurance company about claiming for the stolen

stock, see if Dani's heard anything overnight, and I need to figure out
how to stall the bank. The ute's been hard to start and the garden's an
absolute disaster.'

Elliot held up a hand and laughed, 'Okay, okay! I think that's
enough for the moment. I'll make sure Tui Dancer's okay and then take
a look at the ute. You do your errands and we'll see where we are at
morning smoko. All right?'

Bridget drained her coffee and stood up. 'Perfect. Can I borrow
your car?'

Elliot grinned and said, 'The keys are in it.'

It was close to ten o'clock before Bridget finished her chores and
returned to the homestead. The sun was slanting through the open
doors of the stables and she could see Elliot's legs sticking out from
beneath her ute. As she entered she heard a loud metallic clang. Elliot
wriggled out with a large wrench in his hand and looked up at her.
'Hey, you're just in time,' he said. 'Step in and give 'er a try.'

Bridget had bought the ute when she bought the farm. She hadn't
been able to pay much and it showed: it was faded red, had high
mileage and showed the dings and scrapes of a hard life. But it had
been remarkably reliable, until recently. She opened the ute's door and
sat behind the wheel. She turned the ignition key and after a couple of
hesitant coughs the engine caught and grunted into life. She revved it a
few times and then let it idle as she slid back out of the cab. Elliot had
stood up and was wiping his hands on a rag, listening carefully to the
engine.

'That's amazing,' said Bridget. 'What was the problem?'

'The timing was out and the solenoid was sticking. I didn't have a
strobe so I couldn't do a proper job on the timing, but it'll get you to
town.'

'But it sounded like you were pounding on something.'

'Yeah, just the solenoid. I didn't really fix it, just jarred it loose. You
should start thinking about replacing this thing.'

Bridget laughed and said, 'Yeah, and I should think about a trip to
Hawaii, too. When I win the lottery.' She reached into the cab and
turned off the engine. It died with a rattle and left the smell of exhaust

heavy on the air in the confined space. The two walked to the door and stood in the sunshine for a moment.

'Thanks a million,' said Bridget. 'You don't know how much I appreciate your help.'

'Hey, it's the least I can do.'

'Where'd you learn to fix motors like that?'

Elliot paused and looked over her shoulder at the hills not yet burned summer brown. 'Oh, you know. You have to learn to put your hand to anything when you're on the farm. And I was in the army for eight years. They taught me some practical things along the way.'

'Really? You were in the army? I'd never have guessed. You've never mentioned it before.'

Elliot shrugged. 'Not much to talk about, actually.'

'What did you do? What was your rank?'

'Nothing very glamorous, I'm afraid. I was just a foot soldier. Made sergeant before I left, but fat lot of good that did me. Playing nursemaid to new recruits wasn't my cup of tea.'

'So you were never in a battle?'

'Now, I didn't say that. I was in Malaya in '51 and '52. Saw plenty of action during the Emergency. I was promoted to sergeant at the end of my tour. Most of the boys in my unit were on their second tour and the senior officers had been in the Second World War. It was a good mob to be with, tough and experienced. That's why I couldn't face the prospect of peacetime soldiering back in the UK.'

'So you came to the land of opportunity, met Beth, and stayed'.

'Yep, that's about it. But enough about the past. Are we going to have a cup of tea, or what?'

'Of course,' Bridget answered. 'What's the time?' She looked at her watch and exclaimed, 'Damn! I need to go to town to sort out the insurance on those cows. I tried to call earlier but they put me on hold and I gave up after listening to music for ten minutes.' She started walking briskly towards the house. 'I won't be long. Go ahead and take a break. You know your way around. Make yourself that cup of tea and I'll be back soon. There are biscuits in the tin on top of the fridge.' She broke into a trot and disappeared around the front of the house. A few seconds later Elliot heard her start the engine in her ute and drive away. He shook his head and walked slowly towards the house.

—————

Gordon arrived at his desk at 8.30 a.m. He hadn't slept well, thinking about the sale of the paper and how he could track the rustlers. He made a cup of instant coffee in the tearoom and returned to his desk. His eyes felt scratchy but his mind was still active, as though it had kept running at full speed even when he had eventually fallen into a restless sleep.

He killed time doing the crossword puzzle in the paper until his watch said 9.15. He then found the number he was looking for in his address book and reached for the phone on his desk. It rang four times before it was picked up and a warm, husky voice said 'Inland Revenue Department, Phoebe Long speaking. How may I help you?'

The voice always made Gordon think that Phoebe could make a fortune with telephone sex. 'Hey, Phebes, how's it going? Gordon here. How's life at the IRD?'

'Gordon! Good to hear from you. I'm doing pretty well. What are you up to?' The warmth deepened, if possible. She was genuinely glad to hear from him.

'I'm okay. You know, some ups, some downs, but things are going okay. How's your backhand draw coming along?'

Phoebe laughed. 'Superb. Simply superb. I made the top five in the district finals and qualified for the nationals in Auckland.' Phoebe was 57 and at least twelve kilos overweight but she was the life of any party and had a passion for bowls. 'What can I do for you? I know a reporter wouldn't call just to socialise.'

It was true that Gordon never called just to chat but he knew that it would never affect their relationship. He had won Phoebe's undying friendship eighteen months earlier when the provincial bowls and rugby teams had both won their championships and he had seen to it that the bowls team got the main picture and the big headline. He had done a few feature articles on some of the bowlers, including Phoebe, and the club membership was at an all-time high.

It was Gordon's turn to laugh. 'Yeah, you know me too well. I wonder if you could help me with a little problem. I'm trying to track down a shady business deal and I was wondering if you could assist. I'm after a guy who's selling stolen meat and the only chance I can see that we can nail him is to look through his tax returns.'

Phoebe cleared her throat and said, 'You know that's illegal. I could lose my job if anyone found out.'

'I know, and if you say no I'll understand. But it's important. And I'm working with the cops on this one.' Gordon wasn't sure that talking to Dani would really stretch to 'working with the cops' but he didn't have time to worry about it. 'I don't want anything in writing,' he said. 'I just want you to help me sift the evidence and see if there's anything there. If we find something then I'll go to the police and let them take over.'

Phoebe's voice turned wary. 'I don't know. This would be a big step for me. There's this little thing called the Privacy Act that says what you want to do is a no-no. A big no-no. Why don't you go to the cops first and get their okay on this?'

'That would take forever. You know how that goes. I'll be lucky if the cop on the case has an hour a day to spend on it. It'll take him a week to fill out the preliminary paper work only to decide to call it' a "no-victim crime" and to shelve it.' Gordon shifted the phone to his other ear and continued, 'Phebes, I know what you'd be risking. But if you don't then I'll probably lose my job. You didn't hear this, but the paper's going to be sold and most likely all our jobs are going down the tubes. If I can break this story then I have a chance to stay on with the new owners. Or maybe get a job with a national paper.' Gordon hesitated for a moment and then continued softly, 'So it's a big deal for me. But if you say no I'll understand. There's no point in us both losing our jobs.'

'Oh, hell,' Phoebe said resignedly. 'Get your worthless ass over here. If you lose your job I'll just feel guilty so I may as well stand in the dole queue with you.'

There was relief in Gordon's voice when he replied, 'Thanks. You're the best. I'll be there in a tick.'

'Yeah,' she said, 'well don't hurry too fast. My supervisor doesn't go to lunch until midday. You get here after that and we'll see what we can do in the hour she's gone. And if we find anything you can buy me dinner afterwards.'

Gordon laughed and said, 'You've got it. The best restaurant in town. I'll be right there.'

————

Hugh brought his Range Rover to a stop outside Bridget's house and got out. As he did, Elliot opened the kitchen door and walked to the edge of the veranda. 'Morning, Hugh. Everything okay today?'

Hugh walked around the front of his vehicle and shook hands with Elliot. 'Sure thing,' he said. 'I just came by to see how Tui Dancer's doing.'

Elliot gestured towards the stables. 'I checked him out this morning and he seemed fine. But you should have a look.'

The pair walked towards the stable and Hugh asked, 'Where's Bridget? I expected to see her this morning.'

'She had to go to town. She said something about the insurance on her stolen cattle.'

'Hmm,' Hugh mused, 'good luck with that. Most policies are so strict that it's bloody tough to collect. They suspect you of killing the animals yourself.'

Elliot slid the stable door open and followed Hugh into the dim interior. They both walked over to where Tui Dancer was held. The big stallion stuck his head out the top half of the door and watched them approach. Hugh pulled an apple out of his jacket and a folding knife from his trousers pocket. He began cutting the apple and feeding slices to Tui Dancer. 'Hey old man. How you doing?' he asked. He fed the horse the last of the apple and put his knife away. He opened the bottom of the door and entered the stable, running his hand over the horse's back as he moved forward. He called to Elliot over his shoulder, 'Could you hand me the body brush – the soft one – and the curry comb, please?'

Elliot found the brushes on the bench and handed them to Hugh, who started using the body brush on the horse with a circular motion and cleaning it occasionally on the curry comb. Since Tui Dancer hadn't been worked for a few days his coat was pretty clean, but the massaging motion of the brush stimulated the skin and was part of his daily routine.

Elliot watched for a few minutes, then cleared his throat and said, 'Bridget was a bit vague about exactly why Tui Dancer is here. I mean, I get the secrecy thing and I know it's none of my business, but what's wrong with him? I'm no expert but he looks healthy to me.'

Hugh interrupted his brushing to reach down, lifted the horse's left forefoot and examined it thoroughly, muttered, 'He'll need shoeing soon' and let the foot fall back to the floor. Resuming his brushing he said, 'You're right, it's none of your business. But for your information, Tui Dancer is here for a check-up. His performance has dropped off and we don't know why. I want to run some tests; figure out what's wrong. We hope that it's nothing serious and he's back on the track soon.'

Elliot nodded and thought to himself, *That's a press release, not an answer*. But he just smiled and said, 'Thanks. I'll leave you to it. Sing out if you need anything.'

Hugh replied 'No worries. I'll be away soon.'

———

Fraser finished the last of his coffee and pushed the cup aside. He lit a cigarette and leaned back from the table. Dennis was reading the front page of the paper open on the table beside him. Venus was also at the table, drinking a mug of milky tea. The kitchen was old but functional, tidy but not clean. The cupboard doors were painted dark green and the cupboards and walls were a grimy lemon. The linoleum floor was worn to the white backing except where the original pink and grey swirl pattern was preserved along the edges of the room and where it peeked out from under the stove and fridge.

A courier had arrived that morning with a small package addressed to Fraser Lyman. He'd taken it into his bedroom and opened it. Inside was a stack of one hundred dollar notes. There was no return address on the package or message inside. He'd smiled as he put a few of the notes in his wallet. He put the package in a drawer behind his underwear and went to the kitchen. 'What's the time?' he asked.

Dennis looked at his watch. 'High noon.'

'Time to take a drive.'

Dennis muttered 'Shit' as he drained his tea and wiped his mouth on his sleeve before hurrying after his partner. Venus took the time to dump the last of her tea in the sink and rinse the mug before following them out the back door.

———

Barbara had just finished lunch and was drying the dishes when she heard a car pull into the drive and crunch to a stop on the gravel outside the barn. She kept the tea towel in her hand as she stepped out of the dark interior of the kitchen and into the daylight on the porch. She could see two men sitting in the front seat of an old Falcon station wagon. A young woman sat in the back. The car had been originally pale green but it was now faded almost white, and specked with rust. There was quite a bit of glare on the windscreen but she could see that the two occupants in the front seat were wearing wrap-around sunglasses and had longish hair.

With no obvious signal they opened the doors at the same time and got out. They kept their eyes on her as they stepped to the front of the car. The girl got out of the right rear door and moved up behind them. The driver looked around the farmyard, not with the critical eye of a potential buyer but as a connoisseur would eye a favourite painting. His passenger glanced briefly at the barn before the group walked across the gravel to stand in front of her. 'Can I help you?' Barbara asked.

The driver pushed his sunglasses onto his forehead and looked Barbara in the eye as he pulled a pack of cigarettes from his shirt pocket and shook one loose. 'I don't know. I hope so.' He stuck the cigarette in his mouth and dug a book of matches from his trouser pocket. 'We're looking for Mr Jacobs. Is he around?'

Barbara didn't answer straight away. She watched while the match flared and the driver lit his cigarette and blew a stream of smoke into the morning air. The driver's lips were curled into a slight smile but she sensed that the man was neither amused nor light-hearted. The passenger stood at the driver's shoulder, half a step behind and with his arms crossed on his chest. The girl watched with no expression on her face. Barbara gripped the tea towel more tightly and unconsciously twisted it into a short garrotte. 'No, he's not here. What do you want? What can I do for you?'

The driver took another long drag on his cigarette before answering. He stuck out his hand and said, 'Hi, I'm Fraser. This is Dennis,' he pointed to Dennis, 'and Venus.' Barbara ignored Fraser's hand and looked at the others. An average guy, surfer hair and designer stubble, T-shirt and jeans, clean-ish. A girl, young but maybe not as young as she looked, long brown hair in a ponytail, dark eyes and eyebrows, pale lips, a T-shirt and cut-off shorts.

Fraser dropped his hand and went on. 'We're looking for work. We hear you're looking after that famous horse and we figured that you might need some help.' He lifted a thumb towards his companions. 'We've had experience handling horses and reckon we're the right blokes for the job. Venus grew up on horses.'

Barbara frowned and the slight creases in her forehead deepened. She shook her head and said, 'I'm sorry. You've made a trip for nothing. We're not looking after any famous horse. And we don't need any help at the moment.'

It was Fraser's turn to frown. He drew on the cigarette and looked around the yard again. 'You sure? I mean, we heard it from a reliable source that his trainer's sending him here. And a horse like that's going to need plenty of looking after. Your husband's a busy man and he can't expect to look after that horse on top of all his other work. We've been around horses all our lives and have looked after the best. We know about exercise. We know about feed. We know about hygiene.'

Barbara shook her head again. The two men in front of her looked like a lot of things, but horsemen wasn't one of them. The woman, maybe, but given she was with the other two she reckoned probably not. Barbara repeated, 'Look, I'm sorry but I can't help you. I don't care what you've heard but the only horse here at the moment belongs to us. On the rare occasions that we need some help we always get someone we know. In our business we can't afford to take on strangers. As you're so familiar with horses I'm sure you can appreciate that.' Barbara swung the tea towel in her hand and said, 'Now, I've got a lot of things to do and I'm sure you do, too.'

'Sure, Mrs Jacobs. I guess we figured wrong. But since we've driven all this way out here can we at least have a look around? As I said, we're really keen on horses and it would mean a lot to us if we could see what goes on inside a top stable.'

Barbara's face hardened as she got irritated at the persistence of these strangers. 'No, I'm afraid that won't be possible. My husband is a vet, not a trainer. There's nothing to see. So if that's all then I really have to get back to work.'

Fraser took a last look at the barn, dropped his cigarette butt and ground it into the earth with his shoe. 'Okay. I guess that's that.' He turned to the others and said, 'I know you're disappointed but you heard what the lady said. Guess we might as well head back to town.'

They turned away but stopped as Bridget's ute came into sight and slid to a stop next to their car. Fraser's eyes narrowed as Bridget bounced out and trotted over to them. He definitely liked the way things were moving inside the close-fitting trousers and shirt. And there was something else. Something familiar about her.

Bridget gave the characters standing near Barbara a long look as she approached. There was no one she recognised or, by the look of them, anyone she cared to meet. Barbara's body language, arms akimbo and feet solidly spread, told her that these weren't likely to be friends of hers, either. She stopped a little in front of Barbara and said, 'Morning, Barbara. Hugh around?'

Barbara smiled and replied, 'I expect him back any minute. What can I do for you?'

'I need a couple of things from Hugh's supplies. Can you help me find them, please?' Bridget looked at Fraser, Dennis and Venus and said, 'Oh, sorry. Am I interrupting something?'

Barbara said, 'No, it's okay Bridget. I'll be with you in a second. These folks were just going.'

Before anyone could move, Fraser stuck out his hand to Bridget. 'I'm Fraser, ma'am. And this is Dennis and Venus. We heard about the vet looking after the famous racehorse and all, and just came around to see if there was any chance of work.'

The flashback came to Fraser the instant he touched her hand. The hair was longer, the face a little fuller, more mature. But it was definitely her. There was no doubt this was Bridget Tronheim, one of his secondary school teachers.

Bridget was thinking quickly about what the man had said. About looking after a famous racehorse. Wondering if he really knew anything about Tui Dancer and, if he did, how he knew it. She had to be careful not to say anything at all about Tui Dancer. She took his hand reflexively and felt the firm, dry, grip test her own lean fingers. Not trying to crush her hand like some macho jerks she'd known, but probing nevertheless. Testing her. Assessing how far she was willing to go. She watched the lazy smile on Fraser's face; a smile that touched the eyes but didn't warm them. She pursed her lips slightly as she looked at him, waiting for him to release her hand. She thought, *He isn't half as smooth as he thinks he is. But he's got* something, *all right.* She looked more closely. *Something ... different, but something* familiar *as well.* Suddenly she jerked her hand back and unconsciously wiped it on her jeans.

Fraser's eyes never left her. 'Ms Tronheim? Is that you?' he asked. 'It is, isn't it? Wow, it's been a long time. How you doing?'

Bridget sensed the blush start to rise from her throat and felt even more uncomfortable. 'Ah,' she said, 'Fraser. What a surprise. It certainly has been a long time.' She fought to keep her composure and thought, *Not nearly long enough, you creep.* She kept her face neutral, resisting the urge to put her hands in her pockets.

'Hey,' said Fraser, with an almost cocky grin on his face, 'it's great to see you. What are you doing here? You're not teaching anymore?'

Bridget felt her blush flare again. 'No,' she replied, 'I'm not teaching anymore.' She continued in her mind, *because of you, you prick.*

Fraser reached out and brushed a strand of hair behind her ear. 'Pity. You were a great teacher.'

Barbara stepped forward and said, 'Come on, let's go to the barn.' She looked at the three strangers and said, 'That's it for now.' She gestured towards their car. 'I think it's time for you to leave.'

Fraser watched Bridget's body move as she and Barbara walked slowly towards the barn. He smiled and turned to Dennis and Venus and said, 'Okay, let's roll.' He got in the car and started the engine. Before he engaged the clutch he called out to Bridget, 'Hey, Ms Tronheim, I like your longer hairstyle.' He laughed and waved as he turned the car and drove down the drive.

———

Hugh had to swerve to avoid an old Ford Falcon as he turned into the drive to his house. 'What the hell?' he muttered as he regained the driveway. He pulled to a stop next to Bridget's ute and saw Barbara and Bridget walking towards the barn. They stopped and waited while he parked his car. Hugh hurried after them and asked, 'Who the hell was that?'

Barbara moved to him and they hugged briefly. She stepped back and said, 'I don't know. I've never seen them before. They just showed up and said they wanted a job. They said they'd heard about you looking after a famous racehorse. I said there was no famous horse here and told them to piss off.'

Hugh rubbed his chin thoughtfully. 'Hmm,' he said, 'it's probably just a coincidence but I don't like it. How could they know anything? None of us would have talked to them. I'm sure the owners and Max have kept their mouths shut. But I don't like it. This is exactly the kind of thing I was afraid of – why I decided to put Tui Dancer at Bridget's.'

Barbara gestured at Bridget and said, 'One of them, the guy who did all the talking, said he knew Bridget.'

Hugh looked at her and asked, 'Is that true? Do you know him?'

Bridget nodded slightly and murmured, 'Yeah, I know him. Or I knew him. He's just a kid from my old school. I haven't seen him in years. I didn't recognise him until he said he recognised me.'

Barbara reached out and touched Bridget's arm. 'That wasn't just a kid. I saw your face. You were shocked when you saw him. Did he do something to you?'

Bridget was silent for a long moment, deciding what to say. 'Teaching feels like another life. I never expect to see my old students. Fraser was …' she struggled for the word. *Different? Special? Trouble?* What could she say that wouldn't lead to more questions? Finally she said, 'Fraser was just another kid. Outspoken, but just another kid.'

Hugh looked at her. He could tell this was only part of the story but decided not to pursue it. If Bridget wanted to tell him sometime then he'd be glad to listen but he wasn't going to worry about some school escapade that happened years ago. 'Okay,' he said, 'what do you think about what they said? Do they know about Tui Dancer?'

Barbara and Bridget both thought for a moment before replying. 'I don't know.' said Barbara, 'In spite of what they said they didn't seem to know anything about horses. I think they were fishing for information. I don't think they actually know anything about Tui Dancer, much less know he's here.'

Bridget shrugged. 'I couldn't tell either. As far as I know, Fraser's never had an interest in horses. But it's been a long time and I have no idea what he might be up to now. He's a tricky bastard and you don't want to underestimate him.'

Hugh nodded and said, 'Okay, thanks. I don't believe in coincidences but I guess they have to happen sometimes. We'll carry on and keep our eyes open. We're taking precautions and it probably doesn't matter what these guys know or don't know.'

———

At exactly 12.05 p.m. Gordon tapped on Phoebe's door. He entered when she waved him in without looking up from her screen. He pulled a spare chair closer to her desk and tried to decipher the information that flashed across her computer screen as her hands flew across the keyboard and manoeuvred the mouse. What he saw looked like summaries of savings records, but he couldn't be sure.

'What a day!' Phoebe exclaimed as she shut down her application and turned to face Gordon. 'Your little problem is not what I need right now but let's see what we can do.' Before he could reply she spun her chair around to face her terminal again and continued, 'Now, you're interested in stolen meat and tax returns. That sounds like butchers to me, right?'

Gordon leaned closer and said, 'That's my best guess at the moment. Any help you can give will be great.'

'Okay,' she murmured as she began to type again. 'Let's see what we can find.' Once again her fingers danced over the keyboard, bringing screens of information flashing before them, faster than Gordon could follow. 'We'll cross-reference the employment category registration from the government insurance records with our returns to see what we can find about local butchers.'

Several minutes passed while she mumbled curses at the slow network and then she sighed and leaned back. 'Okay. We have a list of eighteen individuals and companies in this region. Now, we'll extract the names of the owners and link them with our database and see what we see.'

Several more minutes passed and her curses centred on linked lists and common fields. Finally a list appeared of names and a series of numbers and Phoebe relaxed again. 'Right. We have financial details for twenty-three people associated with those companies for the last ten years, both corporate and personal. What shall we look for?'

Gordon shrugged and looked helpless. 'You're the expert. What would you look for?'

'Hmph,' she grunted, 'this is not really my line, you know.' She looked across the top of her computer, focusing on a spot far away. 'We'll look for a sudden change in income. But there could be lots of legitimate reasons for a change and if the guy's smart it probably won't appear on his accounts. Don't hold your breath.'

This time the mouse did the work and in seconds there was a graph with coloured lines scratching paths across the screen. Some were flat, some sloped up, some sloped down and others wiggled across the graph like demented serpents. Phoebe studied the graph closely before pointing to it with her finger. 'See? Most of the accounts are relatively steady but thirteen of them are all over the place. There's no way we could track down that many suspects without a lot of work.'

Gordon shook his head. 'No, that's not going to be possible. If we can't find it easily then I'll have to take it to the cops and leave them to do the donkey work.' He looked at Phoebe: 'Is that it? Any other ideas?'

She sat still and thought for what seemed a long time. Gordon looked at his watch: 12.45. Phoebe's supervisor would be back from lunch soon and they would have to stop. His grasp at a break would be a failure.

Phoebe began tapping a fingernail on the keyboard and nodded her head slowly. 'Hang on. There may be another way into this thing.' Her fingers began to fly across the keys again and she spoke as tables of figures appeared and disappeared on her screen. 'Let's get back to basics. What are we looking for? Someone with excess cash they're trying to hide. This guy has exactly the same problem as the big-time dope dealers. Only he has twenty thousand or so a year to launder, not twenty million. Which should make it harder to detect, only he doesn't have the resources to set up elaborate schemes in the Channel Islands and the Caribbean.

'Now, say our man has twenty grand. That's a lot of money if it's tax-free but not enough for him to be willing to part with some of it to legitimise the rest. So what does he do? He does the best he can. Buying everything he can with cash and running the rest through his business and home accounts in small amounts so they don't attract attention. But if we're lucky, we'll find that the sum is greater than the whole.'

Gordon looked puzzled. 'What do you mean?'

Phoebe smiled as she continued to work at the computer. 'A great man once said there are lies, damned lies and statistics. What I hope is that we'll get a lead on our man by statistics. I'm going to add it all up, look at the complete accounts of all our suspects – bank accounts, credit card records, tax records, declarations, the lot – to get a picture of the pattern of their financial activity. What I hope is that when we look at the final list something will stick out. Someone with more expenses than income, say. Or unexplained bank deposits. It may be a flop but it's the best I can do.'

'Okay,' said Gordon, 'I've got my fingers crossed.'

They sat in silence for ten minutes while Phoebe coaxed information from databases and Gordon watched the data slowly accumulate in neat rows and columns. The orderly rows of digits, neatly spelling out this person's greed, that person's tragedy, another person's generosity, made him depressed. *Is it really so easy? Is there no privacy anymore?* Gordon wanted this answer badly but suddenly knew he wasn't going to feel the usual surge of excitement if it appeared.

At last Phoebe sat back from her screen and began to study the rows of numbers on her screen. 'Here we go.' The screen slowly scrolled up, the numbers flowing across Gordon's vision without eliciting any recognition. Then it paused, went back up, back down, and stopped. Phoebe was frowning at the screen.

'Got something?' asked Gordon.

'I'm not sure,' she replied. 'Could be. There's lots of scatter, of course. But so far only one account has stuck out. Most of the accounts have total traceable purchases averaging about 50% of their income and savings of about 10%. The rest will be accounted for in cash transactions. The total traceable purchases for this account are only 30% and savings are about 30%. Now, this guy may be very frugal, or he may have another source of income.'

'What's his name?'

Phoebe scrolled the screen to the right and read it aloud. 'Mr Miller, Mr B. Miller.' She glanced at Gordon. I can't print any of this out for you. I've taken too big a chance already. This is strictly off the record, between you and me.'

Gordon scribbled the name in his notebook and made a patting motion with his hand. 'And the address?'

'Damn,' Phoebe muttered, 'I guess it's in the phone book anyway.' She read out the address and Gordon added it beneath the name in his notebook.

He looked up and gave her a big smile. 'Don't worry, Phebes. Chances are this guy is totally legit. I'll make a few enquiries and see what I can find, but no way is anyone going to trace anything back to you.'

Phoebe said, 'I hope it was worth it.' She shut down the program and pushed back from her console.

Gordon stood up and extended his hand. 'Thanks a million. I owe you a big one for this.'

Phoebe shook his hand and watched him reach for the door. 'No worries. Don't forget dinner. And remember us next season.'

———

Once they were out of the drive Dennis looked hard at Fraser. 'Fraser? What the fuck's going on? I thought we came here to find a goddamned horse, not to chat up some chick.'

Fraser dropped his sunglasses over his eyes and said, 'Well, you've got to find your fun where you can. She's a bit older than me but I'm sure we'll get on just fine.' The tailgate of the old Ford rattled terribly and Fraser had to shout to be heard.

Dennis said, 'Right. What did you say back there? She was a teacher?'

'Yes, she was definitely a teacher.'

'So what? The world's full of teachers. What's so special about her?'

'What's so special is that she was *my* teacher. My sixth-form teacher, to be exact.'

Venus piped up from the back seat, 'No way! She was your teacher?'

Fraser grinned and looked at Venus in the rear-view mirror. 'Yeah, she really was my teacher.'

Dennis looked at Fraser and asked, 'So? Who cares if she was your teacher? What does that have to do with getting this racehorse that you're so hot about?'

'Well, it makes it more interesting. Much more interesting.'

Dennis just shook his head and turned to look out the window. Fraser was a good mate but he was fucking weird sometimes.

After a few kilometres of silence Fraser asked, 'Do either of you have any thoughts about that little scene back there?'

Dennis scowled at him. 'What do you mean? Seemed like a fucking waste of time. We didn't even get to see the bloody horse. You were so busy sniffing after your ex-teacher that all the blood must have flowed from your brain to your dick. For all we know the bloody horse may not even be there.'

Fraser pulled a cigarette from his pack with his teeth and grinned at Dennis as he pushed in the lighter. 'Of course the bloody horse isn't there. It's probably at Bridget's.'

The lighter popped out and Dennis watched as Fraser lit his cigarette and took a long drag. 'The fuck you say? It's at Bridget's? How do you reckon that?'

Before he could answer Venus said, 'Elementary. The vet's wife was uneasy. She didn't even acknowledge the existence of the horse, much less show him to us. And she wasn't going to let us anywhere near her stables.'

Dennis was sceptical. 'Yeah, but would you show a million dollar horse to a stranger?'

Fraser cut in and said, 'Probably not, but then Bridget shows up and wants to pick up something from the vet's supplies. She was acting squirrely, too, and it wasn't just the excitement of seeing me again. I don't know what else they might be sharing but I'll bet they're sharing a certain horse.'

Dennis watched more scenery roll past. 'Well, you may be right. What do we do next?'

Fraser blew smoke and said, 'I think it's time to have another chat with our good friend and business partner Barry.'

———

Dylan Cassidy sat behind his big desk, elbows on its surface and fingers templed in front of him. Bridget sat across from him in a large, hard chair. She'd met Dylan when her previous bank account manager had retired and introduced her to his replacement. She'd had a few meetings with him, negotiating loans to keep her farm operating. She knew his easy, confident smile, the firm handshake and fashionably long, straight, dark hair. The thousand-dollar suit and the power tie. His youth. Most of all she knew the way he touched her when he ushered her in or out of his office. The way he stared at her breasts instead of her eyes. How her negotiations were always more successful when she dressed in a short skirt and high heels. Every time she sat in this office she thought that when her friend had retired from the bank and walked out the door she'd started a long slide towards trouble.

It wasn't that Dylan was incompetent – he was incredibly competent. Every form was filed and every report submitted. But those forms and reports recorded her losses, not profits, and he was now asking for payment of her outstanding loans. Bridget had just spent an hour going over her financial details with him, trying to get him to understand the realities of farming's cash flow.

'That's all very well, Ms Crawford,' he said, dropping his hands to the desk, 'but I really don't see how you will be able to repay the bank's money.' Bridget looked at him without speaking. She'd used up all her words in the last hour. 'Unless you can make a substantial payment in the next month,' he continued, 'then I'm afraid we will have no choice but to start proceedings to seize your farm.'

'My farm,' she repeated. 'Seize my farm?'

'Yes, that's correct. If we don't have an assurance that you will be able to repay the money you owe then we will seize your farm.'

Bridget wanted to cry or scream, but forced herself to sit in the chair and look at him. She waited a long moment before she was sure her voice was under control. She stood up and stepped forward until her legs pressed against the front of his desk. 'Dylan,' she said, 'you will seize my farm when hell freezes over. The bank will get its money. You will have been disbarred or defrocked or deflowered or whatever it is that happens to corrupt bankers before I leave my farm. Don't get up. I know my way out.'

———

Bridget parked her ute in one of the angled parking spots outside a row of small shops in town. Through the front window she could see that the hair salon was busy, the three hairdressers fussing over clients. The name of the salon, Streaks Ahead, was painted in fancy lettering on the big plate glass window and in smaller lettering on the door. The bell above the door chimed as she pushed it open and entered. She was immediately struck by the smells of soap, hair dye, hair spray and a faint note of something overheated. Smells familiar from her youth. Her mum, Caroline, turned from the client she was working on – it looked to Bridget that she was in the middle of a complicated dyeing job – and said with a smile, 'Good morning, dear. Good to see you. How are you?'

Bridget couldn't remember her mum without a smile on her face. Not when her husband left; not when Bridget quit teaching, not when Gordon left Bridget. Nothing seemed to affect her – she refused to give in and carried on as though all was still well. 'God didn't put us here to have fun,' she used to say. Bridget had responded, 'But you don't believe in God, mum.' Her mum had just laughed and said 'You take your support where you can find it, dear.'

'Mum,' said Bridget, 'I need a haircut. Right now.'

'Well, um, of course, dear.' Caroline glanced at the clock on the wall and said, 'I can make a start on you while Mrs Conway's dye is setting.' She turned to the woman with foil wrappers in her hair and said, 'Don't worry, Sylvia, I'll get back to you as soon as that's set.'

The woman looked up from her magazine and said, 'Don't worry about me. I'm in no hurry. See to your daughter.'

Caroline fussed for a moment, organising towels, scissors and the bottles and tubes on her bench. She brushed the last few hairs off the seat and turned to her daughter. 'Okay. What would you like, dear?

'Blonde. That's what I want. Blonde.'

Caroline regarded her daughter in the mirror. She didn't know what was going on but could tell it was serious. Bridget had always ridiculed hair dyeing; had been outspoken about how false it was. For her to consider it now was a big deal. She ran her hands up through her daughter's hair. *Blonde? Well, it was only temporary.* Nonetheless, she looked at her daughter and her forehead creased as she asked, 'Are you sure? Blonde? That's a big change.'

'Yeah,' said Bridget, 'I've decided it's time for a change. I want to go blonde.'

'Well, okay, dear,' Caroline sighed, 'if that's what you really want. Have a seat and we'll give you a shampoo first. This is quite sudden and you've always been disparaging about women who dye their hair.'

Bridget felt her mother's strong fingers in her hair and massaging her scalp. With her eyes closed she saw Fraser's intense blue eyes and thick blond hair. She saw him standing in the hard light of Hugh's drive and heard him say, 'Ms Tronheim, I like your longer hairstyle.' Then her memory jumped further back in time and she saw unruly blond hair falling across those same blue eyes half shadowed by the elm tree outside the school gym, 'Ms Tronheim, you've got the prettiest hair I've ever seen.' She involuntarily shook herself and dragged her thoughts back to the present. 'Mum, just cut the damned hair.'

The fingers stopped for a moment and Caroline asked, 'Are you all right dear?'

CHAPTER 6

Cathay Pacific flight 113 touched down at Auckland at 1.10 p.m., ten minutes ahead of schedule. The flight from Hong Kong had been uneventful, aided by tailwinds. The Boeing 777 taxied to the gate and, shortly after it stopped, the doors opened and the passengers began to disembark.

Wang Qiang walked steadily along the concourse, just another body among the throng of other arrivals. He was dressed casually in dark slacks, a polo shirt and scuffed white trainers. He had a small flight bag slung over his left shoulder.

Luo Tao had been seated near the rear of the plane and was toward the end of the stream of travellers. He was also dressed casually, in jeans and a sweatshirt with SuperDry Japan printed on it. He was wearing Nike sports shoes and a cap with the New York Yankees logo. He pulled a small piece of wheeled carryon luggage.

There was a long queue for travellers with foreign passports. Mr Wang and Mr Luo waited patiently, shuffling forward as the line slowly advanced. Both men passed through immigration, collected their luggage and cleared customs without incident. They exited the arrivals hall and moved to an area away from the bustle of cars, buses and taxis.

There was nothing about Wang that would attract attention: average height, medium length hair, ears that lay close to his head, face full but not plump, eyes medium brown, nose straight and full. His lips were slightly bow-shaped, almost feminine. His body looked stocky but, with his loose clothes, it was impossible to tell whether it was muscle or fat.

Wang watched Luo approach. He was a little taller than Wang and younger by at least ten years. He wore glasses with dark frames and narrow rectangular lenses that did little to hide the traces of childhood acne. His hair was similar to Wang's though cut a little shaggier on the sides and his eyes were a darker brown. His body was solid but it was apparent from the width of his shoulders and narrowness of his hips that there was no fat on him.

Wang said in Chinese, 'Are you ready? We have much to do.'

Luo replied, 'Of course. The sooner we are finished the better.' He looked up at the clear blue sky and gestured broadly with his right hand. 'What an amazing place. Did you see the colour of the ocean before we landed? And the green of the fields and trees. This is a land of primary colours. And what about those steaks in the back of the airline magazine? I want to get one of those before we leave.'

Wang smiled sourly and said, 'Yes, it's quite a change from the brown haze of home. But don't get comfortable. We're only here for a few days.'

'Okay,' Luo replied.

Wang looked around and gestured back towards the terminal. 'Come on, the car rentals are this way.' He turned and moved off, Luo trailing a little behind.

———

'Did I instruct you to go to the vet's?'

The voice in the receiver was icy. Fraser swallowed and said uncertainly, 'No.' He swallowed again and regained his confidence and said more firmly, 'No. I used my initiative. Isn't that why you hired me?'

'I hired you to do exactly as I say. Your initiative is not required.

You do not know what's going on. Your bumbling efforts could cause a problem. I do not like problems.' The voice was silent, then said, 'Did you find the horse?'

'No. I don't know,' Fraser said. He ran his hand through his hair. He was thinking rapidly, trying to stay one step ahead. What the voice had said was true – the one thing he was sure of was that he didn't know what was going on. He decided to keep his mouth shut as much as possible and only answer questions.

'Well? What *do* you know?'

'Look, we went to the vet's place. That's where you said the horse would be. We asked around but there was no sign of the horse. And his wife said it wasn't there.'

'Then let me ask you this: was there any security in sight? Any guards or alarms? Any sign of anything out of the ordinary?'

'There was what looked like an alarm box on the side wall of the barn but there was nobody there but the vet's wife. There were no guards that we could see. It looked ordinary. Like a farm. Or a stud. Or whatever they call a horse farm. Oh, and a woman showed up as we were leaving.'

'A woman?' the voice queried. 'What was she doing there?'

'Her name's Bridget Tronheim. Except she's called Bridget Crawford now. She must have got married. She used to teach at my school. I'm not sure what she was doing there. She said she needed something from the vet's barn.'

The voice was silent for a moment, then said, 'So, a million dollar horse is supposed to be there but there is no sign of extra security. And a woman shows up and says she needs something presumably for a horse.' There was another long pause. 'Does that suggest anything to you? Do you think it's possible that the vet is trying to be clever? Do you think these things could be telling us where the horse is? Do you think that you should perhaps make a visit to this teacher?'

Fraser congratulated himself. The voice had reached the same conclusion he had. He answered, 'Sure, I get it. The vet's moved the horse to her place. That's why they were so relaxed and there was no sign of security.' He smiled and continued, 'It would be a pleasure to continue my conversation with Ms Crawford.'

'Very good. Then go get the horse. There's no time like the present.'

'You may be right, but I need to do a recce of her place to see if the horse is there. Unless you know what security she has? If the horse is there then we'll plan how to get it.'

There was silence on the phone for a moment, then the voice said, 'Very well. Make your reconnaissance. But time is short.'

'Yeah, but I hear time is very long in prison. If we're caught then we're the ones who will go to jail, not you. Don't worry, I want this over as quickly as you do.'

'Actually, on consideration a short delay in getting the horse might be worthwhile. There are other resources that will be available to help you soon. I'll be in touch.'

The call ended abruptly and Fraser slipped his phone back into his pocket. He turned back to the car and saw that Dennis and Venus were about to enter the back door of the house. 'Hold it!' he called out. 'Back to the car. We have another visit to make.'

Gordon sat in his car outside the IRD office and drummed his fingers on the steering wheel. He had a thread. A thin, frayed strand of a clue that might or might not lead him to the rustlers. Phoebe had given him the name of a butcher who could be involved in the rustling scheme. There were any number of reasonable, perfectly legal explanations for his financial records. But it was the only lead Gordon had and, as a reporter, he knew he had to follow it up.

Then why, he asked himself, *am I so reluctant to start the bloody car and go to talk to this guy? This story get me right out of this backwater town. I could land a job as an investigative journalist on a real paper, or even for a TV network. Isn't that what I want? Independence, free parking and no rush hour for impossible deadlines and crowds? No more interviews with third-division netball teams? No more articles on the champion ram at the annual field days? No more lattes made with instant coffee?*

But even if I find out who the rustlers are it won't get Bridget's cattle back. Can she survive the loss? Norman said things aren't going well for her but I haven't seen any sign that she's in trouble. And I haven't seen any signs of her having a relationship with someone. What had Norman said – 'it was not a prospective relationship'?

The tempo of Gordon's fingers on the wheel quickened. He didn't need to be Sherlock Holmes to conclude that Norman thought she was seeing a married man. Gordon's mind ran over all her friends but he couldn't think of anyone it might be. Bridget had lots of married friends. In fact, *most* of her friends were married but he couldn't think of anyone who she seemed particularly friendly with. She'd do anything for Elliot, but Norman hadn't been talking about that kind of relationship. Gordon didn't see how she could possibly have the time or energy to work the farm and have an affair. Particularly a clandestine one with a married man.

He started the engine but didn't put the car in gear. His eyes were focused far beyond the Toyota parked in front of him. *What if she is having an affair with someone, married or not? Do I care?* That stopped him for a minute. He hadn't answered that one before the next question came to mind. *And if I do, is there anything I can do about it?* Bridget had made it pretty clear when he'd last seen her that she wasn't ready to forgive and forget. She hadn't given him any chance to talk to her since he'd returned from Australia. He finally put the car in gear, released the brake and pulled out from the curb without looking. The butcher could wait. He needed to interview Bridget for the article anyway.

———

'Can you give me a hand here?'

Elliot looked up from skipping out the droppings from Tui Dancer's stable. 'Sure. I'll be right there,' he called out.

The sound of a car coming up the drive reached them and Bridget turned and looked to see who was approaching. A dusty white Honda rolled slowly into the yard and parked near the stables. Bridget folded her arms and frowned as the motor was switched off and Gordon emerged. He looked warily at Bridget, then glanced at Elliot and finally swept the entire yard with his eyes as if searching for snipers. Elliot moved up beside Bridget and said softly, 'I think I'll shoot off now.'

Bridget nodded absently but her eyes didn't leave Gordon. He shuffled from behind the car and moved circumspectly towards her. She still had her hand up, shading her eyes, and he couldn't see their expression. When they had been married, that had been his secret weapon. Bridget was an expert at concealing her emotions. Except for her eyes. As he stepped closer he squinted, trying to get even the faintest hint of her mood. 'Afternoon,' he said.

'Gordon,' she nodded stiffly in response.

'Like your hair.'

'Uh-huh.'

'You look good. As a blonde, I mean.'

'Uh-huh.'

'Everything okay?'

'Is that a professional question?'

'Is that the way you want it?'

'Isn't that the way you want it?'

Gordon scratched his ear and looked tired. 'Shit. I don't know. Can we start again?'

'This conversation or our lives?'

'For Christ's sake! Can you just give me a break? Can you unbend for just one minute and talk to me? Can you stop answering a question with a question and avoiding me? Can you talk to me like a person? Like I was someone you once cared about?'

Bridget put her hands in her trousers pockets as she answered. 'No, I don't think so,' she said coolly. 'Is there anything else I can do for you?'

Gordon clenched his fists and shut his mouth determinedly. After a moment he almost visibly sagged and said resignedly, 'Okay. Okay.

That's fine. I'm sorry to have bothered you. I wanted to apologise. To tell you what a fool I was. I know I can't regain your respect. But I want my own. I also wanted to talk with you about your missing cattle. But maybe another time.' He turned to walk away and Bridget put her hand out and touched his shoulder.

'What do you want me to say? That it's okay now?' She removed her hand from his shoulder and brushed her hair from her forehead before continuing. 'Well, I'm sorry. That's not the way it works. I did care for you once. Of course I did. But that seems like a long time ago now. Life isn't like one of those TV scenes that you can reshoot if you don't like the way it turned out. We can never go back to being the way we were. I was angry when you left. Angry and hurt more than you can imagine. But that's over now. I've stopped thinking about it and found other things. I don't hold a grudge or think badly of you. There's really nothing for us to say about it.' She patted the pocket in her shirt and looked at Gordon. 'Do you have a cigarette?'

He looked at her blankly. 'A cigarette? No, I don't have a cigarette. You stopped smoking years ago.'

'Yeah, but I think I've started again.'

Gordon looked away, but he wasn't seeing the landscape. 'I talked with Dani about the theft of your cattle.'

'Good,' said Bridget, 'I hope she finds the bastards.'

Gordon desperately wanted to tell her what he and Phoebe had discovered but he knew it was too early. He didn't really know anything yet and he didn't want to get Bridget's hopes up if he was wrong. 'She gave me the facts. Is there anything else you can tell me?'

'Like what?'

'Like how you're feeling? Like what the theft meant to you? You know, the human side. That's what people want to read.'

'I don't care what people want to read. How I feel is pissed off. And that's neither surprising nor any of their business.' Bridget wiped her hands on her trousers and said, 'Now, unless there's something else, I have work to do.'

———

Bridget looked at herself in the mirror. She wasn't sure she liked being blonde but she had to admit it made her look different. She went into the kitchen to get a glass of wine before dinner and heard a car pull up on the gravel outside her house. She put the bottle back in the fridge and stepped to the kitchen door. She recognised the car immediately. It was the Falcon that she'd seen at Hugh's earlier in the afternoon, and the same three people were getting out of it.

Fraser closed the driver's door and squinted up at her. 'Hey, you look great. What have you done with your hair?'

Bridget reflexively raised her hand and then jerked it back to her side. 'Fraser. What are you doing here?'

'You know, I really like the blonde look. I used to fantasise about you being blonde. Man, this really brings back memories.'

'Yeah, well you only bring back nightmares. What do you want?'

'Well, it was so good seeing you this afternoon that I thought it would be good to have a proper catch-up. You know, have a cup of tea or a beer and talk about old times. What we've been doing, and things like that.'

'You're crazy. Why would I want to talk about old times with you? I don't know what you're doing and I don't care. Obviously what happened back in school had a big effect on you. I get that. And you think that somehow everything now has to revolve around it.' Bridget pulled out a pack of cigarettes, shook one free and lit it. She took a deep drag and blew out a long plume of smoke. 'But that's bullshit. The world's moved on. I've moved on. There's nothing for us to talk about.'

Fraser gestured at Venus and Dennis. 'My mates and I have come a long way to see you.' He looked around at the house, stable building and gardens. 'You have a beautiful place. What do you guys think? Is this place great or what?'

Dennis grinned and said, 'You bet. I'm a landscape gardener and this has to be in the top ten places I've seen.' Venus gave Dennis a strange look but kept her mouth shut. If she remembered correctly, his landscape gardening career had lasted five weeks, and had mostly involved digging trenches for irrigation.

Fraser said, 'There you go. Now, Bridget, what do you say? You sure you can't at least give us a tour?'

Bridget took another drag on her cigarette and said, 'What are you doing, Fraser? You fucked up my life but I always thought you'd be successful at *something*.' She gestured at her farm and then at the trio in front of her. 'What are you doing here? What are you doing with them?'

Fraser smiled and said, 'Well, yeah, I guess I was successful at something.' He paused reflectively for a moment and then looked into her eyes. 'I went to university, you know. Got the education, got the degree. Double major in literature and commerce.'

He paused again and said, 'Can I bum a cigarette?' Bridget wordlessly held out her pack. He stepped forward and extracted one, then returned the pack. She gave him her lighter before he asked for it. He lit his cigarette, blew smoke and said, 'I was good, really good. All the big accounting firms were after me. I took a job at one: I thought I had it made – six-figure salary straight out of uni. Bought a car. Had a nice flat. The whole nine yards.'

Bridget said, 'Yeah? So what happened?' She nodded towards the clapped-out car. 'You're sure as hell not working for an accounting company now.'

Fraser raised his cigarette and watched the smoke curl up and blow away in the light breeze. 'No, I parted ways with my employer. They thought I'd misappropriated some of our client's money.'

'And had you?'

He shook his head. 'Nope. But my boss had. I was young and stupid and greedy. I had no idea what he was doing. Or that he'd set me us as his patsy in case the shit hit the fan. Which it did.'

'So? Why didn't you fight it? Get a lawyer? You said you were bloody good.'

'Yeah, but he was better. He'd fit me for the box and there was no way out. Believe me, I had sleepless nights for weeks trying to find a way out. I went to two lawyers and they just said I was fucked.'

'What did you do?'

'I quit before they could fire me. But of course New Zealand's a very small place and word got around. No one would hire me.'

Bridget regarded him coolly. 'So … what? What are you doing now?' She nodded towards Dennis and Venus. 'What's with Bonnie and Clyde? I know you're up to something. What is it?'

Fraser smiled and said, 'Sorry to disappoint you, Bridget. Like I told you and the vet lady this morning, we're just looking for some honest work.' He waved his hand and said, 'And we'd really like to see your beautiful farm.'

Bridget dropped her cigarette and ground it out with her boot. 'Bullshit. Look, Fraser, just leave. Okay? Just leave.'

Fraser shrugged: 'Sure, if that's what you want. Maybe another time. It's been great catching up with you.' He turned to Dennis and Venus: 'I guess we'd better go.' He started the car and pulled forward until he could look up at Bridget from his window. 'I really like your hair,' he said and drove away.

———

Barry Miller was in the back of the shop and didn't see Fraser and Dennis walk through the door. He was working his way through a hogget, turning the solid carcass into a pile of chops and roasts. He hadn't had lunch and was wondering whether he'd have time to nip along for some fish and chips, or whether he'd have to make do with a bread and butter sandwich. He heard the bell ring as they walked in and called out, 'Be right with you!'

Fraser smiled slightly, nodded to Dennis and walked around behind the counter. As he passed by the chopping board he picked up a boning knife and tapped the side of the blade lightly against his palm as he entered the back room.

Barry had just finished removing one of the back legs and turned as Fraser walked through the door. He froze in the act of putting his knife back in the holster at his waist. He still had his chain mail glove on his left hand.

'Hello, Barry,' said Fraser. He stood just inside the door, still with that small smile on his face. Barry saw Dennis move up behind Fraser's shoulder and stand in the doorway looking at him. Barry jammed his knife into the holster and took a step forward.

'What the fuck are you doing here? I thought we agreed you'd never come here!'

'Now, now,' Fraser said, 'calm down a minute. Aren't you glad to see us?'

'Glad to see you?' Barry exclaimed. 'Am I glad to see a rabid dog? You guys are nothing but trouble. I should have never had anything to do with you.'

'Ah, that's what Faust said, too. But it's too late for that kind of thinking now. And anyway, this is our farewell. In a way.'

Barry paused and looked at Fraser suspiciously. 'Farewell? Bullshit. You guys never go away.'

'No, really.' Fraser's smile broadened and he spread his arms slightly. The blade of the boning knife gleamed in the overhead lighting. 'We're getting out of this business. We just stopped around to say goodbye.' He made a small bow and stood back up with a flourish of the knife. 'And to ask for a final favour.'

Barry's eyes strayed to the knife held so casually in Fraser's hand. He sighed heavily and rubbed his big hand over his eyes. 'What is it this time?' he asked dully.

Fraser stepped forward and clapped him on the shoulder. 'I knew we could count on you! Compared to all the things you've done for us already it's really nothing at all.' Fraser stepped over to the bench where Barry had been working on the carcass and idly poked some of the chops with the point of his knife. 'We just want you to look after an animal for us. No big deal. No killing this time. Just do your farmer thing and make sure it stays nice and healthy until we ask for it back.'

Barry looked puzzled. 'Look after an animal? This is crazy. What are you two idiots up to this time? The only animals you guys care about are the ones in paddocks with unlocked gates.'

'You underestimate us.' Fraser looked Barry in the eye. 'The beast in question is not just any old animal. We're not talking a lump of beef or a side of lamb here. We're talking a once-in-a-lifetime experience.

We're talking big. Something you'll tell your grandkids about.' Dennis stifled a laugh and Fraser shot him a quick look. 'Well, maybe not. But it will be an experience you'll never forget.'

Fraser stood in front of Barry and tapped him softly on the chest with the knife. 'You're going to have the privilege of looking after Tui Dancer.'

Barry looked stunned for a moment and then shook his head vigorously. 'Uh-uh! No way, man. Even *I* know about that horse. You must be out of your bloody mind. Do you know what that horse is worth? You're crazy to even be thinking about stealing him.'

Fraser smiled. 'Hey, who's said anything about stealing? Dennis and I have come into some resources and we're looking for a suitable investment. We thought that, as we're high-risk sort of guys, a racehorse would suit our style. And if we're going to enter the business then we thought we might as well start at the top. Right, Dennis?'

Dennis straightened slightly and responded, 'You bet. I can't see us wasting time on some old nag when we could go for a horse like Tui Dancer.'

Barry looked back and forth between the two men, a look of dismay still on his face, as Fraser continued: 'It's a straight business proposition. There are a few details to sort out with the owners but we expect to have the horse any day. We're short of storage space is all and of course when we need some farming help who do we think of – none other than our old mate Barry! Now of course, if you are seriously not interested in helping us then Dennis and I could understand that. After all, you're not used to the world of big business the way we are. But maybe instead of worrying about some of the grey areas you should think about what an anonymous phone call might have to say about your little sideline.' He raised his eyebrows and broadened his smile.

Barry put his hands over his eyes and his head drooped. 'Oh my God,' he said, 'what have I done?'

———

A puff of night air moved the curtains, giving a moment's relief from the heat of the kitchen. It brought the smell of jasmine and roses and dew-wet grass. The dim moonlight gleamed off the polished surfaces but provided no illumination to the room.

Bridget wrapped her arms around Hugh and held him tightly to her, burying her face in his chest. Hugh, caught off guard by her action, took a moment to respond. He wrapped his arms around her and stroked her hair with one hand as he held her to him. They stood in Bridget's kitchen, holding each other without speaking.

'Wow,' Hugh said finally, 'I like the welcome. But I suspect it's not entirely out of gladness to see me.'

Bridget shook her head silently against his chest and didn't look up. Hugh continued to hold her until he felt her back begin to relax and she moved away. Bridget switched on the kitchen light but didn't turn to look at him. She studied her reflection in the window, sharp against the blackness outside.

'And changes. Changes are good. I like the new hair colour,' Hugh said. 'Was it something you saw on TV?'

Bridget turned to him and shrugged. 'No. I don't know. I mean I'm not sure why, really. It just seemed like time. For a change.'

'Okay, I love the greeting and I think your hair looks great. But what's going on? Is there something I should know?' Hugh's thoughts oscillated between concern for Bridget and for Tui Dancer. He felt strung too tightly and knew it wouldn't end until Tui Dancer was off his hands.

She wiped her eyes with her hands before looking up at him. 'No, it's nothing really. I'm just being silly. I'm okay now.'

Hugh reached out, gripped her arms gently and squeezed slightly. 'Balls. You're never upset over nothing. Now tell me what it is and we'll see what we can do about it.'

Bridget smiled ruefully. 'This is a problem you can't do anything about. Gordon came to see me today. He wanted to talk about us. About him and me, that is, not about you. I told him there was nothing to say, and that was it. He left and I went back to work.'

'Well, that doesn't sound too traumatic.'

'Seeing Gordon is never easy but that's not all that happened. After he left, Fraser came by. You remember we told you about him? That guy who showed up at your place with another guy and a girl?'

'Oh, yeah, I remember. Sounded like he was a cocky little bastard. What did he want?'

'Yeah, well he showed up here this afternoon. He only stayed for a few minutes before I told him to bugger off.'

'I can imagine *that* conversation,' Hugh said.

'The thing is,' said Bridget, 'I can't figure out why he was here. He said it was just to catch up. He saw me at your place and wanted to talk to me. But I don't think that was it. He didn't really say much and he kept looking around at the yards and buildings.' Bridget eased away from Hugh's touch and crossed her arms over her chest. 'It's too much of a coincidence. He shows up at your place talking like he knows about Tui Dancer and then he shows up here with no good excuse.' She shook her head. 'I don't like it, Hugh. Something fishy's going on.'

Hugh smiled, turned and put his arm across Bridget's shoulder. 'You may be right, but so what? They may be sniffing around but they don't know anything. They can't do anything. Forget about Fraser. Forget about the people with him. Just focus on what we have to do.' He paused and Bridget saw him swallow before continuing. 'You know I'll never be able to thank you for what you've done. I know we said there were no ties between us. But, well, you're very special and I'm not sure that's still what I want.' He looked away and then back at her, staring directly into her eyes.

Uh-oh, thought Bridget. *No, no, no. This isn't supposed to be happening. I don't need this.*

Hugh continued, 'I've been thinking about us a lot and when this is all over I want to go away with you. I've got some opportunities in Asia but we can go anywhere you want. We'll do whatever you want. We'll leave all this bullshit behind and just relax. Enjoy being together. I know it's out of the blue, but what do you say? Would you come with me?'

Bridget looked at Hugh for a long moment. She looked at those dark brown eyes and firm features and thought about how good he made her feel. How safe and loved. She thought about her mortgage and the stolen cows and the asshole Fraser who was turning her life upside down. She thought about Barbara and Gordon and Elliot: how they would be affected and what they'd think. She thought about how good it would be to just walk away and start over again. *Again?*' she thought, *could I start over again?* She stepped forward and wrapped her arms around Hugh. 'I don't know,' she said. 'I don't know. There's so much going on right now that I don't know what I want.'

Hugh held her against his chest and said reassuringly, 'Okay, that's okay. I just wanted you to know how I feel. I hope you'll say yes but at least think about it.' He released her and turned her gently towards the door and said, 'So, how's Tui Dancer doing? Shall we have a look?'

Bridget sighed and said, 'I guess.' She reached up and squeezed his hand. 'Yeah, let's check on him.'

CHAPTER 7

Dennis looked nervously at Fraser and asked, 'Why are we going back to that lady's place? I know that mystery man who told you about Tui Dancer didn't tell you to go. You didn't get a call from him. Are you sure this is a good idea?'

Fraser took a long drag on his cigarette, blew the smoke out of the car window and said, 'Relax, Dennis, everything's under control. This is called showing initiative. It's what you do to earn extra credit.' He tried very hard to forget the voice's words: 'I hired you to do exactly as I say. Your initiative is not required.' He'd never been good at following instructions.

Venus piped up from the back seat, 'I don't have a good feeling about this. We haven't talked about what we're doing. We have no plan. We have no idea what's going on. This is real life, not high school. Nobody's after extra credit. You're totally full of shit.'

'Okay, okay, hang on a minute. Think about it. What do we know?' Fraser asked. He didn't wait for an answer before continuing, 'We know Tui Dancer's there. We know that there's no security system. We know that there are three of us and Bridget's on her own. We know that any of these things could change at any minute, so now's the best chance we have. If we wait then they could move Tui Dancer. Or they could bring in security. Or do some other thing that will make it harder for us to get the horse. I know there are things we're not sure about. Where do we get a trailer? Who's going to keep Bridget under control? What do we do if someone else is there? We should have a detailed plan but sometimes you can overthink these things. Like Sun Tzu, Homer Simpson or somebody once said, "Planning is good, but action is better." Trust me. You just follow my lead and we'll be right.'

'Trust me?' said Venus. 'Isn't that what Butch Cassidy said to the Sundance Kid?'

———

The old Falcon station wagon crunched up the drive, stones pinging against the underbody, and stopped near Bridget's house. Bridget stepped out onto the porch and frowned as three now-familiar figures emerged from the car.

Fraser took a step towards the house, gave her a slow smile and raised his hand. 'Hey, Bridget, long time no see. How you doing?'

Bridget glanced at the other two. The guy and the girl stayed by the car, their bodies shielded by the doors. She looked back at Fraser. 'Mr Lyman. You are like shit on my shoe. It seems no matter how hard I try I just can't get rid of you. I told you that there's nothing for us to talk about.'

Fraser lowered his hand and took another step closer. His smile was intact when he said, 'Whoa, I think we got off on the wrong foot. I know I probably should have called ahead and told you we were dropping by, but I didn't have your number and I thought you'd be glad to see an old friend.'

'You are neither old nor a friend. Why don't you cut the crap? What are you doing here? Two visits in two days is not an accident.'

'No, you're right. It's no accident. And it's not because I enjoy your company so much, either. Since you ask so nicely, I'll tell you. We've come for a horse.'

'A horse?' Bridget wrinkled her forehead. 'What horse? I don't have a horse for sale.'

'Ah,' Fraser lifted both hands from his side, palms up, 'there's a small misperception. You see, the horse we're after isn't yours, and it isn't for sale.'

Bridget felt a sinking feeling in her stomach but struggled to keep her composure. Her thoughts were racing. *Do they know about Tui Dancer? How could that be possible?* She bit her lower lip and glanced again at Fraser's companions. They stood patiently, listening, serious expressions behind their sunglasses. Their hands were in sight on top of the door frames but she sensed they were ready to move at a moment's notice. She said, 'I'm sorry, I don't understand. Why did you come here for a horse that isn't mine?' She shook her head and said, 'This is bullshit. Get back in your car and get off my property. I don't have a horse or anything else that you want. If you're not gone in one minute then I'm calling the police.'

Fraser ignored her threat and said, 'Really, are you saying you don't have Tui Dancer in your stables?'

Bridget felt the blood drain from her face. This was impossible. No one knew Tui Dancer was here. She brought her hand up to cover her mouth and slowly shook her head again. Her brain was numb. Finally she managed to say weakly, 'No. No, the only horses here are mine.'

Fraser gave her a slow smile and said, 'Come on. You can't bullshit me. And the Catholics are right you know. Confession brings such relief.' He stood close to Bridget, looking directly into her eyes. He could see the fear in them and felt an almost sexual surge of excitement. He said, 'When we visited your friend Mr Jacob's place there was no security, no extra staff. No sign of anything out of the ordinary. Does that seem odd to you? It seemed odd to me. And it got me to thinking. And the more I thought about it the more it seemed pretty obvious that the horse wasn't there.'

'But that's true here as well,' Bridget objected. 'I don't have any security or staff, either. Why did you come here?'

'Yes, that's the point. The horse is supposed to be at Mr Jacob's place so that's where the security should be. But instead the horse is here, where it's not supposed to be. And any security here would only draw attention, so there's none here, either.' Fraser smiled almost gently and said, 'When you showed up at the vet's acting a little strange I decided it was worth coming to have a chat with you, to see if Tui Dancer might be here.' He paused and continued, 'Really, you did very well. But our last visit convinced me that you have Tui Dancer.'

He brought his right hand up and stroked her jaw line. Bridget flinched but didn't step away. Fraser brought his lips close to her ear and whispered, 'You are really very beautiful. Maybe one day we can pick up where we left off.'

Bridget didn't move for several seconds. She desperately wanted to protect Tui Dancer but she was running out of options. Fraser was obviously convinced Tui Dancer was here. She couldn't see how she could persuade him otherwise. And she couldn't throw him off her property – there were three of them and one of her. She wished Hugh was here. She wished Dani was here. She stepped away from Fraser without a word and walked around him. Her boots kicked up small clouds of dust as she strode towards the stables. Fraser watched her and turned to gesture for Dennis and Venus to follow as he moved in her wake across the hard-packed dirt.

Bridget opened the sliding doors of the stable block. When they entered, her horse Blackbird stuck his head outside his stable and looked at them. 'Is that him?' asked Fraser. 'Is that Tui Dancer?' He pulled a crumpled envelope from his pocket and scanned it.

Bridget thought quickly. Despite a little height difference there was quite a strong resemblance between Blackbird and Tui Dancer but no one who really knew them would be fooled. However, she was sure that neither Fraser nor Dennis knew anything about horses, and Venus had seen neither horse so far. She glanced at Tui Dancer's box and prayed that the door was latched. She prayed that he would stay quiet for the next few minutes. 'Yeah,' she said, 'that's him.' It broke her heart to put Blackbird in peril but she knew she had to protect Tui Dancer at all costs.

Fraser looked back and forth between his scribbled notes and the horse. 'Black with a white mark on his face and two white legs.' He gestured to Bridget, 'Get the horse out of the stable so we can see him properly.'

Bridget went to the back of the building and took a headcollar off the wall. She went to Blackbird's box and released the lower part of the door, putting her hand on Blackbird's forehead as she did so. 'Good boy, good boy,' she said as she entered and fitted the headcollar. She led him out and his hooves clattered as he moved onto the concrete floor.

'Okay,' Fraser said, after walking around the horse, 'looks good to me.'

'Which legs are supposed to have the socks?' asked Venus.

Fraser looked at her and then back to his paper. 'It doesn't say. Why?'

'I don't know. It probably doesn't matter. But there are four legs and it would be good to know which ones are supposed to have the socks.'

Fraser thought about that for a second and said, 'Yeah, well, we've got a black horse with a white forehead and two white legs. That's good enough for me.'

It was crowded in the stable block with the four people and the horse and Bridget's ute. 'Right,' said Fraser, 'we've found what we've come for. Unfortunately it seems we're a little short of transport. I'm afraid we're going to have to requisition your ute, and your trailer.'

'You bastard,' Bridget hissed.

'Now, now, don't be like that,' said Fraser. He turned to Dennis. 'Let's get that ute out and hook up the trailer. Venus, are you okay with looking after the horse for a minute?'

'I guess,' Venus said and took the headcollar. She moved close to the horse and smoothed her hand down his flank. She thought back to her decision to get involved. This was the moment of truth. *What the fuck am I doing?* she wondered. *This is no longer a game. This is a real horse and these guys are really going to steal him. And what does Fraser think he's doing? He's not anonymous. He knows this woman for God's sake. The cops will be after us before we're halfway down the drive. Not just some anonymous robbers, but* us. *This is nuts. Should I bail before it's too late?*

Fraser looked at her quizzically for a moment and said, 'Hey, it looks like Dennis was right. You've done this before.'

Venus shrugged and said, 'I know a bit.'

Fraser grabbed Bridget's upper arm and began moving her outside. 'Let's go. Let's give them some room.'

Dennis got into the ute. The key was in the ignition and Bridget cursed herself for being so trusting. He started the engine, put it in gear and eased through the double doors. The trailer was parked on the left side of the building and he pulled forward far enough to reverse back to it. Fraser pulled Bridget over to the trailer and began guiding Dennis back towards it. When the ute was close to the trailer hitch Fraser banged on the tailgate and Dennis stopped abruptly.

Fraser looked at Bridget and said, 'Come on, give us a hand.'

'You've got to be joking,' she said and folded her arms across her chest.

He gave a short laugh and began rocking the hitch towards the ball. Dennis got out of the ute to help and together they quickly got the trailer attached to the vehicle. Dennis got back into the ute and pulled forward parallel to the front of the stable block until the trailer was adjacent to the main doors. Fraser moved Bridget back inside and left her while he unlatched and lowered the trailer's rear door. 'Okay,' he said, 'now, let's get him in here.'

Venus felt caught up in events. Her mind was in a turmoil and she still hadn't decided whether to go along with the theft or flee the scene. With all eyes on her and no decision made about what to do, she led the horse out of the stables and to the rear of the trailer. The rear door formed a shallow ramp that sloped up to the floor of the trailer. There were several thin wooden slats attached across the ramp to prevent slipping as horses entered and exited the trailer.

Venus led Blackbird up the ramp and into the trailer. She stepped left as he entered and when he was fully inside she attached the lead rope to a cleat in the front of the trailer. When she was done she walked back down the ramp. Dennis helped her to lift it and close the latches. Bridget watched with a mixture of sorrow and jubilation as they did so. 'Well,' said Fraser, 'as always, it's been a pleasure.'

'You won't get away with it, you know,' Bridget responded. 'I'm going to call the cops as soon as you're gone.'

'You may call the cops, but not right away.' Fraser said, 'By the time you do we'll be long gone.' He stood in front of her and put his hands on her shoulders. 'I have to check that you don't have a cell phone.' He ran his hands down her body, feeling her breasts and the curve of her waist and hips before finding the cell phone in the back pocket of her jeans. Bridget felt herself blush at the unwanted intimacy but didn't move. 'Just like old times, eh?' he said with a smirk.

'I'll get you for this, you bastard,' Bridget said, her voice trembling with emotion. Fraser knew very well where her cell phone was. He must have seen its outline in her pocket and he'd only frisked her to humiliate her and reinforce his ascendency over her. As angry as she was with him she was even angrier at herself because she'd responded involuntarily to his touch.

Fraser used his index finger to push beneath the cell phone and ease it up out of the tight pocket, giving her bottom a pat as he did so. He dropped it on the ground, said 'Oops' and stamped on it with his boot. 'Sorry,' he said, 'I hope you're insured.'

Bridget was beyond words and just glared at him. She was powerless to resist as he moved her further back into the stable block and left her by the workbench. 'You're a clever woman and I'm sure you'll get out of here soon.'

'You can run but the cops will find you, you bastard,' Bridget said, 'I'll see you pay for this.'

Fraser gave her a thin smile and said 'I don't think so. By the time anyone catches up with us the horse will be long gone and it will just be your word against mine. Again. And we know how that worked out last time. Do you really think the cops are going to believe you when they learn the whole story? When I tell them that you're still out to get me?'

He gestured to Venus and said, 'Take a quick look around the building and make sure it's secure.' As she moved off he reached out and plucked Bridget's sunglasses from where she'd pushed them up into her hair. He smiled as he put them on his face and said, 'Thanks, I need a new pair.' Bridget jumped towards him and swung her fist at his face but he easily deflected the blow and wrapped his arms tightly around her. He held her for a moment and then slowly released her. She stood silently, staring sightlessly at the floor. Fraser backed to the front of the building and stepped through the big doors. She heard his laugh as the board fell into place, locking her inside.

Through the doors Bridget heard Venus say, 'All good' and the door to the ute slam shut before the engine revved and they set off down her drive.

'Fuck,' she said. 'Fuck, fuck, fuck.'

———

'Hugh! Hugh! Thank God!' Bridget almost shouted into the phone. She'd tried repeatedly to reach him but had been unable to get through. She'd been frantic by the time he'd finally answered. 'They were here! It was terrible! They took Blackbird. They were after Tui Dancer but they took Blackbird.'

'Hey, Bridget,' Hugh soothed her, 'I'll be right there.'

Hugh pulled to a stop in front of Bridget's house and before he could close the Range Rover door she had run out of the house and hugged him tightly. Hugh put his arms around her and tried to comfort her. 'It's okay. It'll be okay. Just tell me what happened.'

Over her head he looked at Constable Painter and Elliot. They had also come out of the house and were standing on the porch. Bridget had been talking with the constable, who had her notebook and pen in her hands. Elliot was standing behind Dani, hands in his pockets. They watched impassively as Bridget and Hugh embraced.

It had taken Bridget ten minutes to break a window and crawl outside. She'd run to the house to call the police but her phone line had been cut. After only a moment's thought she'd run back outside and headed off at a steady trot towards Elliot's farm. When she'd reached his house she'd called out and Elliot had appeared almost immediately from inside. 'Bridget,' he'd exclaimed, 'what's the matter?'

It was a few seconds before Bridget collected her breath sufficiently to answer: 'They've taken my horse. They've taken Blackbird.'

Elliot had rushed to her and taken her arm to support her as he'd urged her into his house, where she'd used his telephone to call the police. Dani had taken the details and said she'd be there as soon as she could. When she'd hung up Bridget collapsed into a chair and put her head in her hands. Elliot had heard the story as she'd related it over the phone. 'Right,' he'd said, 'you need a good cup of tea. Then we'll drive back to your place so you can go through it again with Constable Painter.'

Bridget had looked at him bleakly and said, 'Thanks. I'd rather have a whisky but I'd better not.' By the time she and Elliot returned to her farm Bridget was feeling calmer and was ready to go through the story again with the constable, who'd arrived a few minutes earlier and had spent the time looking around the stables and farmyard, making notes in her notebook.

––––––

Dani sat across the kitchen table from Bridget. She'd accepted a cup of coffee, hoping sharing it would calm Bridget down. Bridget had been clearly distressed when she'd called forty minutes earlier, reporting the theft of her horse. Dani had asked enough questions to put an APB out for a red Toyota ute towing a trailer before getting in her cruiser and driving to Bridget's house.

'Fuck,' Bridget said, 'I don't know how much more I can take.' She reached for a pack of cigarettes, shook one out and lit it.

Dani cocked an eyebrow and said, 'I didn't know you smoked.'

Bridget blew a long stream of smoke towards the ceiling and said, 'I don't. Except when I want to kill somebody.' She caught the look in Dani's eyes and realised some things cops just don't joke about. But she also decided that she didn't care.

Dani cleared her throat and looked at the notes she'd made in her notebook. 'Right, so do I have it correct? Two guys and a girl show up. They are after a horse and they steal yours, what's his name ...?' Dani flipped through her notes looking for the name.

'Blackbird,' said Bridget, 'his name is Blackbird.'

'Right, Blackbird. So these guys show up, take your horse, lock you in the stable block and drive away? Is that about it?'

Bridget took a long drag on her cigarette and thought, *Is that it? Is that it? Is that a summary of having a maniac whisper in my ear and feel my breasts and steal my ute and take my favourite horse? Of being so afraid I thought I'd pee my pants? Of feeling helpless and, God forbid, weak?* She stubbed her cigarette out in an ashtray and said, 'Yeah, that's about it.'

Dani cocked her head at Bridget and twisted her pen in her hand and said, 'I'm not a rookie cop anymore. I've interviewed hundreds of victims and perpetrators. Why is it I think you're not telling me everything?'

Bridget studied the table for a long moment. Her strong brown fingers rested on the worn timber surface and the smell of fresh coffee still lingered in the kitchen. What could she say? She'd promised to keep Tui Dancer's presence at her place a secret. True, Dani was a cop but that didn't change her reluctance to talk about it. And Fraser … damn, he was the last thing she wanted to talk about. Even though it was years ago and she was innocent, the incident with Fraser was too painful to expose willingly.

She studied the young constable across the table from her. She was slender, but Bridget got the impression that this meant Dani had the strength of a long-distance runner rather than a gym bunny. Her lips were on the thin side and smiled readily, a feature not shared by her eyes, which were light blue and shone with an intensity that belied her otherwise easygoing, reassuring manner.

Bridget decided that stonewalling would only make Dani more curious. She sighed and said, 'You're right, I should have told you earlier.' She paused for a moment then resumed, 'I know the guy who came here. Not the two people who were with him, but the guy in charge. He was a student of mine about ten years ago.'

'What? You know him? Why didn't you say so earlier? We could have a search out for him as well.'

Bridget reached for another cigarette but didn't pull it out of the packet. Her hands fidgeted nervously with it before she replied: 'I'm sorry. I really am. But it's messed up. And I really don't want to go through it again.'

'Go through what?'

Bridget took a deep breath and let it out. 'His name's Fraser. Fraser Lyman. He was a brilliant kid, but trouble. But not the only one. Another student accused me of improper behaviour.'

'That doesn't sound good.'

'No, it wasn't. It's not something I'm proud of and I don't talk about it.' The discussion was causing Bridget considerable discomfort. 'I was accused of having a relationship with one of my students. It got messy. Very messy.'

'I can imagine. I don't see how something like that could end up well for anyone.'

'That's for sure.'

'And how was Fraser involved? Was he the student you were accused of having the relationship with? I bet some of those boys could be pretty forward.'

'No, it wasn't Fraser.' Bridget sighed and continued, 'It wasn't … it wasn't one of the boys in my class – it was one of the girls.'

Dani raised her eyebrows. 'Wow. That's very twenty-first century.'

Bridget chuckled with no real humour. 'Yeah, I guess. It was this girl, Karen Voss. I thought she was okay. Not the brightest in the class but not a troublemaker, either. Then out of the blue, near the end of the term, she went to the principal and accused me of making sexual advances.' Bridget felt herself blushing and had to let her thoughts settle before she could continue. 'I still have no idea why she did it. She was doing okay in the course and was going to pass.' Bridget paused, sighed and continued, 'I denied it of course but the school board had an investigation and it came down to her word against mine. I couldn't prove I wasn't there when the alleged advances took place.'

'So what happened? How was Fraser involved?'

'He gave me an alibi.'

'An alibi? That must have been a relief. How come you didn't bring it up in the first place?'

'Because that wasn't true, either. I couldn't believe it. I was going through the investigation and thought things couldn't get worse when this kid from another class steps forward and says he can verify that I couldn't have made advances on Karen.' Bridget looked down and drew her hand across her forehead. 'Fraser had been one of my students the previous year, so he knew me. He was a bit of a strange kid. Incredibly bright but unmotivated. I don't think he ever studied, but was still near the top of the class. From the things he said, I think he had a bit of a crush on me. He had a way of saying things with a bit of innuendo. Nothing I could object to, but it was clear what he meant.

'Anyway, Fraser knew me and we had this, this history. When he said that I couldn't have been with Karen because I was with him it was a shock. But in a twisted sort of way it seemed inevitable. At least he said that it was he who came on to me, so I wasn't the instigator of the relationship. But that was no real consolation. I was accused of having relationships with not just one, but two students. It was all total bullshit but Fraser actually made my position worse. It might have been possible for me to successfully deny Karen's accusations, but who would believe that both students were liars? Where there's smoke there's fire, right?'

Bridget straightened and pushed her hair back. 'I did the only thing I could. I had a long talk with the headmaster, telling him that none of the accusations were true. At the end of that meeting I gave him my resignation, which spelled out what I'd said so it was on the record.'

Dani closed her notebook and looked at Bridget for a long moment, seeing her in a new light. 'Sounds like he's a real shithead. What you've told me may help us understand what's going on but the rights and wrongs of what happened ten years ago aren't relevant today. I'll get on the phone now and put out a notice to be on the lookout for this guy Fraser Lyman. You don't have a photo of him by any chance, do you?'

Bridget shook her head: 'Not in this lifetime.'

Dani nodded and continued, 'That's okay. If we can't find something online then we'll get a photo from the school. Can you give me the name of your school?'

'Yeah, sure,' Bridget said. She stood up from the table and went to the counter where a pad and pen lay by the phone. 'I'll write it down for you.'

———

It took several minutes but eventually Bridget disentangled herself and stepped back from Hugh, pushing her hair from her face. She took a deep breath, looked Hugh in the eyes and said, 'It was Tui Dancer. It was Fraser and those two friends of his. They came here about nine and said they wanted Tui Dancer.' Her eyes went wild for a second and she glanced at the stables before returning her gaze to him. 'There was nothing I could do. They *knew* Tui Dancer was here. They gave me a cock and bull story about knowing he wasn't at your place so he had to be here, but it sounded like bullshit to me. It's been driving me crazy. Not many people knew he was here. I'm sure neither of us said anything. Do you think it could have been one of the guys in the horse van?'

Hugh knitted his brow: 'Shit. I don't know. I can't see the drivers telling anyone. I don't think they even knew it was Tui Dancer. All they were told was to move a horse to my place, and then to yours.' He shook his head. 'That may not matter now, anyway. Tell me how they took Blackbird.'

Bridget had composed herself by then. 'Well,' she said, 'I just told all this to Constable Painter.' She nodded in her direction and continued, 'Those guys really are total idiots when it comes to horses.' She reached for Hugh's hand and pulled him into the stables. Dani and Elliot followed a few steps behind. Bridget pulled Hugh to the back stable and looked in the top half of the door. When he saw her, Tui Dancer quickly came over and stuck his head out. Hugh gave him a firm pat on the neck and Bridget said, 'When we got in the stables Blackbird stuck his head out and of course they looked at him.' She shook her head, 'You know, they look a bit alike but anyone who knows horses would have seen instantly that he wasn't a million-dollar stallion. They had a description on a piece of paper that said Tui Dancer was a black stallion with a white mark on his forehead and two white legs. They read that, looked at Blackbird, and said they had the right horse.'

Hugh said, 'But wait a minute, Blackbird has socks on his left foreleg and right hind leg, not both forelegs.'

Bridget smiled grimly, 'I know. But their description must not have included that detail. They had obviously never even seen a picture of Tui Dancer. I told you, these guys are idiots.' She put her hands in her back pockets and continued to stare at Tui Dancer. 'So they took my ute and trailer and drove off with Blackbird. It's been hours now and I haven't heard anything. I doubt they'll be fooled forever.' She looked at Hugh and he could see the fear in her eyes. 'I'm scared. It's lucky that Tui Dancer's okay but I'm scared they'll come back.'

Hugh put his arms around her again and held her tightly. 'I'm bloody lucky, but you must be devastated. Blackbird is a hell of a horse. We'll do everything we can to get him back. I think you're right, though. These guys will be back.' Without releasing Bridget he turned his head and looked at Dani. 'Constable? What do you think? What are you going to do to catch these guys?'

Dani tapped her notebook into her left palm and said, 'Mr Jacobs, Ms Crawford, this is a terrible crime but at the moment there's not much more I can do. I've already put out an alert and this will of course be a priority for our investigations. But you know there are only four constables in the district and we can't afford to be here full-time.'

Bridget had turned to look at Dani. She nodded and said, 'I know. I know you'll do the best you can. We don't expect you to babysit us.' She patted Hugh's hands that now rested on her shoulders. 'We'll be fine.' She looked at Elliot and said, 'We've got lots of friends who will help.'

Dani gave all three of them a look and said, 'Right. Well, I don't think there's anything else I can do here. Unless you can think of something then I'd better get back to the office and try to make some progress there. I understand your concerns but I'd be surprised if they came back. They know that you'll take more precautions and they won't be able to surprise you next time. I doubt they're completely stupid.' She held out her hand and Bridget took it. Dani's hand felt small and warm and strong. 'Don't worry,' she said. 'I'm very sorry you have to deal with this. I know you've been through a lot in the last few days. Losing your cattle and then your horse. We're going to get these guys.' She nodded to Hugh and Elliot and walked back to her patrol car.

Bridget reached out to Hugh and Elliot. They took her hands and looked at her. 'Thanks to you both for being here. I know the police will do what they can, but your help means a lot to me.'

Elliot was the first to say, 'No worries. You know we're always here for you. I reckon I'll hang around a while and make sure you're okay. Maybe even stay the night.'

Bridget laughed hollowly: 'Hey, you don't have to do that.'

Hugh shook her hand gently and said, 'Just be quiet for once and listen to some good advice. Your safety is the most important thing.' He dropped her hand and stepped back into the main entrance of the stables, from where he stood looking at Tui Dancer's box. The horse had moved back inside and was no longer visible. Hugh said, 'I'm a little worried about Tui Dancer, though. The constable's probably right and these guys won't come back, but they were willing to take some big risks last time to get him. And it's only luck that it didn't work.' He shook his head and frowned. 'As the constable said, these guys aren't stupid. They're smart enough to have planned a very bold robbery and they had the balls to almost pull it off.' Turning back to Bridget he added, 'I think we need to move Tui Dancer back to my place. No offence, but my idea of hiding him in plain sight obviously didn't work. I think I'd be happier if he was in my stables. I'll organise extra security to make sure something like this can't happen again.'

Bridget nodded, 'Sure. I understand. I'm sorry I didn't do a better job.'

Hugh laughed grimly and said, 'Bridget, you did a terrific job. Without you they'd have taken Tui Dancer for sure. But I can't ask you to take risks for me again. You were lucky once. I don't want you to have to be lucky again.'

Bridget shrugged and said, 'Okay. Then you'll have to go home and

get your trailer. They took mine, remember? And Hugh, can I borrow
your old car? They took my ute as well.'

———

Bridget walked angrily through the door of her mother's salon. She'd
finished her chores in town, including getting a replacement cell
phone. She'd avoided the bank – she had no idea how she would find
the money she needed to keep her farm going and seeing Dylan would
only have fuelled her anger.

Her mother was busy behind the reception desk and looked up
when the door chimed. She immediately sensed Bridget was upset and
stood up. 'Darling! I didn't expect to see you so soon. What's the
matter?' she asked, stepping around the counter.

Bridget stormed past her, heading for one of the hairdressing
chairs. 'Nothing,' she said angrily. 'Nothing's wrong, mum.'

Caroline's forehead wrinkled with worry and she followed her
daughter to the chair. 'But, honey, something's obviously happened.
What is it?'

Bridget sat heavily in the chair and stared at her mother in the
mirror. For a moment she saw Fraser there, laughing as he slammed the
main stable door closed on her, and she heard him say, 'I really like
what you've done with your hair.' Her whole body went tense and then,
with a sigh, she looked down, losing some of the awful force that had
possessed her when she entered. 'It's okay, mum. Really. It's just, it's
my horse. It's this guy. It's difficult.' She hesitated and looked again at
her mother's concerned face in the mirror. 'I need a haircut.'

Caroline stepped forward and placed her hand on her daughter's
head, feeling the soft hair beneath. She looked at Bridget in the mirror.
The face showed the usual resolute strength that characterised her only
child, but she also saw a shadow of vulnerability in her eyes,
something she hadn't seen before. She caressed Bridget's head for a
moment and said softly, 'Oh well, if it's just a guy then it must be
okay.'

Bridget laughed wryly, remembering that was one of their standing jokes when she was growing up. Her mother had been frank about her father's departure, not sparing Bridget from any of the details. She told her about the drinking, threatened violence and infidelities. Whenever a boy had behaved badly with Bridget – behaviour that had ranged from not returning her calls to sleeping with her best friend – her mother had defused her grief and anger by saying 'Oh well, what can you expect. He's just a guy.'

Now she turned and looked at her mother and said, 'You remember that guy from school? The one who claimed to have had a relationship with me?' Even now, years after the event, her face flushed with embarrassment when she thought about it.

'I'm not likely to forget *him*,' Caroline said.

'Yeah, well, he's back. He showed up at Hugh's the other day. And then yesterday …' Bridget paused and swallowed; the event had been so shocking that she still had problems talking about it. 'Yesterday,' she continued, 'he showed up at my place and stole Blackbird.'

Caroline stopped fussing with her scissors and brushes on her bench and looked at Bridget in shock. 'What!' she exclaimed. 'Oh no! You love that horse! How could he do it? How did he get away with it? Did you go to the police?'

In a strange way her mother's outrage and concern relieved Bridget and she was able to speak more openly about what had happened. 'Yes, I went to the police. The constable said she'd do whatever it takes to find the horse and arrest Fraser and the others.'

'That Fraser,' Caroline almost spat, 'I knew he was trouble from the start. With that smile and those eyes I knew he was only interested in one thing – and it wasn't school.' Bridget started to say something but her mother held up a hand and continued, 'I know, I know. We've talked about this before. But why did he come back after all this time? And why did he steal your horse? I mean, Blackbird's a fine horse and all but it's not like he's going to win the Melbourne Cup.'

Bridget looked at the worry and anger in her mother's eyes and wondered how much she could tell her. She shook her head slightly and said, 'I don't know. I really don't. There's something else going on and Fraser's involved somehow. I can't really talk about it. But he's back and he's, well, it's kind of complicated.'

Caroline picked up a smock and laid it across Bridget, fastening it behind her neck. 'Well, if you can't talk about it then I guess I can't help you.' She stood behind Bridget and held her head gently in her hands and looked at her daughter in the mirror. 'If I remember correctly it was complicated last time, too.'

Bridget wasn't sure it was possible but it felt as though she was blushing even more. 'Mum, it's not just my horse. When he was at my house he said things. He's trying to get inside my head. He said he wants to pick up where we left off.' Bridget paused. She couldn't say that her response to Fraser's actions included fear, because she didn't really know where they'd left off: that her feelings ten years ago had been equal parts anger and guilt; that she was afraid that, in spite of everything he'd done, he'd still have some sort of influence with her.

Caroline continued to prepare her equipment for the haircut, placing several pair of scissors on a folded white cloth. 'Well, I know that you and he didn't do the things he said you did, but I also know that something was going on in that head of yours. You never said anything, but I think he wasn't just another student.' She fluffed Bridget's hair, looking at it critically. 'You say he's come back? Fine. But just remember, darling, the guy's a total tosser. I wouldn't piss in his ear if his brain was on fire.'

Bridget looked in shock for a moment at her mother's reflection in the mirror and said, 'You're right. But I still want a haircut.'

'Okay, dear. What do you have in mind?'

Bridget pointed to a poster on the wall showing a model with a long, blunt wavy bob. 'That's it, that's what I want.'

Caroline looked from the poster to her daughter and her forehead creased as she asked, 'Are you sure? That's a big change. Are you sure you don't just want a good trim? You've had it long since, well, since …'

'Yeah, since I stopped teaching,' Bridget finished for her. 'It's time for a change. I want it short.'

———

Bridget was just finishing her haircut when Barbara Jacobs entered the salon. Bridget heard the door chime and could see in the mirror that Barbara was dressed casually in jeans, white silk blouse and black jacket. Bridget thought that, even in her fifties, she still looked like a model. Not for the first time Bridget wondered why Hugh had strayed from the nest. And not for the first time she avoided coming to a conclusion.

'Caroline!' Barbara called out as she entered.

'Barbara!' Bridget's mother responded. 'How good to see you. Just take a seat. I won't be a minute.'

Barbara sat in one of the chairs in the front of the salon and picked up a magazine. She flipped idly through the pages, but Bridget could see she wasn't thinking about the articles. Barbara kept glancing at her and Bridget wasn't sure if it was her new blonde look or something else that drew her attention.

Caroline used her scissors to make the finishing touches to Bridget's hair and then said, 'There you go, honey. I hope it's what you wanted.'

Bridget cocked her head and looked in the mirror: 'It's perfect, mum. Just what I needed.' She smiled at her mother and said, 'I knew I could count on you.'

Caroline looked unconvinced: 'Well, it's a big change. I hardly recognise you.'

'Yep, that's what I need. New looks for a new chapter.' Caroline removed the apron and brushed a few loose hairs from Bridget's clothes as she stood up. Bridget leaned forward and kissed her mother on the cheek. 'Thanks, mum. I don't know what I'd do without you.'

Caroline looked both flustered and pleased and said, 'It's nothing, dear. What are mothers for?' She put a hand on Bridget's shoulder and squeezed gently. 'Run along now. I need to get started on Mrs Jacobs.'

Bridget walked towards the door and, as she did so, Barbara stood and took a step forward, the magazine still in her hands. The older woman was smiling but to Bridget the edges looked fragile, like a crystal glass teetering on the edge of a shelf. Bridget felt her insides tense. *What does she know?* she thought. And then, *We can't have this discussion in front of my mother!*

Barbara gave Bridget a long look and said, 'Wow! I really like what you've done with your hair. It's perfect!'

Bridget nervously pushed her hair behind her left ear and said, 'Hi. Thanks. Good to see you. You look as good as ever.'

Now it was Barbara's turn to look down at her clothes, touch her silvery grey hair and glance sideways at Bridget's mother. 'Oh! Not really, I'm way overdue for a haircut.' She reached out towards Bridget but her hand stopped before she touched her arm. 'Actually,' she said, 'I'd really like to talk with you. Could you spare a minute? Please?'

Bridget's heart sank. She wasn't ready for this. *Shit,* she thought. *What was she going to say? Sorry for fucking your husband?* Her smile felt glued to her face and she was sure Barbara would see the anxiety in her eyes when she said 'Sure.' She gestured feebly at the chairs in the front of the shop. 'Here? Or …?'

Barbara said quickly, 'Let's step outside, shall we? It's a lovely day and we don't want to disturb your mother or the other customers.' She moved to the door and went outside, holding it for Bridget to follow. On the street Barbara paced back and forth for a moment, obviously searching for a way to start the conversation. Finally she turned and looked at Bridget. 'Can I talk to you woman to woman?' She held a hand up as though to wave away Bridget's objections. 'I know, it's not like we're close friends. But the truth is I don't have any close friends.' Barbara looked away for a second and resumed, 'We moved here ten years ago and Hugh's done all right. He's out and about all the time, meeting people. But I haven't made many friends. Everyone at the dairy factory's nice but I don't want to socialise with people at work. And the girls in the bridge club are great but I don't think I can talk to them about this.'

Bridget suddenly had an almost out of body experience. This was all too surreal. The wife of her lover was asking if they could be friends so she could talk about – what? 'Um, I don't …' she mumbled but Barbara was hitting her stride and took no notice.

She was looking into Bridget's eyes as she said, 'I know what you've been through and I know you'll understand. It's no secret that Hugh and I are going through a rough patch.' She sighed and looked away for a moment before returning her gaze to Bridget. 'I married Hugh because he's such a classic alpha personality. He oozes charm and confidence. There's nothing he won't try or can't do. He's taken me on an amazing journey and he's made me feel valued even though it's been his show.'

Barbara paused again and then continued: 'Hugh always needs a challenge. If things are too easy then he gets bored. And when he gets bored he loses interest in everything – his work, his sports ... even me. We've been through a few of these episodes. The kids were good for reinvigorating him. His rugby was, too, until his knee finally gave out.' Bridget listened with a sort of sick fascination, seeing Hugh through this new lens. Suddenly some of his behaviour began to make more sense. Perhaps even his attention to her.

'He hit a bad patch a couple of years ago,' Barbara continued, 'and nothing seemed to be able to get him back to normal. He became focused on making money. I think that he thought if he had enough money then he could leave his job and do whatever exciting thing he wanted to do.' Barbara gave a bitter little laugh, 'But I have no idea what he thought he would do that he'd enjoy more than working.' She shook her head: 'Hugh always has lots of ideas but he isn't very good at sharing them. Until he's decided what we're going to do.

'Look, the long and the short of it is that recently Hugh's been acting even more remote than usual. When I try to please him, or even get his attention, it's like I'm not even there. I've been racking my brain but for the life of me I can't think of anything I've done to offend him. What about you? You see quite a lot of him. Have you noticed any changes? Does he seem to be acting differently to you?'

Bridget wanted to say 'Well, he's not much interested in foreplay anymore, which pisses me off,' but instead she said, 'Oh, I'm so sorry. I haven't really paid much attention, but I don't think I've noticed any difference. Of course, he's been pretty wound up about Tui Dancer. That's all he's talked about the last few times I've seen him. Maybe that's it? He's so worried about Tui Dancer that he's not paying attention to anything else?'

Barbara forced a smile. 'Oh, of course. I'm sure you're right. That damned horse. That's probably what it is. He's certainly been worked up over him. You know, I don't think Hugh's been quite the same since he started looking after him. He's had other big-name horses before but none of them have affected him the way Tui Dancer has.' Barbara looked off into space and continued, 'You know, it was Tui Dancer that got Hugh out of his last bad patch. When he started looking after that horse it was as if he flipped a switch and was suddenly back to his old self. But it didn't last.' She looked back at Bridget. 'This time it wasn't one of his usual mood swings. It wasn't like he was bored. This time he's excited but also sad and, maybe, well, *scared*. Which is impossible because he's never afraid.' Barbara shook her head again, 'I'm sorry, I know this isn't making any sense. I shouldn't have bothered you.'

'Barbara, something's wrong and you're clearly upset. I don't think it's just the horse. What else is bothering you?' *My God*, Bridget thought, *Why did I ask* that? *I don't want to know what's bothering Barbara!*

Barbara took a deep breath and seemed to brace herself. 'I think Hugh's having an affair.' She paused, perhaps startled that she'd managed to say it out loud. Then, as though gaining strength once the barrier was broken, she hurried on. 'We have separate bedrooms,' she said almost aggressively. 'It started because Hugh was working such long hours and kept waking me up when he got home at some godforsaken hour. It got so I wasn't getting any sleep and it was affecting my work. So he started sleeping in the spare room, but we still made time for sex.' She held up a hand and said, 'I know, I know, it's not like we're newlyweds.'

'But ...' Bridget tried to interrupt but Barbara was rolling and couldn't be stopped.

'Once a week, once a fortnight was okay. In fact, it was good. Maybe better than before because it was something we looked forward to.' Bridget groaned inwardly. This was way more information than she needed. 'But recently even that stopped. I didn't think much about it at first. I mean, we were both so busy that it was easy to just slip into the routine – work, eat, sleep. Then one day I thought I'd make a real effort. Get things back on track, if you know what I mean. I got dressed up and put on makeup and made his favourite dinner. And waited. He said he'd be home by six but it was after eight before he showed up. The thing is I wasn't even annoyed. I just wanted to please him. So we had dinner; it was overdone but the wine was nice. After dinner, when I suggested we go to bed he said he was too tired. Too tired! Isn't that what I'm supposed to say?' Barbara took a ragged breath, clearly emotional from what she was saying. 'That night we went to bed as usual but in the morning I started thinking. And wondering. So I began paying more attention to his hours, his moods, his …,' she hesitated, 'smells. I was doing the laundry a couple of months ago and bent over the basket to get a pair of his briefs. And suddenly I realised that they smelled. Like sex.'

Barbara broke off and looked away. Bridget was paralysed, wondering how much Barbara knew, what she was going to say next. Barbara continued softly, 'The funny thing is I wasn't angry. Or surprised. I was just sad. I still love him but obviously that isn't enough anymore. And his actions made sense. Not only did he have Tui Dancer, he had a lover. And he found it both exciting and scary. Scary that he was no longer in control. That there was someone who could expose him.' Barbara paused before continuing, 'At first I wanted to know who it was; who had taken him? Who was better than me? Was she young? Was she attractive? Was she sexy? But then I realised it doesn't really matter. Whoever she is, I'm not going to compete with her.' Barbara looked directly into Bridget's eyes. 'That's when I thought of you.'

Bridget felt a spasm of fear blow through her and thought, *Oh, fuck, here it comes*, but Barbara continued, 'You've been there. Your husband ran off with someone else. You know what it's like to be unwanted. To be rejected. To be not good enough. But you didn't make a fuss. You didn't make a scene. You just carried on as though nothing had happened. You just got on with your own life. I thought about that and looked at you for inspiration. For strength. I mean, if you could do it then so could I.'

Bridget shook her head. She knew she should keep her mouth shut and mumble supportive phrases. This conversation wasn't going anywhere she wanted to go. But before she could stop herself she said, 'You have no idea. When Gordon left I was a mess. Hell, I'm still a mess. I was so dumb I didn't have a clue he was even looking at other women, much less fucking one and deciding to leave me. Believe me, I wanted nothing more than to make a fuss. But I found out he was leaving the day he shot through to Australia and you can't make a scene if there's only one actor. Well, you can but it's not very satisfying.' She shook her head again and said, 'So don't look to me for inspiration. I'm no role model.' Bridget couldn't totally lie to Barbara and she struggled, thinking of what to say to her. 'Look, you're a fabulous woman. You're smart, gorgeous and still young. If there's someone else there's no way she's better than you. And the loss is his.'

Fuck, she thought. *Do I mean that? And if so, then what does it mean for Hugh and me?*

Barbara reached out, took one of Bridget's hands and squeezed it gently. She smiled sadly and said, 'Thanks. See, I knew I could talk to you about this. You can't imagine how much you've helped me.' She gave Bridget's hand a final squeeze before turning back to the hairdressing shop. 'I've got to run. Your mum will be wondering where I've gone.' As she opened the door she looked back over her shoulder and said, 'Thanks again. See you later.'

CHAPTER 8

Dennis swung the ute into the drive and they bounced slowly along it towards the buildings huddled under a group of trees a few hundred metres away.

'Pull around behind that shed on the right,' Fraser gestured. He was sitting next to the door and had reached across Venus when he pointed to the right. 'Let's get this thing out of sight and then I'll go find Barry.'

Venus' head swivelled back and forth as they edged up the drive. A grey weatherboard house with white trim stood off to the left. It had a low-pitched corrugated iron roof, also weathered to a dull grey colour, and a carport on the left end of the house. A few shrubs struggled in the narrow flowerbed that hugged the walls. Four concrete steps led to a front door with three panes of glass. There was no sign of life, though a child's bike and a trampoline were on the front lawn. Unkempt curtains blocked much of the view inside. 'Not exactly Southfork, is it?' Venus asked. Both Fraser and Dennis looked at her blankly and she muttered, 'Forget it.'

A medium-size corrugated steel shed with four bays, the three on the left open and the one on the right with a roller door, stood behind the house. A large John Deere tractor was parked in one of the bays. The others held farming implements, drums of chemicals and a stack of fence posts.

To the right of this shed stood a much larger steel building, the roof of which was two storeys high. Two large roller doors were set in the front wall, one in the middle and one towards the right side. Both were closed. A small, lower-roofed annexe was attached to the left side of the building: a small door and an aluminium window indicated that this was some sort of office.

Dennis followed the drive to the large open space in front of the main building. The area was paved with gravel and a gravel path curved past the right-hand side of the building. Dennis slowly followed the path to another large gravelled area at the rear. A shipping container, a boat and trailer and a rubbish skip were along the outer edge of the parking area. There was a large roller door at the left side of the rear of the building, in line with one of the doors at the front. A small door was set in the wall adjacent to the large one. Dennis stopped the ute in front of the large door and looked across Venus at Fraser for instructions. Fraser said, 'Okay, back the trailer up to the roller door. We're just about done.' He got out of the ute and stood to one side, ready to direct Dennis if he needed help.

Dennis put the ute in gear and shook his head slightly. 'Bloody control freak.'

'Pardon?' Venus asked. 'What was that?'

'Nothing,' said Dennis as he let out the clutch and swung the ute and trailer away from the building. As he straightened up he said, 'Look at that guy, just waiting for me to make a mistake.' He gestured with his head towards Fraser. 'I could back this fucking trailer between his ass cheeks but he'd still be there telling me to lower my right hand a little.'

'Maybe he's just being careful.'

Dennis snorted, 'Fraser thinks everyone else is a fuck-up. That he's the only person he can rely on to do anything right. I mean, I know I really am a fuck-up sometimes but it doesn't mean he has to treat me like one all the time.'

Venus didn't say anything, just watched as Dennis skilfully backed the trailer up to the large roller door. He stopped the ute, set the emergency brake and shut off the engine. In the sudden quiet Venus could hear the wind in the tall poplar trees that lined the edge of the paddock adjacent to the parking area.

'Okay, okay, let's get this door open and show Tui Dancer his new home,' said Fraser.

Dennis and Venus got out of the ute and walked to the back of the trailer. Fraser had already unlatched the rear ramp and together he and Dennis pulled it down until it was fully open. The three of them stood together and looked into the gloom of the trailer. The horse's coat shone even in the dim light and his head pulled sharply against the headcollar. Fraser stepped forward slowly and moved until he could reach the knot fastening the lead rope. He worked the knot loose with his left hand while he smoothed the horse's neck with his right hand.

Dennis said, 'I thought you didn't know anything about horses.'

'I don't,' Fraser replied, 'but I figure if you treat them like women you can't go far wrong.' He glanced at Venus and barked a laugh.

'Uh,' she said, 'I think you may find there's a difference between your average woman and a highly strung five hundred kilogram racehorse with a penis as long as your arm.'

Fraser was now intent on getting the horse out of the trailer and he ignored her. He slowly urged the horse to back up, rubbing his neck and saying, 'It's okay big boy. Easy. Easy now. That's it. Keep going. Almost there,' until the horse was at last standing on the ground near the roller door. Fraser grinned at the others and said, 'See, easy-peasy. Now, one of you grab the rope while I find Barry.'

Fraser and Venus looked at Dennis, who held up his hands and said, 'Hey, don't look at me. I don't even like Western movies.'

Venus sighed and reached for the lead rope. 'Okay. Give it to me,' she said. She stood close to the big horse, stroked his neck and then started walking him slowly around the yard.

Fraser had just stepped towards the small door in the building when they heard the snap of a relay and the big roller door started to rise. It clattered and shook as it rose, revealing first two sets of feet and legs and then the rest of the two men who stood facing them. The sunlight highlighted them, in contrast to the unlit gloom of the large shed behind them. They were obviously Asian, probably Chinese, Fraser thought. The one on the left was older, maybe early forties, but his smooth skin and full head of dark hair made it hard to tell. The one on the right was younger, maybe late twenties or early thirties, he guessed. Both were wearing dark trousers and light-coloured sports shirts. Their arms were bare and Fraser saw that the older one had a faint tattoo on his right forearm. Both wore sturdy black lace-up shoes with thick soles.

No one said a word until Barry appeared from the right side of the door, wiping his hands on a rag. 'Hey,' he said. 'You, uh, got the horse I see.' He paused, facing Fraser, a step in front of the Chinese pair. Fraser could see his eyes were frightened but there was no sign in his voice. 'He's a beauty all right.'

Fraser interrupted him. 'Wait a minute. Who the fuck are these guys? I do not want to see strangers right now. They make me nervous. Very nervous.'

Barry glanced over his shoulder and said, 'Yeah, well, they showed up this morning and said they'd wait for you. I don't know who they are but I figured if they knew you were coming then it had to be okay. No one else knows you're coming here, do they?' he asked anxiously.

'Fuck no,' said Fraser, 'no one knows shit. I've never seen these guys before and I sure as hell haven't told them anything about what we're doing.' He looked at the older man on the left and raised his voice, 'Hey, you, what's your name? What the fuck are you doing here?'

The older man remained placid, no sign of emotion on his face. He stepped forward into the full sunlight and swept his eyes across the group. He wasn't large but his presence exuded a sense of power or menace that made even Fraser pause. Fraser was no stranger to trouble and he usually found he could outthink his opponents or use his own ruthlessness to intimidate them. He suddenly wasn't sure that was going to work with this pair.

The man took another step forward and said, 'You may call me Mr Wang.' He gestured towards his companion: 'This is Mr Luo.' He reached into his pocket and pulled out a cell phone. He pressed a button and held it to his ear. After a moment he held it out to Fraser and said 'For you.'

In spite of his Oriental features the man spoke with an English accent. Fraser took the phone and moved a few steps away before putting it to his ear. He couldn't hear any sound on the phone. No breathing. No background noise. 'Yes?' he asked.

'Mr Lyman,' said a familiar voice, 'how good to speak with you again.' Although he'd been expecting a call, Fraser felt a chill run through him when he heard the voice. The voice continued, 'You've met my associates. I assume you're ready to get the horse?'

'Um,' Fraser said, 'we've already got him.'

There was silence on the line. 'You have the horse? You've retrieved him from Ms Crawford's stables? Without instructions? Didn't I tell you to do as you are told? That additional resources would be available? '

Fraser looked at Venus holding the horse and said, 'Yeah, but there was no way for me to reach you for instructions. We did the recce and saw there was no security so we decided we should just do it in case something changed. And we were right. There were no problems. Tui Dancer's right here. We're about to put him in the shed for safekeeping.'

There was a long silence on the phone. 'Well. I guess success is its own justification. But you are on thin ice, Mr Lyman. Very thin ice. You may have been successful this time but there will be serious consequences if you disobey me again.' The voice paused and then continued, 'The gentlemen you've just met have my complete confidence and are authorised to act on my behalf. Now, one final detail and I think we're done. Please return the phone to Mr Wang. I need a photo to confirm that you have Tui Dancer. There is a great deal of money at stake and there can be no mistakes.'

Fraser handed the phone back to the older Chinese man, who spoke briefly into it before disconnecting the call. He gestured to Venus and said, 'Move the horse, please. More this way. So I can get a picture.' Venus swung the horse around until he was broadside on to the man and held him steady while the photo was taken. The man then pressed buttons on the phone, sending the photo as a text message.

Venus looked at Fraser and asked, 'What's going on? Who was that on the phone?'

Fraser just shook his head and didn't reply. They all stood in the sunshine, waiting for the call confirming they had Tui Dancer. Fraser looked at Wang and asked, 'Where are you from?' When the man shrugged and didn't reply Fraser asked, 'Where'd you get the accent?'

'Imperial College London. I got a first in biomedical science.'

'Uh-huh,' Fraser said, 'you and Venus here will have a lot to talk about. She's doing a Ph.D. in computer science.' *This is getting weirder by the minute*, he thought. *What were these two Chinese guys doing here? What was a Chinese scientist doing here? Give me my money and I'm out of here.*

Finally the phone rang. The older man listened for a few seconds, grunted a reply and held the phone out to Fraser, who took it and held it to his ear.

'Mr Lyman,' the mocking humour of the earlier call was gone and the voice was hard as ice, 'I'm afraid there's a problem. The horse you stole is not Tui Dancer.'

CHAPTER 9

'But that's impossible,' Fraser exclaimed, 'we went to Bridget's farm. The horse was there, just like you said. It matched the description. It's *got* to be the right horse.' Dennis and Venus almost visibly flinched when they heard this, looking first at the horse and then each other, eyebrows raised in surprise.

There was silence on the phone for a few seconds before the voice continued, 'Regardless of what you say, the horse you stole is not Tui Dancer. Tui Dancer is a larger animal and has socks on both his forelegs, not one on his left foreleg and one on his right hind leg. I don't know what horse you have, but there's no doubt he's not Tui Dancer.'

Fraser's thought back frantically, recalling the scene at Bridget's farm. *The bitch!* he thought, *she tricked me. She knew I had the wrong horse. She's probably still laughing at me.* He brought his thoughts back to the call and said, 'Okay, but if we got the wrong horse it's partly your fault. Your description wasn't good enough. Black horse, white face, two white feet. That's what we agreed.' Before the voice could respond he continued, 'But that doesn't matter. I said we'd get the horse and we'll do it. We'll go back to that bitch's farm and get Tui Dancer. There will be no mistake this time.'

There was another pause on the phone before the voice said, 'So very typical of your generation, always blaming someone else.' The voice sighed and continued, 'But, very well. I don't care whose fault it is. I want that horse. You have one more chance. But make very sure you get it right this time.' Fraser didn't think it was possible but the voice got even harder. 'My associates will go with you to see that there are no more mistakes. No more mistakes. I'm counting on you.'

Fraser swallowed, looked at the horse standing by Venus and said grimly, 'Don't worry. We won't be fooled again. What should we do with this one?'

'I don't care. Take him back, turn him loose. That horse isn't important. Let me speak with Mr Wang.'

Fraser passed the phone back to the older Chinese man who spoke briefly and nodded twice before hanging up. He returned the phone to his pocket and gestured towards Venus, 'Bring the horse. Give him to Mr Luo.'

Venus looked anxiously at Fraser and said, 'Okay, this is freaking me out. What's going on? Did you say this isn't Tui Dancer? How's that possible? Is there something we should know?' She looked at Dennis and asked, 'Do you know anything about this?'

Dennis shook his head and said, 'Nope. All I know is I trust Fraser. He's always been right in the past.'

The horse jerked his head and sidestepped, sensing Venus' unease and pulling her slightly away from the others. 'This is bullshit,' she said, 'I don't know who these guys are. I don't know who was on the phone. This is not the plan we had earlier.'

Fraser moved to her side and put an arm around her shoulders. 'Hey, relax. Everything's okay. Well, almost okay. We got the wrong horse but we'll go back and get the right one. Just look at this as a test run.' He squeezed her shoulders and continued, 'Next time will be even easier. I didn't tell you about these guys because you didn't need to know until now.' *And because I didn't know they were part of the plan either*, he thought. 'They'll come with us and give us a hand; make sure we get the right horse this time. Now, give the horse to the Chinese gentleman and we'll be on our way.'

Venus shrugged his arm off her shoulders and said, 'Save your crap for someone who still listens to it. I don't care what you say, I don't like it.' She continued to pat the horse and calmed him down so he stood quietly by her side again. 'You want me to give the horse to these guys? They don't look like horsemen to me.'

'I know,' said Fraser, 'but trust me, you have to do it.'

Venus looked at them all and then slowly walked the horse to the younger Chinese man. 'Here,' she said and handed him the lead rope. It was suddenly very quiet. The silence dragged on until two blackbirds erupted from the hedge by the shed, calling to each other. The younger Chinese man took the rope and looked at the older man for instructions. The older man spoke briefly in Chinese, nodding his head towards the interior of the shed. The younger man nodded once and turned, pulling the horse behind him into the darkness.

'Hey,' said Venus to the older man, 'what's going on? What did you tell him? What are you doing with that horse?'

Wang just looked at her and when she started to follow the younger man and the horse he stepped in her way and grabbed her arm. 'Stay here,' he said firmly. Venus tried to shake free but the man's grip was surprisingly strong and she couldn't escape him. The other three men stood still and watched as Luo disappeared into the shed. No one moved for what seemed an eternity, but was actually no more than a minute. Suddenly there was a loud crack and a flash of light inside the shed that made them all jump. All except Wang.

Venus started shaking her head and looked at him and shouted, 'No! No! You couldn't have! What have you done?' She started crying and pulling against his grip and this time he let her go. She started to rush into the shed but stopped just at the entrance, unable to go inside. Her eyes were wide with horror as Luo appeared beside her in the doorway, a pistol in his right hand. He nodded to Wang and stepped past Venus into the sunlight.

Dennis' eyes were also wide and he muttered 'Jesus!' Fraser seemed impassive and didn't say anything, but even he was shocked by the casual violence. *Fuck*, he thought. *Where did they get guns? No one said anything about guns.* Barry's face had gone white and he was too shaken to speak. He was used to death but for him killing was a job, to provide meat to his customers, not just because it was convenient.

Wang's cell phone rang and he pulled it from his pocket. He didn't speak a greeting but listened for a few seconds, murmuring acknowledgement several times before hanging up. Venus was still sobbing quietly when Wang turned to Fraser and said, 'Okay, we can go now. Let's get the right horse this time.'

———

Fraser was driving the Ford station wagon with Venus in the front seat and Wang in the back. Dennis was driving Bridget's ute with the trailer still on the back, with Luo beside him in the front. There was no sign of the gun. None of them had seen where the younger Chinese man had put it: they were all on edge, just knowing he had it somewhere, and had no compunctions about using it.

Dennis wanted to ask about the horse but was afraid to do so. In a nervous attempt to strike up some kind of conversation, he opted for the time-honoured opening question for all travellers: 'What do you think of New Zealand?'

Luo looked at him for a moment and Dennis was beginning to wonder if he understood English when he said, 'It is very primitive.'

Dennis looked puzzled. 'Primitive? What do you mean?'

'It is full of sheep and cows and grass and trees. It is primitive.'

'Oh, I think you mean rural,' said Dennis. 'Primitive means, uh … forget it.'

Dennis pulled out his pack of cigarettes and offered them to Luo, who took one and then gave one to Dennis. He lit both cigarettes and they smoked in silence for a few minutes. Then Dennis gathered courage and asked, 'Have you shot lots of horses?'

Luo said, 'A few. Not so many.'

'What's it like to shoot a horse?'

'Horse, pig, man – all the same. You pull the trigger and they fall down.'

Dennis was still processing this remark when Luo said, 'I saw an advertisement for steaks in the airline magazine. At least this thick.' He held his hand up with his fingers about four centimetres apart. 'Can you take me to a place where I can have a steak like that?'

Dennis glanced at him and said, 'I don't know. Maybe.' He paused for a moment and then said, 'I bet you like it rare, right?'

Fraser was about to make the turn that would take them back to Bridget's place when Wang grunted, 'No. Go straight.' He had his phone out and was looking at their position on a map app.

Fraser looked at him sharply in the rear-view mirror and asked, 'What? What do you mean, go straight? Aren't we going back to Bridget's place?'

'No. We're going to the veterinarian's farm.'

Venus turned to look at him and said, 'What? Why are we going there? Isn't Tui Dancer at Bridget's farm?'

'Ah,' sighed Wang, 'why must you always ask questions? Always who? What? When? Why? I think you need to just relax and let some adventure into your life.'

Fraser and Venus exchanged a look and then returned their gaze to the road in front of them. 'Adventure? Adventure my ass. This is totally fucked,' said Venus. She realised she didn't understand Wang at all. *Who the hell is this guy? Things are getting out of control. This is way more adventure than I bargained on.*

Venus glanced at Wang who was watching them impassively from the back seat. 'Hey, bio-man,' she said, 'what are you doing here anyway? Why would anyone need a scientist to steal a horse?'

Wang shrugged and Venus thought he was going to ignore her questions, but then he said, 'I am here because it is not just any horse that we are going to steal. It is Tui Dancer.'

'What difference does it make which horse it is? Who are you, anyway?'

Wang shrugged again and said, 'You ask too many questions. You will know what you need to know when the time comes.'

Venus looked forward through the windshield. *I'm so fucked,* she thought. *What am I going to do? I helped steal that horse. I was there when that bastard shot him. It was cool being with Dennis and I thought Fraser was starting to like me. But this is just so fucked. These Chinese guys are from another planet. Fraser says I can walk away but what's the guy with the gun going to say? Do I want to find out?* She had a sudden yearning to be back in the safety and security of the university, even if it meant dealing with her touchy-feely advisor. From where she sat now his libido seemed like a very minor problem. But in reality, sitting in the car on the way to steal another horse, she felt that she had no choice at all.

Fraser glanced at her and lowered his voice, 'Stay cool, Venus.'

Venus looked at him and thought, *Wow, that's probably the closest I'll ever get to an apology from him. Or an explanation.* She didn't respond, just turned her head and looked out her window at the countryside flashing past.

Fraser focused on his driving but part of his mind was replaying the scene in the shed. As much as he tried to forget it, the events kept going through his mind. Hearing the final shot over and over. Shooting the horse had suddenly taken the whole affair off in a new direction, one he hadn't planned and one he wasn't sure he could control. Fraser had shot a few rabbits and possums, but that was just having fun with his mates. It was sport. Shooting that horse, that was something else. He wasn't sure what it was but he was sure it wasn't sport.

As they wound through the countryside, the rolling paddocks impossibly green, broken only by the occasional trimmed windbreak or stream, Fraser's thoughts drifted to Bridget. He thought of her hair in the sunlight as she'd shaded her eyes to see them as they'd arrived at her farm. Of the smooth swivel of her hips in her tight jeans. Of her body when he'd held her before locking her in the stable block. He thought of Bridget in school: how hot he'd thought she was; how he used to try to flirt with her; how she always seemed so cool, never responding but never telling him to stop, either. He wasn't sure why he'd made up the story of them being together. But thinking about it now released a stew of emotions, an equal mix of embarrassment and power and lust. And he remembered that was exactly why he'd made it up. Because that girl Karen Voss was a bitch and being with Bridget was one of his fantasies. He was sorry in a way that things had turned out as they had. He had wanted to help her, not make her leave school. He'd missed her the following term. He'd even found out her address and gone by her house once, but by then she'd moved and he couldn't find out where she'd gone.

When he'd seen her again at the farm he couldn't believe it. She was more beautiful than ever and still had that air of unobtainability about her that he found irresistible. He was surprised to discover that his infatuation had changed, though. He was no longer a schoolboy enamoured with his teacher. Now he needed her to want him.

Part of him knew this was ridiculous. She'd quit teaching because of him for God's sake. She was a mature woman with a farm and a mortgage. But another part of him didn't care. It was that part that drove him to compliment her hair, run his hands over her body, take her sunglasses. He'd flirted with her before and he was flirting with her again. Her reactions so far could hardly be called even ambiguous, but he was patient and willing to see what happened.

He pulled a cigarette from the pack in his shirt pocket and felt for his lighter. *Fuck it,* he thought as he lit the cigarette, *I'm screwed no matter what. If the Chinese dude doesn't shoot me then Bridget probably will.*

————

After settling Tui Dancer in the middle box in Hugh's barn Bridget, Hugh and Elliot walked back out into the hot sunshine. Bridget asked, 'Where are the other horses? You usually have a full house needing attention.'

Hugh sighed and glanced back in the barn. 'I've been so worried about this deal with Tui Dancer that I haven't taken on any other horses. I thought I had everything planned. But it never occurred to me that someone might want to steal Tui Dancer.' He shook his head. 'Damn, that was close. I don't know what I'd have done if they'd taken him.'

Bridget reached out and put her hand on his arm. 'I'm really sorry. I didn't want to let you down.'

Hugh covered her hand with his and patted it softly. 'Don't be silly. You did all you could. Besides, Tui Dancer's here. He's okay. You're the one I'm worried about. They took Blackbird and I know how much he means to you.' Hugh removed his hand and rubbed his palms together. 'Look, you've both gone beyond the call of duty but I wonder if I could impose on you one more time?'

Bridget looked at Elliot, who gave a small shrug and then looked back at Hugh. 'Well, I guess so. What is it?'

'I just remembered that I have to go to town. The insurance people are all over Tui Dancer's visit. They okayed his transfer to your place but I know I'll have to see them in person to explain why he's coming back here. It won't take long but I don't want to leave Tui Dancer alone. While I'm in town I'll organise some extra security, too. And a few days ago I promised Barbara I'd take her out to dinner tonight. After all I've put her through I really don't want to let her down. Could I impose on you to babysit Tui Dancer until we get home? We won't be late.'

'Well, I guess I'm free,' Bridget said, 'what about you, Elliot?'

'Fine with me. I don't have any plans.'

Hugh gave a big grin and said, 'Great. Thanks, guys. I owe you big time for this.' He strode to his Range Rover, started the engine and waved as he drove out of the driveway.

———

It was after five o'clock and Bridget and Elliot were on Hugh's porch having a cup of tea when the small caravan arrived, the Falcon and Bridget's ute towing a trailer.

'Fuck,' said Bridget, 'that's my ute.'

'Uh-huh,' said Elliot, 'looks like trouble. I'll call the cops.'

Elliot stood up from the small table but before he could move Luo got out of the ute, pulled a gun and pointed it at him. Wang had got out of the back seat of the station wagon at the same time and said, 'Don't move, please. I would hate for my associate to have to shoot you. When he gets nervous there's no telling what he'll do.'

Bridget looked at Luo's eyes and steady hand and thought she'd probably never seen anyone less nervous. Fraser, Dennis and Venus got out of the vehicles and stood behind Wang. Fraser looked as cocky as ever but Bridget watched his eyes, saw him glancing at the gun, and suspected he wasn't quite as confident as he seemed. Bridget thought the girl looked uncomfortable but she kept her mouth shut and stood alongside the others.

'Who are you?' asked Bridget. 'What do you want?'

Wang slowly climbed the steps to the veranda and stood facing her. 'Ah, tea,' he said, 'what a splendid idea. As lovely as it would be, we're not here for a social call and really can't stop for a chat.' He held out his hand and said, 'Your cell phones, please.'

Reluctantly Bridget and Elliot reached in their pockets, pulled out their phones and handed them to Wang. He turned and tossed them to Venus who, taken by surprise, managed to catch Elliot's but dropped Bridget's.

'Right,' said Wang, 'now that the formalities are out of the way, shall we press on with the business at hand? Would you be so kind as to take us to Tui Dancer?'

Bridget and Elliot exchanged glances and Elliot asked, 'What do you mean? Who's Tui Dancer? We don't know what you're talking about.'

'Really, sir, I don't think you can pursue that line. We have reliable information that Mr Jacobs is looking after Tui Dancer.' Wang gestured towards Fraser, Dennis and Venus and said, 'My colleagues visited this farm and Ms Crawford's farm yesterday looking for him.'

Bridget took a step forward and said loudly, 'Yeah, and they took my horse. Where is he? What happened to him?' She looked at Fraser and said, 'You can't get away with this, you bastard. I've already been to the cops and they're out looking for you.'

Fraser smiled: 'Yes, but they haven't found me, have they?'

'Answer my question!' Bridget shouted. 'What have you bastards done with my horse?'

Wang replied with no show of emotion, 'I'm sorry, but you can't worry about your horse now. We are here to find Tui Dancer. My colleague has a gun. You can help us get the horse or we can shoot you and find him ourselves. It's entirely up to you.'

Elliot put his hand on Bridget's shoulder and said, 'It's all right Bridget. Listen to what he says. I don't think he's bluffing about shooting us.'

There was silence for a long moment. Bridget looked at the gun in Luo's hand and realised that Blackbird wasn't coming back. Something inside her suddenly snapped. She didn't care about Tui Dancer. She didn't care about the gun. She just wanted to hit the bastards who'd killed her horse. Through his grip on her shoulder Elliot had felt Bridget tense and before her intended leap started he'd wrapped his arms around her from behind, hugging her back to his chest. She struggled briefly but he held her tightly and didn't let her escape.

Finally she relaxed in his arms and he felt her body start to shake with the release of tension. He let go of her slowly and eased her around, back into his embrace. 'It'll be okay,' he said softly. 'You have to be strong now. It's almost over. It'll be okay.'

Finally she regained her composure and slowly pushed back from him. She rubbed the back of her hand across both her eyes, smearing tears across her cheeks. She looked at the two Chinese men and said dully, 'He's dead, isn't he? My horse. He's dead.' She waited, but no one spoke. Finally she forced herself to stand erect and said, 'Okay. Okay, you win. He's in the barn.'

Wang gestured and said, 'Good. Lead the way, please.'

Bridget and Elliot led the group to the barn. The door was open and they entered and walked to Tui Dancer's stable. The upper door was open and the horse's head was out, watching them approach. Wang said, 'I think this time we'll make sure we have the correct horse. Open the door, please, and lead him out.'

As Bridget did this Wang pulled his cell phone from his pocket. Bridget led Tui Dancer out and stood him in the centre of the barn. Wang took a picture and said, 'Excellent. Please put him back.' He fiddled with his phone and said, 'Okay. I've sent the photo to verify the identity of the horse. We will make no mistakes this time so I expect the response will take a while. We'll go to the house to await confirmation of his identity and that they're ready to receive him. You will stay here with the horse.'

The two Chinese men, Fraser, Dennis and Venus filed out as Bridget put Tui Dancer back in his stable. Wang turned from the open door of the barn, looked back at Bridget and Elliot and said, 'Very good. I thank you for your cooperation. Once everything's checked out we'll take the horse and be on our way.'

Elliot said, 'What about us? Are you taking us, too?'

'Goodness no,' replied Wang, 'what would we want with you? Once we have the horse you'll be free to go. We may have to tie you up or something to give us sufficient time to get away but that's all. He stepped back and his accomplices closed the main doors. There was a loud clunk as the board fell into the brackets on the outside of the doors, locking them in. Bridget and Elliot looked at each other. 'Is there another way out?' asked Elliot.

Bridget shook her head. 'I don't think so, not easily.' She gestured towards the two small windows. 'Hugh sometimes has drugs in here so he put bars over the windows to stop burglaries. There's another door on the first floor for loading hay into the loft but it's a long drop and it opens over the front of the building. They'd see us for sure if we tried to use it.'

Elliot walked slowly around the interior, straining to see in the dim light. 'Okay,' he said, 'it looks like we're not going anywhere in a hurry.' He headed right, towards the storage area at the back of the building behind the office and operating rooms.

Bridget trailed behind him, waiting for her friend to speak. The room was clean but still smelled of oil and petrol and steel and wood shavings. The smells reminded Bridget of her father's shed, a space he'd made his own; a space he'd shared with his only daughter. She remembered him cursing as he banged a knuckle changing the oil on his old Massey Ferguson, and the hot snap of the welder as he repaired the tines on the cultivator. She'd loved the time she'd spent in the shed. Perhaps the confidence working with her father had given her, learning how to fix whatever was broken, had helped her decide to take the risk and keep her farm.

Elliot walked to the back of the barn and looked at the accumulation of stuff piled on the floor, on the workbench and on the shelves against the back wall. A hammer, large screwdriver, pliers, crescent wrench and a socket set were on top of the bench and a battered tool box was on the shelf beneath it. A shovel, rake, fork and sledgehammer hung on the wall. To the right of the bench, in the corner of the barn, were a lawnmower, petrol can and a small chainsaw. A large plastic drum at the end of the bench was half full of trash. Adjacent to the mower were partly used bags of compost, bark, fertiliser and cement. Several plastic buckets were upturned beside the bags, and garden implements hung on nails on the back wall. Shelves held painting gear, motor parts, two batteries, spools of wire, and irrigation supplies.

Elliot looked to the left where saddles, headcollars and lead ropes hung on the wall near the horses' boxes. A bench below them held combs, brushes and a hoofpick. Bags of horse feed were stacked beneath the bench.

Watching on, Bridget laughed nervously and said, 'It's a total mess. Hugh says he keeps meaning to clean it up but it never becomes a priority.'

Elliot smiled and observed, 'Sometimes procrastination can be a good thing. You know what they say, one man's junk is another man's treasure.'

'Yeah, well, I think most of this is just junk, not anybody's treasure,' Bridget replied. She ran a hand through her hair and suddenly felt very afraid. 'What's going to happen? We're in big trouble, aren't we?'

Elliot turned and looked straight into Bridget's eyes. She'd never seen him so serious. 'I can't lie to you. These are not good people. But we're not out of options yet.'

He walked to the front of the building and peered through the gap between the doors. Bridget's ute and trailer were just visible, parked to the left of the barn. There was no sign of any activity around the barn or the house. Elliot turned back to Bridget and said, 'That guy in charge is a smooth talker but you saw what happened when they arrived. Do you have any doubt that he wouldn't have told the younger guy to kill us?' Bridget shook her head and he continued, 'I saw men like him when I was in Malaya, not all of them on the other side.' His face turned even more serious. 'From my experience, when you're dealing with people like this, people operating outside the normal bounds of society, there comes a time when you have to decide how far you're willing to go. Whether you can throw away the rules. No thoughts about what's fair or right.' He paused for a moment and moved closer to Bridget. He continued softly, 'You see where this could go, don't you? Once we start, you see where it could go?'

He watched her closely and saw her lips thin slightly as she pressed them together, the only sign of tension on her face. She returned his gaze, weighing her anger against the truth in his eyes. She nodded once and said, 'Yeah, I can see it. Fuck it. Fuck these guys. We're going all the way.'

'You're sure?' Elliot asked. 'You're sure you can do it? Whatever happens it's going to be bad. Worse probably than you can imagine. This is not a reality TV show. I don't care what the Chinese guy said, these guys are used to violence and won't hesitate to harm us. Maybe kill us. Are you sure you're ready for that?' Elliot knew that Bridget really had no clue what was coming. Unless she'd experienced real violence before there was no way she could truly comprehend what they faced. But he also knew that they had no choice and he needed her to agree to help.

Bridget tried not to show her shock at Elliot's mention of killing. She'd known on some level that was what he'd been talking about. But it was one thing to consider killing in the abstract and something else to come out and say it. And mean it. She clasped her hands in front of her to steady them and thought about all that had happened in the last few days. After some time she looked up and asked 'Do we have a chance?'

Elliot didn't answer her immediately. Instead he said, 'There's obviously some history between you and Fraser. Is there something I should know?'

Bridget shifted uncomfortably before replying. 'Well, yeah, I was one of his teachers in secondary school.' She looked away and swallowed. 'Actually he was the reason I left teaching.'

Elliot just raised an eyebrow so she continued. 'Long story short, another student accused me of sexual advances and he gave me an alibi. They were both lying and it became a complete mess.' She shook her head and continued, 'I explained all this and I think the headmaster believed me but it was bad, really bad, and the whole thing got so toxic that I decided I had to leave the school. I was so distraught that I left teaching altogethcr, the thing I loved most.'

'That must have been hard,' said Elliot.

Bridget looked wistful for a moment. 'Yeah, it was hard to leave teaching. It's what I'd trained for and what I'd always wanted to do. And it was hard to be unable to defend myself. Fraser knows the truth but everyone else probably still thinks I was guilty of something, even if they're not sure what it was.'

'Wow. This guy is a real little shit. He screwed with your life once and it looks like he's back to do it again.'

'I don't know what's going on but I have no doubt that I'm part of Fraser's plan. Nothing he ever did was straightforward.'

Picking up on this, Elliot said, 'So let me ask you, do you think they'll kill us? What's your bottom line? What do you think Fraser will do? What do you think the others will do?'

Bridget furrowed her brow and pondered the question. Eventually she responded: 'I don't think Fraser would kill us. He's dangerous but I can't see him going that far. Killing people is a big step.' She took a deep breath and added, 'But I don't know about those Chinese guys. They frighten me. That guy looked pretty comfortable with a gun. I think they're capable of anything.'

Elliot said, 'I think you're right. I think they're the real danger. But I don't think they'll kill us if they don't have to. They want Tui Dancer but I don't think they want a string of bodies across the countryside. I think something's going on that they want kept quiet, and murdering people is not the best way to achieve that. So chances are we'll be okay, but we can't afford to be wrong.'

'I know. But I can't just sit here and let shitheads like this get away with it. I'm scared but we can't give up.' Bridget moved to Elliot and put a hand on his shoulder. 'But this is my fight, not yours. You don't have to do this.'

Elliot smiled, almost peacefully. 'Civilisation is a very thin veneer. A straitjacket that's sometimes a pleasure to shrug off.' He turned and walked to the bench on the back wall of the barn. 'Everyone's heard about the effects of war on soldiers. Shellshock, post-traumatic stress. There are lots of terms for the emotional injuries they suffer from what they've done and seen. But did you know that a large number suffer from withdrawal after the adrenalin rush? Have a secret, shameful longing to live it again?'

Bridget stood beside him, scanning his hard, lined face. 'Is that you? Do you want to go back to battle?'

He smiled again and shook his head. 'No. I don't fall into either of those categories.' He turned his face towards her and smiled grimly. 'No, I want to be involved but my reasons are far simpler. I just don't like shitheads, either.'

———

Elliot rubbed his hands together and said, 'Right. Let's think this through logically. They want to steal a horse that's locked in the barn with us, correct?' Bridget nodded and he continued. 'They said that once they have the horse they'll leave us and disappear. Our first question is, do we believe them?'

Bridget pondered the question. Eventually she responded, 'As I said before, they're bloody dangerous but I don't see why they'd lie about harming us. As they said, once the horse disappears we won't be able to prove anything.'

Elliot smiled grimly. 'I think you're right. So, if we assume that they won't kill us then what's our best course of action? If we want to stop them stealing Tui Dancer then we don't have many options. We can't get out of here. And even if we could disable the ute – let the air out of the tyres, drain the fuel, drain the radiator – that would only delay them.'

He continued, 'So we need to do something in here that not only disables the ute but also makes it impossible for them to continue their plan.' He rubbed his chin thoughtfully and continued, 'And even though we said there were no limits, there are a couple of things that I think we can agree are out of bounds.'

'Such as?' Bridget asked.

'Such as keeping us, Tui Dancer and the shitheads from being collateral damage to whatever action we take,' Elliot replied. 'Suicide missions never appealed to me. And, if it came to them or us I'd choose us.'

'I agree,' Bridget said. 'They're expendable, we're not, but it's better if everybody walks away.'

Elliot's eyes moved around the building. 'Hugh's mess is filled with treasures and we have plenty of things here to make a surprise or two. Unfortunately an AK47 isn't one of them, so getting them to surrender when they come back isn't an option. A hammer or a crowbar isn't going to be very useful against a gun. But we've got everything we need to make some serious noise.' He walked over to Bridget and grasped her arms, 'I've got to ask you again. Are you sure you're up for it? Once we start we're committed. We can try to control the damage but there's always going to be a chance someone will get killed. Including us.'

Bridget swallowed and asked, 'What … what do you have in mind? I don't care about them but what are the chances that we'll get hurt?'

As he'd walked around the barn Elliot had made a mental inventory of its contents and a plan was coming together in his head. He shrugged and said, 'Hurt, killed – there's no way to tell. We're going to make a bomb and that's inherently dangerous. And uncertain. But there's no doubt it's our best option. IEDs have become the trademark of asymmetric warfare.' Elliot looked around the barn, 'And you can't get much more asymmetric than being locked in a barn while our opponents are outside with guns.'

'IEDs?' Bridget looked puzzled. 'I know about IUDs but I don't think I've heard of IEDs.'

'IEDs – improvised explosive devices. I'm sure you've heard them mentioned on TV. The roadside bombs used in Iraq and Afghanistan were IEDs. Bloody effective because they can be made to look like anything. But like I said, they're also very dangerous to make. The successful ones make the news. The ones that blow up the bomb-makers don't.' He moved back to the workbench and continued, 'The way the media goes on you'd think IEDs were invented in Iraq or Afghanistan, but they've actually been around forever. The Romans probably faced IEDs when they invaded Gaul.'

'Actually,' Bridget said, 'I think gunpowder didn't make it to the West until the Middle Ages.'

Elliot just grinned and started clearing a space on the workbench. 'Whatever. Well, we'll be careful but you have to realise the risks we're going to be taking. The bomb we're going to make is a bit like baking a cake. The recipe's simple but if we have an accident then it's *bang!* and it's all over rover. Or it could go off the way we plan but not have the desired effect – which could piss those Chinese guys off enough that they might come back and kill us before we can get away. Or it could fail to go off entirely and then they'll do whatever it is they have planned for Tui Dancer.'

Elliot could see that, despite her determination, Bridget had gone a little pale. He continued quickly and gave a grim smile. 'Or, of course, everything could go the way we plan and the shitheads are defeated and we go back to living our ordinary lives.'

Bridget looked at him wanly. 'Ordinary? Bombs and guns aren't part of ordinary. Do you really think we could go back to living ordinary lives? After this?' She shook her head and held up her hand before he could answer. 'No, forget it. We'll worry about the future when it comes. What's the plan? How are we going to stop these guys taking off with Tui Dancer?'

Elliot stepped back to the workbench. 'Okay. First, the bomb has to be big enough to be sufficiently devastating that it makes it impossible for them to proceed with their plan. That means that if we're not going to kill ourselves or Tui Dancer then we can't explode it here in the barn.'

'You can't make a small bomb?'

'I'll make it as small as I can but you've got to understand that this isn't a munitions factory. I'm going to be guessing at quantities and if I'm out by even a small amount then it could be devastating in an enclosed space like this. Besides, there will probably be lots of sharp things flying around and it would be hard for us to avoid getting hit this close to the explosion.

'So, if we can't explode the bomb inside then we need to explode it somewhere outside. Hopefully somewhere close to Mr Fraser and the Chinese gentlemen. But if we make the bomb in here then how do we get it to explode outside, when and where we want it? And that's really two problems – how do we get the bomb out of here? And then how do we get it to explode when we want it to?' He looked at Bridget and said, 'The only practical option I can see is to somehow attach it to your ute. And use some sort of fuse with a timer.'

'Jesus,' said Bridget, 'you make it sound impossible.'

Elliot responded, 'Difficult, I agree, but I hope not impossible. An IED has five components – a container, a charge, a fuse, a switch and a power source. Anyone who goes to the movies knows motor vehicles are a wonderful source for most of them. The battery's a perfect power source and there are lots of bits and pieces that can be used as a switch. And of course the petrol tank is always there as the charge. But we can't get to the ute so those easy options are out.

'What we need is something we can carry out and put in the ute without them recognising it as a bomb. I've got an idea for that but we also need a fuse. A timer would be great, too.' He looked again around the barn. 'There's no clock here. I could probably use my watch but even if I could, I don't think a clock timer is going to work for us. We can't predict when to start the countdown. They could put Tui Dancer in the trailer at any time and drive away, or just sit in the yard waiting for a phone call.'

Picking up a bucket, Elliot said, 'Let's think about the fuse while we make the explosive. We're going to make a fertiliser bomb. It's low-tech and not particularly high-yield but it's tried and tested by terrorists everywhere.'

'Great,' Bridget muttered, 'it's good to know that I'm following in the footsteps of Che Guevara.'

'Probably more in the footsteps of the IRA and the Red Brigades,' said Elliot, 'but let's not quibble.' He picked up the sack of fertiliser and poured some into a bucket. He eyed the amount critically and poured in a little more.

'You've done this lots of times before, right?' Bridget asked anxiously.

'Well, I've watched a couple of YouTube clips.' Elliot glanced up and saw the shock on Bridget's face and quickly continued with a laugh, 'Heh, that's a joke! The army taught us lots of useful skills. We blew up a few things on the range. Fortunately, I never had to use those skills in Malaya but they did come in handy on the farm here. Blowing stumps in the early days.'

'Blowing up stumps? Wasn't that dangerous?'

Elliot chuckled, 'You'd never get away with it now. Health and safety officials would have a coronary. Beth used to hate it but, like most things, it's really only dangerous if you make a mistake.'

He put down the fertiliser bag and picked up a garden trowel and the can of petrol. 'Now this is the tricky part,' he said, 'it's like the three bears. Too much fuel and the mixture is too runny. Too little and it doesn't readily explode.' He began to pour the petrol into the fertiliser and mix it carefully with the trowel. He stopped pouring, put the can down on the bench and continued to stir the blend slowly. 'And then there's baby bear,' he smiled, and tipped the bucket so Bridget could see the stiff material inside, 'when the mix is just right.'

'Now we need a detonator,' he continued. He looked around the barn again and shook his head. 'If we're going to have remote detonation then the easiest option is an electric detonator. So the first thing we need is a battery.'

Bridget pointed to the shelves along the back wall and said, 'There are a couple of car batteries there. They're old but they're probably not flat yet.'

Elliot shook his head. 'They are too big and heavy for what we need. We'll have to carry our device out to the ute, remember, making it look like something else. I don't think a car battery could be part of that plan.' He swivelled around and kept shaking his head. 'We need a small battery but I just don't see anything …' As he finished the sentence, he looked up over the workbench and spotted a smoke alarm fastened to the ceiling. 'You beauty!' he exclaimed and clambered up onto the bench. He removed the smoke alarm from its mount and said, 'Thank you Hugh, for being safety conscious. Here, take this will you?' He passed the alarm to Bridget and dropped back to the floor.

He put the smoke alarm upside down on the workbench and Bridget saw a small rectangular battery in the back. 'We have to hope that Hugh replaces the battery every year,' Elliot said, 'but it's easy enough to check.' He grabbed a couple of rags, put them over the alarm and pressed the button on the side of the casing. A piercing wail blasted out of the unit, somewhat muted by the rags but still very loud. 'Bugger,' he said, 'we had to do it but I hope no one heard us.'

He removed the battery from the casing and put it on the bench. 'Okay,' he said, 'we have a power source. Now we need something for a spark.' He grabbed the box of car parts and looked inside – it held a greasy carburettor, a distributor, a timing chain and a handful of nuts, bolts and washers. 'Bugger,' he said again, 'we really could have used a coil.'

Bridget looked puzzled. Elliot answered her unspoken question: 'A coil boosts the battery voltage high enough to fire a sparkplug. Without one we can't use the sparkplug from the mower or chainsaw as a detonator.'

Bridget said, 'Okay, I get it. We need something that gets really hot, hot enough to set off the fertiliser, right? I have an idea.' She pointed to the box of paint supplies. 'Hand me that box, would you?' Elliot reached up and brought the box over to the workbench.

Bridget rummaged around inside, pulling out several paintbrushes, a roller and tray, two tins of enamel paint and a couple of paint-spattered rags. At the bottom she found three packages of sandpaper and a box of steel wool. Her eyes lit up and she said, 'Bingo!'

This time it was Elliot who looked puzzled. Bridget explained, 'One of my nephews loved science and used to take great delight in showing me some of the experiments his class did in the lab. His favourites involved lots of smoke and bad smells. I remember this one experiment when he touched a battery to steel wool and it started to burn. I mean, it was crazy and seemed impossible but he explained it all to me. I understood it at the time but I don't have a clue how it works now.'

She pulled a small piece of the steel wool from the box, fluffed it slightly and placed it on the bench. 'But that doesn't matter. Have a look at this.' She picked up the battery from the smoke alarm and touched the terminals to the piece of steel wool. The strands around the terminals immediately began to burn with a small, intense flame, like little glowing fireflies, sending off sparks. The burning continued until the entire piece of steel wool was consumed, leaving behind darkened strands in the same shape.

'Holy shit,' said Elliot, 'that's amazing – and just what we're looking for. Bridget, you and your nephew are brilliant.' He gave Bridget a quick hug and continued, 'Right, we've got our explosive and detonator, now all we need is a fuse.' He walked to the back of the shed once more and picked up one of the car batteries. 'We can use the acid in the battery for part of the fuse, but we need something for it to eat through, something to provide a delay.' He glanced at Bridget and asked, 'I don't suppose you have a condom on you, do you?' Bridget blushed and shook her head. He sighed and said, 'Oh well, they're so useful but no one ever seems to have one when we need it.' Bridget continued to look shocked and Elliot grinned. 'It's okay. I don't care about your sex life. Condoms dissolve in acid and can make a perfect fuse.' He went to the rubbish container and dumped it on the floor.

'What are you doing?' asked Bridget in surprise.

'If we're lucky we'll find what we need for the fuse.' Elliot quickly sorted through the rubbish, tossing most of it back in the container. He set aside a small plastic drink bottle and a crumpled piece of aluminium foil. He then picked up another bucket and put it upside down on the bench. He took a Phillips screwdriver from the tool box and the hammer from the bench top and used them to punch a hole in the bottom of the bucket. He then used a large screwdriver to pry off one of the caps on the top of the battery. As he worked he explained,

'We'll put acid in the bottle and close the top with the foil. The acid will eat through the foil. When it does it will complete the electric circuit and set off your trigger.'

'Seems simple,' said Bridget.

'It is,' agreed Elliot, 'in theory. But believe me, there's a lot that can go wrong.'

After a moment's pause he said, 'Okay. I'm going to need your help now.' He pointed to the bucket and bottle. 'We want to get the battery acid into the bottle. I want you to hold the bucket over the bottle so the hole is lined up over the bottle's mouth. While you do that I'll pour the acid from the battery into the bucket.'

Bridget struggled for a moment, balancing the bucket on the narrow mouth of the bottle, and then said, 'Okay.'

Elliot lifted the battery over the bucket and tipped it on its side. Battery acid poured from the hole in the top of the battery. It didn't take long to slow to a stop. Elliot gave the battery a shake, getting a little more acid into the bucket before setting the battery back onto the bench. 'Right,' he said, 'how much did we get in the bottle?'

Bridget put the bucket on the bench and lifted the bottle for their inspection. It was about half full. She looked doubtful. 'Is that enough?' she asked.

'We only need a little,' Elliot replied, 'as long as the sulfuric acid is still there.'

'How do we know that?' asked Bridget.

Elliot broke off a small piece of aluminium foil and said, 'Let's see.' He dropped it in the bottle of acid and watched. Nothing happened for a few minutes.

'Shit,' said Bridget, 'looks like the battery's a dud.'

'Hang on,' cautioned Elliot, 'give it a little time.' And on cue bubbles began to form around the scrap of aluminium. In a short while the reaction stopped, leaving a lump of black material on the bottom of the bottle. 'Well, I guess we're in business,' he said.

'Okay, but that only took, what, a couple of minutes? We have to have a longer delay than that.'

'You're right. We'll have to use more layers of foil.'

Elliot then used the Phillips screwdriver to make two small holes in the bottle top. He cut three pieces of wire and stripped the insulation from their ends with pliers from the bench. He carefully stuck one end from two of the pieces of wire through the holes in the bottle top, making sure they didn't touch on the inside. With equal care he stacked four pieces of foil together, put them over the top of the bottle and poked them down a centimetre or so into the bottle. He then gently screwed the cap about one turn on the bottle. 'Well,' he said, wiping his forehead, 'that's our fuse. When the acid eats through the aluminium it will complete the circuit with the two wires. Whatever you do, keep the bottle upright. We don't want the acid to touch the aluminium foil until we're ready.'

'Do you think four sheets are enough?' asked Bridget.

'Damned if I know,' Elliot replied. 'We don't want the thing to go off next to us but we don't want it to go off near innocent people, either. I'm hoping four layers will dissolve before the bastards get down the drive, but there's no way to tell.'

Bridget licked her lips: 'I guess that's all we can do.'

Elliot placed his hand on her shoulder and gave a gentle squeeze. 'Don't worry. It will be okay.' He scanned the items laid out on the bench and said, 'All that's left is putting it together into something they won't recognise as a bomb.' He turned and looked across the barn. Tui Dancer had stuck his head out of the stable and was looking at them. 'Tui Dancer's a pretty special horse, right?'

'I guess so. What do you mean?'

'I mean he gets special feed, special exercise, special medical treatment?'

'Well, no different from any other racehorse.'

'But it wouldn't be unusual if you, as the person charged with Tui Dancer's welfare, was concerned about his feed?'

'Noooo,' said Bridget slowly, 'I guess not.'

'Good. Then when the time comes you're going to insist that if Tui Dancer leaves here he has to take his special feed with him.'

Bridget looked puzzled, 'But I don't think he gets special feed. I think Hugh uses normal feed unless the horse has colic or something.'

Elliot grinned and said, 'You're probably right. But do you think these jokers will know that? We need to get the bomb onto the ute. The only thing I can think of that's big enough to hold it is a bag of feed.'

Bridget smiled. 'Ahh. Now I get it.'

'Right. You tell them that Tui Dancer needs his special feed and keep saying it loudly until they agree to let us put it in the back of the ute. We'll take a couple of bags out of the barn, including one with our little package inside. We'll put that bag on its side, starting the reaction between the acid and the aluminium. After that all we can do is watch.'

Elliot walked over and grabbed one of the feed bags and manoeuvred it to the empty stable at the back of the barn. He pushed open the door and dragged the bag inside. He opened it with some difficulty and poured about half the contents behind the door. He walked back into the barn, closing the stable door behind him. He gave the bag to Bridget and said, 'Hold it open while I put our surprise inside.'

He buried the ball of fertiliser mix in the remaining feed and then pushed the bottle in beside it, being careful to keep it upright. He then connected one of the two wires from the bottle to one battery terminal and the third wire to the other. Finally he took the battery and steel wool and pushed them into the fertiliser ball, making sure the loose ends of the wires from the bottle and battery were in contact with the steel wool. He folded the extra wire on itself and pushed the bundle into the feed. Having done so, he stood back and regarded the bag. 'It wouldn't pass close scrutiny but let's hope it doesn't come to that.'

Bridget licked her lips, looking back and forth between Elliot and the bag. 'Fuck, this is the scariest thing I've ever done.'

'Yeah, well, it's right up there with me, too,' admitted Elliot.

'Shit, there are so many things that could go wrong. It could be a complete dud or it could blast the ute and trailer into orbit.' Bridget ran her hand through her short blonde hair.

'Yeah, you're right,' Elliot agreed. 'But I think it's going to work.'

Bridget looked surprised. 'Oh, really?' she asked, 'Why? Why are you so confident?'

'Because it has to,' Elliot replied.

CHAPTER 10

Barbara and Hugh were seated at a small table in the only decent restaurant in town. Barbara touched her napkin to her lips and lifted her wine glass. She tilted it towards Hugh and smiled. 'To us,' she said. Hugh put down his fork, touched her glass with his, and replied in kind.

'That was nice,' Barbara said, 'I enjoyed my meal. How was your steak?'

'Fine,' replied Hugh. He eyed the wine remaining in the bottle, but he was driving so decided he'd give it a miss. He'd arrived a little late and they'd hardly had time to catch up before they'd ordered and their meals had arrived. Now he could feel the pressure of the day start to ease and he smiled at his wife across the table. 'How were things at the office today?'

Barbara smiled back and shrugged. 'Okay. No dramas. I went for a haircut this afternoon and ran into Bridget.'

Uh-oh, thought Hugh. *This isn't going anywhere good. I didn't notice her haircut and she's been talking with my mistress.* His vocal response was more positive: 'Hey, it looks great! I was going to say something earlier but the light's a little dim in here and I wasn't sure ...' His voice trailed off and he looked guardedly at his wife.

She just smiled again and shook her head, making her short grey hair float briefly in waves before settling back in place. 'It's okay. I know you have a lot going on. Hair's the last thing on your mind.' She took another sip of wine and changed the subject. 'How's Tui Dancer? Everything going okay at Bridget's?'

Hugh looked uncomfortable for a moment. 'Um, there was an incident at Bridget's and I decided Tui Dancer would be better off with us.'

'Incident? What sort of incident?'

Hugh hesitated, then said, 'Someone stole one of Bridget's horses.'

'Someone stole one of Bridget's horses! That's ridiculous. How? Why? She didn't say anything to me. What's going on?'

'Well, we're not sure but it's possible they were after Tui Dancer. Bridget's horse looks a little like Tui Dancer but we really don't know why he was stolen. It turns out Bridget knows one of the thieves.'

'What? That's crazy. She knows him? What kind of robber steals from someone he knows?' Barbara looked at Hugh sceptically: 'You're not bullshitting me, are you?'

Hugh shook his head. 'No, I wish I were. It's stupid but true. There's something going on and I decided it would be better to keep Tui Dancer where we could keep an eye on him.'

Barbara lifted her glass and stared into the wine that remained. 'What time did this happen?'

'I'm not sure. Maybe ten? Half past?'

'I wonder why Bridget didn't say anything about this when I saw her this afternoon.' Barbara turned the glass in her fingers. She lifted her eyes to Hugh's and asked, 'You're doing okay, dear? There's nothing you want to tell me?'

Hugh looked at her and thought frantically, trying to come up with an answer. He was used to Barbara's conversational swings but this was leading him into dangerous waters. *What was she really asking? Had Bridget said something to Barbara?* He said, 'No, just the stolen horse. That's it.'

'Okay,' Barbara said thoughtfully. 'I just got the impression from Bridget that you were under a lot of pressure. I'd understand if you needed a release.'

Holy shit, thought Hugh. *What does she know? What did Bridget say?* He said, 'Uh, thanks. That's great. I think everything's under control now but it's good to know you're there for me.' He paused for a moment and continued: 'I know it's been hard. I've been a proper shit recently. But if this thing with Tui Dancer comes off then I'll make it up to you. We'll take some time off and just relax.' Even as he was talking Hugh felt himself break out in a sweat. He thought about this promise to Barbara. He thought about asking Bridget to leave with him. He thought about what he had to do for Tui Dancer. What was he thinking? There was no way all of these things could happen. Suddenly he remembered a quote he'd read in school, something about believing six impossible things before breakfast. He brought his thoughts under control and mentally squared his shoulders. *Fuck it,* he thought, *dealing with the impossible is what I do.*

Unaware of Hugh's inner turmoil Barbara said, 'That sounds great. I think we could both use a break.' She reached across the table and took his hand. 'Don't worry. I understand everything. We'll work something out when this is over.'

———

'Back, back, back a little more.' Fraser was rotating his hand, directing Dennis as he backed the trailer towards the barn door. 'Okay, that's it!' he called out and raised his hand, signalling stop. Dennis stopped the car, turned off the ignition and got out. The sun was just dropping below a layer of low cloud that had formed and the evening light was like a yellow bruise, throwing long, strange shadows across the ground.

Fraser clapped his hands and said briskly, 'Okay, let's go, let's go. Let's get that horse out of the barn and into the trailer. Dennis, you get the horse. You, Wang, keep an eye on Bridget and the old geezer. Luo, you help him. Venus, get that trailer open.' He clapped his hands again and said, 'Come on, come on. We've wasted enough time here.'

It had taken thirty minutes to get confirmation of Tui Dancer's identity and then another twenty minutes to reach Barry and confirm that he'd finished his preparations for Tui Dancer. Fraser grew increasingly frustrated as the delay lengthened. The bloody vet could return at any moment. A client could drop in for advice. Hell, the horse could have a heart attack and die. It was with a great deal of relief that he finally got Barry's call that all was ready.

Dennis was standing next to Venus. He leaned close to her and whispered, 'Yeah, and he's the one that's been holding us up 'til now.' Venus just gave him a quick smile and stepped over to the trailer. Dennis unlocked the barn doors and pushed them open, letting the sun, low on the horizon, pour into the dark interior.

Bridget and Elliot were standing by the workbench. They didn't move when the doors opened. Dennis moved inside and headed for Tui Dancer's stable. As he entered, Wang and Luo walked towards Bridget and Elliot, stopping a few metres away. Their hands were folded in front of them and their eyes were unwavering, their faces blank. Unconsciously, Bridget reached over and took Elliot's hand. Fraser strode into the barn with a big grin on his face. 'Bridget, I'm sorry that our visit will be so brief but we really have to run.'

Dennis unlatched the stable door and opened it. Fraser glanced over and then returned his gaze to Bridget and Elliot. 'As I said earlier, I do apologise for our earlier misunderstanding. Once we have Tui Dancer we'll bid you farewell and we'll never see each other again.' He moved close to Bridget and reached out, running his hand through her short blonde hair. She turned her head slightly, cocking it away from his touch, but otherwise didn't move. 'The new haircut really suits you.'

Bridget looked at him coldly and said, 'You know, I really liked you once. You were smart, interesting and exciting.' She shook her head free of his hand and continued, 'And in spite of what you did to me I felt no animosity for you. Stupid as it was I couldn't hate you. In a twisted way part of me still admired you. But you know what? Now I see you're just a little shit who couldn't make it in the real world. I'll be happy when you're finally where you belong – behind bars.'

Fraser's smile dimmed for a moment but quickly returned, though his eyes showed no mirth. 'Bridget, Bridget, I had no idea that you felt that way about us. If I'd known I might have made other plans. Plans that included you. But, well, I'm sorry I've been such a disappointment.

Life's full of disappointments. The loss of your horse was a disappointment. The loss of Tui Dancer is going to be another.'

'No, the loss of my horse was a crime,' Bridget retorted hotly, 'and you'll never get away with Tui Dancer.' She stepped towards him quickly and tried to hit him in the face, but he turned slightly and took the blow on his shoulder. Luo growled and took a step forward but Fraser held up a hand and stopped him. He reached out to touch Bridget again, but she moved away and avoided his hand. 'Ah well,' he said, 'it will take more than you and an old farmer to stop me.' He dropped his hand, pivoted and the charm disappeared. He growled at Dennis who had stopped with the horse and watched the interchange, 'Dennis! Wake up! Get that horse into the trailer.' He followed Dennis and Tui Dancer out of the barn.

Elliot kicked Bridget softly and whispered, 'Feed.' Bridget brought herself under control and gave him a quick nod. She stepped forward, trying to go around the Chinese pair, but Luo sidestepped to stop her. She raised a hand and called out, 'Hey! Wait a minute.' Fraser turned and looked at her quizzically.

'Look, if you're going to take Tui Dancer then you've got to take some of his feed.' She gestured towards the bags standing against the back wall. Fraser's look turned to scepticism and she hurriedly continued, 'Racehorses are highly tuned animals, sensitive to all aspects of their environment. Giving them the right food is essential for their well-being. At least let us put a couple of bags of his feed in the ute so I'll know he'll be okay.'

Fraser thought for a moment. He wasn't sure the feed thing wasn't bullshit, but if it kept Bridget quiet then he couldn't see the harm. 'Okay. You and the old man can put some horse chow or whatever the fuck is in those bags in the ute. But no funny business. We've got our eyes on you.'

Bridget nodded her thanks and walked to the back of the building. Elliot joined her and together they leaned over the feed bags. Elliot whispered, 'Well done. You take the feed and I'll get our device.' They each picked up a bag and carried it to the back of the ute. Bridget lifted in her bag, placing it towards the front of the vehicle, just behind the cab. She stepped back and watched closely as Elliot lifted his bag and put it carefully on its side next to the first one. He stood up and they exchanged a look before walking back to the barn. They picked up the last two bags of feed and put them in the back of the ute, one on top of each of the first bags.

Bridget felt a drop of sweat form on her forehead and she wiped it away with the back of her hand. *Fuck,* she thought. *This is the dumbest thing I've done in my entire life.*

Dennis and Venus brought Tui Dancer from the barn towards the trailer. The Chinese pair moved into the yard, keeping an eye on Bridget and Elliot and the loading of the horse. Venus led Tui Dancer up the ramp. When he was fully inside she attached the lead rope to a cleat in the front of the trailer. She looked at Tui Dancer and the open space in the trailer. 'Wait a minute!' she called out. 'I want another lead rope. This is a big trailer and I don't want him moving around too much.'

Fraser frowned and said, 'Okay, but hurry up. We've taken too long already.'

Venus dashed out of the trailer and back into the barn. She went to the wall by the loose boxes and took a lead rope from a hook. As she was turning to leave she spotted a lunge line coiled on another hook. She thought quickly – she didn't know where they were going, but chances were they would need to exercise the horse. That would be easier with a lunge line so she grabbed it as well and ran back out of the barn.

Tui Dancer was standing quietly when she re-entered the trailer. She clipped the second lead rope to his headcollar and tied it to another cleat. She cocked her head and decided she was much happier that the ropes held Tui Dancer more safely. She put the lunge line on a hook at the back of the trailer and walked down the ramp. She and Dennis lifted the ramp and secured it in position.

Fraser stepped in front of Bridget and said, 'That's it. If you'll get back in the barn then we'll close the doors and be on our way. You'll find a way out soon enough. Or the veterinarian will return and let you out. We just need a little time to disappear.' He gestured to the Chinese pair, 'You two, see that they're locked in.'

Wang and Luo moved forward and Bridget and Elliot retreated before them. They stood just inside and watched as the doors closed and they heard the board fall into place, locking them in. A moment later they heard the vehicles start and the sound of tyres on gravel as they moved up the drive. Bridget turned to Elliot, put her arms around him, hugged him tightly and said, 'I hope we did the right thing.'

Elliot in turn put his arms around her and tried to comfort her. 'We did the only thing we could.' His words sounded hollow even to him, but he knew all they could do now was wait.

———

Fraser led the way up the drive in the Falcon with Wang in the front passenger seat and Venus in the back, followed by Dennis and Luo in the ute. Sunlight filtered through the trees lining the drive, shadows crawling over the bonnet and windscreen. Venus was staring out the side window, watching the tree trunks flit past her gaze. A hawk drifted above the paddock beyond the trees, its head swivelling as it looked for prey in the grass.

Fraser stopped when he reached the junction with the highway. Paddocks across the road were dotted with sheep and rose to a small ridge a couple of hundred metres away. Fraser looked carefully both ways. It wasn't crucial but he would prefer that they weren't seen leaving Hugh's driveway. There were no other vehicles in sight so he pulled out, turning left onto the paved road. In his rear-view mirror he could see Dennis following about thirty metres behind. He saw Dennis turn and say something to Luo just as a large explosion shot skyward from the back of the ute. He had a momentary glimpse of a red fireball bursting upwards before everything disappeared in a cloud of dirty grey smoke.

Fraser slammed on the brakes and shouted, 'What the fuck?' as he opened the door and jumped out of the car. Wang and Venus didn't see the explosion but, at the sound, both their heads jerked up and twisted backwards to stare at the ute and trailer behind them. It took them several moments to process what had happened and, by the time they'd jumped out of the car, Fraser had run back and was hauling open the driver's door.

Dennis was slumped over the steering wheel, blood oozing from cuts to his neck and the back of his head where the glass from the rear window had been blown forward. Fraser shook him and yelled, 'Dennis! Dennis! Wake up!' Smoke still engulfed the back of the ute and he couldn't see the trailer. His first thought was that the petrol tank was going to explode. 'Dennis,' he yelled again, 'you've got to get out of here. The whole thing may explode.'

Dennis' eyes opened but it was clear that he was still in shock, probably deafened by the blast, and couldn't hear what Fraser was saying. Fraser grabbed his hands and heaved him out of the cab, dragging him towards the Falcon. By that time Wang had opened the passenger door: it was clear that Luo was similarly injured and Wang had to drag him free, too.

Venus ran past them and through the cloud of smoke towards the trailer. Broken glass crunched beneath her shoes as she ran past the ute. The smoke began to disperse and it appeared that there was no fire and little likelihood of another explosion. To her relief the front of the trailer, though discoloured by the blast, was intact. She could hear Tui Dancer moving around violently inside, whinnying nervously and kicking the tailgate.

She paused long enough to turn and yell, 'Fraser! Hey, Fraser! Tui Dancer's okay, but we need to get him out!' She ran to the back of the trailer and struggled with the latches. The breeze blew a cloud of smoke past her and she coughed and closed her eyes. She only paused for a moment and had just freed the tailgate when Fraser appeared at her side and helped to lower it. Inside they could see Tui Dancer pulling on the ropes that tied him to the front of the trailer, moving sharply left and right, clearly agitated. The sight of five hundred kilograms of nervous horseflesh caused them both to pause.

'Fuck,' said Fraser, 'what do we do now?'

Venus said, 'Just stand back and don't get hurt.' She grabbed the

lunge line that she'd hung in the rear of the trailer and moved quickly
to the small access door on the front left-hand side. She opened the
door and studied Tui Dancer. He had stopped whinnying and was
quieter, only occasionally stamping his hooves on the wooden floor,
but his eyes were still wide and she could see him trembling. Venus
stepped into the front of the trailer and stood very still, making
soothing noises to calm the horse. Tui Dancer was still frightened but
began to settle. She slowly reached out and attached the lunge line to
the headcollar. The horse jerked his head away but not as violently as
his earlier movements had been. Venus then reached for the closer lead
rope and slipped the quick-release knot from the cleat on the front wall
of the trailer. She could feel her pulse pounding and her hands were
wet with sweat. She imagined her eyes looked as wild as Tui Dancer's.
She started thinking of all the things that could go wrong but, before
she could dwell on those thoughts, Tui Dancer shuffled sideways
giving her room to grab the other lead rope and release it. The two lead
ropes dangled from the headcollar and she gripped the lunge line
tightly as the big horse backed restlessly away from her. She let the
line slip slowly through her hands as Tui Dancer worked his way
backwards. As he reached the top of the ramp she started walking back
slowly, staying well away from the horse but keeping a firm grip on the
rope. As soon as Tui Dancer sensed the top of the ramp and freedom
from the trailer he picked up speed, scrambling rapidly down the ramp.
Venus moved with him, hoping she could hang onto the line.

Once down the ramp Tui Dancer steadied himself and swung to the
left, away from the trailer. Venus gave the horse the entire ten metre
length of the lunge line and pulled gently on it, pulling his head around
and slowing his movement. She continued to make soothing noises and
moved with the horse, getting him to focus on something other than the
terror in the trailer. She had begun to think that he was about to settle
when Tui Dancer tossed his head, almost tearing the line from her
hands and pulling her off her feet. However, she held on and
maintained her balance and kept moving, kept talking, kept soothing
until the big horse finally came to a stop. His neck was wet with sweat
and his nostrils still flared but his eyes regarded Venus with something

nearer to their normal steady gaze than the terrorised gleam they'd had in the trailer.

Fraser had moved well away when Tui Dancer had left the trailer and now slowly approached Venus, keeping a sharp eye on the horse at the end of the line. 'Fuck me,' he almost whispered 'how did you do that?'

Venus gave him a look and said, 'Shut up and stay where you are. We're not done yet.' She returned her gaze to the horse and went back to talking softly, her voice a monotone, forging a tenuous link between them. She slowly began to approach Tui Dancer, moving her hands up the line as she got closer. She could smell the sharp scent of horse and sweat and fear. Tui Dancer snorted and took a step back and shook his head and Venus paused until he settled again before continuing her approach. Finally she was close enough to reach out and touch him gently on his neck. Tui Dancer rolled one eye towards her but made no effort to escape. She moved even closer, keeping a close eye on his hooves, and continued to stroke his neck and make soothing noises.

Eventually she said, 'He's okay now but it wouldn't take much to spook him again. I want to take him away from here. Where were we going before the bomb went off?'

Fraser looked at her speechlessly for a moment, as though she was speaking a foreign language. 'What are you talking about? The ute and trailer are wrecked. The horse isn't going anywhere.'

'Shut up, you idiot, and listen to me,' she replied viciously. 'We only have one chance to get him out of here. Now are you going to tell me where we were going or not?'

Fraser shook his head in bewilderment. He had no idea what Venus had in mind but he was still in shock, too, and couldn't argue with her. 'The farm. We're going to the farm. Where we took the last horse.'

Venus took the lead ropes that still hung from either side of Tui Dancer's headcollar, knotted them behind his withers and led him a few metres to stand beside the front of the battered ute. She unclipped the lunge line and let it fall to the ground. Shortening her grip on the lead ropes, she stepped up onto the ute's bumper and sprung nimbly onto his back. Tui Dancer fidgeted, sidestepping stiff-legged away from the ute as Venus settled on his back.

'Okay,' she shouted over her shoulder. 'The farm, that's northwest of here, right? Past the agricultural store and the farm with the derelict barn?'

Watching in amazement, Fraser managed to call back, 'Yeah, yeah, that's right. The letterbox says Miller.' It was suddenly clear to him that what Dennis had said about Venus' experience with horses was no exaggeration.

Venus turned Tui Dancer's head to the left and got him pointed towards a gate on the far side of the road. 'Gate!' she yelled at Fraser. 'Open the gate!'

Fraser ran to the gate and swung it open towards the road.

'See you there,' she called out and kicked the horse into motion.

Fraser stood in awe, mouth open, as Tui Dancer went from stock-still to a full gallop in three strides. Venus was leaning forward, keeping a firm hold of the lead ropes, using them as substitute reins. Fortunately for her, although Tui Dancer moved on strongly, he was no longer in panic mode and responded to her directions after a fashion. Even so, with no bit in his mouth, and without the aid of saddle and stirrups, it needed all her skill and strength to retain even a semblance of control and avoid being pulled over his head.

He didn't slow as he galloped across the paddock, his hooves throwing clods of the soft earth high into the air. 'Fuck me,' said Fraser as he watched them disappear over the rise.

At that moment Wang came around the trailer and called out, 'Where's the horse? Where's the goddamned horse?'

Fraser pointed across the road and said, 'He's gone. Venus is riding him. She'll take him to Barry's.' *I hope,* he added silently.

Wang paused and composed himself. He said, 'Someone is sure to have heard the explosion. The police will be here soon. What do we do now?'

Fraser dragged his gaze back to Wang. He saw Wang's composure and in a flash he was entirely focused on what needed to be done. He moved quickly towards the wrecked ute and said, 'It's a total fuck-up. Let's get out of here.'

———

Hugh's Range Rover slammed to a stop next to the wrecked ute. He stared hard at the scene before him – the ute just about blown in half and the front of the trailer dented and scorched. The smell of burnt … something … was heavy in the air and a few wisps of smoke still rose from the twisted metal at the back of the ute.

He got out of his vehicle and walked slowly around the wreck. There was no sign of anyone, either in the ute or on the ground. He moved to the back of the trailer and saw that the tailgate was down and that there was no horse inside. Finishing his investigation of the scene he jogged back to the Range Rover and got inside. He eased past the wreck and sped down the drive. He skidded to a stop by his house and leapt from the car. He looked around at the buildings and yards but saw no sign of life.

'Bridget! Elliot!' he called out. 'Are you here? Are you okay?' He stood still and listened and then heard faint voices calling back. He ran to the barn, fumbled with the latch and finally pulled the doors open.

'Bridget! Bridget, my God! What happened?' he said as the door opened against its stop. The last of the sunlight flooded the interior of the barn as Bridget ran out and threw her arms around him and hugged him fiercely. She felt his solid strength and couldn't hold back the tears. Hugh held her and ran his hand through her short hair saying, 'It's okay now. It's okay.' He looked over her shoulder at Elliot and raised his eyebrows enquiringly.

Elliot explained, 'The guys that took Bridget's horse came here and took Tui Dancer. There were five of them. Four guys, two looked Chinese, and a girl. We rigged a bomb in the back of the ute to try to stop them getting away with Tui Dancer. We heard it go off but don't know what happened.'

Bridget stopped crying and loosened her grip on Hugh, pulling back just far enough to look up into his face. 'I'm so sorry. They got Tui Dancer. We did our best but they took him away.'

Hugh held her close again and said, 'It's okay. We'll get him back.' He looked at Elliot and said, 'Your bomb went off, all right. I drove past Bridget's ute and trailer at the top of my drive. They're a write-off.'

'What about Tui Dancer?' Bridget asked anxiously. 'Is he okay? Is he hurt?'

Hugh shook his head, 'I don't know. There was no sign of him. Or of any of them. The trailer wasn't badly damaged and the tailgate was down, but that's all I know. I didn't take time for a good look. The police can do that. I didn't see any bodies or pools of blood, so I guess they all escaped somehow.'

Elliot raised his eyebrows. 'Hmmm, that's interesting,' he said. 'The horse is gone. Everyone's gone. But it's only been a few minutes since the explosion. They couldn't have found another trailer in that time. How the hell did they do it?'

Hugh said grimly, 'We'll worry about that in a minute. First of all, you're sure you're both okay?'

Both Bridget and Elliot nodded. Bridget said, 'We're fine, we're fine. They locked us up but didn't harm us.'

'If you're okay then I need to call the cops. It's only been a few minutes, you say?' asked Hugh. Elliot nodded and Hugh continued, 'Then if we hurry the cops may have a chance. They'll need to talk to you to get details of the thieves and their car but that won't take long.' He turned away, pulled out his cell phone and dialled 111.

As he dialled Barbara drove up in her car. She jumped out and ran to Hugh. 'Hugh! What's going on? Is Tui Dancer okay?'

Hugh pulled his phone from his ear and called to her, 'Somebody tried to take Tui Dancer but we don't know yet what's happened. Bridget and Elliot were locked in the barn when I arrived.' Barbara ran to him and was hugging him as he got through to the emergency number.

Bridget reached for Elliot's hand and, when he took it, she started pulling him up the drive. 'Come on,' she urged, 'I have to see what happened.'

'Sure,' he replied, 'I want to see this as well. I can't believe that the bomb went off and Tui Dancer's gone.'

Together they hurried up the drive, only slowing when the wrecked ute and trailer came into view. Bridget walked up to the trailer and looked inside. As Hugh had said, there was no sign of blood or violence. She joined Elliot where he was looking at the shattered rear end of the ute.

'Well I'll be damned,' he said, 'it actually worked.' He shook his head in amazement. 'We stopped the vehicle and didn't blow everyone to kingdom come.'

'It's incredible,' said Bridget. She raised her hand, palm out, and they exchanged an awkward high five. 'If we just had the horse you'd be a hero.'

Elliot shook his head again. 'I don't get it. I really don't get it. How could they take Tui Dancer without transport? It's not as if horses can fly.'

Bridget looked carefully at the scene, seeing the wrecked ute and trailer, the road disappearing to the left and right, the open gate and paddock across the road. She slowly turned to face Elliot. 'No, but they can run.' She turned back to look carefully at the pasture on the other side of the road. 'As Sherlock Holmes says, once you eliminate the impossible, whatever remains must be the truth. If they didn't drive away and he didn't fly away then those bastards must have ridden him away.'

Elliot looked at her, revelation flooding his eyes as well. 'You're right,' he said, 'it's crazy but you must be right.' He looked more closely at the area around the rear of the trailer. 'Hey,' he called out, pointing to the ground. 'Here, look at this. What do you think?'

Bridget knelt and looked at where the dirt had been churned up. 'I don't know. It could have been done by a horse. Or it could have been something else entirely.'

They both looked around again. 'Whoever took him must be a hell of a rider,' said Elliot.

They were standing by the front of the ute when Hugh drove back up the drive and stopped behind the trailer. He got out and walked up to join them, looking at the wrecked vehicles as he walked past. Bridget took his arm when he reached them and said, 'They must have ridden Tui Dancer away. It's the only explanation that fits.'

'What?' said Hugh, 'That's impossible.'

'I know it's hard to believe, but it's the only thing that fits. It's the only way they could have moved Tui Dancer away from here.'

Hugh shook his head and looked at the surrounding countryside. 'Damn. I guess you're right. Shit. How do we know which way they went?' He scuffed his boot in the dirt by the front of the ute and wiped his hand back through his hair. 'Damn. It's a hell of a thing but you did the best you could. The cops will be here soon. It's up to them now.'

———

It was fully dark and Fraser and Dennis were almost back at Barry's farm. They'd been driving around the roads in the district, trying to spot Venus and Tui Dancer. They knew the cops would be looking for them and they didn't really want to be out, but they needed to get Tui Dancer back.

Shortly after they'd arrived at Barry's farm, before Fraser could plan what to do, he'd received another phone call from the voice. 'Mr Lyman,' the voice began. As always there was little intonation but even so it managed to convey disappointment. And irritation. Or maybe that was just Fraser's nerves. 'What am I going to do with you?' Before Fraser could respond the voice continued, 'I understand that your latest attempt to secure Tui Dancer was also unsuccessful. Is that correct?'

'Um, no,' replied Fraser, thinking rapidly. How could the voice already know what had happened? 'That's not quite right. We got the horse from the vet's place all right.'

'So I'm mistaken? The horse is in your possession now?'

'Well, not exactly. He's still, um, in transit.'

———

Venus shifted on Tui Dancer's broad back, trying to relieve the ache
that ran from her own back to the soles of her feet. She'd pushed the
horse hard for the first few kilometres, when she had to, until she
thought she was far enough from the wreck to avoid immediate
detection. At that point she slowed Tui Dancer to a walk but only let
him stop twice to drink from streams that cut across the rolling
landscape. The paddocks were large and although she often saw flocks
of sheep they were not heavily grazed. She only saw one homestead
and gave it a wide berth.

She'd used the sun as a guide, keeping it on her left flank as it
neared the horizon. She crossed a small road, seeing no traffic, but she
knew it wasn't the one they'd been on when they drove to Barry's. The
sun had set a while ago and she relied on her namesake, Venus, low in
the west, for guidance. The stars were scattered across a clear sky
when she paused on the top of a low ridge and looked ahead of her. A
road was visible as a grey line along the centre of the broad valley
before her. It was hard to be sure in the darkness but she was pretty
certain it was the road to Barry's farm. She didn't know if the farm lay
to the left or right but decided she'd worry about that when she reached
the road. She urged the horse forward and felt his fatigue as he began
the walk down the slope.

In spite of the strangeness of her situation and the terrible events
she'd escaped she couldn't help marvelling at the peace of the world
around her. She could hear frogs and crickets starting their evening
chorus and smelled a pungent mix of sweat, dust and dew. A bitter
tinge of smoke still clung to her clothes and reminded her of the awful
sight of the wrecked ute. A cold pang of panic lanced through her as
she thought of the dead horse and the injured men. She wondered why
she was riding Tui Dancer back towards them. She thought briefly of
turning around and looking for a town or a house or anyone who could
help her get out of this mess. But she knew that wasn't a real option; it
could only lead to questions she couldn't answer. And she was too tired
to face another long ride, especially in the dark. She thought of just
turning the horse free and fleeing back to her university life. But as
much as she feared what was to come she couldn't just leave Dennis to

deal with the situation on his own. It's not that she loved him or anything, but regardless of the consequences, she couldn't let a mate down like that. She wasn't sure what she thought about Fraser but, even if he was a shit, she wasn't happy leaving him to the mercy of the Chinese. So it was with mixed feelings that she slipped off the horse, opened the gate and stepped with him onto the road. A smell like fireworks or gunpowder suddenly filled her nostrils and a halo of bright light glowed at the periphery of her vision. She slumped forward against Tui Dancer's withers, too tired to decide which direction to go next. She heard a vehicle approaching from the left. Her first inclination was to hide but her fatigue and her ambivalence about what she should do rooted her to the spot. She turned Tui Dancer to face the vehicle and waited.

———

Fraser drove up the long grade, the headlights illuminating the road, fences and verges in the dark. Hitched to the rear of their vehicle was the trailer Barry kept for his daughter's pony, which Fraser had 'persuaded' him to lend them. They set off shortly before dark in the hope of, first, finding Venus and Tui Dancer, and second, finding them in one piece. Dennis was the first to spot them. 'Hey! There's something up ahead. It looks like a person and a horse.'

Fraser eased off the accelerator and in a moment also spotted them. 'Well fuck me running,' he muttered. 'She pulled it off.'

He stopped a few metres short of Venus and Tui Dancer, the pair illuminated like actors in hot spotlights. The harsh headlight beams highlighted Tui Dancer's sweat streaks and drooping neck and Venus' wild hair and tense posture. Dennis lunged out of the car and said, 'You beauty! You bloody beauty!' He ran to her side and reached to put an arm around her waist. 'Come on, come on now. I can't believe it. You made it.'

Venus began trembling and brought her arms up to hold Dennis close. Suddenly she went limp, overwhelmed by the ride, the pain, the fear of what might come next. Dennis held her and did his best to comfort her. 'It's okay, it's okay,' he kept murmuring, running his hands across her back while he supported her.

Fraser grabbed the lead ropes Venus had knotted for reins, unclipped one, and held Tui Dancer while he watched Venus and Dennis embrace. He began to walk Tui Dancer slowly towards the trailer. He called to Dennis, 'Let's get moving. Open the trailer.'

Dennis reluctantly let go of Venus and lowered the trailer ramp. Fraser led Tui Dancer cautiously into the trailer. He secured the long doubled lead rope rather untidily to a ring at the front of the trailer then exited, raising and locking the rear ramp. Venus stood shakily, holding herself with her arms across her chest, looking around her as though wondering where she was. Dennis was grinning like an idiot, but Fraser sensed some of the turmoil she faced.

'Venus,' Fraser said softly, 'hey, Venus.' He took a step towards her and reached out a hand to touch her shoulder. 'You made it. You and this beautiful horse made it.' He squeezed her shoulder gently and sidled a half step closer. 'You're amazing, girl. I don't think anyone else could have done it. When you took off across that paddock and disappeared over the hill I thought we'd never see you again. You and that horse,' Fraser paused for a second, 'you've both got heart.'

Venus had been looking down but, at that, she looked Fraser in the eye and said, 'You have no idea. You have no fucking idea how special that horse is.' She glanced at Dennis and then back to Fraser. 'I don't know what's going on, but get this straight. I don't like those other fuckers. I don't like what they did to that horse. And I won't let them do it to Tui Dancer.' She looked back and forth at the two men again and raised her voice, 'I almost didn't come here. I almost went to the cops. I almost said fuck it and just left you with them.' She glared at the two men and went on more quietly. 'But I didn't. I don't know what's going on but I know that someone has to look after this horse. You two are totally useless so that leaves me. From now on I'm Tui Dancer's shadow. He doesn't go anywhere without me. Nothing happens to him without my say-so.' She looked again at Fraser and Dennis and nodded once. 'Let's get out of here.'

She took a step towards the car and the pain in her thighs was so great she faltered and almost fell. She felt as though she'd been split in two. She'd had pain from riding before but nothing like this. Then again, she'd never ridden any real distance across country bareback, either, let alone as far as this. Dennis reached out to help her but her look froze him and he just watched as she hobbled to the car and eased herself into the back seat. She was so stiff and sore that she had to use her arms to lift her legs into the car.

Fraser and Dennis exchanged a glance and Fraser shrugged, walked over and got behind the wheel. Dennis went to the back of the trailer and made sure the door was secure before getting into the front passenger seat. He turned and looked at Venus and said, 'For the record, we're not totally useless. We found you didn't we?'

Venus just stared at him until he turned back toward the front of the car.

———

It was fully dark by the time Fraser pulled the car and trailer to a stop behind Barry's shed. The big roller door was open and light spilled into the parking area from the fluorescent fittings high in the ceiling. Barry was standing in the centre of the opening with his arms folded on his chest. Fraser stopped the car and let Dennis and Venus out. He then drove to the rear of the parking area before reversing the trailer back to the roller door.

'That's it!' shouted Dennis, holding up his hand when Fraser was close enough. Dennis moved to the back of the trailer as Fraser shut off the engine and got out of the ute. Venus limped slowly into the light coming from the barn.

'Where'd you find them?' Barry asked.

'Not far,' said Fraser, 'Venus did an awesome job of getting here.' Barry looked appraisingly at Venus as she turned to watch Dennis open the rear door of the trailer.

Dennis let the door swing to the ground. Tui Dancer stood quietly inside, too tired to fidget. Dennis started to enter the trailer but Venus stepped forward and pushed him aside. 'No, I'll do it,' she said, 'I want to do it.'

She moved up beside the big horse and patted him gently on his neck as she went to the front of the trailer. 'Easy boy, easy there boy. It's okay now,' she said softly as she released the still-knotted ropes from the cleat at the front of the trailer. She gently and slowly guided Tui Dancer back out of the trailer. In no time he was standing calmly on the ground. The lights from the shed highlighted the sharp definition of his muscles and the sweat streaks on his coat. Holding the knotted lead rope, Venus looked at Fraser and asked, 'Where do you want him?'

Barry stepped forward and said, 'In here. I've set up one of the pens for him.' Venus followed Barry inside, moving gingerly, and turned right along an open area between large pens spaced along the rear of the shed and smaller ones in the centre of the open area. Barry stopped at the first pen along the back wall and pointed, 'In here. He'll be okay here.'

Venus led Tui Dancer into the pen and looked around. It was made of heavy steel bars, strictly utilitarian but clean. She nodded to Barry and said, 'It'll do. For now.'

CHAPTER 11

Bridget was seated across the desk from Dani. She'd just finished giving a summary of the events to the constable and Dani was flipping back through her notes. A small tape recorder lay on the desk between them, a blinking red light showing that it was recording.

Without looking up from her notebook Dani said, 'Okay, let me get this straight. You were looking after this million dollar racehorse for Mr Jacobs. A gang of four men and a woman showed up and tried to take the horse. Three of them, including a man known to you, had stolen your own horse the previous day. They were accompanied by two gentlemen probably of Chinese origin. These people locked you in the barn while they awaited instructions. And while you were locked in you and Mr Hayes made a bomb and set it to go off in the back of the ute. The bomb *did* go off when the thieves got to the end of the drive. Mr Jacobs released you from the barn and called for help. When you got to the road the ute and trailer were there but the horse and the gang were gone. Is that a fair summary?'

Bridget shifted in her seat and said, 'Uh, yeah, but it wasn't really like that.' She looked flustered for a moment and continued, 'It wasn't as simple as you describe. I mean, these guys were scary. Elliot and I thought they might kill us and take the horse. The guy I know, Fraser, is bad enough, but the Chinese pair he had with him were a whole other story. Those guys were hard. We were sure they'd shoot us if we didn't do exactly what they said.'

'Let me get this straight,' Dani asked, 'they had guns? Did you see guns?'

Bridget nodded: 'Oh yes, there were definitely guns. At least one gun.'

'Okay,' said Dani, 'I'll put a warning in the APB that they are probably armed. We have to assume the worst here.' She flipped forward in her notebook, frowned slightly and continued: 'Now I need to ask a few more questions about the bomb.' She looked up and stared at Bridget. 'You probably broke a dozen laws doing what you did. You know you could have killed five people and a valuable racehorse. You can't resort to violence without thinking about the consequences.'

Bridget felt her face start to go hot. She forced herself to take a deep breath before replying but even so her voice was tight and more forceful than usual. 'Hang on just a minute. Who's the victim here? Are you saying I don't have the right to protect myself and my property? These criminals invaded Hugh's farm, threatened me and Elliot and then stole a horse that had been put in my care. If we did nothing then they would have got away with it. Hell, it looks like they got away with it anyway.'

'But you can't just take the law into your own hands,' Dani replied. 'That's what the police are for. And regardless of how bad they are, you don't have the right to kill anyone.'

Bridget was unimpressed: 'It's not like they gave us one phone call. And we didn't have time to get a fucking permit, okay? I mean, these guys stole my horse and I'm sure they killed him. They were about to steal another one. I couldn't just sit there and let them get away with it. And besides, Elliot's very experienced with explosives. He knew he could make a bomb that would stop their getaway without hurting anyone.' She reflected briefly that this wasn't quite what Elliot had said but this wasn't the time to worry about details. 'And he was right. We stopped the bastards and it looks as if no one was hurt. But we didn't stop them stealing the horse.'

Dani replied wryly, 'Yes, I've had a preliminary interview with Mr

Hayes. I'm seeing him again immediately after we've finished. I expect we'll have an interesting discussion about his explosive qualifications.'

Bridget wanted a cigarette but knew she couldn't smoke in the police station. She sat back in her seat and asked, 'So are we through here?'

Dani closed her notebook and folded her hands on top of it. 'Just one more question. You say you think someone rode Tui Dancer away from the explosion site. Do you have any idea which of them could have done that? And where they might have gone?'

Bridget thought for a moment and suggested, 'I think it must have been the girl. I don't think Fraser has had any experience with horses. And the Chinese guys looked like city types. The other guy is a possibility but I'd go for the girl. There was something about her. She was quiet and stayed in the background but seemed to know what she was doing when they loaded the horse into the trailer. As to where they may have gone, I don't have a clue. It couldn't be too far. Tui Dancer's a racehorse, not a cross-country horse.'

Dani stood and moved towards the door. 'Okay, that's it then. If we need any more information we'll give you a call.' She held out her hand and smiled as Bridget stood and joined her. As Bridget opened the door Dani said, 'And, please, you've had two run-ins with these guys. Leave it to us now, okay?'

———

Bridget felt safe for the first time in days. She lay in bed with Hugh's strong arms around her, felt the warmth of his body pressing against her from behind. She pressed back softly with her bottom and felt his hardness.

The day had seemed an endless round of interviews and conversations she neither wanted nor needed. Dani had dropped her off at home after dark, too tired and distraught to eat. She'd poured a glass of wine and was standing in the dark kitchen when car beams had swept across the windows, throwing the room into harsh relief before they were extinguished as the car stopped outside her house. Seconds later there was a knock on her door and she heard Hugh call out, 'Bridget? Bridget, are you home? Why are the lights off?'

Bridget put her glass on the counter, but didn't move. She heard Hugh knock again and then try the knob. She heard the latch click and sensed the door swing open. Hugh called out again, 'Is anyone here?'

This time she moved to the light switch and turned it on as she called out, 'In here. In the kitchen.'

Hugh stepped from the dark of the lounge into the now illuminated kitchen. He stood just inside the door and looked at her for a long moment. Her eyes were red and her whole body drooped. He raised his arms to her and said softly, 'Oh my darling. What's happened to you?'

She ran across the kitchen and threw her arms around him. She felt his own burly arms enclose her and draw her into his body. Once again she was transported to a safer place by his words, his smell, his strength. She heard him mumbling soothingly into her hair and felt his hands holding her to him, but was barely conscious of either.

Suddenly she took half a step back, placed her hands on either side of his face and kissed him. Softly at first and then with a powerful need. He responded by picking her up and carrying her to the bedroom. They fell into bed with their clothes half undone. They were caressing and kissing and then it was all right.

Afterwards they'd lain together and had drifted into a light sleep. It lasted less than half an hour before Bridget woke shaking, the memories of the day once again fresh and sharp in her mind. It had taken some time to regain control, remember where she was, who she was with, and slowly the trembling had stopped.

She felt Hugh shift behind her and felt his hand cup her breast. For a moment she was tempted but she knew this wasn't the time. She gently disengaged from Hugh's touch and rolled to face him. His eyes were open and stared into hers. She ran her fingers lightly along his cheek, feeling the bristle of his beard. 'Thanks,' she said softly.

'Any time,' he responded, 'like now?'

Bridget tousled his hair and swung towards the edge of the bed. 'No, not now. You have to get home to Barbara and I have to get some sleep. I have to go back to the police station early to see if I can identify any of the others in the gang.'

On the porch Bridget hugged Hugh and said, 'Thanks for coming. I mean it. I really needed you tonight.'

He brushed her hair and replied, 'No worries. There's nothing I want but to keep you safe.'

Bridget watched his taillights disappear down her drive and felt her spirits ebb. *Safe*, she thought. W*ill I ever be safe again?*

———

Bridget walked through the door of Streaks Ahead. The day before she'd been angry and had hardly noticed anything around her. Today she didn't notice anything, either, but it was because of an immense lethargy. She knew this was the natural consequence of the adrenalin rush of the previous day, but that didn't make it easier to manage. Every scene was etched in her memory and the knowledge that Tui Dancer was gone was almost more than she could bear. She wanted to be home, resting, but she knew she had to be here.

Her mother looked up when the door chimed and exclaimed, 'Darling, I didn't expect to see you again so soon. You look awful. What's happened? Is there anything I can do?' She rushed to her daughter and hugged her tightly.

Bridget just stood for a moment, feeling her mother's arms around her and felt herself relax. She slowly reached up and pulled free from her mother's arms and turned to look at her. 'I'm okay, mum. Really. It's been a tough day though.' She gave her a wan smile and said, 'You're not going to believe it but I need another haircut.'

Caroline looked at her daughter for a long time before urging her towards one of the hairdressing chairs. 'Before I do anything you're going to tell me what's going on,' she said. She moved until she stood in front of Bridget and then leaned back against the counter. 'I'm your mother and I have a right to know.'

Bridget shook her head slowly and said, 'Okay, mum.' She paused and looked up at the ceiling while she composed her thoughts. She brought her eyes back to her mother's face and continued, 'You remember that guy I told you about, Fraser? Well, he and some of his buddies came to Hugh's farm yesterday and stole Tui Dancer.'

'He stole Tui Dancer?' said Caroline. 'First he stole your horse and then he stole that famous horse that Hugh's looking after? That's terrible. But I don't get it. What's going on, dear?'

Bridget shook her head again and replied, 'I don't know either. I think he stole my horse by mistake. But it's even more complicated than that. Elliot and I were at Hugh's farm when they came for Tui Dancer. We made a bomb and put it in the ute they used to take him. The bomb exploded at the end of Hugh's drive but by the time we got there the horse and everyone had disappeared. Tui Dancer hasn't been seen since.'

Caroline sensed that there was much more to the story. She picked up an apron and draped it over her daughter, fastening it at the neck while she thought about what she'd heard. 'Okay, sweetheart, you were involved with bad people and the horse is gone and I can see why you're upset. But why are you *here*? You've had two haircuts in two days. Why do you need another one?'

Bridget looked down in her lap. The one thing she didn't want to talk about was why she was there. She wasn't sure *she* knew exactly why she was there, so how could she tell her mother?

Finally she said, 'Mum, I don't know why I need a haircut. But every time I see that guy he comments on my hair; how great it makes me look.' She looked up at her mother and admitted, 'As hard as I fight it, as much as I know he's a total wanker, that he fucked up my life once and is doing it again, he gets inside my head and I don't know … I don't know …'

When she saw Bridget close her eyes Caroline wrapped her arms around her and said, 'It's okay, sweetie, it's okay.' She stepped back and continued, 'Don't forget that you're the one with a farm and a life and he's the one with nothing, trying to steal what you've got. It doesn't matter what he does or says, you're a good person.'

'Thanks,' said Bridget, 'I hope you're right. But I still want a haircut.'

Caroline sighed: 'Okay, dear. What do you have in mind?'

'I want it dyed. I want it platinum. Maybe a fringe? What do you think?'

Caroline regarded her daughter in the mirror and ran her hands through her hair. The previous cut had turned out spectacularly well, she thought. The shorter hair and bit of curl brought out Bridget's best features. *Platinum?* she thought, *It could look pretty hot.* 'Okay, honey. We'll go platinum. But I don't think we need a fringe.'

———

Bridget was early for her follow-up appointment with Dani so she went to the café for a coffee. She'd no sooner found a table than Gordon slid into the chair across from her. 'Mind if I join you?' he asked.

'No. Yes.' Bridget was still flustered from the day and night before. Her head was filled with the terror of the theft of Tui Dancer, the relief of spending the evening with Hugh and the knowledge of what Barbara had said to her. 'Just go away,' she finally managed to say.

Gordon held up a hand with two fingers extended. 'Two minutes. I swear. That's all I need. Just give me two minutes and I'll be gone.'

Bridget didn't have the energy to fight him so sighed and agreed, 'Okay. Two minutes. I have to leave in a minute to go to the police station anyway.'

Gordon pulled out his notebook and pen and began, 'First, wow! What's with the hair? It looks … great. But very different.'

Bridget held up her hand to stop him. 'We're not talking about my hair. What else is so important?'

Gordon tore his gaze away from her hair and looked into her eyes. 'The police. The crimes. That's what I want to talk to you about. I hear that two horses have been stolen, one from your place and one from Hugh's. And that you know one of the guys who did it.'

Bridget's mind was whirling. How had word of the thefts spread so quickly? She didn't think Dani would have gossiped, but once the APB had gone out there was probably no way the events would have been kept secret. Gordon could have heard about it from any number of people. The waitress brought her coffee and Bridget fiddled with the cup while she decided what to say. Gordon wasn't just a reporter, he was her ex-husband and she didn't want to say anything that would make her look weak or needy. She took a sip of coffee and said, 'Yeah, people came and stole some horses. Unfortunately I happened to be there both times.'

Gordon waited for her to continue and when it was clear she wasn't going to say anything else he prompted her: 'Yes? And? Who were they? What did they do? Why did they take *your* horse? Come on, you can't clam up and tell me nothing. This is a small town. It will all be on the street by tomorrow. Give me a break for the paper.'

Bridget took another sip of coffee, put her cup down and looked Gordon in the eyes. 'Okay, here it is. You remember that little shit who caused me such grief at the school? The one who said he was having an affair with me?'

'Yeah, sure. How could I forget that?'

'Well, he and some of his mates showed up at my farm two days ago and stole Blackbird.' Bridget felt her voice rise uncontrollably as she continued, 'They stole him and then they killed him.'

Gordon looked shocked and puzzled. 'What? That's crazy. Why would they steal Blackbird? And why would they kill him? That makes no sense. And the guy, the one you know, what was his name ...?'

'Fraser,' Bridget said, forcing herself back to some measure of calmness. 'Fraser Lyman.'

'Yeah, Fraser. He made no effort to disguise himself?' Bridget shook her head. 'That's really weird. Why would he take a horse that, no offence, isn't that valuable? And let you know who did it?' Gordon drummed his fingers on the table for a moment before continuing. 'And you say he came to Hugh's the next day? And stole another horse? That's just off the charts bizarre. Or stupid.'

'Well, what can I say?' Bridget shrugged. 'The guy's arrogant and cocky as hell but he isn't stupid.' She took a sip of coffee then added, 'And he still thinks there's something between him and me.'

'And is there?'

Bridget prefaced her answer with a rude sound and continued,

'What do you think? There *never was* anything between us! I don't know why he said those things back then and I don't know why he's still living in his fantasy world.'

Gordon nodded understandingly and said, 'Yeah, I get that. But you've got to admit you've acted a little strangely recently.' He gestured at her hair and said, 'I don't think you've ever changed your haircut before. And now it's, what, three changes in three days?'

Bridget felt herself start to blush and unconsciously touched her platinum hair. 'That's bullshit. I've been thinking of a change for a while. The stress of the last few days made up my mind, that's all.'

Gordon looked sceptical but decided to ignore it. 'Okay, so what else can you tell me about what happened?'

Bridget asked, 'What do you want to know?'.

'Everything,' Gordon replied. 'Who else was involved besides this Fraser guy? What other horse did they steal? When did they steal the horses? Why did they target you? That'll do for a start.'

Bridget looked away to compose her thoughts. After a few moments she looked back at Gordon and said, 'Fraser was there both times. The first time it was him with another guy and a girl. All about the same age. The three of them took my ute and trailer and Blackbird. They acted like complete idiots but I couldn't stop them.' She toyed with her coffee cup and continued, 'The next day they came to Hugh's. The same three, Fraser and the guy and the girl, but this time they had two other guys with them, looked like they were Chinese.' She looked at Gordon and said, 'Those two, man, they were the real deal. They weren't amateurs like the others. I'm sure they're the ones who killed Blackbird. They were at Hugh's to make sure they got the right horse.' Bridget stopped and bit her tongue. *Stupid, stupid, stupid*, she thought.

Gordon's eyes lit up and he wasted no time following up on her slip. 'Right horse? What do you mean they made sure they got the right horse?'

Bridget licked her lips and thought frantically about what she could say. 'Look,' she started but had to stop and compose herself before going on, 'I really can't talk about this. All I can say is I was helping

Hugh look after a horse. Somehow these people found out the horse was there and they came and stole him.'

'Come on, you have to tell me more than that!' Gordon exclaimed. Several of the other people in the café turned and looked at him and he lowered his voice. 'This could be important. You said they came back to get "the right horse". What's so special about him?'

Bridget shook her head and looked down again. 'I can't. I promised not to tell.'

Gordon looked out the café window but he didn't see the pedestrians on the footpath, or the cars passing on the street. His mind was racing, looking for hints and connections. He slowly started nodding and looked back at Bridget. 'It was Tui Dancer, wasn't it?' Bridget shook her head but Gordon carried on before she could voice her denial, 'It's gotta be Tui Dancer. We reported that he was taking a break from racing to have some tests. Hugh's the horse's vet. You and Hugh are pretty close …' a sudden thought passed through his head and he wondered *exactly how close*? He made a mental note to come back to that thought later but he didn't pause, '… and if he needed to move Tui Dancer for some reason then you're the one he'd turn to. No question.' He was becoming animated again, 'Fuck! They thought Tui Dancer was at your place but stole the wrong horse. When they realised their mistake they came back to Hugh's and stole Tui Dancer. Shit! He's gotta be, what, if not the top horse in New Zealand then at least in the top three.' He reached out and took Bridget's hands in his. 'Look, you've got to tell me what's going on. What are you and Hugh doing about it now?'

Bridget was angry with herself for not keeping her mouth shut, and angrier that Gordon had figured out so quickly what had happened. 'I can't,' she kept repeating, 'I just can't.'

Gordon and Bridget looked at each other without speaking. Then Gordon got up and looked down at Bridget and said, 'Okay. Okay. I'll find out another way.'

The bell on the door clanged as it closed behind him.

CHAPTER 12

Fraser and Wang had started talking quietly as soon as Tui Dancer arrived at Barry's shed. Dennis tried to help Venus put Tui Dancer into the pen but he was more of a hindrance than a help. Venus insisted on lining the pen with hay bales for the horse's safety and Fraser smilingly agreed, over the objections of the Chinese pair. Dennis helped her move and stack the bales until they stood shoulder-high. When she was satisfied with the bales, Venus undid the headcollar, intending to give Tui Dancer the freedom of the pen.

However, no sooner had she done so than Wang stepped into the pen with a hypodermic syringe in his hand and told Venus to hold the horse steady while he took a blood sample. She refitted the headcollar and gripped the knotted lead ropes tightly while Wang moved up along the horse's right flank. He ran his hand along the horse's back as he slowly stepped towards Tui Dancer's head. Venus made soothing noises to the nervous horse. She could feel his hot breath on her left hand, sensed the increased breathing rate and saw the occasional nervous twitches of the big stallion's skin. She gently rubbed behind the horse's ears as she watched Wang rub the side of his neck, looking for a vein. He applied pressure to the neck and gave a small grunt of satisfaction when a vein swelled into view. He brought the syringe up and deftly inserted its long needle through the skin and into the vein.

Tui Dancer jerked his head slightly but immediately relaxed. With the needle in place Wang slowly withdrew the plunger. Venus watched as dark red blood filled the syringe.

In a few seconds the syringe was full and Wang withdrew the needle. As he examined the syringe he handed a handkerchief to Venus and said, 'Apply pressure to the vein for at least one minute.' Venus pushed the cloth firmly against the site. She felt the deep pulse of the horse's heart and started counting.

After Wang moved away with the syringe Dennis came up behind her and stood looking at Venus and the horse. 'I was surprised to see you earlier,' he said softly. He reached up and ran his fingers gently through the hair at the back of her neck. 'I thought you'd either fall off and lose the horse or you'd ride him away like you said. To the cops or somebody. Maybe back to the vet.' Venus moved her head beneath his fingers but didn't say anything. 'I'm glad you came back, though,' he said, 'I'm really glad you came back.'

Venus turned and looked up into his eyes. Dennis looked so, so innocent. She didn't love him but she liked him. She liked him a lot and she couldn't leave him with Fraser and the Chinese pair. He wasn't really bad but these guys could make him do things that he wouldn't dream of doing on his own.

'You're very sweet,' she said, touching the side of his face, 'I can't let anything bad happen to Tui Dancer. And I can't let anything bad happen to you.'

Dennis laughed nervously and said, 'You're worried about something bad happening to me? No way. You've seen Fraser. You *know* him. Fraser's smart and he's very careful. He's my mate and we look after each other.'

Venus continued to look into Dennis' eyes and shook her head slowly. 'You have no idea. Fraser is definitely smart but the only thing he looks out for is himself. Believe me, you may think he's got your back but when the shit hits the fan he's going to put a knife in it. And if you don't believe that, then think about those Chinese guys. They're going to make sure Fraser does exactly what they tell him to do. And you mean less than nothing to them.'

Dennis looked across to where Fraser was still talking with Wang. Luo stood in the background, eyes focused on Tui Dancer but watching everyone's movements. 'Those guys? You think Fraser's going to do what they say?' He shook his head and said, 'No way. No way. Fraser's in charge. If those guys cause trouble he'll tell them to fuck off.'

'What planet are you on?' Venus asked. 'Have you forgotten that they have a gun? Probably one each? That they shot that horse?' She gripped his arm and said, 'Fraser's able to look after himself, that's true. But those guys do violence for a living. They aren't here to listen to some Kiwi wannabe. They're here to do a job and go home. Anyway they have to. I don't know exactly what they're here for but I do know that if anyone gets in their way they're ready to shoot them, too. Like they did that poor horse. No questions. No hesitation. Just pull the trigger and sleep well at night.' She continued, 'So don't tell me that Fraser's in charge. That things are under control. They're not. They're out of control. I like you and I love that horse but if you're not careful, if *we're* not careful, then we're not going to walk away from this. We're going to be dead.'

———

Wang handed the syringe to Luo, who put it in a padded envelope and sealed it.

Fraser asked, 'You're mailing the blood sample to a lab?'

Wang replied, 'No. Mr Luo will take it back to Hong Kong for testing.'

Fraser cocked an eyebrow in query: 'Really? He's going all the way to Hong Kong? Personally? What are you testing it for? You know we're not a third-world country. We have labs that can test blood here.'

Wang looked at him coolly: 'Our lab is the only one we trust. He will take the sample back and let us know the results as soon as they are ready.'

Fraser noticed that Wang hadn't answered his question about what they were testing the blood for, but it was obvious he wasn't going to get any more information. 'Okay,' he said, 'it must be an important test to go to all that effort.'

Wang ignored him and turned to Luo. They had a brief exchange in Chinese before Luo turned and headed for the back of the shed.

Dennis called out, 'Hey, Luo! Are you flying first class? Maybe you'll get a steak on your flight.'

Luo stopped when he heard Dennis call to him but he didn't respond. He just grinned and gave him a thumbs up and walked out the roller door. Dennis returned the thumbs up and muttered underneath his breath, 'Thank God. One of the crazy motherfuckers gone.'

Venus looked at him and started to say something, but just shook her head and turned back to Tui Dancer.

Fraser watched the interplay between Luo and Dennis without comment. He heard the car start and saw the sudden glow of reflected light as the headlights came on. He saw the car drive past the open shed door and heard the sound of its tyres on the gravel drive fade as it went away.

———

Gordon turned off his lights and eased to a stop on the shoulder of the road. He'd waited until dark to drive to the address Phoebe had given him, hoping that a car parked by the side of the road would be less conspicuous at night than during the day. He was about a hundred metres south of the drive. He could see a mailbox on a post and a glow of lights from a house about fifty metres up the drive. The curtains weren't drawn and the light spilled across the porch in front of the house. Further back he could just make out a large shed or barn, the corrugated iron roof silver in the moonlight. He thought he could see a faint light coming from the back of the building, but he wasn't sure.

When he was younger he'd been used to long stakeouts, waiting for a story to develop. But reporting on bingo games and school sports didn't require those skills and now he found it hard to just sit and wait. He wished he had Phoebe's computer skills and wondered if this could really be the place he was looking for. He had a sudden dismaying thought: he realised he had no idea what kind of cattle Bridget had lost and would probably not recognise stolen cows even if they were here.

He'd kept the windows rolled up to maintain heat in the car but now he felt the night chill start to invade him. Even if he knew what her cows looked like and this was the place to which they'd been taken, he knew it was unlikely they were still in the shed. They were probably hamburgers by now. He began to feel foolish. Journalism might not need the same level of evidence that the law did, but just thinking he was right wasn't enough. He had to have proof of some sort that Bridget's cows had been here. As he waited his mind wandered and he wondered if perhaps there had been too many things in his life that he hadn't thought through. He wondered if he'd have left Bridget if he'd thought it through.

He'd been waiting about an hour when he heard an engine start and saw headlights come on behind the shed. The vehicle came down the drive towards the road, not slowing as it passed the house. Gordon prepared to duck if it turned his way, but when it reached the road the vehicle turned north, away from him. He had only a brief look at it but he could see that it was a sedan, possibly dark blue or grey. The taillights dwindled and disappeared when the car went around a bend.

He waited another thirty minutes and there was no sign of life on the farm. The house lights continued to shine across the porch and, though he was now convinced there was light coming from the back of the shed, he hadn't seen any change in its intensity. There were no more cars, no movement of any kind.

Fuck it, he thought, and got out of his car. Not only had his stakeout skills waned, he had become more impatient. He was no longer content to watch. He was going to have a look at the house and shed. He wouldn't know if there was anything there if he didn't go to have a look.

He buttoned his coat as he moved slowly and quietly along the road and up the drive. He walked on the grass verge to reduce the sound of his steps. There were scattered clouds in the sky, dimming the light of the moon as they passed in front of it. The stars pulsed with light in the gaps between the clouds.

Halfway to the house he moved away from the drive, heading towards the darkness adjacent to the house. The lawn was unmown and neglected and he glided across it. He put his palm on the weatherboards and felt their cool hardness in the darkness. He eased towards the front of the house and dropped to his hands and knees as he reached the front porch. He peered around the corner and saw nothing on the porch. The nearest lighted window was a metre away. He slowly lifted his head and took a quick look into the room.

To the right he saw a weary sofa and armchair facing a dark TV. Two prints in simple frames hung on the far wall. Doors led to the right, towards the front door, and to the back of the house. There was no one in the room. He listened carefully for a minute but there was no sound from inside. He pushed himself back and stood at the corner of the house. He thought about the lack of activity and then decided it didn't matter. The shed was his priority, not the house. He retreated across the lawn the way he'd come and headed up the drive.

Between the moonlight and the faint houselights he felt quite exposed. But there was no sign of anyone watching and he wanted to minimise the time spent out in the open, so he decided to stick to the side of the drive.

There were no lights or other signs of life along the front of the shed. As Gordon continued slowly towards the back the light grew brighter and he was forced to move away from the drive to stay in darkness. A few poplar trees grew along the drive and he worked his way along them towards the rear of the building.

When he was level with the rear wall he paused again. The cool blue light of overhead fluorescent bulbs spilled out through an open roller door. Behind the shed was a large gravelled area. A blue six-metre long container with Mitsui OSK Lines painted on the side was just to his right. On the far side of the gravelled area was a rubbish container with its top closed, and a boat trailer with a small aluminium runabout on it. In the back of the area was a Ford Falcon with a white trailer.

Gordon listened and at first heard nothing but the recurring night sounds that had accompanied him up the drive. Then, after a few seconds, he was sure he heard something else, the low hum of conversation. He couldn't make out what was being said but at least he knew there was someone in the shed. He had to see more. He had to see what was going on in the shed.

Without taking his eyes off the open door he backed cautiously away until he was sufficiently hidden from the light, and then sidestepped towards the container. When it was between him and the door he changed direction and moved forward in its shadow. He moved to the corner of the container and dropped to his stomach then inched his way forward until his eyes cleared the base of the container and he could see through the shed's doorway. He ignored the sharp stones digging into his hands and body and concentrated on what he was seeing.

He was closer now, so the voices were louder, but he still couldn't make out what was being said. At first all he saw was the inside of the shed, a large open area with what looked like animal pens disappearing out of sight to the right, and the dull metal of the front wall rising in the background. There was no movement, no sign of life other than the low sound of voices.

He looked around the rear of the shed for another sheltered spot that might offer a better view of the interior, but before he could do more than start his examination a man stepped into the middle of the doorway. Gordon froze and pressed himself even harder to the ground. He slowly turned his head so that only one eye looked directly at the illuminated figure.

It was a young man, early- to mid-twenties Gordon estimated, with medium length dirty, curly blond hair. He was wearing blue jeans, a white T-shirt with something on the front that Gordon couldn't read, and a dark nylon jacket. His features were angular and looked menacing in the deep shadows cast by the lights above and behind him. He stepped further out into the gravelled area and pulled a pack of cigarettes from the pocket of his jacket. He took one from the pack and pulled out a lighter. He lit the cigarette and took a drag, holding the smoke and letting out a long jet before returning the lighter to his pocket. He stood there for several minutes, smoking silently and looking into the darkness.

At first Gordon was afraid that the man would see him, but it became obvious that he was lost in thought and wasn't looking for threats. Nevertheless Gordon knew how much a face stands out, even in poor light, so he kept his head still and firmly on the ground and only exposed as much as was necessary to keep an eye on the man.

Half the cigarette was gone when Gordon was surprised to see another man step into the doorway. This man was Asian, medium height and weight, wearing dark-framed glasses He stepped up beside the first man and said something that Gordon couldn't hear. In a second it was obvious that he had asked for a cigarette, as the first man retrieved his pack, gave one to the second man and lit it for him. They stood together, looking into the darkness and smoking without speaking.

Gordon was becoming increasingly puzzled. Was the first guy B. Miller? If not, then who was he? And who was the Asian guy and what was he doing at a farm in the middle of the night? It was obvious from his dress and his relationship with the first man that he didn't work on the farm. Was he involved with the rustling? Or was he someone totally innocent? A friend of the family perhaps?

Whatever was going on, Gordon didn't have enough information to decide whether this was where Bridget's cows had gone or not. He had to look into the shed. He risked a look around for another spot that would give him a better view, but there was nothing. If anything the other options were worse, giving less of the view he'd hoped for. He was resigned to failure when a young woman appeared in the doorway and called out, 'Fraser! Hey Fraser, you'd better come and look at this.'

The first man spun around and looked at the young woman. Gordon heard him say, 'What is it?' and the woman respond with, 'I don't know but you'd better come look.' She turned and disappeared into the shed. The first man dropped his cigarette and ground it into the earth with his shoe before following her inside. The Asian man continued to smoke for a few seconds before he, too, ground out his cigarette and went inside.

Fuck, thought Gordon. *There are at least three of them and one of them's a woman. Didn't Bridget say one of the gang that had stolen her horse was a woman?* He had to know more. Taking no time for conscious thought, he jumped to his feet and ran to the left side of the doorway. With his heart pounding he inched forward and looked inside.

The pens he'd seen extended the length of the building. As he'd suspected, fluorescent lights hung from the exposed steel rafters beneath the roof. Their overlapping illumination cast strange, diffuse shadows across the floor. He saw all this in a glance but his gaze was immediately drawn to the group of people clustered at the back wall of the shed. They were looking at a large horse in a pen that was lined with hay bales. The animal was distressed, tossing his head and moving jerkily. Gordon could see it was a black horse, with a blaze on its forehead. He felt his palms go sweaty and his pulse start to race as adrenalin hit his bloodstream.

I don't see any cattle but that sure as hell looks like Tui Dancer. Gordon didn't know what was going on, but his first instinct was to get some proof of what he saw. He backed away a short distance from the roller door and reached carefully into his pocket for his cell phone. He'd photograph the people and the horse and take the images to the police. Whatever was happening here was likely to be a big story for the paper, and if it was big enough then it might save his career from skidding even further off the rails.

He drew his phone from his pocket, turned it on and started the phone app, shielding the lighted screen from anyone in the shed. He crept back towards the roller door and brought the phone up for a photo. Just as he pressed the button to take the picture his sweaty hands slipped on the case, the phone fell from his grip and hit the gravel with a sharp crack. Gordon's eyes were on the people in the shed and he saw the woman lift her head sharply and look towards the doorway. Without another thought he grabbed the phone and stood, tensed, ready to move away as quickly and as quietly as he could into the darkness.

Dennis looked at Venus and said, 'What? What is it?'

Venus listened for another few seconds and shook her head.

'Nothing, I guess. I thought I heard something outside but I guess not.' She looked into the night for a moment longer before returning to the discussion with the others about what to do while they waited for news from Hong Kong.

———

Bridget looked up when she heard the sound of tyres on her driveway. She'd stopped for a cup of tea and was feeling sorry for herself. *How could I be such an idiot? Dani's right. How could I have thought making a bomb was a good idea? Why did I agree to get involved with Tui Dancer anyway?* She had no sooner thought of this question than she knew the answer. *Because Hugh asked me.* This led to more introspection. *What does Hugh mean to me? What do I mean to him? Is he serious about leaving Barbara? Does that matter? Does Barbara know about us? Would Hugh say anything?* She was in this downward spiral of self-criticism and uncertainty when she heard the car arrive.

She got up from the kitchen table and went to the door, arriving there in time to see Hugh's Range Rover pull to a stop. He got out and grinned when he saw her and walked rapidly up the porch steps. He took her in his arms, held her close and said, 'I missed you. Are you okay?'

Bridget burrowed closely into his shoulder and didn't say anything. How could she tell him that there was nothing wrong exactly, but neither was anything right. Everything was a muddle and what she wanted more than anything was for the last few days to disappear and for a return to her normal life. But she knew this wasn't going to happen. She was pretty sure she loved Hugh and was pretty sure he loved her, but life had already taught her the unhappy consequences of 'pretty sure'.

It seemed to her like forever but in reality it was a very short time before she stepped back and gave him a wan smile. 'Not a good day?' Hugh asked.

Bridget shook her head and almost laughed. 'No, not a good day,' she replied.

'Well,' said Hugh, 'maybe I can make it better.' He paused for a second and then said, 'I've heard from them. The guys who took Tui Dancer. They called me a little while ago.'

Bridget's face mirrored her shock. 'What?' she exclaimed. 'They called you? What did they say? Did you tell the cops? What are we going to do?'

Hugh held up his hands and said, 'Hang on, one thing at a time. They told me they have Tui Dancer. That he's okay. That they'll return him if we pay what they demand. And no, I haven't been to the cops. They said that if the cops get involved then they'll kill Tui Dancer and disappear.'

Bridget brought her hand to her mouth and gasped. 'Oh my God. What are we going to do? Tui Dancer's okay, but what are we going to do? How much is the ransom?'

Hugh stepped close and held her. 'It'll be okay. They've given me twenty-four hours to raise the cash. They'll know there's a limit to how much I can get in that short time. We'll take this a step at a time. We'll get the money. We'll arrange to meet with them. Then we'll see what happens next. Remember that they don't want a dead horse any more than we do. They want the cash and a safe exit – we want Tui Dancer safe and sound. I'm sure we'll work something out.'

Bridget sighed: 'I hope so. I really hope so. I don't want anything to happen to him. One dead horse is enough.'

Hugh said, 'Right. I'm counting on you. They said they'd call back tomorrow afternoon. I know it's asking a lot but I'd really appreciate it if you'd come with me when we make the payment. It will be dangerous but you know one of them and at this point any edge we can get might be crucial.'

Bridget was surprised, but strangely pleased as well. Other than looking after Tui Dancer Hugh had never asked her for help before. Their lovemaking was full of desire and respect, but if Bridget was honest there was never an indication that Hugh *needed* her. Was this a sign of his commitment to her? The thought that she might be able to help was thrilling, but the realisation that this was a situation that Hugh thought he might not to be able to handle on his own was frightening.

In spite of these feelings going through her mind Bridget didn't hesitate before saying, 'Of course. I'll do whatever I can.'

Hugh gave her a relieved grin and said, 'Thanks. I knew I could count on you.'

Bridget put a hand on his shoulder and said, 'I'll help, but I want Elliot there, too.'

'But ...' Hugh started to object but Bridget cut him off.

'He got me – he got *us* – out of a real jam. It wasn't his fault that Tui Dancer got away. I'd feel better if he comes with us.'

Hugh thought for a moment and said, 'Okay. If you're sure that's what you want. And if he agrees to come.'

'Thanks, Hugh. I'll give him a call and see what he says. But I'm sure if he can help then he'll say yes.'

———

Gordon had waited at the shed doorway long enough to see the horse settle and the group of people start to disperse. He felt terribly exposed and was relieved when he felt he could turn from the doorway and move back along the side of the shed towards the house and the road. He was just as careful about not making noise or being seen as he'd been when he arrived, but he was now familiar with the area and made better time back to his car.

He got into his car as quietly as he could, started it and reversed slowly away from the drive with his lights off. The moon was still up and the road was a pale ribbon behind him. He was halfway back to town before his pulse returned to normal and he was no longer sweating.

His first instinct was to drive straight to the police station and report what he'd seen. But the drive back to town gave him time to reflect and, after some consideration, he decided he'd be better off waiting until morning. There was no one on duty at this time of night and an attempt to talk to the cops now might immediately escalate the matter to an emergency.

And what did he really know? What could he say? How could he explain why he was interested in B. Miller? How could he explain how he had got B. Miller's address? The unwritten rule of Phoebe's assistance was that it would never come back to bite her, so he could never tell the truth about why he was at the farm. And what had he seen that was a cause for alarm? He'd seen some people who might or might not look like the gang that stole cattle and horses from Bridget. He'd seen a horse in a shed that might or might not be Tui Dancer. He couldn't imagine what a group of people would be doing with a horse in the middle of the night that was legitimate, but that didn't mean he should report it to the police. No, if he went to the cops now they'd listen to him and thank him for his efforts and go back to sleep. Or worse, they might get excited, go to the farm and scare whoever was there into flight, breaking Gordon's one thin thread towards solving the crime and getting a story.

He eventually decided that his only chance was to wait and bypass the proper channels and have a quiet, off the record, chat with Dani Painter. They'd helped each other out a few times in the past and he knew she had a pragmatic view towards criminal justice and due process. So, as soon as he'd got home he'd texted her and suggested a meeting the next morning. She'd texted back that she could have a coffee at 7.30.

Gordon was early and was sitting at a table in the window of the café across from the police station by 7.15. He was scrolling through the messages on his phone when he saw Dani pull her police car up in front of the station, get out and walk across the street towards him. He stood as she entered the café and signalled to the waitress, who nodded and began working the espresso machine. Both Dani and Gordon were regulars and she knew they wanted a long black and a flat white.

'I'm sorry, there's a lot on and I can only spare a few minutes,' said Dani as she reached the table.

Gordon looked at Dani as she sat down across from him. 'Thanks for meeting me,' he said, 'I know you're busy and I won't keep you long. Something's come up and I could use your advice.'

He could see the sudden interest in Dani's eyes, but they were both silent for a moment while the waitress put their cups on the table. Both were aware of the potential value of their relationship and Gordon knew he'd have Dani's full attention while he told her what he'd seen. He knew Dani was ambitious and he'd previously managed to give her a couple of tip-offs about things he'd heard that had helped her arrest record. She'd also helped him a few times get a scoop on a story and in terms of favours he figured they were about even.

Once the waitress had left and they had taken a sip of their coffees, Gordon looked at Dani and said, 'This has got to be off the record for now. I think there are things that you'll find useful, but some of it has to stay between us. Is that okay?'

'Sure,' Dani said, 'same rules as always. Nothing we say goes beyond this table unless it's evidence of an imminent crime.'

'Good,' said Gordon. 'I think I have evidence of something, but I don't think it's an imminent crime.' He turned his cup on the saucer a few times while he considered where to start. 'You remember those cows that Bridget lost last week?' Dani nodded and he went on, 'Well, you know Bridget's still kind of special to me and I wanted to do something to help her. And I wanted a good story for the paper, too. So I thought about how to track down cattle rustlers.' He had another sip of coffee before continuing, 'I couldn't see any way to find the rustlers themselves but I thought there might be a way to track down who they were selling their cattle to. Through their financial records. You know, look for butchers who have unexplained income, or lifestyles that don't match their declared income.'

Gordon paused in his story and Dani said wryly, 'I think this may be the part that I don't want to know about.'

Gordon gave a brief smile of acknowledgement: 'Uh, yeah. Let's just say that I did a little browsing on the computer, a friend did a little browsing on the computer, and we found something interesting. A local butcher whose finances are, let's say, unconventional. The incomings don't seem to match the outgoings.' He held up a hand and said, 'I know, I know, this isn't proof of anything. I'm just telling you what happened.' He drained the last of his coffee and continued, 'Right. I have a local butcher who is a person of interest, as you'd say. But I've got nothing substantial. So I went by his shop and found nothing out of the ordinary. Steaks, chops, chickens, just the usual stuff you'd expect to find. It was a dumb idea. I mean if the guy's clever enough to be hiding his handling of stolen meat then he's not going to be dumb enough to label it that way in his counter. But I got to see him. At least I assume it was him because he was in charge of the shop. Big guy, solid, arms like hams. Short hair.'

Gordon noticed that Dani had finished her coffee and asked, 'Another one?' Dani shook her head and he went on with his story. 'Anyway, last night I went out to his farm to have a look.'

Dani put her hand over her eyes and shook her head. 'Uh oh – is this another part that I don't want to know about?'

'No, this part is okay. Except maybe I was technically trespassing but other than that it was all legit.' Dani rolled her eyes and he went on. 'I got there after dark, about midnight. There were lights on in the house and I thought maybe some in the shed but nothing was moving. About 1.30 a.m. I heard a car start up and saw it come from behind the building, down the driveway and leave, heading north. So I waited a while longer and nothing happened. About 2.00 a.m. I decided to have a nosey around, see if anything suspicious was going on. I walked up the drive and had a look in the house. Nothing. I backed off and carried on up the drive to the shed. I went around the back and had a look. Nothing. A roller door was open and there were lights on inside but I couldn't see anything. I heard voices but I couldn't make out what they were saying. I waited a little longer and two guys came out the doorway and had a smoke. One's probably not local, looked Chinese.'

Dani perked up at this and asked, 'Chinese? Are you sure? Could he have been Korean? Or Japanese?'

Gordon thought for a minute and said, 'No, I'm pretty sure he was Chinese. I mean, he could have been from anywhere – Malaysia, Thailand, hell, he could have grown up in New Zealand – but he looked Chinese. Anyway, the next thing a young woman came to the door and called out to them and they disappeared back out of sight into the shed.'

'Tell me you didn't go look in the shed,' Dani said.

'So I went to look in the shed,' Gordon continued, 'I went up beside the doorway and looked inside. And I saw a horse. A black horse. Prancing around in some sort of pen. And there were four people standing around. The three I've already described plus another guy who looked like a hippie or a surfer.' Gordon paused to get his phone from his pocket. 'Actually, I have a photo.'

'A photo,' Dani repeated. 'Of course you have a photo.'

Gordon scrolled through his phone, pausing once or twice, and then held it out to Dani. 'Here you go. Four people and a horse. Just like I said. The focus isn't too good because I just pointed and shot. I didn't have time for anything fancy.'

Dani took the phone and looked at the photo. As Gordon had said it showed four people standing in a rough semi-circle looking at a dark, probably black, horse. The focus definitely wasn't good enough to get a clear look at the people's faces, but it was obvious that there were three men and one woman and that one of the men was Asian. There was nothing exceptional about either of the other two men; both were average height and weight with light-coloured hair. The horse was moving and even more out of focus than the rest of the photo. Dani thought about what Bridget had said about the gang that had stolen her horse and Tui Dancer. First, there'd been two guys and a girl, then those three plus two Chinese men. Two guys, a girl, a Chinese man and a horse wasn't a perfect fit but it was enough to get her attention.

She handed the phone back and said, 'Okay. You've got four people and a horse in a shed. And no cattle at all, let alone Bridget's cattle. Where's the probable cause of a crime?'

Gordon had obviously had the same thoughts. 'What did Bridget tell you about the gang that stole those horses? She told me that the first time there were two guys and a girl and the second time the same trio plus two Chinese dudes.' He tilted the phone her way again. 'What do we see in this photo?'

'Yeah, yeah, that occurred to me, too,' Dani replied, 'and the missing joker's not a real problem. He could be anywhere, maybe taking a piss.' Dani shoved her coffee cup away and said, 'I suppose you're going to tell me that's Tui Dancer in the photo?'

Gordon grinned: 'I've never seen him but if I were a betting man then you're right, I'd bet that's Tui Dancer. The photo doesn't show it but when I saw him in the shed he didn't look like just another horse. The way he moved, the way he looked – I don't think he's just another horse.'

Dani drummed her fingers on the table and looked out the window, processing all the things Gordon had told her. Her fingers slowly stopped and she looked back at Gordon. 'I think you're right but you know there's nothing I can do, don't you?'

Gordon didn't say anything and Dani shook her head in annoyance. 'Shit, there's nothing here I can use. I can't use the financial thing, right?' Gordon shook his head and she continued, 'And even if I could use your photo, taken while trespassing, the judge would need more than just a coincidence in the makeup of the people to issue a warrant. And without a warrant there's nothing I can do. Officially.'

Gordon had been becoming more and more despondent as he saw his evidence dismissed, but his eyes lit up at Dani's last statement. 'Officially?' he asked.

Dani hesitated and said, 'Officially I need a warrant to follow up on what you've told me. Unofficially, I'll see what I can do. I'll at least drive by the place. Maybe make a routine community watch visit. Maybe say I'm looking for a woman and a horse fleeing from the police.' Dani stood up. 'Look, I've got to go. No promises but I'll see what I can do.'

Gordon stood as well and held out his hand. Dani took it and shook it once and turned to go. 'Thanks,' Gordon said, 'anything would be a help.'

———

Dani turned into the drive and parked the car in front of the farmhouse. It was quite ordinary, grey weatherboards and a darker grey roof, but appeared to be tidy and well maintained. She stepped out of the car and walked to the small covered porch. The front door had pebbled glass to let in light but maintain privacy. There was no bell, so she knocked on the door frame and waited for a response.

A few seconds later a shadow behind the glass showed someone was approaching and a woman's voice said, 'Hello?'

'Good morning,' Dani replied, 'I'm Constable Dani Painter. Can I speak with you for a minute, please?'

The door swung open and Dani was faced with a middle-aged woman, about 45 she guessed, with a solid, strong build. Not fat, but she was never going to win a beauty pageant. She had sensible brown hair, straight and cut to the bottom of her ears. She stood with one hand on the door, ready to close it, and the other on her hip. 'Yes?' she said. 'What do you want?'

Dani quickly decided that she wasn't going to get invited in and adapted her approach accordingly. 'Mrs Miller? Are you Mrs Miller?'

The woman nodded curtly: 'Yes. What do you want?'

'Mrs Miller, there's been some criminal activity in the area and I wondered if you've seen anything unusual. Maybe some strangers hanging around? Cars parked in strange places? Anything like that?'

Mrs Miller shook her head, 'No, I've seen nothing unusual. We mind our own business and don't take any notice of our neighbours. Or anyone else.'

'I see,' said Dani. 'I'm particularly interested in a young woman riding a horse. Have you seen anyone riding a horse in the neighbourhood?'

Mrs Miller gave her a strange look and shook her head again. 'No. No horses. No girls. Nobody.'

Dani looked towards the large shed up the drive behind the house. She pointed to it and asked, 'Do you mind if I have a look around? You have a large property. It's possible someone came on your property without you knowing it.'

Mrs Miller stepped out onto the small porch, crowding Dani's space. 'What's going on, constable?' she asked. 'I'm not answering any more questions until you tell me more about why you're here.'

Dani smiled and said, 'I'm sorry. At this stage all I can tell you is we're looking for a girl and a horse. We think she was heading this way and I want to be as thorough as I can. I'd really appreciate it if you'd let me look around. I promise I won't disturb anything.'

Mrs Miller folded her arms across her chest: 'Sorry. Like I told you, I don't know anything about a girl or a horse or anything else. I don't want you snooping around my property, either. So you'd better get back in your car and piss off.'

Dani dropped her smile and gave the woman a long look. She tipped her hat and turned away. 'Okay. Thank you for your time. One of my colleagues or I will be back with a warrant soon. And then we'll have a thorough search, not just a look around.'

Dani got back into her car, backed onto the drive and drove out to the main road. In her rear-view mirror she could see Mrs Miller standing on the porch watching her drive away.

———

Gordon was sitting in his office at the newspaper, working on a story about the weekend's netball tournament, when the phone rang. He answered it: 'Crawford.'

'Is that you, Gordon?'

He recognised Dani's voice and immediately dropped the article he was working on. 'Yeah. Hey, how'd it go?'

Dani cleared her voice and replied, 'About how I expected. I spoke with Mrs Miller. She denied any knowledge of anything and told me to piss off.'

Gordon stifled a laugh: 'Really? She told you to piss off? That took some balls.'

'Yeah,' said Dani, 'she's not exactly public-spirited. I tried to get a look around but she wouldn't let me. I threatened to get a warrant but she didn't budge.' Gordon heard Dani sigh. 'I'm sorry. That's all I can do unless we have more evidence. It sucks but my hands are tied.'

'No worries,' said Gordon, 'you tried.' He was silent for a moment, thinking what to do next. 'You say you could do something if you had more evidence?'

'Yeah, probably. But it would have to be good.'

'Uh-huh. Okay. I'll see what I can do.'

'Hey! Don't go and do anything stupid. We'll find a way ...' Dani stopped when Gordon disconnected the call. She put her phone in her pocket and said, 'Shit.'

Gordon leaned back in his chair and reflected on what Dani had just told him. He could think of only one thing to do next, so he grabbed his coat and bag, left his office and drove to the Millers' farm.

———

Hugh arrived at Bridget's house at lunchtime. They kissed but both were too edgy to put much into it. They had a light lunch and sat at the kitchen table drinking tea and waiting for the call. At 2.37 p.m. Hugh's phone rang. He answered, 'Yes, this is Hugh Jacobs.'

Bridget strained to hear the conversation, but all she could hear was Hugh's voice. Hugh glanced at Bridget and she saw a bead of sweat appear on his forehead. 'Okay,' he said into the phone, 'I get it. You want money. Just don't hurt the horse. How much money?' He was silent and looked despairingly at Bridget. 'I don't have that kind of money,' he said, 'you'll have to give me some time.' After a brief pause he said 'Look, I can't get one million dollars. I've been working on this all day. I can't get in touch with the owners. I can get two hundred thousand by tonight. That's the best I can do.'

He listened for what seemed like a long time and then pulled the phone away from his ear and turned it off. 'Shit,' he said, 'they want a million dollars or they're going to kill Tui Dancer.'

Bridget looked distressed. 'Oh no. What are we going to do?'

Hugh looked grim. 'I'll get as much money as I can. They gave me directions to the handover point. It's a farm in the district. And they said no cops.' He ran his hand across his forehead. 'Hell, what am I going to do? This has turned to total shit.'

'Do you need money?' Bridget asked. 'I've got a little and you're welcome to have it.' She didn't mention that strictly speaking it wasn't her money, it was the bank's money that she'd borrowed. She remembered Dylan's threats and demands and smiled in spite of the situation. The thought of using the bank's money to pay the ransom seemed appropriate.

Hugh smiled wanly and shook his head. 'No thanks. I'll get all I can and hope it's enough.' He stood up abruptly and reached for her. He held her tight for a minute and then let her go. 'I'd better get a move on. It's going to take all afternoon to get the money together.' He stepped towards the kitchen door and said, 'They said to be there at nine o'clock. It's a bit of a drive and I don't want to leave anything to chance so I'll be here about eight.'

'Okay,' said Bridget. 'I'll be ready. Good luck.'

'Thanks,' said Hugh over his shoulder, 'see you soon.'

'I love you,' said Bridget as he disappeared out the door, though she wasn't sure he heard her.

CHAPTER 13

Elliot had driven to Bridget's house and they were both waiting when Hugh pulled up at eight o'clock. Bridget got in the front seat of his Range Rover and Elliot got in the back. They were all grim and there were no hellos, just nods of greeting.

They were silent on the drive. Hugh drove slowly, as though reluctant to reach their destination. Glimpses of the pastoral scenery flashed by her window, highlighted by the headlights, but Bridget didn't see them. She kept thinking about Fraser. She knew he was wild and wasn't surprised that he was involved in a dodgy scheme, but this seemed too big, too organised for him. She couldn't see him bringing together a million-dollar heist. He thrived on a little chaos, **he** got off on the thrill of uncertainty, but that wasn't the feeling of what was going on. Whoever was behind stealing Tui Dancer knew what they were doing. They were totally ruthless and minimised risks. *It's those Chinese guys*, she thought, *they represent whoever's really behind this.* And that was scary. She'd seen them in action and knew their limits of morality lay way outside normal. She shivered and tried not to think about what might happen.

Elliot, in the back seat, watched Bridget and Hugh. Bridget was obviously nervous and upset. Elliot didn't know what she was thinking; her thoughts were far away. Hugh, on the other hand, was keyed up, but not as nervous as Elliot thought he might be. After all, how many times in your life do you have to deliver a huge ransom to a bunch of criminals? He looked at the battered leather briefcase on the floor behind Hugh's seat and thought even if it was full it didn't look like enough. Not enough to satisfy the Chinese guys. They looked like take-no-prisoners type of people, not interested in negotiations or excuses. The Range Rover went over a large bump and Elliot raised his hand to steady himself. He watched Hugh's firm hands on the wheel and wondered if there was any chance they would get Tui Dancer back.

It was warm and the windows in the vehicle were down. Bridget could feel and smell the night outside – the fertile dampness under the trees, the soft squawk of an unseen bird, the spicy fragrance of a pine plantation. The stars were blazing overhead by the time they approached their destination. Hugh drove even more slowly for the last kilometre, stopping as he read the name on a large letterbox. Elliot looked between the two heads in the front seat and saw Miller in white letters.

'This is it,' announced Hugh. 'Everybody ready?' He glanced at Bridget but didn't wait for a reply before turning into the drive. The Range Rover's headlights swept across a lawn and an unremarkable farmhouse as they made the turn. The big tyres tossed stones into the wheel wells as Hugh drove slowly up the drive and towards a large shed just visible through the darkness. 'That's it,' he said, 'they said to go to the rear of the shed.'

———

Fraser heard the car pull up behind the shed. The driver turned off the lights and engine and everything was quiet. He was sitting on a folding chair near Tui Dancer's pen, with Venus sitting beside him. The old Chinese guy was in the office and Dennis was standing in the open doorway. He didn't move as the car pulled up a few metres from him.

The driver's door opened and a big guy got out. Maybe not so much big as solid, Fraser thought. He opened the rear passenger door and got out a leather briefcase. As he did so the front passenger door opened and Bridget stepped out. She was highlighted in the light from the shed, her short platinum hair looking exotic and sexy. *What is she doing here?* Fraser thought. *This wasn't supposed to be part of the plan.*

'Bridget!' Fraser called out. He was smiling as usual but his lips were thin and the smile forced. 'I really hoped I wouldn't see you here.'

Bridget looked up and saw Fraser inside the shed. She stepped forward, giving Dennis a wide berth. The place looked spotless but its smell struck her, a mix of urine and shit and straw, the legacy of Barry's cattle, and a hint of diesel exhaust. She looked more closely at Fraser and thought she saw something – maybe fear – in his eyes. 'Yeah, well, we just couldn't stay away,' she replied.

Fraser looked past her and saw her elderly friend get out of the back seat of the car. *Oh fuck,* he thought, *this just gets worse.* He looked back at Bridget and said, 'Uh-huh. You couldn't stay away – you couldn't stay away from what?'

Bridget's heart was pounding but she tried to look casual as she pointed over her shoulder and said, 'We've come along with Hugh. He's got the money and he wanted witnesses to make sure there were no surprises.'

'Jesus Christ,' said Fraser. 'You shouldn't be here. You should stay far away from here. This doesn't have anything to do with you.'

Bridget tossed her hair and said, 'Actually, it does. I've been involved since you stole my horse ...' She saw Fraser flinch and look away but pressed on, '... and killed him. I've been doubly involved since you stole Hugh's horse. Or at least the horse that was in his care. The horse that I was responsible for.' She stepped closer to him and asked, 'What's going on? This bullshit isn't like you. I can't see you being in charge of something involving guns and murder.'

'He's not,' said Hugh from behind her, 'I am.'

Fraser recognised Hugh's voice instantly. It was the voice on the phone, the voice that had given him instructions. And threats. Fraser looked at the briefcase and replayed what Bridget had said, and in a flash everything fell into place.

Bridget whirled and looked in astonishment at Hugh, her hand to her mouth. He stood in the doorway with the briefcase in his left hand, no sign of emotion on his face. He handed the briefcase to Dennis and stepped into the shed.

'Hugh?' Bridget gasped. 'What ... what are you saying?'

'That I'm in charge.' This time he let a small smile appear and he moved towards her.

'But ... but I don't understand. What do you mean you're in charge? What about Blackbird? What about Tui Dancer? That was all you?'

Hugh shrugged. 'Well, not just me,' he said. 'It didn't all go quite as we intended.' He grimaced slightly and said, 'Blackbird wasn't part of the plan, but we got there in the end.'

'But if you're in charge then who called you on the phone? Who told you to come here?' Bridget asked. She pointed to the briefcase. 'And what about the money?'

Hugh smiled grimly: 'No one called me. There are dozens of apps that fake calls. The hardest part of faking a call is remembering to stop talking to let the non-existent other person speak. As to the money,' he gestured to Dennis, 'show her.'

Dennis clicked the latches on the briefcase and opened it. It was empty.

Bridget's mind reeled in confusion. 'There's no money,' she said, bewildered, 'but, if there's no ransom then what are Elliot and I here for?'

'An excellent question, my dear,' Hugh said, 'you and Elliot have proved to be remarkably resourceful and, what shall I say, inconvenient. I decided that for this last phase of our little caper it would be best if I knew where you were and kept you from interfering.'

'And that's all?' asked Elliot. 'You just want to keep an eye on us? There's no plan to kill us?'

'Kill you?' Hugh said incredulously. 'Why would I want to kill the woman I love?' He faced Bridget and continued, 'There's another reason why you're here, Bridget. I asked you once if you'd come away with me. You said you weren't sure. Well, now it's time to decide. I love you and want you to come, but ...' he paused, 'I understand that it's not easy.' He looked at Bridget as he said this and she had no idea what thoughts were going through his head. *Was he serious? Was he out of his mind?*

'Don't worry,' he continued, 'regardless of what you decide you'll all be unharmed. You'll be kept where we can see you until we're finished. You'll be released when it's safe. I don't care who or what you've seen because your testimony would be irrelevant. I'll go overseas and have a very nice life. Unfortunately I'll never come back to visit you here in New Zealand.'

Fraser stepped forward and said, 'And what about us? We're not going overseas and they've seen our faces.'

Hugh shrugged. 'I'm afraid that's your problem. You chose to be cavalier about your appearance and now that decision's come home to roost. I told you what to do and paid you well. How you achieved your tasks was entirely up to you. Like us, though, you will find that if there is any investigation then it will be your word against theirs. There will be no evidence of any of their accusations. We'll see to that. And anyway, you'll have some time to get away from here before they're released. I'm sure you will make the most of it.'

Fraser felt his temper rise but held it in check. As much as he was beginning to hate this bastard he knew that an element of what Hugh said was right. He should have thought further ahead, planned for a contingency like this. 'But you haven't,' he said, 'paid us well. You haven't paid us at all.'

Hugh smiled and said, 'All in good time. Unlike the ransom money, your money's here and you'll be paid in full tonight.'

———

Wang stood in the quiet of the office, his phone pressed to his ear. The call was from Hong Kong and there was no echo or static on the connection. The voice on the phone said, 'The results are clear. The blood sample is perfectly normal. You can proceed with the final phase.'

Wang said, 'Okay. We are ready here,' and hung up. He put his phone in his pocket and walked out into the shed.

Hugh saw him enter and waved him over. 'Mr Wang, come over here. I think you've already met Bridget and Elliot. They've kept us on our toes, haven't they?'

Wang showed no surprise at seeing Hugh, Bridget or Elliot. He came and stood next to Hugh. He looked at Bridget and Elliot and then turned to Hugh and said, 'I didn't think you'd bring them here. You know how crucial this phase is.'

Hugh said, 'Yes, but as I told our principals, I thought it was better to have them here where we can watch them than outside somewhere causing mischief.'

Wang shrugged, 'No matter. I just heard from our lab in Hong Kong. The blood results are clear. There is no sign of the drug. We are to finish the project tonight.'

Hugh smiled: 'Excellent news! I was sure there'd be no trace but I confess to being a little nervous until we got the lab results. This calls for a celebration later.'

He turned to Bridget and Elliot and said, 'I'm sorry, but you two need to just do as you're told now. We have a few final things to do and I don't want you getting in the way.' He gestured to Fraser, 'Would you and your team look after these two for a while? Just keep them out of the way. Make them a cup of tea or something. If they cause any trouble then let us know.'

Before Fraser or Venus could move, Bridget stepped forward and said, 'This is insane. What's going on? Why is Tui Dancer so important? What do you mean there's no sign of the drug? What drug? Have you done something to Tui Dancer?'

Hugh was silent for a moment and then smiled and said, 'Well, my dear, I guess there's no reason not to tell you.'

Wang hissed, 'Shut up, you fool! No one can know about what we're doing!'

Hugh waved him off, 'Nonsense. That's the beauty of what we've done. It's absolutely undetectable. And once Tui Dancer is gone it doesn't matter if Bridget or anyone else knows. If she talks then either no one will believe her or they will never be able to prove anything.'

He walked to Bridget and cupped her cheek with his palm. She flinched away and then stopped, her face immobile. 'I asked you to come away with me,' Hugh said, 'but I knew it would be like this. It would never be the same between us once you knew about Tui Dancer. And you couldn't come away with me without knowing that.' He dropped his hand back to his side. 'You want to know what's going on? It's very simple, really. We've developed a way to make a horse run fast. Or make him run slow. We've been testing it for over a year and it's now 100% reliable. And as I said, totally undetectable.'

Bridget looked at him scornfully. 'Why? Why would you do something like that?'

Hugh said, 'Obviously the drugs were developed to make a few people lots of money. But do you mean me? Why did I help?' He gave a small shrug: 'The challenge? The money? It doesn't really matter.' He put his hands in his pockets and walked a few steps, his eyes on the ground. 'I was approached about a year ago by a famous horse breeder from Hong Kong. He wanted my advice on improving some of the medical procedures of his stud. I was flattered, of course, and agreed to help him. I went to Hong Kong – you remember I was gone for six weeks last year – and while I was there he talked to me about some other ideas he had. Ideas that were, shall we say, unorthodox.'

'You mean illegal, don't you?' said Elliot.

Hugh ignored his comment and continued, 'In his own way, this man is a visionary. You have to understand that, at the level of competition we're talking about, these horses are like Olympic athletes. Changes in performance of even one percent, if that, are all that's required to make a difference between winning and finishing out of the money. There are numerous ways to influence a horse's performance, probably more than those used in the Tour de France. Everything's been tried, from drugs that improve oxygen uptake to drugs that inhibit pain response.

'The problem with traditional doping methods has been that they are relatively easily detected. My Hong Kong contact wanted to know if it was possible to find drugs that would affect a horse's performance but would be undetectable. Undetectable, not because a test hadn't been developed – that would merely continue the arms race between performance enhancement and testing. No, what was needed was something new – something outside the scope of all existing tests, something that would have modest but significant effects on horse performance.

'We began doing experiments and, after considerable effort, found two new drugs that affected performance: one that improved it and one that impaired it. Not by much; just enough to make a difference but not so much as to attract attention. The exciting discovery was that extreme physical activity removed all trace of the drugs from the horse. Tests after every race showed no sign of the drugs in the horse's blood, urine, hair, anything. It was as though the drugs were never there. They were literally undetectable.'

Hugh raised his hand and pointed a finger at the ceiling, 'But there was one problem. The amount required and the time it took for the drugs to have effect varied from horse to horse. This could be evaluated by administering the drugs during the horse's training, varying the amounts and timing until the metabolic uptake of the drugs was understood. These tests were done. It took time but we documented what was necessary to get the required performance of the horses. And then there was just one hurdle that remained before we could fully exploit the potential of the drugs.' He walked over to Tui Dancer's pen and looked at the horse for a few moments, then turned back to Bridget. 'That's where Tui Dancer came in.'

Elliot said, 'I get it. You needed something more than a lab test.'

Hugh nodded: 'That's right. It's one thing to get results during training and something else to demonstrate you can deliver results for a whole season.'

Bridget said, 'So Tui Dancer was your guinea pig.'

'Exactly,' Hugh replied, 'we needed a good horse we could race for a whole season, but one in a low key environment. A place where less money was riding on the outcomes and there was likely to be less oversight if there were any problems.' He held up his hands. 'New

Zealand fits the bill perfectly. We have a very active racing industry and, although some fine horses come from here, the races themselves are virtually unknown on the international scene. If something went wrong we were confident we could contain and manage the situation without compromising the global standing of the syndicate.'

'And were there?' Bridget asked. 'Any problems?'

Hugh shook his head. 'Nope. Everything worked perfectly. We worked out Tui Dancer's metabolic uptake during his training and then used the drugs to influence his performance throughout the season. With a little chemical assistance Tui Dancer won or placed in every race he entered for the first part of the season. He was tested repeatedly and nothing unusual was ever discovered. Then I'm sure you noticed how his performance suddenly dropped in the last few races? The reason was simple. He hadn't been pushed too hard as some people speculated. He'd been given the other drug. Again he was tested and nothing was found.'

'And you were a part of this?' Bridget asked with contempt. 'You thought this was a good thing to do?'

'Good, bad, such emotive terms sometimes,' said Hugh.

'So that's it?' asked Elliot. 'You've finished your experiment and now you'll scuttle back to your master in Hong Kong?'

'Pretty much,' Hugh replied, 'there are a few details still to work out,' he gestured to Fraser, 'like paying Mr Lyman and his associates, but that won't take long. Then we'll be on our way and you'll be free to go. Isn't that right, Mr Wang?'

'Yes. The boss said that once we're through here we pack up and return to Hong Kong.'

Hugh looked at Bridget and offered, 'Last chance. Say the word and we'll go together.'

She looked at him in disbelief and shook her head. 'I can't,' she whispered, 'you know I can't.'

Hugh looked at her for a long moment and then clapped his hands and moved forward. 'Right. Then let's get this done. Fraser, Mr Wang, come to the office with me and we'll get you sorted out. Dennis, you and Venus look after Bridget and Elliot. Make sure they're … safe.'

Hugh, Fraser and Wang walked across the shed and disappeared into the office. Dennis said, 'Move over there, by the horse.'

Bridget and Elliot moved towards Tui Dancer's pen and sat on the folding chairs. Venus went with them and leaned on the door to the pen. Dennis walked to the open doorway and stood, watching the three of them and the parking area outside.

———

Elliot said softly, so only Bridget and Venus could hear him, 'You know what happens next, don't you?' Bridget and Venus looked at each other and shook their heads. 'You don't really think the Chinese guys can let Tui Dancer or us leave here, do you?' asked Elliot. 'No way. I don't care what Hugh says, none of us are leaving here alive.'

Bridget and Venus looked shocked. 'What do you mean?' whispered Bridget with alarm. 'You heard what Hugh said. They don't care about us. They don't care about Tui Dancer. Nothing can be detected. Their scheme is perfect. There's nothing we can do to stop it.'

Elliot shook his head and said, 'Hugh may believe that, I don't know. But I don't think these Chinese gangsters were sent here just to check on the blood tests. Horseracing is serious business to these Asian gamblers. We're talking millions, probably tens of millions of dollars they stand to gain if they succeed with this plan. We can't underestimate them. They're smart enough to know that nothing's perfect. I don't care what Hugh says, there's always a chance that those drugs might be detected. Believe me, these guys know how to manage risks. And that's what I think this Wang bloke's here for. To eliminate risks. And If Tui Dancer's dead, then he's no risk.'

Venus moved a step closer and asked, 'Are you serious? You really think they'd kill us? And Tui Dancer?'

'Tui Dancer, for sure,' Elliot replied. 'No one found any sign of their drugs during the racing season but they can't take a chance of anyone getting suspicious and asking too many questions. As long as Tui Dancer's alive then there's a chance the scheme might be discovered and traced back to them. And there's always human error –

someone may have slipped up somewhere and left a trace of what they've done. This is the age of the Internet. If anyone digs hard enough then they might find links from Tui Dancer back to a lab in Hong Kong. I don't care how perfect the scheme is, the one thing they don't want is attention that might lead to questions about other aspects of their business. So Tui Dancer has to disappear, probably a victim of a tragic accident while in Hugh's care.'

Venus remembered the dash across the road and the surge of power beneath her as Tui Dancer accelerated across the first paddock. 'No!' she cried. 'They can't kill Tui Dancer.'

Elliot raised his hand and gestured to Venus to lower her voice. He looked at the two women and said, 'Well, they will. And they'll kill us, too, for the same reason. We're loose ends that can only cause them trouble, no matter how hard it might be for anyone to believe what we say. As long as we're alive, we're a risk. It doesn't matter how small it is, we're still a risk.'

Bridget brought her hand to her mouth. Her eyes were large and round with fear. 'You can't mean that. This is New Zealand, not some Third World war zone. They'd never get away with it.'

Elliot reached out and gripped Bridget's shoulder. 'Believe it. They brought their world with them. I think they've done this before. I think they're very good at their job. Wang will kill us and all he has to do is delay our discovery until he's left the country. Once he's back in Hong Kong he'll disappear.'

'Shit,' said Venus, 'I didn't sign on to any of this. Dennis or Fraser never said anything about murder. But what can we do? That guy Wang has a gun.' She gestured helplessly. 'We've got nothing.'

They were silent for a long time, not looking at each other. Finally Elliot leaned close to Venus and said softly, 'If you could get his pen open and got on his back, could you ride Tui Dancer out of here?'

Venus opened her mouth and closed it again. She thought about Dennis, Fraser, Hugh and Wang. She thought about how her body hurt and how her study break wasn't turning out quite as she'd expected. She looked at the concrete floor of the shed and the large open door at its rear and the empty blackness beyond the lit parking area. She looked at Elliot and said, 'Sure.'

Elliot inclined his head to indicate that both women should move closer, but he kept his eyes on Dennis, still standing in the doorway.

Elliot waited until they were close enough to hear and then said softly, 'Okay, this is what we're going to do.'

———

The generator stood against the back wall of the shed, near the roller doors. It had been purchased to provide emergency power in case the main electrical circuits went out. It had two wheels and a handle in the front for moving it around and was the size of a very large suitcase. It was faded red with a generous coating of oil, grease and dirt in places. Next to it were a 20 litre plastic petrol can and several coiled black exterior extension cords.

Elliot drifted towards the doors and stood looking out into the night. Dennis was standing in the doorway. He watched Elliot approach and turned with a scowl. Elliot ignored him and pulled a coin from his pocket, flipping it idly as he continued to stare out the doorway. He slowly edged closer to the door until Dennis barked, 'Get back inside! You're not going anywhere yet.'

Elliot jumped slightly as though startled from his reverie and dropped the coin. It rolled across the floor and stopped under the generator. Elliot gave Dennis an apologetic smile and walked over to retrieve the coin. He knelt down in front of the generator and groped with his right hand for the coin. He put his left hand on the petrol can, as though for balance. The can moved easily and he felt the slosh of petrol inside. He estimated that the can was less than a quarter full, with plenty of room in the top for a combustible fuel-air mix. His body blocked Dennis' view of the petrol can and, as he scrabbled beneath the generator, he swiftly unscrewed the plastic top and put it behind the generator. Once the cap was off he grabbed the coin and held it up in triumph. He smiled at Dennis as he stood and then slowly walked back to the others and nodded.

Bridget exhaled and thought about what she had to do. As Elliot rejoined them she walked to the doors and gestured to Dennis to come to her. He hesitated, not sure if he should talk to her. Bridget brought her fingers to her mouth and asked, 'Do you have a cigarette? I'm dying for a smoke.'

Dennis smiled in relief and sauntered over to her. He pulled a pack of cigarettes from his shirt pocket, shook one loose and offered it to her. "You know this is bad for you, don't you?' he asked with a small grin as she took the cigarette. 'You know smoking kills.'

'You have no idea,' Bridget said as she lifted the cigarette towards her lips. 'Do you have a light?' Dennis pulled a plastic lighter from his trousers pocket and lit Bridget's cigarette. He watched her take a deep drag and blow the smoke past him towards the open door.

'Thanks,' said Bridget. She moved away from the door, standing several metres back from the opening. She turned her back on Dennis and looked into the shed. Dennis returned to his spot in the doorway, trying to keep an eye on anything that might appear outside and on Bridget smoking behind him. She took infrequent puffs, trying to make the cigarette last as long as possible. She saw Elliot reach out and touch Venus' arm. *Uh-oh,* she thought, *show time.*

Venus had watched Elliot distract Dennis as he removed the top of the petrol can. She watched him walk back towards them and nod. She watched Bridget get a cigarette and start smoking. She felt Elliot's touch on her arm and suddenly wanted to be sick. She thought about the other horse that had been shot in this place. She looked at the gate of Tui Dancer's pen and thought about how long it would take to open it and get on his back. She looked at the bare concrete floor and thought about whether the big horse's hooves would find traction. She studied the darkness outside and wondered how far she could get before someone caught her and shot her, along with the horse.

Venus had no illusions. No matter what the vet said, she thought the old guy was right. This was going to be a cleanup operation. The Chinese guy was here for just one reason. The syndicate behind this escapade didn't want any witnesses to how Tui Dancer had been used to test their doping programme. Elliot's plan was crazy. If the slightest thing went wrong then she'd be dead. But if she did nothing then she'd be dead for sure. So, if crazy was the only other option, then it would have to do.

The feeling of nausea quickly passed, but Venus continued to stand without moving for several long seconds, long enough for a look of concern to appear in Elliot's eyes. Then, with an almost visible wrench she turned on her foot and walked to the gate of Tui Dancer's pen. She moved neither quickly nor slowly, but purposefully. She was confident that this would attract the least attention from Dennis and she needed to project an air of confidence when she mounted Tui Dancer. Both Dennis and Tui Dancer would be alerted by haste or stress, either of which would result in disaster.

She reached the gate, opened it quietly and stepped inside. As far as she could tell Dennis hadn't noticed her movements yet, but it was only a matter of time. She moved to Tui Dancer and stroked the horse on the muzzle and neck, murmuring softly to him as she moved down his left side. He jerked his head up and down to her touch and took a half step sideways, pushing her against the wall of the pen. Venus had a moment of panic as she thought she would be crushed, but relaxed when the pressure eased and she discovered she could still move. Taking advantage of the fact that the horse's movement had helped to conceal her, she reached for the headcollar, which she had hung on a ring, fitted it carefully and slipped the knotted lead ropes over Tui Dancer's withers, then ducked beneath his neck and clipped the free end to the other side of the headcollar. She raised her hand and gripped a handful of Tui Dancer's mane, took a deep breath and launched herself up onto his back. He snorted and shuffled as he felt her weight but quickly settled beneath her.

She was now clearly visible above the sides of the pen, lit by the overhead fluorescent lights. Every second of delay only increased her danger so she gripped the knotted lead ropes firmly and urged Tui Dancer forward with her legs. He instantly responded and stepped through the gate.

Bridget had watched Venus enter the pen and mount Tui Dancer with growing terror. *No, no, no!* she thought. *I'm not ready yet.* She was supposed to have moved closer to the generator, but once she'd taken the cigarette and had Dennis' attention she'd forgotten to move. She looked anxiously at the petrol can, now standing at least four metres away. The opening beckoned but was less than three centimetres in diameter. She glanced at the cigarette in her hand. It was short; she'd smoked it almost to the filter. She saw Venus and Tui Dancer come out of the pen. She saw Elliot start to move forward. She saw Dennis turn to look at her and his eyes slide past to see what was happening behind her in the shed. She lifted her hand and prepared to make the goal shot of her life.

As they came out of the pen Venus felt her fear of the crazy people in the shed fall away, to be replaced by the need to try once again to remain on top of a fleeing horse and attempt to guide him to safety. Establishing some degree of stability, she urged Tui Dancer to turn left and then kicked him hard with her heels. She felt Tui Dancer jump beneath her, startled at this unexpected signal to run. His feet slipped once, twice on the smooth concrete and then she felt him gather himself beneath her and launch himself towards the open door.

When Elliot had seen Venus mount Tui Dancer he started moving towards the door, diagonally away from the generator and petrol can. He glanced behind and saw them come out of the pen and he began to run.

Bridget focused on the petrol can and felt everything go quiet. When she had been playing netball competitively, even in the noisiest home games, she'd been able to shut it all out and see only the net. She didn't take her eyes off the opening as her hand came up, she cocked her wrist, and tossed the cigarette.

Dennis couldn't believe his eyes when he looked over his shoulder and saw Venus come out of the pen on the horse's back. He spun towards her, saw Venus kick the horse and saw Tui Dancer start to gallop towards him. His mind was warning him frantically to get out of the way, but he was slow, way too slow. His eyes widened with fright as the horse closed on him. It was one thing to watch a horse race around a track – it was something else to stand in front of a charging stallion and try not to get crushed or trampled to death. The stallion was still accelerating as Dennis turned to jump out of the way.

The cigarette thrown by Bridget spiralled towards its destination, dropping in a perfect parabola into the open top of the petrol can. In a split second the can exploded with a roar and a huge ball of flame.

———

Gordon had been edging closer to the open shed doorway, moving carefully because he could see a young guy in the entrance, looking into the darkness. He knew, however, that it was very difficult to look from light into darkness and that if he avoided sudden movement, or reflecting the light from the shed, then he would be very hard to see. Earlier he'd seen Elliot and then Bridget stand near the doorway. He'd seen Bridget get the guy to light her cigarette and then disappear back inside. He wanted to see what was going on in the shed, or at least try to hear what was being said. He wanted to call the cops. He wanted to call Dani, but he knew he needed something more than just a Chinese guy and a few of his associates in a place where they didn't belong.

He had lifted his foot to take another slow step towards the shed when he heard a loud clatter and saw a horse emerge from the shed, galloping hard. He heard the change in tone as the hooves left the concrete for the packed stones of the parking area. Before he could turn, the horse was gone, vanished into the night. He was still trying to figure out what to do next the night erupted with an enormous explosion and he was blown off his feet.

He was back up in an instant and stood uncertainly, ready to run but unsure in which direction to go. There was no sign of the guy in the doorway – he was there one second and gone the next. A large cloud of black smoke was billowing from the shed and he could see the glow of flames somewhere inside. He was slightly deafened from the blast but thought he could hear yelling.

Two very loud gunshots, their noise amplified by the acoustics of the shed, made his decision for him. Without another thought he spun and sprinted into the night, following the horse and the mysterious rider.

———

The explosion had blown Bridget off her feet and singed her hair and face. She felt as though she had the worst case of sunburn ever but, as she raised herself onto one arm and peered around her, she was grateful to be alive. She coughed as a cloud of thick smoke briefly engulfed her and she wiped her eyes with her free hand. The fire was dying down, the generator a scorched metal skeleton. Across the doorway she saw Dennis lying in a huddle on the floor, not moving. Further into the shed she saw Elliot rise to his feet, obviously less affected by the blast than she was. She saw him start to run towards her and was about to push herself to her feet when two more explosions rocked the building, smaller than the petrol can but loud enough to cause her to fall back to the concrete floor.

Elliot had dropped to the floor when he saw Bridget toss the cigarette towards the petrol can and had drawn himself into as small a ball as he could before it exploded. As a result he largely avoided the shockwave and the flames went over his head, leaving him relatively unscathed. As soon as he judged it safe he got to his feet and started running towards where Bridget lay on the floor. He hadn't gone more than a few metres when the concrete near his feet exploded and he heard sounds he hadn't heard since Malaya. Elliot knew what gunfire meant and he knew what shots at his feet meant – either the person was a bad shot, in which case the message was he would keep firing until he hit Elliot, or he was a good shot and the message was 'don't fucking move or I'll kill you'. Elliot hoped it was the latter and froze.

Hugh and Wang were about twenty metres away, both with pistols in their hands. Wang stood in the classic shooter's stance, feet wide apart and both hands on the gun's grip. A whiff of smoke came from his gun's barrel, hardly visible in the reduced light of the smoke-filled shed. 'Mr Jacobs,' he ordered, 'cover these two while I see what the fuck's going on.'

Hugh nodded, stepped sideways and lifted his gun towards Bridget and Elliot. 'I've got them,' he said.

Wang lowered his weapon and relaxed slightly. He stepped cautiously towards the crumpled form of Dennis. Smoke still filled the shed, though it was beginning to thin as the breeze blew it out the doorway. He reached the fallen man and kicked him lightly on the shin. There was no response, but when Wang looked more closely he could see the slight rise and fall of his chest. 'He's okay,' he called back to Hugh, 'he's still breathing.' *Okay* may have been an exaggeration. Blisters were already appearing on the exposed parts of Dennis' body, but compared to being dead any sign of life was okay.

The fire was out and the smoke was rapidly dispersing; that which hadn't risen into the high roof space being sucked out of the shed by the breeze. Hugh pivoted where he stood, his gaze first moving to Tui Dancer's pen. His brows contracted briefly when he saw the open gate and no sign of the horse. He saw Wang also look at the empty pen and give him an angry look.

'Where is the horse?' Wang asked in a low growl.

'I have no idea where the fucking horse is,' Hugh replied calmly. 'Dennis and Venus were supposed to be watching them.' He gestured towards the body on the floor. 'Maybe he can tell us – when he wakes up.'

'This is not acceptable!' Wang shouted. 'I demand that you get the horse right now and we finish this business once and for all!'

Hugh was silent for a moment and then continued his examination of the shed. Wang, Bridget and Elliot formed a frozen triangle. Behind them Fraser stood in the door to the office space. His face was ashen and blank. He was clearly in shock and Hugh watched him as he began walking stiffly towards the others.

Everyone was accounted for except that crazy bitch Venus. Suddenly Hugh knew exactly what had happened. It was Venus who had ridden Tui Dancer away from the wrecked trailer and he now had no doubt that she'd ridden him away from here as well. God only knew how she'd done it, *why* she'd done it, but at that moment Hugh didn't care. He wanted, he *needed*, to get Tui Dancer back and Fraser was his starting point for information.

Wang shouted again, 'Where is the horse? I hold you accountable for this!'

Hugh looked at Wang and said, 'We will get the horse back.' He turned to Fraser and said loudly, 'We seem to be missing a horse and one of your associates. I suspect that these are related. Do you have anything to tell us?'

Fraser had moved towards them and stopped a few metres short of Wang. He looked blankly at Wang and said, 'You tried to shoot them. I saw you try to shoot them.'

Wang shook his head and said, 'I'm sorry to disabuse you, but if I'd tried to shoot them they would be dead. True, I fired my pistol but it was to get their attention. Mr Jacobs asked you a question. What is your answer? Do I need to get your attention?'

'What?' said Fraser, and looked quickly at Bridget and Elliot. 'What do you mean? No, you don't need to get my attention.' The shock of the explosion and the pistol shots was wearing off and Fraser was starting to realise that he might be in deep shit.

Wang stood in front of Fraser and put the barrel of his pistol against his left shoulder. Fraser looked panicked but couldn't move. 'Hey!' he exclaimed nervously. 'What's going on?'

Bridget looked on in horror as the scene unfolded before her. In the real world, people didn't carry guns or shoot at each other. Her fists clenched and unclenched repeatedly as the stress built inside her.

Elliot watched the action with a clinical eye, judging distances and angles and assessing probabilities. He had no weapon but was uninjured and was ready for any opportunity that presented itself.

Wang said, 'Now. We need to find Tui Dancer. You will help us. I know that bitch of yours has ridden him from here. If you tell me where she's gone then we can go there and bring him back. If you don't tell me where she's gone then I will have to hurt you.'

Fraser's eyes grew wild and he tensed, ready to flee. 'I don't know where she's gone. You've got to believe me! She was Dennis' friend. I don't know why she'd run. I don't know where she'd run to. I wasn't even out here. I was in the office talking to you!'

Wang looked thoughtful for a moment. 'Very well,' he said, his voice rising, 'you say you don't know where she's gone. You say you don't know where she's taken the most valuable horse in New Zealand?' His last words were almost a shout and he paused to bring himself back under control. 'This woman has helped you to steal Tui Dancer, not once but twice. And you say you have no idea where she's gone. Is that right?'

Fraser closed his eyes and nodded. He was almost crying. 'Yes, yes, that's right. I have no idea where she's gone.'

Wan looked at him for a moment and said, 'Well, that's too bad.' Then he shot Fraser through his left shoulder.

The sound of the shot and Fraser's scream were almost too much for Bridget. She felt faint and swayed before she regained control and steadied herself. Elliot quickly stepped to her side and wrapped his arms around her, keeping her steady on her feet.

Fraser fell to the floor and clutched his shoulder with his right hand. Blood welled thickly from both the entry and exit wounds and he was weeping openly now, maintaining a constant moan as he rocked back and forth. Wang stood over him, smoke coming from the pistol that was now aimed at Fraser's head. Hugh stepped to Fraser and knelt beside him. He moved close to his right ear and said, very quietly so only Fraser could hear, 'Fraser. Hey, Fraser. Listen to me. This guy is a psycho. Believe me, if you want to walk out of here alive then you have to tell us what you know.'

He gripped Fraser's chin in his hand and turned his face towards him. Tears and snot stained Fraser's face, and his eyes were dull with fear. Hugh studied the face for a moment and said, 'I don't think he knows anything. He'd be talking by now if he did.'

Wang didn't say anything. He gestured for Hugh to stand up and took his place, kneeling by Fraser. 'Mr Fraser, do you understand the situation? Do you understand the question? I'm going to ask you again and I hope that you answer this time. Next time I may hit something more important.' He adjusted his position, placed his hand on Fraser's good shoulder and gave it a light squeeze. 'So here we go. One more time. I want you to tell us where the horse has gone.'

Fraser continued to weep and shook his head and said over and over, 'No, no. I don't know. I don't know. I don't know.'

Wang looked thoughtful for a moment and then stood and gazed down at Fraser. He looked at Hugh, who averted his head and stepped away. Wang adjusted his stance and pointed his pistol at Fraser's right knee.

As Hugh moved away Bridget broke free of Elliot's arms and ran towards Wang, shouting, 'No! You can't do this! It's barbaric! Can't you see he doesn't know where they've gone?'

Hugh reached out and grabbed her as she tried to get to Wang and Fraser. 'Hey!' he said, 'Bridget! Take it easy.' He pulled her close to his chest, overpowering her attempt to pull free. He ran a hand across the hair at the back of her head, soothing her like he would a skittish horse, although she was way beyond soothing. He felt her stop struggling and stand stiffly against him. 'There, that's better,' he said and let her move a short distance from his body. He kept one hand loosely on her shoulder and looked into her frightened brown eyes. 'Really, I had no idea you cared so much for this lad. I thought he was the man who ruined your life and that it was you and I who had something special.'

Bridget was in turmoil. Here was the man she'd been sleeping with for months, the man she thought she loved – the *married* man she thought she loved. The man whom she'd trusted and who now held her with one hand and held a gun in the other. And on the floor was the man who had tempted her before betraying her and destroying her career. Who had re-entered her life and brought her nothing but anger and violence and now this, this moment when she honestly didn't know if she'd walk out of this shed alive or wind up dead on the floor. The man who, in some perverse way, still somehow stirred her crazy side and made her run towards a stranger with a gun.

Her eyes were wide as she stared at Hugh, then looked over at Fraser, who had struggled to his feet. Wang stepped back a step and now had his gun aimed at Fraser's chest. She shook her head and said shakily, 'Don't shoot him. Please don't shoot him.'

'Actually,' said Wang, 'I think we're done with Mr Fraser. But we have a few questions for *you*.' He swivelled and pointed his gun at Bridget. Hugh, looking startled and confused, took a long step sideways, away from Wang's gun.

'Wh-, what?' Bridget stammered. 'What do you mean? I don't know anything.'

'That's for us to discover, my dear,' said Wang

Hugh looked anxiously back and forth between Bridget and Wang. 'Wang?' he said. 'What's going on? There's no need for a gun. I'm sure she will cooperate.'

Wang ignored Hugh and his eyes drilled into Bridget's, 'Now, you heard what we asked Mr Lyman. It's a very simple question. Where have Venus and Tui Dancer gone? Just tell us what you know and we can all move on.' He smiled sadly at her and waited for her to speak.

Bridget looked frantically from Hugh to Wang and back. 'I don't know!' she wailed. 'I only met the girl here. I don't know anything about her. How could I know where she's gone?'

Wang replied patiently, 'The girl obviously didn't escape on her own. Mr Elliot was part of the plan. You were part of the plan. It makes sense that you would have discussed what she would do once she left. And that's what I want to know. What did you decide when you planned Tui Dancer's escape? Where have the girl and the horse gone? Tell us what you know.'

Bridget was almost hyperventilating, breathing more rapidly than she had after sprint training. 'No,' she begged, 'don't do this. Please don't do this. I don't know where they went. We only had a plan to get out of the shed. That's all. There was no plan for what to do next. None of us really thought we'd make it, so what was the point?' She looked pleadingly into Wang's stony brown eyes.

Wang was silent for a moment, as though considering what Bridget had said. Then he sighed and said, 'I'm sorry, I have no choice. You have no idea what forces are at play here.' He straightened his shoulders and said, 'So, one last time. Tell us where Venus and Tui Dancer have gone.'

Bridget was crushed. There was nothing left, no place to go. A maniac was demanding a response to a question to which she didn't know the answer. And if she didn't answer, then he was prepared to shoot her. And as if that wasn't enough, the man she thought she loved was just standing there. Making no attempt to protect her or save her. How had she come to this? How had she been so wrong about someone? She thought about the men she'd been involved with, one way or another – Fraser, Gordon and now Hugh – and marvelled at how badly she'd chosen. Could she have picked three men more likely to screw up her life? She felt a brief flush of shame, but this was almost immediately replaced by anger. She felt the rage swell up inside her. Rage against the injustice of her life but most of all rage against this man who had said he loved her and who was now going to let her die.

Bridget straightened and felt her face harden. 'Fuck you!' she screamed. 'Fuck you, you fucking asshole!' She could only see his face, the thick eyebrows, broad nose, firm cheeks, strong neck, and she started to lunge towards him. From the corner of her eye she sensed movement as Wang lifted his gun. Once again the shed echoed to the heavy sound of a gunshot. She felt a hot burning sensation under her right arm and everything went black.

———

Elliot had started to run towards Bridget, but stopped at the sound of the gunshot. He stared in disbelief at the two bodies on the floor. Bridget lay face down at Hugh's feet, her legs sprawled awkwardly and her arms still stretched towards him. Her shirt was torn and bloody and a pool of blood was slowly forming beneath her. Elliot wasn't sure if she was alive or dead, but it was certain at the very least that she was badly injured.

Next to her, closer to Wang, Fraser lay face up on the concrete, his face remarkably serene. His shoulder wound was a ragged mess but the large pool of blood beneath him showed that the second injury was much more severe.

Elliot was stunned by the rapid sequence of events. Fraser had lurched between Bridget and Wang just as the gun went off. The bullet went through his heart, bounced off two ribs and emerged, its velocity much reduced, to enter Bridget's body below her right armpit with enough force to knock her off her feet. The bullet had started to tumble when it left Fraser's body and it made a large irregular wound in Bridget's chest that was now dripping blood onto the concrete floor.

Even though he'd been expecting the shot, Hugh was paralysed. Before him lay two bodies, probably both dead. He stared at Fraser and Bridget and saw no signs of life. Just blood. Blood everywhere.

He turned to Wang and screamed, 'You idiot! What have you done? Tidying up the project was supposed to be discreet, not a bloodbath. What part of your instructions didn't you understand?' He looked at Bridget's still body and muttered, 'I'm sorry.'

Wang looked at him without emotion. He ignored the bodies at his feet and lifted his gun towards Hugh. 'My instructions were very clear,' he replied, 'leave no witnesses.' He pulled the trigger and shot Hugh in the centre of his chest.

———

Dani turned into the drive and slowed but didn't stop as she passed the house. She didn't need another encounter with Mrs Miller. She proceeded slowly up the drive, pulling over and parking before she got to the big shed. She got out of the car and looked around. There was no sign of life and no sounds. There were lights in the windows of what looked like an office area on the left side of the shed. She could see a glow coming from the back of the shed and assumed that a door was open there. She moved cautiously forward, her feet making only the lightest sound on the gravel drive.

As she approached the front corner of the shed there was a commotion and a horse exploded across the parking area and fled into the darkness. Before the horse disappeared there was an enormous explosion and the area behind the shed was suddenly lit like day. In the flash she saw Gordon standing near the rear corner of the shed then blown off his feet by the blast.

At the sound of the explosion Dani flattened herself against the side of the shed, half crouched, ready to run in either direction. She began to move towards the back of the shed but froze again at the sound of two loud gunshots. Before the echoes had died she saw Gordon take off running, following the horse. *Jesus Christ*, she thought, *what the hell is going on? Gordon said they had guns but I never thought they'd actually use them.*

In the quiet after the gunshots she could hear voices inside the shed, too indistinct to tell how many but definitely more than one. She pulled her baton from her belt and tugged at her stab-proof vest. Dani thought of the radio in the car and wished she'd brought a portable one. She knew the smart move was to go back to the car and call for backup, but she was afraid that innocent people might still be in danger and every minute might make a difference for them. Her indecision was resolved when there was another shot and a scream.

––––––

Gordon ran faster than he'd ever run on the cricket ground. After a couple of hundred metres he stopped, turned back to the shed and crouched, gasping, with his hands on his knees, trying to catch his breath. He had just straightened when he saw a bright flash in the shed and heard another gunshot.

He was frozen by indecision. *Where the hell are the cops? Where the hell is Dani?* He walked in a circle, clawing at his head with his hands. He was a journalist, not a cop. Or a hero. This must be something someone else can deal with. He froze when he clearly heard Bridget's voice coming from inside, directed out the doorway by the acoustics of the shed. He clearly heard her yell 'No! You can't do this! It's barbaric! Can't you see he doesn't know …,' the end of the sentence fading beyond hearing as the breeze shifted. Suddenly he realised there was no one else – he was the only one who could deal with the situation. In an instant he started sprinting back towards the shed.

He reached the outer limits of the illuminated area and slowed to a walk, this time edging right around the parking area where the shadows were a little deeper. He looked into the shed and saw Bridget in Hugh's arms, Elliot standing between them and the doorway, that crazy fuck – what was his name, Fraser? – clutching his hand to a bloody shoulder, and a Chinese guy standing slightly behind them with a gun in his hand.

Guns, blood – the scene was way beyond anything Gordon had experienced before. What was going on? Had the Chinese guy shot Fraser? Was he about to shoot Bridget and Hugh? He became even more confused when he saw Hugh step away from Bridget and saw that he, too, had a gun. Then the Chinese guy pointed his gun at Bridget and he saw her sag. He could see that she and Wang were talking but their voices were too low for him to make out what they said. Then he heard Bridget suddenly scream 'Fuck you! Fuck you, you fucking asshole!' and leap towards Hugh. He saw Fraser lurch towards her and Elliot start to run towards them and then the Chinese guy pulled the trigger and Bridget and Fraser fell to the floor and lay very still.

Gordon was in shock. *Oh fuck. Oh fuck.* The woman he loved lay motionless on the ground and he'd been unable to do anything to stop it. In anguish he looked up at the sky and squeezed his eyes shut. He felt anger build inside him. He didn't know what was going on but he wasn't going to let Bridget's death go unavenged. Deep inside he knew this was insane, but sometimes rationality has to take a back seat to emotion.

He opened his eyes and retained enough sense to know that he didn't have a chance if he just ran yelling into the shed. The Chinese guy would shoot him as coldly as he'd shot Bridget. He looked around for a weapon, an idea, anything – and he saw Dani step around the corner of the shed.

She saw him in the same instant and flashed a hand signal at him. He didn't need to be a SWAT member to know it meant 'don't move'. She eased forward until she reached the edge of the doorway, knelt, lowered her face to the ground and peeked into the shed.

They both heard Hugh scream, 'You idiot! What have you done? Tidying up the project was supposed to be discreet, not a bloodbath.

What part of your instructions don't you understand?' But they couldn't hear the man's reply before he shot Hugh in the chest.

Dani quickly ducked back and tried to control herself. She'd counted four bodies – a guy by the doorway, Fraser and Bridget, and now Hugh. This wasn't an incident; this was a butcher's shop. Elliot looked to be the only one alive besides the Chinese guy and, based on what she'd seen, she didn't give him long. She took a deep breath and then another and felt herself grow calm, knowing what she had to do. She thought about where the Chinese guy was; where Elliot was; where Gordon was. She stood and looked at Gordon and started gesturing to him.

Gordon stood still, his anger dissolved in an instant at the sight of another brutal death. He felt empty, lost, with no clue what to do. All he wanted was to walk away alive from this terrible place. It seemed to take ages for his brain to engage when he saw Dani stand and start gesturing to him. She patiently repeated herself and suddenly he understood what she had in mind. *Oh no,* he thought. *Oh no.* But then he realised that there are limits to fear. He was already so terrified that the thought of what she wanted him to do couldn't make him more scared. So it was with resignation and desperation, rather than hope, that he nodded and prepared for his role in what came next.

———

When he was debriefed Elliot couldn't say exactly what had happened. He huddled in a blanket provided by the ambulance first responders and sipped a cup of sweet, milky tea. He rubbed his forehead and said, 'Look, I'm sorry. I told you about Fraser getting shot, then him and Bridget getting shot, and then Hugh getting shot. Nothing can prepare you for that. A war zone isn't like that. This Chinese guy was like some kind of machine. Cold, really cold.'

Elliot stopped for another sip of tea before continuing. 'So Hugh got shot and I saw him stand for a moment, a look of complete surprise in his eyes, before he fell face down on the concrete. I saw his gun fall from his hand and slide across the floor towards me. The next thing I know the Chinese guy is looking at me and raising his gun. There's no expression on his face, no smile, no frown, no nothing. He takes a step towards me. I feel time slowing down. I mean, it was weird. It was like every breath took a minute, even though I knew I was gasping.'

Elliot paused for a long time and eventually Dani asked, 'Okay, the Chinese guy stepped towards you. What happened next?'

Elliot looked up at her and waited another long moment before continuing. 'Like I said, everything was in slow motion. He took one step and his gun was coming up at me. He took another step, this time over Bridget, and his gun was pointing right at my face.' Elliot shook his head slowly and said very softly, 'I knew it was the end. This guy had just killed three people and had a gun pointed at my head. I had nothing. Nowhere to run, no weapon to fight with.'

He looked across the room at the other person huddled on a chair, also with a blanket across his shoulders. He nodded in his direction and said, 'And then this idiot runs into the room and shouts something daft like 'Fuck your mother.'

'It was "Fuck you, mother fucker",' Gordon interjected.

'Whatever,' Elliot continued. 'He runs in and screams and gets the Chinese guy's attention. Just for a second, but enough for him to move his pistol from my face towards Gordon. I turn far enough to see Gordon spin and run back out the door. The Chinese guy fires and I see Gordon flinch. I'm pretty sure he's hit but it mustn't be too bad because he keeps running and ducks left out of sight.'

'Bad enough it hurts like fuck,' said Gordon, 'he shot me in my writing hand.'

Dani looked over at Gordon and said, 'We'll get your statement next.' She switched her gaze back to Elliot and said, 'Go on. The Chinese guy shot again and Gordon disappeared. What happened next?'

Elliot looked at her a little oddly and said, 'Well, I think you know what happened next, my dear. The fucking Light Brigade came through the door and saved the day. Saved my ass. Saved Gordon's ass too, I wager.'

Dani said, 'In your own words, sir, what happened after Gordon disappeared out the doorway?'

Elliot put his cup down and said, 'The Chinese guy was bringing his gun back down to bear after shooting Gordon when a police constable ran into the doorway from the other side. She had her baton in her hand and when she was inside the door and had a clear view of the Chinese guy she threw it as hard as she could. It hit him in the hand and ricocheted into his face. He dropped his gun and put both hands to his face. I dropped to the floor, grabbed Hugh's gun and shot him twice in the chest.'

Gordon looked over at Dani and said, 'Funny, word around the club is you're a star batsman, not a bowler. Do you want me to have a word with the selectors?'

Dani ignored Gordon, finished writing in her notebook and looked up. 'Mr Hayes, I can't officially thank you for saving my life. And I won't ask you if you think you used excessive force.'

Elliot looked at her and said, 'Excessive force? If I'd had a wooden stake I'd have driven it through his fucking heart.'

———

The hospital room was dark, the only lights coming from the instruments at the head of the bed. Bridget lay on her back, slightly propped up with a pillow, with the covers pulled up to her chest. Her left arm lay on top of the covers, a cannula stuck in the back of her hand. The room was quiet, no beeps or clicks from the instruments or sound of footsteps or conversation outside. There was almost no smell, just the faintest sense of soap or bleach or some other cleaning agent.

Gordon sat beside the bed with a view of Bridget and the door. His eyes were tired and his hand hurt like hell. He desperately needed sleep but he hadn't been sleeping well since the incident in the shed. Too many memories of his terror; too many echoes of gunshots and screams; too many graphic images, among them Bridget lying bleeding on the floor. He still couldn't believe she was alive. The bullet had passed through Fraser and entered her chest underneath her right arm, but it had been slowed enough that it lodged between her ribs. She had a nasty wound and would be in the hospital for some time, but it wasn't life-threatening.

Gordon remembered what he thought when he saw Bridget. He'd thought she was dead and he felt an overpowering sense of grief. The whole incident had left him feeling raw and emotional and vulnerable and, in the days since it happened, he found himself weeping for no apparent reason. Sitting beside her bed he sensed these feelings easing and he watched her breathe with a calmness that was new to him.

Other than when she'd been sedated for the operation to remove the bullet from her ribs, Bridget had been awake since she'd arrived at the hospital. Gordon had called every day to get an update on her condition. Even though, shortly after the operation, the doctor had said it would be okay to visit, he had put his visit off. He desperately wanted to see her but didn't know what to say. It was worse than when he'd first met her after her team had won the regional netball championships. He'd bumbled through an interview and, in a moment of madness, had asked her if she'd like to have dinner. He'd been amazed when she'd said yes, and even more amazed when a year later he'd asked her to marry him and she'd said yes again.

He still didn't know what to say, but knew that if he hadn't come to see her tonight then he might never come. She'd been asleep when he arrived and he sat watching her, the cowardly part of him hoping she'd stay asleep so he wouldn't have to talk with her.

Without warning, her eyes fluttered and opened. She stared straight ahead without blinking or moving, as though coming back to her body from a long journey. Then she slowly turned her head and looked at Gordon. Was there a sign of recognition? Perhaps a small smile? Gordon wasn't sure.

'Hello,' Bridget said softly, her lips barely moving. Gordon marvelled at how wonderful she looked even in a hospital bed. Bridget licked her lips and said a little more strongly, 'I guess I have to thank you for saving my life.'

Gordon's gaze never left her eyes. 'Um, it's actually Dani and Elliot you should thank. I didn't do anything really.'

'That's not what Dani tells me. Nor Elliot, either. I've been waiting to see you. To thank you. I guess you've had a lot to do since ... since what happened.'

'Yeah, sure. It's been pretty hectic. Once the police and ambulance came and I knew you and Elliot were all right I sort of collapsed. One minute I was jazzed, full of adrenalin and bouncing off the walls, and the next it was like I'd been hit with a hammer. A cop drove me home and I slept for twelve hours. I had a debrief, same as you probably, and since then I've been writing the story up.'

Bridget nodded and said, 'I heard about your injury. How's the hand? Writing your story could take a while with only one hand.' She paused and pushed herself up in bed. 'You were always a good reporter. I hope you get a good story for your paper. There's plenty of blood, so the city papers should be interested, too.'

'Actually, the local paper's been bought out. The final edition was last week. I got a short article about what happened into it, just the bare bones. But it was enough to attract international interest.' Gordon paused for a moment and carried on, 'Reuters has approached me and asked if I'd work for them. I'd be based in Auckland and would cover all of New Zealand and most of the Pacific islands for them.'

Bridget smiled weakly and said, 'That's great. Looks like you've got your break at last.'

'Yeah, well,' it's great but ... but there's something I was wondering. I'm going to be in Auckland and I ...,' Gordon hesitated again, 'and I wondered if you'd come with me.'

Bridget closed her eyes, but the smile was still on her lips. She was silent for a long while and Gordon felt his pulse accelerate, anxious that he'd exposed himself once again, hoping that she'd say yes, fearing that she'd say no.

Finally Bridget opened her eyes and looked at him, deeply, with nothing hidden. 'Do you remember the day we got married? I remember it was a gorgeous spring day, with clear skies and flowers everywhere. It was just you and me and our best friends and it all seemed perfect.'

Gordon didn't even nod, unwilling to break the thread of her speaking. 'And it was always perfect. We were always happy and having fun.' Bridget shifted her gaze away for a moment and then returned to stare at Gordon's eyes. 'So you can imagine how surprised I was when you ran away with Miss Channel Nine.' She smiled sadly. 'Actually, I wasn't surprised. I think there was some part of us below the surface that knew it wasn't perfect. That's why you ran away and that's why I wasn't surprised.'

'Maybe you're right,' said Gordon, 'but that was years ago. That was many years ago. We've both been through a lot since then. We're not the same people we were then.'

'You think not?' Bridget asked. 'You think we've changed?' She shook her head slowly on the pillow: 'I don't. I don't think people change. Not down deep. Not where it counts. We knew we weren't compatible then and I know we wouldn't be now.'

'But what about what's happened? Don't you think what we've been through has made a difference?'

'If you're hit on the head with a cricket ball, does it make you a different person?' She shook her head again and sighed. 'Hell, I don't know. Maybe you're right. Maybe you *are* a different person. But I'm not. And I know I can't go with you to Auckland.'

They were silent for a minute and then Bridget said, 'I heard how you tracked us down at that farm. That was pretty clever.'

Gordon shrugged: 'I just had the idea. It was my friend who did the computer search.'

They were quiet again until Bridget said, 'Your friend. You think he could do it again? Make another search?'

Gordon frowned: 'I don't know. I doubt it. She's scared, bloody scared. I was only just able to keep her out of this mess.'

'Pity,' Bridget said. 'Getting her to help would have been a start to making up for running out on me.'

Gordon sighed and asked: 'Tell me what you want.'

So she did.

When she was finished Gordon was quiet for a long time, thinking. Eventually he looked at Bridget and said, 'You don't need my friend for that. Sometimes the old ways are the best.' Bridget raised an eyebrow and Gordon said, 'I'm a reporter. I'll just ask. It's a small town. If there's anything to be found then I'll find it.'

He reached out and took her hand in his. A brief look of anguish crossed his face before he regained control. 'Hey, this is way too soon to be talking about serious things like that. We should be focusing on getting you well and out of here. I don't have to be in Auckland for a while so I can help you get settled back in your house. If you want me to. This other thing?' he gestured. 'We can talk about that later.'

'Sure,' Bridget said tiredly, 'let's talk about it later.' She closed her eyes and must have drifted off to sleep because she didn't hear Gordon leave.

EPILOGUE

Bridget watched Tui Dancer circle her mare, Ginger Snap, in the small paddock alongside her stables. The police had found the stallion grazing quietly by the side of the road about three kilometres from the scene of the shootings. An extensive search had turned up no trace of Venus. The police told Bridget that in light of Venus' actions they would still like to talk with her, but she was no longer a subject of their investigations. A week earlier Bridget had received a postcard from Switzerland showing the Lipizzaner stallions from Vienna performing in a stadium display in Berne. There was no message, just the symbol for female, ♀, in red felt tip pen. Bridget smiled when she remembered this was also the symbol for Venus.

The two horses had been sniffing and circling each other for some time. Tui Dancer's penis was fully extended, hanging to his hocks. Ginger Snap had been raising her tail and had urinated twice. She finally stopped and Tui Dancer moved behind her, repeatedly smelling her rear and tossing his head. Ginger looked back at him, first over her right shoulder and then over her left. Tui Dancer leaped onto her back but the angle was wrong and he slipped off.

The two horses circled again, both tossing their heads and neighing. Ginger Snap stopped again. Tui Dancer moved behind her and immediately mounted her, this time getting his forelegs firmly astride her. He shuffled forward, moving his head alongside the mare's neck, using it to control her position. When he covered her he thrust mightily for what seemed an eternity to Bridget but which she later realised was only a few seconds. Then Tui Dancer dismounted, sliding off Ginger Snap's back.

Bridget found it an incredibly powerful and moving experience. After Hugh's death the police wouldn't allow Tui Dancer to leave the district so he couldn't go back to his trainer. They'd asked Bridget to look after him until the case was closed and Tui Dancer's future was determined. Bridget had readily agreed.

She'd spent considerable time with the horse, getting to know him. With all the excitement she'd missed Ginger Snap's cycle and had to rebook her with the stallion at the McKerrow stud. Tests three days earlier had showed that Ginger was about to ovulate and become ready to be covered. Bridget had booked her with a stallion for tomorrow, but she'd decided that today she'd put her to Tui Dancer. She would never again have access to a stallion of his quality.

As she moved the two horses back to their stables she worried briefly about what she'd done. It wasn't exactly illegal; Tui Dancer was in her care after all, but she suspected that, as his ownership was uncertain, it was at least unethical. The stallion of record would be McKerrow's but, if she was lucky, the foal's sire would be Tui Dancer.

She touched her side where she'd been shot, feeling the still tender scar under her shirt, and decided she didn't care. Her farm was secure and soon, she hoped, she'd have a new foal and a new future.

She smiled when she remembered her last visit to the bank. She'd been shown into Dylan Cassidy's office and declined his offer of coffee.

'Ms Crawford,' he'd said, 'how good to see you. I hear you've had some, um, amazing experiences. I'm so glad that you're all right.'

'Dylan,' she'd said, 'cut the bullshit. You only want to know if I'm going to pay you the money I owe.'

Dylan's smile slowly faded and he said, 'Okay. You want to get to the point? Then let's get to it. Do you have the money or not?'

Bridget crossed her legs and said, 'No, I don't have the money.'

'Well, then I'm sorry, but it looks as if I'm going to have to take your farm.'

'I don't think so, Dylan,' she replied.

'What do you mean "I don't think so"?' he almost snarled. 'It's business. It's simple. You either have the money or you don't. And if you don't, then you lose the farm.'

'What,' asked Bridget, 'if there are extenuating factors? Could I keep the farm then?'

'Extenuating factors? What extenuating factors? What could possibly be relevant to your situation?'

'Well, there's the factor that you're a regular visitor at the Kit Kat Club.' Bridget watched Dylan's face and almost smiled when she saw the brief look of fear in his eyes.

'What do you mean?' he blustered. 'I'm certainly not a regular visitor, at that club or anywhere else. And anyway, everything that goes on there is perfectly legal.'

'I'm sure it is,' said Bridget, 'and your wife and daughters no doubt totally understand why you go there.' She paused and then continued, 'But they may be less understanding of your visits to the apartment of one of the Pussycats.'

Dylan opened his mouth and tried to speak, but nothing came out. Bridget ran a hand down the leg of her jeans and silently thanked Gordon. He'd been to every liquor store, bar, club and massage parlour in town, looking for someone who recognised Dylan. Gordon was beginning to think he was going to strike out when the manager of the Kit Kat Cclub said Dylan often went there. He'd talked to the girls and it hadn't taken long to hit the jackpot.

Bridget shook her head and said, 'Kayla's a nice girl and wouldn't have said anything, except my friend offered her an awful lot of money. She doesn't *want* to talk to your wife. But, like you say, it's business.'

Dylan looked at her for a long time. His face and body were immobile, no sign of any emotion. Bridget imagined him running through his options, and finding none. Finally he said, 'What do you want?'

She smiled and said, 'Well what do you know? We may have found some extenuating factors after all. I think it's time to renegotiate the terms of my loan. Is this a good time for you?'

ACKNOWLEDGMENTS

My wife, June Cahill, has provided invaluable encouragement and support for all my endeavours.

This book had a long gestation period. My long-time friend and author Jim Lawler was instrumental in getting me to stop procrastinating and bring it to a conclusion. I was fortunate to have friends who provided valuable feedback on early drafts. Jennifer Hardiman, Ginny Misselbrook, Blair Polly and Rob Jamieson were especially insightful.

Victoria Twead of Ant Press has been great, providing guidance and advice for every phase of editing and publication. I was incredibly fortunate to have Martin Diggle as my editor. As well as his editing skills he has a vast knowledge of horses and horse racing and his contributions have greatly improved the story.

ABOUT THE AUTHOR

Ray Wood was a marine geologist for more than 30 years. He and his wife retired to a small farm on the east coast of the North Island of New Zealand where he spends his time looking after cows and vintage tractors, trying to grow truffles, making artistic gates and writing. His next novel involves commercial fishing in the Ross Sea, ship wrecks and corporate skulduggery.